C000076006

Book _

The Alpha's Rejected Silent Mate

A ROMANCE NOVEL

written by

CAT SMITH

Copyright © 2023 Cat Smith

Cat Smith has asserted her right under the laws of Singapore, to be identified as the Author of the Work.

All rights reserved.

No part of this book may be reproduced or transmitted in any form by any means, graphic, electronic, or mechanical, including photocopying, recording, taping or by any information storage retrieval system without the written permission from the copyright holder.

This is a work of fiction. Names, characters, businesses, places, events, and incidents are either the products of the author's imagination or used in a fictitious manner: Any resemblance to actual persons, living or dead, or actual events is purely coincidental.

Design and composition by CRATER PTE.LTD.

First Edition 2023.
Published by CRATER PTE.LTD. Singapore

AUTHOR'S NOTES

Writing has always been a form of therapy for me. It is an escape from reality, an escape from my mental illness known as Bipolar Disorder Type 2. I make a fantasy world where true love always wins, immortality is normal, and fate always finds you.

I write because I love to read so much and because the stories I write are demanding to be told. They find their way into my mind and trickle out of my fingertips. I spend each day hunched over my laptop, writing about supernatural forces such as werewolves, vampires, and witches. My husband has always supported my writing and been a sounding board when I've needed inspiration or gotten stuck with my writing. He has kept me company when I've been writing long into the night and has been an endless source of comfort to me when I've needed it most. Without his support, I would never have had the courage to begin writing my novels, and I cannot thank him enough.

My editor at Dreame/Stary writing, Tiffany, is always there to assist and warmly encourage me. She is the one who took a chance on my books and has encouraged me throughout the entire process. I could not have done this without her.

The readers that read my book mean so much to me. I especially love to read their heartfelt comments on the app and watch the read counts of my stories increase. I still cannot believe that people are reading my stories.

I am so grateful to everyone involved in making this possible. I am thankful for the many opportunities made possible by the entire Dreame / Stary Writing team. I feel so honored.

All the characters and names are solely from my imagination. Any similarities between this book and any true life story are merely coincidental. This book is not based on real events from my life or anyone else's.

Table of Contents

Chapter 72

Kai's POV

The summit seems to be going well, and I'm careful to keep Winter by my side as long as possible. Except for that one incident involving that drunken bastard of an Alpha trying to force Winter to go with him, the night has run quite smoothly, and Winter, in particular, seems to be having a wonderful time. I'm glad about that, at least. I would have hated being here if she was miserable because bringing her here was not my intention.

She seems to be fitting in, doesn't she, Kai? She doesn't look out of place at all.

I guess so, Storm.

Did you ever think you would fall so hard for your real mate? I told you, all you had to do was give her a chance.

Yeah, yeah, yeah, rub it in, why don't you?

Well, if you hadn't been so stubborn, you jackass.

Storm, you're pushing the friendship line.

Fine, but you should know someone here you didn't want to see again. Disgusting piece of trash that she is. I hope she dies of food poisoning or someone kills her for being mouthy. Urgh. I feel the need to take a shower and get clean.

Who on earth are you talking about, Storm?

I trail off as the familiar scent of perfume hits me, stiffening as I grab hold of Winter instinctively. Well, this was just fucking great. So much for having a good night. This was more than bound to ruin it. Who in the bloody hell had brought her along to this summit?

1

Unless she had suddenly found her mate, but I highly doubt that. Fuck, fuck, fuck. This was the last thing I needed to deal with right now. All my plans for a wonderful evening are going up in smoke right before my eyes. Damnit.

"Alpha Kai," comes her voice, sickeningly sweet, and I close my eyes, take a deep breath and turn with Winter still clutching my hand, a forced a smile on my face. Two can play that game. I can pretend she's not bothering me. How hard can it be?

She looks just the same, clad in a tight, bright red dress that pulls along her chest and shows off her expressive cleavage with killer heels. She's dressed to the nines, a far cry from Winter's outfit that she'd worn for comfort. She's also clinging onto Alpha Liam's arm hard. Her eyes narrowed and calculated as she stared at me and glared hard at Winter. I glare back at her, holding tightly to Winter's hand in a possessive manner that leaves no confusion. Not to mention the mark on Winter's neck that shows she's been claimed by me.

"Hello, Candice," I say between gritted teeth. Now I know why I haven't seen her around the pack lately. She must have left and gone traveling, and Langdon wouldn't have cared enough to inform me about it. She looks too relaxed next to Alpha Liam, whose eyes are hard. I've never liked the man; the feeling is mutual, considering how hard he glares at me.

"Hello," Winter says in a subdued tone, and I watch Candice gasp, surprised that my mate can now speak. She hadn't been anticipating that at all. I fight the urge to smirk at her, pulling Winter tighter and tucking her under my shoulder in a blatant and possessive move that Candice understands, her anger showing on her face. I resist the urge to flick my finger at her. Winter looks annoyed.

"Winter," she coos. "How lovely to meet you again."

Winter stiffens beside me, raises her head, and stares challengingly at Candice. "Really?" Winter says icily. "Because I have to say that it's not a pleasure to see you again at all," she says with a sugary sweet tone as I blink and almost jump in celebration. So Winter's not going to fake niceties. Good for her. Candice is taken aback. I can't help noticing with amusement. She wasn't expecting that type of response. Either that or she didn't know that Winter could talk now.

"Quite a mate you've got there," Alpha Liam finally speaks. "Is she always this rude?"

I scoff. "Only when it's deserved."

Candice bites her lip and fumes. She thought I would be brokenhearted because now she looks disappointed. Ha. I hope she leaves now.

Then her eyes begin blazing. "How nice that Winter can look past your ahem," Candice coughs, "scars. Don't you ever get self-conscious being with him," she adds cruelly, looking over at Winter.

I stiffen. With those words, I'm back to being self-conscious, trying hard not to trace my scars with my fingertips as Candice smirks at me, clearly proud of herself.

"Never," Winter whispers. "His scars prove his courage and bravery. I consider it an honor that he is my mate, and I would never feel self-conscious being beside him. If that's how you feel, I apologize to whoever becomes your mate. Beauty doesn't last forever, and what's inside counts. Pity you haven't learned that yet," she tells Candice before turning to me, Alpha Liam's mouth open in shock. She deliberately ignores both of them.

"Kai, would you dance with me?" she asks, and I beam, taking hold of her hand and shooting Candice a triumphant glance.

"I would be honored," I tell her and walk away without turning around, hearing Candice wail and splutter in the background as I place my hand around Winter's waist and take her hand, moving slowly back and forth to the music; Winter leaning her head against my chest, sparks flying between us.

"I'm sorry about Candice," I apologize. "I didn't know she would be attending."

Winter searches my eyes for the truth and then nods. "I didn't think you did," she says calmly, giggling as I twirl her around. "You can't be responsible for everything Candice does," she said truthfully. "That woman looks like she loves trouble."

She had that right.

The music peters off, and Winter yawns, making me smile down at her. She looks pretty wiped out and swaying slightly on her feet. The poor thing must be exhausted and too afraid to say anything. If I'm honest with myself, I'm pretty wiped out too. Candice had managed to ruin the night for me and probably for Winter. I sigh.

"How about we go back to the hotel room?" I suggest, and Winter nods, letting me drag her to the elevator. We're on the top floor, and damn, I'm so hoping that Candice isn't. That's the last thing either of us bloody need right now.

I help her out of the elevator and take Winter to the last door on the right, using the keycard to open it, opening the door with a flourish and making my mate giggle as she walks in and makes a beeline for the bathroom.

I sit down on the chair and rest my head in my hands. I wanted this to go perfectly, and one night, Winter had to contend with a drunken fool of an Alpha hitting on her and then dealing with running into Candice. God, I'm hopeless at this romantic stuff. I wanted the night without a hitch; it had gone wrong. I wouldn't be surprised if Winter were now angry at me for it. She would have every right to be. Hell, I would be if it was me in her shoes.

But when she comes out, she looks remarkably calm. Her hair is slightly disheveled, making her look even more adorable than she already is. Her eyes are sparkling as she looks at me, and there's something else on her face that I can't quite grasp. Was she upset?

"Kai, I want you to know that even though there was that thing with Candice, I had a wonderful night with you," she says, and I stare at her in astonishment. Did she mean that? I'm almost beaming with pride. She had had a good time then, despite it all. I had pulled it off and given her something to remember.

4

"I'm glad," I tell her honestly. "I thought you would be angry or upset with me for what happened. I did try to give you a perfect night," I say, and she bites her lip, looking at me, her eyes searching for something like she's trying to decide. I wait. I don't want to interrupt her if she has something on her mind or something she wants to say.

"I know I'm not like Candice," she begins, and I stop her right there, holding a hand up to stop her mid-sentence.

"Whoa," I exclaim. "You're nothing like Candice, and I'm grateful for that. Winter, you're so much better than her. You're kind and warm. You care about the pack. You're beautiful and sweet. I could go on and on, but do you get the gist? You're my mate, and you're the one I want now. Please don't think I'm comparing you to Candice because I can tell you she'd come off as the loser."

Winter giggles, her face smoothing out as she smiles. Is that what she was worried about? That I was somehow comparing her to Candice and finding her lacking? There was no way I would ever do that to her. Not in a million years. Now I feel like a right asshole. How long has Winter possibly been feeling this way, and why haven't I picked up on it?

"I guess we should get ready for bed," I say reluctantly, even though I'm looking forward to sleep-cuddling Winter. Storm is the same. As long as we get to hold her, the other thing can wait until she's ready. We won't pressure her to do anything she doesn't want, especially after having gone through such a traumatic experience with that asshole Thomas. The last thing I want is cause her to remember things she doesn't want to.

Winter bites her lip, though, and eyes me shyly.

"Is something wrong, Winter?"

She shakes her head and sits down on the edge of the bed as I stand up. She's avoiding my eyes now, and I swear she's blushing. Something is on her mind.

"I want you to make love to me," she mutters, and my heart skips a beat.

5

Did I hear that right? Had she just said those words to me? She looks nervous, and I have to clarify.

"You want me to make love to you," I say, and she nods.

I hesitate. I don't think she's ready, but I can't deny that my cock is twitching at the thought of taking her.

"If you don't want me," Winter mutters, and I kneel beside her, looking deeply into her eyes.

"Winter, it's not that I don't want you, but are you ready for this? I don't mind waiting if that's what you need. Don't pressure yourself into something that you don't want. It has to be your decision."

She takes a deep breath and stares back, her eyes mesmerizing me. "I want this, Kai, I want you," she pleads, and I'm helpless to resist her plea, even as I shrug out of my jacket.

"If that's what you want," I growl in my throat, "then your wish is my command," I finish, my eyes turning pitch black in response.

"Lie down on the bed," I order, and she obeys.

"Good girl," I whisper, thinking to myself, *let the fun begin.*

Chapter 73

Winter's POV

Kai looks so handsome as we go upstairs to our hotel room. He's been chivalrous the entire night, and I know the whole debacle with that bitch Candice isn't his fault. No one could have anticipated her being there. I hadn't thought of that woman since Kai had broken up with her. She was like a thorn in the side; I must watch her carefully. I don't trust her as far as I could throw her. She's up to something. I can sense it. She's out for blood, but she's not getting mine. I refuse to let her intimidate me, either. Kai made his choice, and that choice was to be with me. Candice was going to have to accept that.

I bite my lip. I've been thinking about this all night and can't hold back anymore. My body is thrumming with desire, and my whole body is trembling, but this is what I want. Now, right here in this hotel room. I speak quietly. "Kai, will you make love to me?" and watch his eyes darken. Of course, the stubborn jackass has to confirm what he's heard for himself, but when he orders me onto the bed, I give a small smile. Something tells me he's been waiting for this, and I didn't need to ask. But he was a gentleman, waiting until I was ready instead of trying to pressure me.

I'm incredibly nervous, but he comes over and kisses me softly, his lips touching mine, his tongue tracing my lips until I open them, his tongue delving inside and caressing mine as I give a low moan. He begins to pull off my jacket and shirt as I sit up and help him, gently pushing me back down on the mattress as he begins to trail kisses down the nape of my neck, his hands gently touching and squeezing my breasts as I jolt from the pleasure rising inside of me.

I've never felt this way before, and it's making me nervous but curious at the same time.

"Kai," I moan, and he slides my skirt down and then my panties as I writhe on the bed. I expect him to come back up, tensing for what I think is about to happen, but instead, he pulls my legs up so that they are bent, firmly holding them in place, so that they are spread wide, staring down at my pussy and licking his lips as I shudder. I feel exposed, but he's staring at me with a wide smile as he likes it.

He bends his head down, and then with a shriek, I feel the coarseness of his tongue as he begins to lick my pussy up and down, slowly, torturously as I pant and wriggle, his hands never letting go of my legs as my hands clutch at the bedsheets. Fuck. I've never felt this good before, and he's showing no signs of letting up, ruthless as he begins to increase the pressure and the intensity, circling my clit as I writhe. Fuck. I'm helpless to do anything but feel the pleasure, and he knows it.

"God, Kai," I pant. "Fuck, oh, God," moaning out loud and getting louder the more the pleasure rises.

"Kai!" I scream his name as I cum, hard against his tongue. Kai never lets up for a second, lapping at my juices as I come crashing back to earth.

"You taste so good," he moans as my heart flutters wildly. Every nerve ending of mine is on fire, and all I can think about is him and him taking me to the bed. I want him with a wildness that scares even me. I'm desperate for him to take his clothes off. I feel incredibly wanton, and it doesn't bother me.

"I want you," I moan and see his eyes darken as he stands back up and wiggles out of his formal clothes. I almost drool at the sight of his strong muscles and taut abdomen, enjoying looking at his body as he gives a low chuckle, seeing my eyes on him.

"Do you like what you see?" he growls, and I nod.

Oh, yeah, I did. "Very much so," I say gently, and he growls in his throat, coming towards me as my eyes widen in disbelief. I gulp nervously.

He's large, incredibly so, and with the width of it, I don't know if it will fit inside me. My mouth goes dry, and he senses my fear. My whole body is beginning to tremble in fear and anticipation. How much is this going to hurt?

"Winter, it's okay," he says firmly, heading over to the bedside drawer and returning with something in his hand. I squint at the shiny packet and realize he's holding a condom.

"It's your choice," he says calmly. "Do you want me to wear a condom? I don't mind either way," he adds.

So he's asking for my benefit. How sweet of him. He'd come prepared, at least.

I have to think about it, but I'm not ready to become a mother just yet and don't exactly want to conceive on my first time doing it. Shifters are extremely fertile. Most get pregnant the first time they do the deed.

"Yes," I whisper and watch as he tears open the packet with his teeth, placing the condom on the tip of his penis and rolling it down the length of him. His eyes stayed on me the entire time, trying to reassure me.

He gets on the bed and leans over me, kissing me softly, hands moving up and down my body. I feel tingles everywhere he touches me, and it's not long until I'm fully aroused again, wanting him something fierce, my own hands beginning to explore every inch of him, one hand even going so far as to touch his shaft as he sucks in a gasp. Did I accidentally hurt him?

"Sorry," I whisper shakily, but he shakes his head, eyes almost pitch black as he stares down at me.

"Don't apologize," he whispers. "You can touch any part of me you want. I like it, baby girl."

I take a deep breath. "I don't think it's going to fit inside me," I say doubtfully.

He chuckles. "Trust me, it will, but I don't want this to be painful for you," he mutters, bending his head down and taking one of my nipples in his mouth as I gasp, kneading my breast with his hand. I arch my back and hiss in pleasure, watching as he does the same to the other breast.

I honestly don't think I can wait any longer. There's this insatiable desire to feel his cock inside of me, and at this rate, I'm going to end up pushing him onto the bed and taking him. Virgin or not.

"Kai," I plead, biting my lip. "God, please, I need to feel you," I end up sobbing, and he nods, quietly shifting himself so that he's right over me.

I can feel his cock at my entrance, and he looks at me, making sure I still want this, before he pushes the tip inside slowly, inch by inch, as I gasp and stiffens, feeling slight pain as he pushes himself inside. I groan, the pain stinging between my legs.

"It only hurts the first time," Kai whispers, kissing me on the forehead and stilling, wiping away the tears in the corners of my eyes. He looks apologetic. "Tell me when you're ready for me to move," he adds, and I nod, panting and clutching at the bedcovers until the pain seems to have vanished completely.

"You can move," I mutter, and he begins to thrust in and out, slowly and gently, as my eyes widen and my hips begin to take over, nothing in rhythm with him. He feels so fucking good, and before long, I'm begging him for more, not recognizing myself.

"God Kai, harder," I cry at him, and he gives a low growl, moving quicker, his thrusts harder as I moan and whimper, crying out his name, my whole body feeling aflame. I'm shameless as I urge him on more, gripping his shoulders and waist with my hands, clawing at him wildly. He's groaning in delight, his hands caressing me all over.

Then I feel it. My body begins to tense up as pleasure builds up to the point that it's almost painful. Kai adjusts his position slightly, his fingers beginning to circle my clit as my back arches and my legs go straight, my mouth opening in a large scream. Fuck. There's no way anybody could sustain this much pleasure and not die from it. I'm certain of it. He's going to kill me at this rate. Then like a wave, my body tenses and then releases as I scream out wildly, the orgasm so powerful and long that I swear I've died and gone to heaven as Kai continues to pound into me, prolonging the orgasm as I sob.

I hear Kai let out a low growl, and then he stills, thrusting once more and growling lowly in his throat, realizing he's come as he slowly withdraws from me. I wince slightly at the feel of his hard cock leaving me and feel pain down below, but this is something I would treasure forever. He had made my first time memorable. I watch him go into the bathroom, presumably to dispose of the condom, and he comes back out with a washcloth which he uses to wipe me down as I blush profusely. He's so gentle, though, and so caring. It's a nice gesture, and I appreciate it, even though I feel slightly embarrassed.

I yawn, feeling exhausted, and drained but incredibly happy. Kai looks concerned. "Winter, how about a bath before you fall asleep?" he suggests, and I stare at him. Is this Kai? Or did I have sex with a stranger? I love the attention he's giving me. I have to admit.

He returns to the bathroom and runs the water as I awkwardly sit up. It takes one glance down at my thighs and the bed sheets to know why he's suggested it. There's dried blood and a lot of it. Now I feel even more embarrassed, but he seems to take it all in stride, picking me up and gently placing me in the water.

"I'll take care of the bed sheets," he tells me, kissing me on the forehead and leaving.

I wallow in the water. It's helping with the slight pain, and I scrub the dried blood off my thighs and legs, making myself all clean while I wait for him to come back.

He knocks on the door. "Come in," I say tiredly, and he brings in a large fluffy towel, draping it over me as I climb reluctantly out of the bath. But if I stay any longer, I'm going to fall asleep. That's how relaxing being in the bath was. We walk back into the bedroom, and I see the sheets have been changed. Kai almost shoves me into bed, taking the towel off and placing bedcovers over me as he gets on the other side.

My eyelids are drooping. God, I'm exhausted, but I still smile to myself. Tonight was perfect. Kai was perfect. I couldn't have asked for anything better regarding my first time. My eyelids flutter closed as Kai gathers me in his arms, snuggling against me, his head tucked into my shoulder as I fall asleep.

To my shock, the last thing I hear before I pass out completely are the words Kai whispers: "I love you."

Chapter 74

Candice's POV

Ha. I saw the look of shock on that bitch Winter's face when I approached her. She went so pale like she was going to be sick, and that bastard Alpha Kai? Well, if looks could kill, I would be dead right now. I feel so satisfied even as I fake a moan like I'm enjoying what I'm doing right now when all I can think about is having my revenge. Wiping the smile off of that bitch's face. My hands clench into fists. God, I hate that bitch. She's reduced me to taking desperate measures. She's such a simple little thing. That's what I don't understand. What on earth does Kai see in her? How is she better than me? How could he prefer her to me? It didn't make sense. None of it made sense.

"God, that feels so good," I moan, my hips on either side of Alpha Liam, who's gripping me with his rather large brutish hands, riding his cock at a furious pace. It's a complete lie, but men can be so fucking insecure sometimes. I guess they aren't that much different than women when it comes down to it.

"Fuck," he mutters, and I grin, knowing I have him right where I want him. "Switch," he growls, and I climb off him and obediently get on my hands and knees as he orders me. I'm not enjoying myself, but sometimes, you must sacrifice to get what you want. This is one sacrifice I'm more than willing to make. Even if there are times I seriously reconsider what I'm doing. Then I remember the smug look on the bitch's face, and I feel incredibly angry again. She won't know what's coming for her. I tense and prepare myself for the inevitable.

He slams into me with a hard thrust, and I almost lose my balance, his hands gripping my waist painfully, his fingers digging in. I hold back my cries. This man enjoys inflicting pain but doesn't like to think he's rough in the bedroom. I don't get it.

"Take that, you little bitch," he mutters, thrusting back and forth as I wiggle my hips and slam back against him, hoping to make this finish sooner rather than later. This is taking longer than I'd like.

If I'm good at anything, it knows how to please a man. After all, I learned how to please that bastard, Kai, didn't I? Men are like putty in my hands, always have been. All it takes is a pretty face and some flowery words; they will do everything for you. Alpha Liam had proved to be no different.

"Oh, God," I moan, my hands clenching into the bed sheets. At least he's well-endowed. Otherwise, I probably would be getting no pleasure at all from this. Not that I'd expected to, it was just a nice surprise, to be honest. I give another moan out loud, trying to keep him pleased.

"You little bitch," he murmurs, changing the pace and the intensity. I let him degrade me. He can do anything he wants if it means he'll help me get my revenge. I don't even care if he gets even rougher. I can take it. There are times when he's extremely rough, and I've encouraged it. I need this man to want me so badly that he's willing to do anything for me. I've finally achieved that goal.

"Fuck, harder," I shriek, and he obliges, grabbing me by my hair and pulling it as he fucks me, little groans coming out of his mouth. I can feel him beginning to tense and know he must be close. Shame. I haven't exactly had my pleasure yet. My hand goes down to my clit, and I massage it furiously, my walls clenching around his cock as he gives a loud growl. I'll be damned if I don't at least get a fucking orgasm from this, that's for sure. The pleasure builds, and I swear, the orgasm rushing over me as my body tenses and stiffens, my cry loud as I cum. This makes him even more excited, and he begins to pound me as rough and hard as he can before he, too, stiffens, thrusting hard one last time and letting out a ferocious growl as he spills his seed into me. I frown. Thank God for birth control, something else he has no idea I'm on. But there's no way in hell that I want to be a mother, not ever.

I hate children, always have. Something I'd lied to Kai about. The bastard loved children. It never occurred to him to wonder why I never got pregnant. Idiot. Especially considering he never once used a fucking condom. He claimed he didn't like the feel of it, but I know it was just in the hopes of having his child. I've never once forgotten to take a birth control pill.

He pulls out and then lies on the bed, panting, his face red from the exertion. It is not a good look, but I force myself to smile at him. "That was the best sex I've ever had," I lie to his face and grin. Men are such simple creatures.

"Better than Alpha Kai's," he growls, looking at me intently.

"Way better," I assure him—men with bloody egos. Everything has to be a goddamn competition. Including the size of their bloody cocks.

Alpha Liam looks pleased. I know he's long been a rival towards Kai, so I chose the man. All I had to do was flatter him and let slip that I was his ex-girlfriend, and Alpha Liam had been all too willing to take me along to the summit as his date and rub it in Kai's face. We've been dating for over a month, and he's been putty in my hands the entire time. Sex is all it's taken to make him amiable to my suggestions. Then again, isn't that all men want? Sex whenever they demand it and a willing woman beneath them? He sure as hell hadn't wanted a proper girlfriend. With the brutish way he treats me whenever we're not having sex, it's no surprise why he hasn't had a serious relationship before. Because truth be told, he's a bit of a dick and a real asshole.

"Alpha Kai is nothing compared to you," I say, stroking his ego and kissing him. He kisses back, his tongue delving into my mouth as I try not to gag. If I'm particularly honest with myself, I can't stand him, let alone his tongue, lips, or any part of him. But my desire for revenge is what keeps me going. I still haven't gotten over that Kai dumped me after so long together or that he's chosen to be with Winter as his mate. She's so pathetic, so weak. He should have dumped her for me. I was the perfect Luna. I was the one who broke up with men, not the other way around. Without me, Kai would be nothing, not even close to the Alpha he was. He should be thanking me for building him up so much and for being able to look past those hideous scars enough to even have sex with him. I know plenty of other girls have rejected his advances because of them. That's one of the reasons why I approached him in the first place. Because I figured he would make me Luna in appreciation of being with him. But he hadn't, and now he had to pay for mistreating me and picking that pathetic bitch, Winter.

"That girl, Winter," Liam says casually as I throw him a scorching glance. "She's the one you told me about, isn't she? The one you want revenge on?"

"Yes," I said heatedly. "She deliberately broke up Alpha Kai and me by lying to the pack. She's not even his real mate," I say with a growl. "She tricked him into marking her. I was in love with him, and she ruined it. She's nothing but a home wrecker," I say, laying it on thick. I even blink back tears from my eyes, fake ones.

It's all a lie, but men hear what they want to hear. This man is no different. They are so oblivious to my lies, but I am one hell of an actress. Perhaps I should have been one as my career.

"His loss is my gain," growls Alpha Liam, and I cuddle him, frowning over his shoulder.

"Yes," I say sweetly. "But I still want revenge on that girl for ruining my life," I add, and he frowns. He looks uncertain, and I know I must push him to do what I want. He'll come around, even if I have to perform certain sexual favors on the Alpha to get what I want.

"I understand that," he says grimly. "I've always hated that bastard Kai. He always comes across as so arrogant. It makes me want to strangle him with my bare hands. It's like he thinks he's better than me," he huffs.

"I know," I murmur. "He's cocky, and by taking revenge, we're hitting him where it will hurt the most. You get revenge on him, and I get mine," I add.

"I like the sound of that," Liam says with a wicked grin, picking me up as I give a shriek and walk to the bathroom. He starts the shower and places me down, joining me inside. I almost want to roll my eyes. Of course, he wants more sex. How could I have thought he was finished? The man was insatiable. Like a teenager with a constant hard-on. With the energy of one as well. I sigh. I guess I'm going to have to do some more acting.

He places me leaning against the tiles, my back towards him, and I roll my eyes. Christ. How much more could he possibly want? He lines his cock up at my entrance and thrusts inside as I give a long moan, my eyes staring directly at the tiles in the shower as I fight to keep my balance on the slippery floor. Not that Liam notices. If anything, he thrusts inside of me even harder.

"That man," Liam pants between thrusts. "Is going to get what he deserves. I promised you, didn't I," he mutters, and I tip my head back, the water rushing over me. I clench my walls and hear him growl, smiling in satisfaction. This will be over soon. Good.

"When will you take care of it," I whisper, meeting his thrusts, rolling my hips backward as I keep up with his hurried pace. "When will I finally have my revenge?" I ask.

"Soon," he growls. "Soon, my love, and that girl will never do anything more to you again," he promises.

I lean my head against the tiles and let him take me, my thoughts on Winter and what I know will happen to her soon. I can't wait to break Kai's heart like he's broken mine. To see the tears stream down his face and the grief as he deals with the death of his mate. I can't wait to see the devastation I unleash on my ex-boyfriend. The worst thing is, he'll never even know it was me. Liam and I had taken care of that and ensured I had an alibi.

Adios, *Winter,* I think wickedly. *You're about to get everything you deserve, you little bitch, and I will have a front-row seat to what happens to you.*

Chapter 75

Kai's POV

I can't believe Winter gave me the most precious gift she had to give me last night. She was so willing and perfect, and her trust in me was humbling. She was so tight. My cock twitches just thinking about it. If she hadn't been a virgin, I might have tried to persuade her to do it more than once. As it was, I was worried that she might have nightmares or bad memories because of that son of a bitch, Thomas, but she slept soundly next to me, snuggled right beside me as I watched her, fascinated and just in awe of this mate of mine. I've done a complete turnaround, but it's for the better. There's no way I can hurt Winter. I don't want to see sadness or grief on her face anymore, only happiness. I don't want to be the one who makes her cry, not anymore.

I'm careful to climb out of the bed. She's still sleeping, and I don't want to disturb her after last night. I shower quickly, deciding to go downstairs to the summit while Winter gets a much-needed rest. However, I scribble her a quick note, not wanting her to think I have abandoned her. I hesitate to wonder if maybe she would prefer to be woken up, but she had so little sleep last night that, in the end, I leave her be and head out the door and downstairs to the meeting room where no doubt, other Alphas, and Lunas are milling about. Who knows how long it will be until she wakes up? She needed her rest after what we did last night. She could meet me later.

My beautiful Winter/mate

Last night was wonderful, and I'm honored by the precious gift you bestowed on me. I will never take it for granted.

I didn't want to disturb you while you were sleeping. I figured you needed your rest. I will be in the meeting room when you can join me. Take your time. There's no rush.

Love your mate,

Kai.

However, I've no sooner gotten into the meeting room, my stomach growling with hunger, the buffet table directly in my sights when Candice stops me in my tracks. I look for Alpha Liam, hoping he will stop this, but there's no sign of him, to my disgust. The last thing I want to do is force myself to talk to this bitch. My hands clench into fists. Storm wants to rip her into shreds, no matter how many witnesses there are. I have to force my wolf and myself to calm down.

She bats her eyelashes at me. As usual, she's dressed in a skin-tight dress that molds to her curves and shows off her assets. Her makeup is perfect, and her heels clack loudly on the floor. To me, she resembles a Barbie doll, and I don't find the look attractive at all. Winter very rarely puts makeup on, and I find I much prefer her natural beauty instead. She's beautiful without it, perfect. I stand still, resigned, wondering what Candice wants now, of all things. Wasn't she dating Alpha Liam? Shouldn't he be glued to her side? Couldn't she just stay with that bastard and leave me the fuck alone?

She puts a hand on my arm, and I flinch, carefully removing it as she pouts at me, her eyes feigning hurt. I almost want to scoff at her pathetic acting. What on earth is she thinking? She knows how much I despise her, so what is she playing at?

"Kai," she breathes. "There's no need for you to act this way towards me. We were boyfriend and girlfriend for a long time, don't you think you could at least be civil towards me? I didn't mean what

I said to you. Your rejection of me just hurt me," she added as I stared at her incredulously. She's lying. I can tell. Besides, screw her. The last thing I want to be is civil to the bitch.

Is she for real? Does she want me to pretend that the insults she threw at me were just because I was breaking up with her? Because there had been an element of truth in them. What on earth is she playing at? What's with all this pretense of hers?

She moves closer, and I must fight the urge to back away. After all, a crowd is milling around us, and the last thing I want to do is cause a scene. The bitch knows it too. Storm, however, would be more than delighted to create a scene, regardless of all the witnesses. I'm tempted to let him. But I must be polite at a summit unless I want to be ostracised by other packs.

"Can't you see that I was in love with you, Kai," she exclaims dramatically. "You were my whole world, and then all of a sudden, you're breaking up with me as though I meant nothing to you," she says, hurt. Like she can talk, considering the insults she threw my way when we broke up.

I shift uncomfortably, noting that several Lunas and Alphas are openly staring at the both of us, disapproving in their eyes. *You don't have the full story,* I want to shout out in my defense, but instead, I grit my teeth and take a deep breath.

"You know that I found my mate, Candice. I couldn't fight the mate bond anymore. I'm sorry if that hurt you, but I'm with my mate now, and I'm happy," I say grimly. God, let her walk away now. Now wishing I wish I'd waited for Winter to wake up. Then I could have avoided this awkward conversation. Next time, I would wake her up.

She begins to sob. Damn, she's a good actress, sounding slightly hysterical. "We were together over a year, and in that time, you could have made me your chosen mate. Why didn't you?" she cries.

I shift on my feet, sighing deeply. "I didn't want a mate," I told her honestly. "And you knew that."

21

"But you chose to be with Winter," she wails. "You chose your mate, even when you didn't want one. So you're lying."

"Yes," I said tightly, "I changed my mind." Thank God I had. Looking at Candice now, I can't believe I ever dated her. She's so shallow, so vain. She never loved me, that I'm certain of. The Luna title was all she was after, and now it's slipped through her fingers— bad luck. I never would have given her the title anyway, so she wasted over a year for nothing.

"We could go back to those happier times," she tries to whisper, and I step back and shake my head firmly, absolutely repulsed by her suggestion. I fight back the urge to vomit.

"My mate and I are marked," I say with a growl, watching her eyes widen in disbelief. How on earth had she not noticed the marks? I look at her neck; sure enough, she's still unmarked, bare of any tattoo. So Liam hadn't made her his chosen mate yet. Interesting. Her moves speak of desperation. Was Liam getting sick of her crap now as well? Or was he just being sensible?

There's the sound of footprints, and Candice's eyes widen before she visibly relaxes. Alpha Liam joins our small group. His eyes narrowed in displeasure. Is he annoyed to find the two of us together? Because I sure as hell didn't start this conversation, and I would be delighted to finish it and get some damn breakfast. My stomach growls in hunger.

"Alpha Kai," Liam says, greeting me with a small nod, his eyes icy cold.

"Alpha Liam," I return, acknowledging him with tight lips and a grim expression. I've never liked this man, but honestly couldn't say why. It was just an instant feeling of dislike, which was mutual, judging by how he spoke to me.

"Candice, my dear," Alpha Liam said with a smile that Candice instantly returned. "I went looking for you when you disappeared from the bedroom. Is something the matter?" he asked smoothly.

Candice shook her head and stared at me with hard eyes. "I was just having a delightful conversation with Alpha Kai," she said tightly, and Alpha Liam took hold of her hand and kissed it. Yuck.

"Well, if you're finished," Alpha Liam said quietly. "Then perhaps we could get some breakfast and sit down together?" he suggested.

She nodded and shot me a look so full of hatred that I couldn't believe her audacity. Then she flipped her long hair over her shoulder and gave Alpha Liam a brilliant smile.

"I would be delighted," she purred, flouncing off as Liam stared at her. He turned to me. His jaw clenched, his eyes narrowed.

"Stay the hell away from my girl," he growls. "She's mine now."

Good riddance, I think to myself.

"You can have her," I growl back, and he huffs and walks over to her as I watch in relief. Finally, some peace. I can finally feed my hungry stomach, which is growling profusely in its desperate need to be fed.

I happily fill my plate with scrumptious treats and go to an empty table. I'm not in the mood for conversation right now. But I've no sooner bitten into a piece of bacon when there's a sudden commotion in the room. I place the bacon down with a sigh and see security bustling toward someone who's shrieking hysterically. Thank God it's not Candice.

"There's a girl in the elevator," the girl screamed. "She's been attacked, and she's bleeding everywhere."

My stomach churns. I push through the crowd towards the elevator, not caring if it's an Alpha. I'm praying that I'm wrong, that my instincts are incorrect for once, but as I reach the elevator, I see her—my God. I'm sick to my stomach. Who would have the guts to do something like this at a summit full of werewolves, for goodness' sake? Fuck. I've failed her yet again.

She's so pale, but the amount of blood everywhere gets me as I get inside, security shooting me wary looks as I kneel beside her. There's so much blood. I don't know what to do, and I feel helpless.

"She's my mate," I yell and turn to them, my eyes pitch black now, my fury visible to everyone. "Find out whoever attacked her and do it now."

Someone squeezes into the elevator with me, and I turn, ready to attack anyone who dares to attack my mate. "I'm a doctor," he says, hands up in surrender. "Let me deal with her. Please," he adds softly, and I grudgingly let him kneel beside her, checking her vitals. My eyes scan the crowds. Whoever has done this to my mate would be answering to me, whether the security team liked it or not. They would be dying a slow, painful death for their treachery and for daring to even lay a finger on my mate, who's now still there as a statue.

"She's still breathing," the doctor announces, and I close my eyes, thanking God she's not dead. Without a word, the crowd disperses to leave me and the doctor alone, the security team swarming away on a desperate chase. They better get to the attacker first because if I got my hands on them, he would scream for mercy and let him die.

Chapter 76

Winter's POV

I wake up and am disappointed to find that Kai has already left and gone to the summit. But he'd been considerate enough to leave a note so that I didn't feel abandoned, and he had wanted me to have a bit of a sleep-in. I couldn't fault him for that. So I slowly climb out of bed and head to the bathroom, wincing slightly at the pain and stinging between my legs. A bath is definitely in order. I smile, though, remembering last night and what happened between us. It's a memory that I'm going to cherish. For the first time, it was perfect. Everything about it was just magical.

I take my time, luxuriating in the bubble bath, closing my eyes as the pain starts to fade again. I can't get the memory of last night out of my mind. Kai had been so gentle and loving; my first time had been more incredible than I had imagined. He was a changed man, and my heart was full of love for this man who showed me what love felt like. I've never felt like this towards anyone before, not even my brother. This love, this adoration, it's all completely new to me, and if I'm honest, it's frightening as all hell. I'm in love, and I can't imagine my life without this man in it. How's that for being obsessed with him? I don't even know if he feels the same way. I know he loves me but just how much? Enough that he can't live without me, either? I hope so. I know he's protective of me, and his wolf, Storm, loves me and Sabriel. I love his wolf as well. I found Storm to be the perfect complement to Kai's personality.

I hum under my breath as I wrap a towel around myself and head into the bedroom. I look at all my clothes with a critical eye. I don't particularly like dresses, but I'm willing to dress up a little, maybe turn Kai's head. If anything, it will show how much I appreciate the man, won't it? Besides, he likes it when I dress up. I see how his eyes light up when he sees me. Then I frown. He lights up no matter what I wear. So it's entirely up to me what I want to wear today. Something nice, I decide, without being overkill. I want to walk around and maybe even dance with Kai again.

I dress in another skirt and dressy blouse, my leather jacket on top. I love this leather jacket. There's nothing it doesn't go with. I finish up with a pair of dressy heels that are short enough, so I won't embarrass myself by tripping over them. Wouldn't that be something for everyone to see? I cringe at the thought of humiliating myself in front of such a large crowd of Alphas and Lunas. Not to mention Kai. I shudder.

I head down to the elevator. It seems lazy, but the last thing I want to do is go down many stairs, especially considering we're on the top floor. Plus, there's the whole heels thing. *It would be dangerous,* I think to myself, to take the stairs in these beautiful shoes. The elevator is empty, except for one person, a young girl in the back corner, keeping to herself. She's wearing a hoodie, so I can't fully see her face and sweatpants. She mustn't be part of the summit then, but she smells like a shifter. I shrug. It's none of my business. I'm not about to judge her on what she's wearing, even if it somewhat surprises me. Maybe she's an Omega brought here to help serve the guests? But then, wouldn't she be wearing a uniform?

"Good morning," I greet her cheerfully as I step inside, but she stares at me rather coldly and stays silent.

Geez, what's up her butt, I think to myself, slightly disgruntled now, as I press the button for the ground floor. I was only trying to be friendly, for heaven's sake. I guess not everyone is in a good mood today.

The elevator lurches, and I grip the railing. Man, I wouldn't say I like these things. I wouldn't say I like small spaces in general, to be fair, anything that seems like a confined space. Always have. The woman remains quiet, and I dismiss her, staring ahead when she suddenly moves. Even then, I foolishly look ahead, assuming she's making her way to the door for when it opens. There's nothing about her that screams dangerous, and that proves to be my downfall.

Instead, I feel something pierce the flesh in my shoulder, and I cry out, my skin bubbling and burning. The woman reaches over and presses the emergency stop button as she pulls the silver dagger out, and I hiss, my eyes wide. This is a trap. This is an ambush, but why me? This doesn't make any sense. I've never seen this woman before in my life. This can only mean someone was paying her to do this to me. I bet it's that fucking Candice. My hands clench into fists even though I'm extremely unsteady. Damn, the silver. It's so potent and dangerous for werewolves.

"Why are you doing this?" I wheeze, but the woman says nothing. Her eyes were just narrow as she stared at me calmly.

I can't shift, I realize, when I frantically try. I can't even hear Sabriel. Something is dripping from the end of the dagger, and the woman gives me a cold smile. "Wolfsbane," I breathe out in disgust. "You laced the dagger with wolfsbane."

No wonder I can't hear Sabriel or mind-link, I realize, which means that I can't mind-link Kai for help. I'm on my own.

The woman lunges towards me, and I sidestep just in time, wrestling with her for the knife. She kicks me in my midsection, and I double over, screaming as the dagger is stabbed in my side and pulled back out. God, it hurts. The pain is excruciating, and it's spreading throughout my entire body. Not only that, but blood is welling up from my wounds and dripping onto the floor. I'm not going down without a fight, however. I won't give her the satisfaction of watching me give up. Besides, I have much to live for, including Kai. This bitch is going to have to work at it.

The next time she rushes me, I slam my fist against her face hard, hitting her directly on the nose as she howls.

Take that, you bitch, I think, with a scowl. I kick her while she's clutching her face, but she doesn't let go of the dagger and drags it down my leg as she falls. Fuck. God, that hurts like a bitch.

I fall to the ground, clutching my leg, watching as she gets back up. There's nothing but coldness in her eyes and determination etched on her face. I feel helpless but stand, putting my weight on the other foot. All I can think about is Kai. I don't want to die, especially when my mate finally shows me how much he loves me. I'm not ready to leave this world yet, and I'll be damned if I let this woman get the best of me. I don't know why she's attacking, but some part of me instinctively knows that someone's put her up to it. Someone whose name is probably Candice. Not that I have time to accuse the woman of that. She's moving around so bloody fast.

She raises her arm and goes to stab me. I grab her arm in midair and twist it, causing her to yelp as I thrust my head forward and hear a sickening crack. Her nose has been broken this time, with a huge sense of satisfaction. The knife has fallen to the ground, and I limp over, bending down to pick it up, wrinkling my nose at the heavy smell of the wolfsbane it appears to be coated in. This woman wasn't taking any chances, was she? The smell is disgusting and fills the air of the elevator.

The woman's eyes widen in horror as she gets to her feet. "Who sent you?" I demanded, even as my voice was hoarse from my yells and blurred vision. I need to know who set this up. I'm always tired of my life being in danger, tired of always looking over my shoulder in fear. This ends today.

The woman shakes her head. "I can't tell you," she says gravelly. "They'll kill me."

They? Was it more than one person who wanted me dead? Are you freaking kidding me? So much for thinking it was just Candice. Who else have I managed to piss off?

"You're coming with me," I growl, shaking my head as spots appear in my vision. "You can tell security everything," I snarl.

I press the buttons for the ground floor, but as the elevator lurches again, she darts towards me, kicking the dagger out of my hand and sending me flying to the floor as the elevator moves.

I watch, trying to scramble to my feet, hands slipping and sliding, as I realize the entire elevator is covered in blood splatters and trails that belong to me. There's a look of hesitation on her face before she plunges the dagger into me again, my hand swinging out wildly as she pulls back.

"It has to be enough," the woman mutters in a low voice, so quiet, I almost miss it. "There's so much wolfsbane in her system that she can't survive this," she breathes. Is she talking to herself?

"Fuck you," I wheeze. I keep swinging out wildly, my legs kicking, but she's too far away to reach now, and I'm not entirely sure.

I have the strength to stand back up right now.

I'm frantically looking towards the doors, the woman hiding in the corner now. Maybe someone will be on the other side, someone who can help me. It's all I can hope for. The elevator doors open with a loud ping, and I lower my head in resignation. There's no one there. The woman looks triumphant, edging out of the elevator. I hear her footsteps racing away as she makes a run for it.

"Help," I rasp out. "Somebody help me…"

Kai, I think woozily. *Kai, please come and find me.* I cough up blood and lie completely down, feeling extremely weak, spots dancing in my vision, which is becoming blurry. I'm a goner. There's no way I'm going to survive this. It would take a miracle. I regret that Kai doesn't know where I am or that I am coming downstairs. I should have mind-linked him. That would have been the smart thing to do. But I hadn't anticipated being attacked at a summit for werewolves, for goodness sake. This should have been one of the safest places to be. I had thought I was safe here—the irony.

My head lowers to the ground. I'm cold now, so unbearably cold. My eyes are beginning to flutter shut of their own accord. I don't have the strength to hold on for much longer. The last thing I hear as my eyes close and darkness surrounds me is a woman hysterically screaming. I wonder if I just got my miracle.

Chapter 77

Kai's POV

I'm ropeable. How on earth did Winter get attacked at a summit full of werewolves, for fuck sake? The security team has dispersed, seeking out camera footage, and the only one permitted even near her at the moment is the blasted doctor. I hover near the bed where she's been placed while the doctor does his best to ignore me and the low grows I'm giving out every few seconds. Storm is dangerously close to the surface, and it's taking all my willpower not to shift and cause a panic. Shifting would be a very bad idea, even if I want to hurt someone right now and cause damage to everything that's in my path. I have to keep Storm back for everyone's sake, even if I'm tempted to let him go berserk. It would serve everyone right.

"How is she?" I demand, and the doctor sighs, looking up at me with a woebegone expression. I tense.

It's not the first time I've asked, and it damn well won't be the last. He can deal with my presence whether he likes it or not. He sees the look in my eyes and speaks with me, trying not to show his impatience. Good, he does not want to push me right now, not while I'm this insanely angry.

"She's resting for now. I've bandaged her wounds up and attached an IV. I'm concerned, though, because there appears to be wolfsbane in her system. I'm trying to flush it out, but it will take a while."

I stop in my tracks. Wolfsbane. No wonder Winter couldn't mind-link me when she was in trouble. The guilt is eating me alive. I should never have left her there in that room. I should have just waited until she got up and escorted her downstairs. I'm a complete imbecile. My hands are clenched into fists. I'm so angry, but much is directed at myself.

A knock on the door, and the security team hustles in. One of them, presumably the head honcho, so to speak, comes forward to speak to me. I glower at him. He better has some goddamn answers for me.

"Alpha Kai," he greets me stiffly. "I would like to speak to you in private," he murmurs, looking at the doctor, who is still hovering over Winter and lying deadly on the bed.

"I don't think this is the right time," I shoot out impatiently, but he merely raises an eyebrow at me.

He's cool as a cucumber. I can't believe it. How does he stay so damn calm?

"I believe you'll want to be here for this. We have the person responsible and are about to interrogate them," he answers smoothly.

That has me whipping my head around fast. They had found who had attacked Winter this quickly. How? *Good job.* I was impressed despite myself.

"Where did you find them?" I growl.

"She was trying to escape through a loading dock. One of my security officers thought her being there was unusual even though she'd dressed in a uniform she probably stole from somewhere. It was lucky he stopped and restrained her. Otherwise, she would be long gone, and we'd never have caught her."

So it was a she, I thought to myself. Interesting. I looked at the security officer directly, liking that he didn't look away. "Take me to this interrogation," I order, and he nods, motioning for me to follow him.

I hesitate in the doorway. The doctor gives me a knowing look. "Nothing is to happen to her," I growl, and he nods.

"Two of my men will stay back to make sure nothing more will happen to your mate," the leader promises, and I have to contend with that as we walk downstairs to an office he pushes open.

31

I'm in shock as I gaze down at a young girl. She looks more like a teenager. She's a shifter because I can sense her wolf, but she looks so young and innocent. Not to mention I've never seen her before in my life, and I'm willing to lay bets that Winter hasn't ever seen this girl before. Well, not until this morning, anyway.

I wrinkle my nose. There's the smell of blood all over the girl, the metallic scent, and my eyes widen in anger as I step inside the office, the leader of the security team directly behind me. As he closes and locks the door, I glare down at the girl. I can smell my mate's blood all over her, and Storm is going nuts, ready to tear this girl to shreds. I must put a mental block up, preventing him from taking control. He's not pleased with me.

She's been restrained with silver cuffs to the table and looks miserable. She's pale, ashen. Her lip is quivering. I feel no satisfaction in this. Something seems wrong about this entire scenario. Still, I advance on her.

"Why did you try to kill my mate?" I thunder, and she flinches, biting her lip but refusing to speak.

God help me for what I'm about to do. I grab hold of her head and smack it into the table. She hits the corner and begins to bleed. I harden my heart. She's attacked my mate. I'm not about to feel sorry for her.

"You attacked my mate," I repeated, and she still said nothing, but I could see her whole body trembling as she sat in the chair, unable to move away due to her restraints burning her skin.

I glance over at the security guy standing there with his arms folded. Finally, I catch a glance at his name badge. It reads Teddy. It's almost enough to make me smile. Imagine a big hulking guy with a name like Teddy. The irony. He seems unfazed by the violence I'm exhibiting toward his prisoner.

"You might as well talk," Teddy says casually, walking over to the table. I hadn't even noticed the knife in a transparent white bag. "We found the knife, and the victim's scent is all over you. There's no way you're getting out of here alive," he said, and even I flinch.

It might seem harsh, but it was a violent attack, and Winter could have died. It still might be because of this girl.

"If I'm going to die, then what's the point of talking," the girl says harshly, and I'm taken aback. So she does have a voice, after all.

"Listen," I say, slamming my hands on the table so hard that it makes her jump. "I've never seen you before, and neither has my mate. That in itself is suspicious. What reason could you possibly have for the attack? My mate's never done a thing to you." At least, I'm reasonably sure of that. Somehow I can't picture Winter having done anything bad toward anybody, let alone hurt another human being. It's not in her nature.

The girl looks away. She looks like she's about to cry now. I narrow my eyes at her. Something's off. You don't attack someone and then cry about it. At least not that I've ever seen, anyway.

"I can't talk," she finally says, not looking at me or Teddy, who now looks extremely interested.

"Why not?" I demand heatedly. "Did someone put you up to this? We can't help you if you won't even help yourself," I add with a low growl. I nailed it. The second I asked if someone had put her up to it, she went paler than a ghost—a dead giveaway.

"I'm going to die anyway. You just said it," the girl said dully.

"Not if you were put up to it," I say with a scowl, glancing over at Teddy, who nods in agreement. The girl looks hopeful but then looks down at the floor.

I grab the dagger, opening the bag enough to show the blade as she flinches. "I will cut your fingers off, one by one, if you don't tell me what I need to know," I threaten.

Now she looks terrified. *Good.* Still, she refuses to speak. Teddy doesn't make a move. He knows this is between her and me.

I force her hand down on the table as she wriggles and squirms. I spread her fingers out and lined up the knife. This will hurt like a bitch, but she needs to start talking.

"One more chance," I say, the dagger raised in my hand.

Tears form in her eyes, but she says nothing.

I bring the dagger down on her finger and sever it completely as she screams. Blood spurts everywhere, and Teddy somehow finds some bandages to bandage it.

"Fuck!" she yells, and I merely raise my eyebrows.

"Talk," I spit out.

She sobs wildly at me. "I can't," she cries out.

"Can't or won't?" I grunt, raising the dagger again as Teddy moves away.

"They'll kill me," she says, and I stop, glancing over at Teddy. "You don't understand," she sniffles. "They have my family, and they'll kill them."

Now we're getting somewhere. Though it pains me, I raise the dagger again. "Speak," I mutter.

She says nothing, and I grimace, severing another finger as she screams and howls, her flesh burning and effectively cauterizing the wound from the silver.

"No more," she pleads, sobbing. "Please, no more."

"Then talk," I thunder impatiently. "Because I will cut every finger off if you don't start speaking. Who has your family?"

She looks away. There are tear stains on her face and tears trickling down her cheeks. When she finally speaks, it's in a wavery, shaky voice full of fear. "Alpha Liam has my family. He told me that if I didn't kill your mate, he would kill them when he got home. I didn't have a choice."

I'm puzzled, though, and a bit suspicious. "Why would he want my mate dead? He's never even met Winter before the summit. We don't like each other, but that's no reason to kill my mate."

"It's that girl," she cries, and I stiffen. "Ever since she came along, he's been different. Changed. He's no longer the nice Alpha he used to be. She wraps him around her finger, and everyone in the pack hates her."

"Candice," I say slowly, and the girl gives me a nod.

"I would bet anything it was her idea. She hates your mate and hates that you broke up with her. It's all she ever talks about," the girl sniffled.

That bitch. I was going to kill her. Teddy was looking nonchalantly at me. "What would you have us do?"

"Alpha Liam is your problem," I mutter. "I want Candice restrained and taken back to my pack. She's not getting off lightly this time, the traitorous bitch. I should have killed her before."

Teddy raised his eyebrows but gave a firm nod before hesitating and swinging his chin towards the young girl sobbing wildly and looking hysterical.

"What's her name?" I ask quietly.

"Chantelle," Teddy said. "What do you want to be done with her?"

Chantelle's head swings around, and she looks at me pleadingly.

"Let her go free. She's already lost two fingers today as punishment, and she didn't have a choice," I murmur as the girls' eyes light up. "Make sure her family is okay as well," I order.

"Done," Teddy agrees, fetching a key and undoing Chantelle's restraints. "But she needs to stay here while we apprehend the other two, and you can't interfere either," he tells me. I nod reluctantly. I have to let them do their jobs. Chantelle is agreeable as well.

"I'll be in the room with Winter when you're done," I say coldly, storming away. I can't wait to get my hands on that bitch Candice and show her what happens to those that try and harm my mate.

She's gone way too far this time. I begin to plot my revenge.

Chapter 78

Kai's POV

Winter is placed carefully in the backseat of the car. The doctors managed to stabilize her condition, and it looks like she'll survive, which is excellent news. Langdon has personally come down with a small entourage of vehicles and warriors, dragging a kicking and screaming Candice out and throwing her into the back of an SUV. The gag in her mouth muffles her screams, which I see with great satisfaction. Oh, and she's doing plenty of screaming. She knows what's coming and what's in store for her. Good. I'm reveling in her terror.

"She has been secured," Langdon said, coming to my side and gazing at Winter, highly concerned. "What are your orders involving her, Alpha Kai? What would you have us do with her?"

"Secure her in the dungeon, but no one touches her. I want Winter to have a say in what happens to her. But she's not getting out of this one alive. It's rather a matter of how slowly she dies instead," I say. "After all the crap she's pulled and the number of times she's hurt my mate."

He gives a nod but looks rather grim. I open my mouth, intending to ask him what's wrong when another voice interrupts me.

"Alpha Liam has been secured, and the elders are on their way," Teddy said cheerfully, clapping me on the back with a wide smile. "Chantelle is on her way back to her family," he adds, and I nod. That's one bit of good news. I feel bad for cutting the girl's fingers off, however. I wish she would have just talked in the first place, but at least we can ensure her family is safe.

"Langdon, this is Teddy, the ahem," I cough. "Chief of security. Teddy, this is my Beta Langdon."

They shake hands.

"I've gotta go, but I wanted you to know you're all set," Teddy said with a low whistle and a shake of his head. "I hope your mate will be all right."

"Doctor says she'll recover," I mumble automatically, not wanting to discuss it.

Langdon squares his shoulders. "We're ready to move out. Two of the other cars will stay back and be your guard on the way home," he explained, as though he hadn't already told me all this in the mind-link earlier. But he looks pale and haggard, withdrawn. Something is amiss. Something is wrong, and I need to know what it is. He's keeping something from me. I can sense it.

"Is something wrong, Langdon?" I probe delicately, and he shakes his head at me, seemingly startled out of his thoughts.

"Nothing is wrong, Alpha Kai," he says politely, and I swat at him.

"Cut it out with the title," I growl, and he huffs a laugh.

Langdon gathers his troops, and they get into their cars in a procession line, leading the way back to the pack house. I get into the driver's seat of my car and glance back over my shoulder at Winter. She was covered in bandages, but already her wounds were beginning to heal. She would have scars from the silver dagger, which pissed me off. Her beautiful pale skin was already covered in traumatic scars, and now she would have even more to look at and remember what happened. My hands clench on the steering wheel. *Damn it! Damn it! Damn it!* I swear in my mind, thumping the steering wheel with my hands. She never should have had to go through what she had in the elevator. It was all my fault.

I let her down. There's no denying it. I wouldn't be surprised if she hated me when she woke up. It's the least of what I deserve. I should have been protecting her. Heck, if I'd been by her side, she probably never would have even been attacked in the first place.

Candice was beyond obsessive, and I wouldn't say I liked that she was still ruining our lives and our chance at happiness. She would pay, but it would never be enough to undo the hurt and all the damage that bitch had caused. Why hadn't I seen just how crazy and obsessive Candice was? Why hadn't I seen her as a threat? The signs were all there. I had just been completely oblivious.

Winter mumbles incoherently and then stills as I start the car. I've got her tucked in and belted up, but I will still not take any chances on accidentally jostling her if I can help it. We could have stayed another night, but Winter's attack had effectively broken up the all-important summit, and I didn't trust that Candice and Alpha Liam didn't have a plan B of some description. She was safer at home, with me and the pack. At least, that's what I'm hoping. I'm starting to doubt my ability to keep her safe at all. Considering I was failing miserably at it.

I pull out, watching in the rearview mirror as the two cars follow behind me, as Langdon promised me they would. I don't need the guard, but for Winter's sake, I added to it. It's cold, slightly chilly. Is Winter cold? Maybe I should stop and pile more blankets on top of her? I hesitate but then turn the heater on in the car. It would have to suffice. The trip is only a few hours. She would be all right. At least she won't freeze to death in that time. Plus, my heater is quite strong before I know it, and the car is toasty warm.

We finally return to the pack house, and I park the car at the front in relief. God, we've made it. My fingers are numb from clashing the steering wheel so hard with my fingers, and my shoulder hurts from constantly looking over my shoulder to make sure that Winter is all right. But I can't help myself. Storm also desperately needs to check on her and ensure she's doing all right. Both of us are feeling overprotective towards her right now.

Langdon greets me before I can gather up Winter, who's sleeping peacefully, her soft snores reassuring. The drive hadn't caused any more damage to her body. Thank God. I give a small smile. The fact that she's sleeping so peacefully despite being in a car is very reassuring to me.

"Everything has been carried out. Candice is in the dungeon, awaiting your arrival," he tells me, and I grin wickedly.

I had gone easy on her the last time because of all our history together, but this time it wouldn't be anywhere near as soft or held back.

"She stays there. I want Winter to have a say in whatever happens," I order, reaching out and stroking Winter's hair, pulling a stray strand of hair back from her face. She looks so vulnerable, so innocent. My guilt is overwhelming me, and it's killing me inside.

"That's been arranged," Langdon says briefly, then hesitates, something flashing across his eyes. Just as quickly, it was gone, and I blinked my own in confusion. I knew something was going on with him.

"Alpha Kai, I have a request that I would like to ask of you," Langdon says quietly, making me stiffen. Never once has Langdon ever asked me for a favor. Not for himself, not for anyone. So this had to be important for him even to bring it up. I straighten. Winter's still snoring in the background, but I'm not walking away from this car. I fold my arms and give him a stern look as he looks away sheepishly. Whatever this request was, it better be good.

"Ask me, and I will tell you if I can grant it," I challenge, watching as he takes a nervous gulp and a big breath. He looks pale, ashen, and I realize he's worried about telling me whatever it is.

"I only ask that I not be involved with torturing Candice," he says, and my mouth drops open in shock.

Was he asking me such a thing? Not once had Langdon ever balked at torturing prisoners, not even female ones, who deserved it. Why was he suddenly avoiding my gaze and looking into the distance? What made Candice so different from the others he'd helped me within the dungeon?

I'm tempted to shout at him for an explanation, but one glance at Winter has me gritting my teeth and clenching my hands into fists instead.

"Explain why," I say tightly.

He looks away, a flush rising on his neck as though deeply embarrassed. He's silent for so long that I'm pondering whether or not he's turned mute.

"I can't be involved in torturing my mate," he whispers, and I stare at him in utter shock.

What the hell did he mean by that? Candice had told me she'd never found her mate when we got together. Had she lied to my face? Oh, God. My stomach churns. How had Langdon felt when he'd watched me be with her? It must have killed him, and he hadn't said anything.

"Candice is your mate," I say numbly.

"Was my mate," he says seriously. "She rejected me the first chance she got. I wasn't far enough in the hierarchy for her," he added bitterly.

Poor bastard. She'd done a number on him, as well as myself.

"Then why," I start, and he interrupts.

"I just couldn't. I can stand by while she's being hurt, but I can't partake in it myself," he hisses, and I nod, my hands relaxing by my sides.

"Why didn't you tell me?"

"I wanted you to be happy, and if Candice made you happy, then I wasn't going to ruin that," he said bluntly. "Even if I hated her guts for it. You deserved better, but you wouldn't listen," he points out.

I might have listened better if he'd told me the truth, I think to myself a little grumpily. He didn't have to protect me. I'm not a damn child.

"I won't make you do it," I promise him, hurting when I see a look of relief in his eyes. I'd put him through the wringer, and he remained loyal. It boggles my mind. "Did you accept the rejection?" I ask and give a hiss when he shakes his head.

"I was too much of a coward," he mumbles, and I shudder.

"So every time we were together…" I trail off.

"I felt it," he finished. God, I feel sick to my stomach.

"You might want to accept the rejection, Langdon," I tell him quietly, trying to persuade him. "Because she's going to die, and that's the last thing you need to feel."

"I know," he says grimly. "I'm going to. It's been more than enough time. I just can't torture her."

I bend back down and undo all the restraints and seat belts off Winter, cradling her in my arms and slowly backing out of the car. Langdon's polite enough to shut the car door closed.

"I'm going to be inside with Winter until she wakes up," I tell Langdon staunchly. "We don't get disturbed unless it's a damn emergency and someone keeps an eye on that bitch Candice the entire time. Do you hear me?"

He nods. "Take care of your mate, Kai," he says wistfully as we enter the pack house. "Mates are precious," he finishes.

Mates are precious, holding onto mine tight as I ascend the stairs. One day, I hope Langdon gets a second chance mate. If anyone deserves it, I think it's him. I pray the moon goddess grants him that gift as I put Winter to bed and snuggle against her.

Chapter 79

Langdon's POV

My initial reaction is shocking when Alpha Kai informs me of Candice's subterfuge and willingness to kill Winter out of revenge for Kai breaking up with her. I've always known that Candice has been nothing short of a detonator ready to go off at any moment. She's always been slightly unstable, desperate to climb to the top, and coveted the Luna position above all else. Nothing, and no one, not even her mate, would get in the way of that. Still, it doesn't stop me from feeling slightly sorry for her. What can I say? The mate bond still works on my side. I curse the fact that I never accepted the rejection. It would have saved me a ton of heartbreak. I guess I'm just a glutton for punishment. *No more,* I decide.

Poor Kai. He looked so shocked when I told him. I think he was hurt as well. But what could I say? Candice had rejected me on sight because I wasn't an Alpha, and she'd set her sights on Kai. I close my eyes and exhale slowly, picturing that day. It's forever imprinted in my memories, a painful reminder that I'll never be able to get rid of, no matter how hard I try…

I'd just returned from another business trip to the Cold Ice Moon Pack. We'd successfully negotiated, yet another treaty, and our pack was becoming stronger under my and Alpha Kai's leadership. I'd been ecstatic to be back home, tired of the traveling and needing some relaxation. It had been a long trip and an even longer visit. I was happy to return to the pack and even happier to be home. I couldn't wait to get to bed in my own house.

I'd no sooner gotten out of the car when the most delicious and amazing scent of caramel wafted towards me. At first, I thought someone was baking, but as I followed it, sniffing out the source, I came across a woman I had never seen before. Damn, she was beautiful. If I'm honest with myself, she still is. Her pale smooth ivory skin and those big eyes blinked up at me in astonishment. Her hair gleamed in the light, and she was a figure to die for. I'd almost been drooling when I stopped where she was walking and touring the pack grounds. I knew instantly why my wolf was going insane in my mind. There was no doubt about it. She was mine.

"Mate," I growled in disbelief and watched her eyes change color, her wolf coming close to the surface. God, I'd been delighted. I'd waited so long for my mate, and now she was finally here. I didn't have to keep looking at each pack I went to anymore. I finally had her. She was all mine. My heart was swelling with joy and contentment. This was what I had been waiting for. The moon goddess finally blessed me with my mate to cherish and love.

But then she took a step back and another, as I stared at her confused. I didn't understand why she looked so hesitant at me. I wasn't going to hurt her. I would never hurt my mate.

"No," she breathed, and I flinched, hearing her disgust and repulsion. "God no, I won't," she said, and my mouth dropped open. She won't what? Won't accept me? Surely she was kidding? She didn't mean what she was saying, did she?

She squares her shoulders and looks directly at me, crinkling her nose and looking like I'm something on the bottom of her shoe.

"I, Candice of the Silver Shining's Pack, reject you, whoever the hell you are, as my mate now and forever more," she spat. I stare at her numbly.

She hadn't even let me get my name out and rejected me on the spot. She flips her hair over her shoulder and storms away as my jaw drops. I hesitate. Should I go after her? Maybe I could convince her to take it back? If she got to know me better, she would see I was a loving mate. Wouldn't that be enough to convince her she'd made a mistake?

But my pride is stung now, and I glumly begin to walk back to the car. So much for that, I think to myself sourly. Should I accept the rejection, or would she change her mind once she'd had time to calm down and collect herself? I lightened. Maybe she was just in shock at the whole thing. She probably just needed time to think things through. I would wait, and I would speak to her again. I would give her time to adjust to finding her mate and overcome her shock. I would cling to the hope that she would return to me and realize she had made a mistake.

But she hadn't been interested, not in the following few days when I'd attempted to reach out to her, snubbing me and turning her face away whenever I tried to utter a word in her direction. I'd finally given up when Kai called me into his office.

I'd hurried to the study, thinking it was wrong that Kai had mind-linked me for something important. I knocked on the door and waited impatiently, feeling sick as I smelt her scent. What was she doing in his office? Did they know each other? Maybe they were friends, I thought to myself, hopefully. In this case, maybe Kai could convince her to give me a chance.

"Come in," *called Kai, and he sounded deliriously happy. My stomach drops. Something's wrong.*

I see Candice standing behind him, hands on his shoulders, a wide smile on her face as he sits there looking relaxed.

"You called for me, Alpha Kai," *I mutter, glaring at Candice. Kai, thankfully, doesn't seem to notice the look I'm giving her.*

"I want you to meet Candice," *he says with a large smile.* "My girlfriend. Candice, this is Langdon, the one I was telling you about. My best friend and my Beta."

I flinch. He has no idea how much he's just hurt me.

So Kai knows nothing about us being mates, then. I open my mouth to tell him but then pause. I can't tell my best friend that she's using him. Not now. Maybe later, when the flush of the new romance has worn off. Otherwise, I may have to try and hint at it, but I don't want him to be unhappy. God knows he's barely dated due to those scars of his that he thinks are hideous. Women can be so cruel sometimes. I have no doubt Candice is going after him due to an ulterior motive, but I doubt Kai will listen to me, and I'm too ashamed to tell him about my rejection.

I hold out my hand and force myself to grip hers. My eyes were cold and icy as I stared into hers. "It's a pleasure to meet you," I say with gritted teeth, ignoring the tingles that travel up my fingers and hands. I almost yank my hand away. Kai looks confused.

"It's so nice to meet you, Langdon," she coos, and I scowl at her. I can't help it.

"Is there anything else, Alpha Kai," I say pointedly. I needed to leave the room before losing my temper and senses. He looks a little surprised at my abruptness but reluctantly shakes his head.

"No, I just wanted you to meet each other," he says sadly. "You may go, Langdon. Thank you for coming."

"I want to go for a walk if that's all right," Candice says hastily. "It's a little stuffy in here, darling," she says, bending down and giving Kai a peck on the cheek while I try not to gag.

"Sure," he says. "I'll just do some paperwork until you come back."

I roll my eyes and walk out the door, almost jogging out of the pack house. I want to be left alone. I'm not in the mood to speak to the bitch right now.

"Wait," she breathes, rushing to me as I fold my arms and glare daggers at her. "Why haven't you accepted my rejection?" she says, annoyed. "I'm not going to change my mind. You might as well get it over and done with," she points out. "Otherwise, it will hurt like hell whenever I'm with him."

"I'll accept it when I want to, not just because you're asking it of me," I snarled back. "Now get the hell out of my sight, you bitch."

She scurried off, looking once over her shoulder before giving me a smirk and kissing me. Arrogant bitch. I hate her now but know I must keep that from Kai. Not that I've ever been good at hiding my emotions...

Now I curse my stubbornness. Ever since that day, I've felt the pain of the mate bond as she slept with Kai more times than I've wanted to count. My heart's been ripped to shreds, and I don't think I'll ever find a true mate to love me. It would have to be a pretty special woman for me to trust her again after what Candice has put me through, that's for sure. I don't know that such a woman even exists.

My footsteps are loud, and my heart is heavy. I trudge downstairs, my head staring down at the ground intently. I should have done this in the first place. I should never have let it get this far. Still, it's a struggle to put one foot in front of the other and keep going until I've reached the bottom of the stairs and greeted the guards. They let me through without a problem. Used to see me in the dungeon whenever we had a prisoner. They give me my privacy.

I stare at her with disinterest. Once upon a time, I would have believed she was the most beautiful woman in the world, and now I feel nothing. I'm completely numb inside. I don't even feel hatred towards her. She's conscious, trussed up like a lamb to the slaughter, but there's still a smirk on her sad face. Does she think I'm going to help her? After everything she's done? She's in for a rude shock.

"Come to see the torture have you, Langdon." Candice sneers, her voice hoarse from screaming. I don't answer,

She tries another tactic. "Langdon, you have to help me," she whispers. "We're mates. You can't let me be killed. I'll even take back the rejection," she promises, and I smirk at her. She was feeling desperate then.

I take a deep breath. "Correction," I tell her gruffly. "We were mates. I've come to rectify that."

Her eyes widen. She wasn't expecting this. But I won't let her be the death of me. She's made her bed. Now she has to face the consequences alone. I steel myself.

"I, Langdon, accept your rejection, Candice," I tell her, feeling something like an elastic band break as my knees buckle and I fall to the ground, the guards crying in the background in shock.

She screams, feeling the same pain that I do, and it fades away just as quickly. The mate bond has been completely severed. It's done. I'm finally free, I think, sadly, but it's come at a cost.

The guards help me to my feet, and I dust myself off, thanking them. I turn away without another word and ascend the stairs, ignoring her screams.

"Langdon, Langdon, don't do this to me."

I'm not doing this to you, Candice, I think bitterly. *You brought this on yourself. You reap what you sow.*

Chapter 80

Winter's POV

F uck, my entire body is throbbing. My head feels like there's a ton of bricks lying on top of it, and my stomach feels like it's been hacked with an axe or something. No, I'm not being melodramatic. It hurts that freaking much. What in the hell happened? Why am I in so much fucking pain? I feel like a truck ran over me.

We got shish kebabbed, Winter.

We got the what now, Sabriel?

We got attacked in the elevator, remember? By a little punk bitch? She used wolfsbane on the dagger. Coward.

Um, I remember. We were going to go and see Kai.

Yeah, you finally got laid and gave up your virginity. Nice going, by the way. Then the morning after, you were taking the elevator to see a lover boy and a woman, well teenager is probably more accurate, attacked us with a knife? Do you remember? Remember Winter?

I remember now. I can see everything so clearly again, in my mind's eye. The knife gleamed in the lights, the wolfsbane dripping from it. The look of desperation on the girl's face. As though someone had put her up to it. The pain and the struggle to fight back. I had thought I was a goner, but someone found me in time. I blink my eyes open and stare groggily around the room. *At least it's not the hospital,* I think grimly. I've had enough visits to the hospital to last me a lifetime. They're probably sick of seeing me as well. The bed I'm in is nice and comfortable, at least.

It looks like I'm in my bedroom, and I turn my head and exhale, seeing Kai slumped in a chair, his head to his chest as he snored away. He looks haggard, like really haggard. He was pale and with more stubble on his chin than normal, like he hadn't taken the time to shave. Has he stayed here by my side the entire time? My lips are bursting with questions. I'm not at the summit anymore. Did this mean they had caught the person responsible for the entire thing? My heart sinks as I think about the fact that the summit might have disbanded because of what happened. Had I ruined it for Kai?

You idiot. You didn't ruin anything. You were attacked, for heaven's sake, Winter. Stop feeling guilty for something you're not responsible for.

But Kai was looking forward to the summit so much.

There will be other ones, and you'll be with him. He'll live.

I wish I could have shifted in the elevator, Sabriel.

Me too, but sneaky, using wolfsbane as a poison. Clever but sneaky. Otherwise, that bitch would have gone down.

My hand reaches below the bedcovers and feels the bandages covering my body, especially my midsection, where I remember getting stabbed. It itches slightly, and I peel it back to see my wound almost completely healed. It's a miracle. It will leave a scar, but considering my body is covered in them, it's no big deal. At least I'm alive.

"Doctor says not to touch that until at least tomorrow," says a gravelly voice that makes me look over at a now wide-awake Kai.

He struggles to his feet and awkwardly walks over to me, gripping my hand as I give him a shaky smile.

"How are you doing?" he asks quietly.

I think for a moment. I don't feel that bad. Sore, tired, and itchy, but on the whole, it could have been a whole lot worse. I could be dead, after all.

"I'm just sore and a little tired," I admit as he gently smoothes my hair back from my face. Good God, I must look like a complete mess.

Nah, girl, we're pretty no matter how messy we are. Nothing makes us look bad.

Sabriel, you have so much confidence.

You could too, Winter. You have to think like me.

I'll try and remember that.

"I'm glad," Kai says in a low voice. Then he startles me even more by exhaling and bursting out. "I should never have left you inside that hotel room, especially after what happened during the night. I should have stayed by your side, and then you never would have been attacked," he grimaced.

I stare at him incredulously. Was he blaming himself for what happened? Because I didn't blame him at all.

"Kai," I say, fixing my eyes on his. "This wasn't your fault. They would have waited for another chance if you had stayed with me. It was going to happen either way. At least this way, you weren't hurt either," I say firmly. I can't bear the thought of him getting hurt because of me.

He looks disgruntled, but I'm beyond caring. What happened during the night is one of the most memorable nights of my life, and I'll be damned if that gets ruined in any way. I stand on shaky feet, trembling, and walk toward the bathroom.

"Let me help you," Kai offers, but I fix him with a glare. Some things should remain private, and doing my business was one of them.

He backs down and sits, reluctantly watching me disappear into the bathroom. I'm shaky, but I can manage on my own. There's no way I'm about to ask Kai for help.

I do my business quickly and smartly and look at my reflection in the mirror as I wash my hands. I'm pale, with dark circles under my eyes. I can see a bruise near my hair line but other than that, I look all right. My hair was disheveled, but that was to be expected after being asleep. I shrug and walk back out, Kai looking relieved to see me again. Like I was going to run off in this condition. *Give me some credit, geez.*

"Did they catch the person responsible? Was it the girl who attacked me?" I say with a quiver in my voice.

Kai's eyes flash black for a moment. What was that I just saw on his face? Was it regret? An apology of sorts?

"They caught the person. The girl who attacked you was put up to it. If she didn't attack you, they would kill her family," he said grimly.

My eyes widen—the poor girl. Now I feel so bad for her. But what did Kai mean by them? Was more than one person responsible for the attack on me?

"They?" I repeat to him, trying to confirm what I heard.

"Alpha Liam and Candice were responsible for the attack on you," Kai said quietly.

Somehow the notion of Candice being behind it didn't surprise me in the least but Alpha Liam? What did he have against me? I'd never even met him before the summit.

"I understand why Candice," I say, stiffening. "But Alpha Liam…" I trail off helplessly.

"He did it because Candice manipulated him into doing it. She's very good at getting men to believe everything she says." He sounds bitter now. "Alpha Liam never stood a chance once she put her sights on him."

I didn't want to ask, but I needed to know. "Where is Candice now? Did they keep her at the summit?"

He shifts his feet and glances down at the ground. This doesn't bode well. What is he hiding?

"About that," he mutters. "I insisted that Candice be brought back here to be punished."

I stare wide-eyed. I must have heard him wrong. Surely, he wouldn't have been so stupid as to bring the woman responsible for me almost dying back to the pack house where I now lived? He was joking.

He flinched from the look on my face and the dawning anger.

51

"Just wait," Kai cries out as I glower at him. "I wanted you to have a say in her punishment, Winter. You deserve that, as the victim, at least, right?"

I can't believe him. Even now, after all this time, he was asking me to deal with Candice again. Did he not understand my desire never to see this woman again? He wasn't going to keep her at the pack house indefinitely, was he? I feel the bile rise in my throat. I can't stand to even look at him now. I'm so incredibly angry. My whole body is trembling with rage.

"Kai," I say, deadly quiet. "I don't want Candice punished. I want her dead, gone, buried forever from my life. Do you understand me? I'm not going to keep her around for your sake," I shout out, frustrated. Men were such idiots sometimes. I just wanted Candice gone. Why was that so hard for him to get?

"Then we kill her," Kai said gently, and I halted. Did he mean that? "As I said, you get a say in the punishment, and if it is death, so be it," he adds. Oh, I want her dead, all right. I'm sick of always looking over my shoulder and wondering what will happen to me. I want to feel safe again; the only way I can is to remove the person who constantly wants me gone. I don't care if it hurts Kai. I want Candice gone forever from my life.

I can hear the sincerity in his voice, and I'm so angry, so bitter towards Candice right now. It's as though she's sucked all the joy and happiness out of me. Why couldn't she have just been happy with Alpha Liam? She still would have had a chance to be Luna. But I knew her kind. She would have been obsessed over the fact that Kai had broken up with her instead of the other way around. But a small part of me is wavering. I couldn't bring myself to kill the rogue before. How can I bring myself to kill another shifter? Or order the death of one? Alpha Liam certainly doesn't deserve to die. Not when Candice had manipulated the man.

"Where is she?" I demand.

"She's in the dungeon," Kai says quietly. "But there's something else you should know," he adds as I almost scoffed. Of course, there was. I wait impatiently for him to tell me. "She was Langdon's mate but rejected him," he said in a rush.

My eyes are flickering now, between normal and going dark, my hands clenched into fists. Had she rejected Langdon? The man was a sweetheart! A little boring but otherwise a perfect gentleman! It didn't take a genius to determine why she'd rejected poor Langdon. Kai had been a much bigger fish to catch, especially if she wanted to be Luna. I feel indignant on Langdon's behalf.

I make a move to storm off, and Kai hurriedly follows the back of me. I stomp out of our bedroom and downstairs in a fit of pique, my footsteps loud in the quietness of the house, my face scowling the whole time. Kai wisely says nothing, opening the door to the dungeon and gesturing me inside. I barely glance at him before stomping down the stairs, almost shoving the guards to the side, trying to get my hands on Candice. I'm so angry, my chest is heaving, and I'm almost frothing at the mouth. The guards look taken aback, and Kai has to reassure them that I'm allowed down here, patting me awkwardly on the back.

I sniff and smell her disgusting perfume wafting toward me from the last cell. I stomp in the direction pointedly and stop in my tracks, staring up at my nemesis with a repulsed look on my face.

I ignore Kai's calls to stay back, to calm down. I don't need to bloody calm down. Christ. He needs to stop annoying me. Her head lifts, and she stares directly at me while I'm glaring at her, my entire body tense.

"I never thought you would have the guts to come down here yourself," she spits out, and I cringe, watching spittle fly across the bars. Disgusting.

"I guess you thought wrong," I say evenly, between gritted teeth. "Now, how about we discuss your punishment?"

Chapter 81

Winter's POV

I look at Candice directly into her eyes, noting her pale appearance. She has dark circles under her eyes that are almost black, but then again, how much sleep can a person get in a dungeon? My bet is not much. She didn't look as beautiful as she normally did. Her black hair was disheveled and looked like a rat's nest, her body suspended above the ground, her arms over her head, silver restraints, and shackles keeping her upright. I could see where the silver was burning her body. There was no smile on her face now, only a grim expression and hatred in her eyes. Hatred, directed at me. I flinch. It's not like I ever did anything to her. My only crime is that I turned out to be Kai's mate. It was enough for her to want to kill me.

"You don't have the guts to handle a punishment," Candice hisses at me, looking triumphant.

I feel Kai's hand on my shoulder and turn towards him. He looks at me apprehensively. "Winter, I can take care of this if you want to go upstairs."

I shake my head at him. I'm tired of being beaten down all the time. I am tired of being treated like shit by other people. I am tired of being constantly underestimated because I'm a nice person. I'm especially tired of women like Candice. So many bullies in the world. When does it end?

"Where's the trolley," I say evenly, and he looks taken aback but motions for a guard to bring one, pushing it right in front of me as Kai gives a nervous gulp. Even Candice is beginning to look worried now. Good. That's what the bitch gets for thinking I won't do it.

54

Winter, you have my support in this, do whatever you feel needs to be done. I won't judge you.

Thanks, Sabriel, but I'm going to block you anyway. I don't want to make you ashamed of me.

I won't, dear heart.

It's still for the best. I can't bear to have you watch what I'm about to do.

I block my wolf for the first time since I began speaking to her. I don't want her to see this. I don't want her to think less of me for finally breaking. I placed the gloves provided on and surveyed the trolley. My head cocked to the side. All the tools glisten on the trolley, beckoning me to choose one.

"Kai, open the door," I say quietly, grabbing a whip with silver threads.

He opens the cell door reluctantly. "Do you want me to come in?" he asks.

"No," I tell him. "I've got this." Or at least I hope I do.

Candice snorts. "Listen to her. She thinks she's suddenly got backbone," she laughs mockingly. The laughter was cut short as I drew back my arm and struck forward with the whip, using all my might. She howls, swearing as I stand there. My face was full of determination.

"You little bitch," she hissed and then screamed as, once again, I hit her with the whip.

I tuned out her little insults, Kai's staring, and the guard's commotion. I focused on one thing. Removing all my anger, resentment, and frustrations from her felt good. Candice also had to have been behind the poisoned tea and the incident in the hospital. I could have died each time because of her. She's never getting another chance to get near me or try again. I won't let her.

I wasn't merciful, and I didn't hold back, striking the bitch, repeatedly, watching her blood trickle down her body and onto the floor, blood splattering the walls and even the ceiling as I ripped her flesh open. When I tried, I stopped. She'd stopped laughing, and she wasn't joking now. She was deadly quiet, sobs filling the air. Even Kai's mouth was open in shock. I guess he didn't think I had it in me. Up until now, I didn't imagine I had it in me.

I placed the whip down on the trolley and then grabbed hold of the small dagger, examining it carefully as Candice blanched.

"I'm sorry," she wheezed. "Please, Winter. Stop, please."

I cock my head at her. "You caused that incident in the hospital, didn't you, Candice? Poisoned the tea as well with wolfsbane that time?" My voice was like a sing-song as I waited. I already knew the answer but wanted her to admit it.

She gulped nervously. "Yes, Yes, I was!" she screamed. "Please, please, show some mercy," she begged. I laughed, openly laughed at her, feeling incredibly powerful.

"You want me to show you mercy," I whispered thickly. "Where was your mercy when it came to me?"

She shut up, realizing nothing she said would dissuade me, tears flowing down her ashen cheeks. I grabbed her long raven-black hair and sawed away at it, cutting it in chunks and letting it fall to the floor. She cried the entire time. I thought I was generous leaving her hair at shoulder length when I could have made her bald instead.

She wore no clothes, and I perused her carefully, circling her like a hunter circles its prey. There. A perfect unblemished patch of skin. Without warning, I thrust the dagger in and began to cut through her flesh, Candice's head thrusting backward as she uttered a mouth-gurgling scream. I took my time, being slow but diligent, wanting my artwork to stay perfect. When I was finished, there was one single word on her back that read "Traitor."

I give her a smile of satisfaction, listening to her weeping as I look over at Kai.

"Winter, are you feeling all right?" he asks, and I look at him, confused.

What does he mean by asking that? I feel perfectly fine. I feel powerful and have never felt better. It was a rush.

I stab Candice in the midsection. "That's for me," I tell her with gritted teeth as she bucks and writhes in her chains. Another stab, this time to her back. "This one's for the girl you used," I snap, a little upset I hadn't asked her name. "And this one," I pause, thrusting the dagger into her back, severing her spinal cord, making her paralyzed from the waist down. "Is for Alpha Liam, whom you manipulated into doing your bidding."

I pause and then remember someone else. "This is for Langdon, the man you rejected," I say, stabbing the knife into her shoulder and gritting my teeth as she screams. Her body can't move anymore, and I back away from her slowly, pulling the knife back out.

I slam the knife onto the trolley and turn back to survey her. Her face looks green, like she's going to vomit, and I'm impressed she hasn't so far. Her body is slumped now, there's no feeling below her waist, but that will fix itself in time. I guess it's the beauty of being a shifter, but it will take weeks to heal completely, not days, and it will be painful—the least of what she deserves.

"Kill me," she whispers, so quiet that I almost miss it completely, my body stiffening as I pick up the words. She has some nerve.

"Kill me," she repeats, and I turn to her, my eyes blazing, my jaw tight, and my hands clenched into fists.

"I wouldn't give you the satisfaction!" I scream, venting all my rage as the guards back away and Kai clenches his jaw. "You ruined my life for nothing," I laugh bitterly. "You were never going to be Luna, you stupid girl. You should have just walked away."

She opens her mouth and spits out blood that I easily dodge. She's panting, her breathing weak.

"What... do... you... want..." she gasps out loud.

I have to think. Even though I'd managed to torture Candice, I still couldn't kill her. Am I a weakling? Or is there something I'm missing to be able to be that cold? Why can't I do it? Why can't I bring myself to kill?

I sink to my knees. "I can't do it," I mumble, frozen solid. "I hate you, despise you and everything you are," I laugh bitterly. "And still, I can't kill you. I guess I'm weak," I mutter, rocking back and forth as her eyes gleam with tears.

"Enough," Kai growls. "Winter might not be able to kill you, but that doesn't mean I won't," he snaps, picking me up and cradling me towards his chest.

Candice says nothing. Her head slumps back down to her chest. But I stop him, raising my head and looking at the woman who looks defeated and broken. What good could come from killing her now?

"Don't," I say quietly as Kai looks at me in disbelief. "Don't kill her."

"She tried to kill you," he growls, and I look away.

"I know," I respond. "But look at her. She's weak now. That wound will take weeks before she can walk again. Do you think she'll try again after this? When will everyone be on the lookout for her? She'd have to be insane to do it."

"I don't know, Winter," Kai growls warningly. "You've seen what she's capable of. Do you want to risk it again?"

I start to sob. I feel so repulsed at myself for what I just did. It was like I had been another person for a few minutes, and my anger and hatred had overtaken me. I need to wash myself and get clean. I can smell her blood on me, making me hysterical.

"Just leave her at the boundary's edge and banish her from the pack," I plead between sobs. "Please, don't make me responsible for someone's death."

"What about the girl whose family she threatened," Kai said in an icy voice.

That stops me momentarily as I look up at him, stricken. I had just remembered that. Shouldn't she also have the right to feel safe and secure?

"I can't kill her, Kai," I whisper, my heart thudding painfully in my chest as I sniffle against his shirt, which I notice, with a wince, is covered in my tears and blood from my clothes.

"I know, sweetheart, but I can't let her live," he finished, and I could see the pain his words were causing. I slump in his arms.

Candice can't be forgiven for what she's done, and the poor girl and her family must be kept safe. What I want is no longer relevant. I still know she will die, but I must accept it.

"Get me out of here," I whisper shakily. I feel so sick for what's about to happen, not just what I've done. How could I?

His hands tighten, and he begins to take me upstairs, but a miserable-looking Langdon meets him at the top. I flinch at the pain on the man's face. My God, this was killing him. Kai hands me to him. "Take her upstairs," he orders, and Langdon gives a shaky nod and turns with me in his arms.

"Langdon, I'm sorry," I tell him, and he looks down at me with the tiniest hint of a smile.

"You have nothing to be sorry for," he whispers.

We both stop as we hear Candice scream out for mercy before. Just as suddenly, it stops, the air around us growing cold and silent. We both know instinctively that Kai has killed her. Without another word, Langdon takes me upstairs as I silently cry into his shirt.

Chapter 82

Kai's POV

I slit her neck. Winter didn't want me to kill Candice, but I couldn't let her live. So despite everything, I made Langdon take her upstairs, and I returned to where Candice was waiting. She sneered at me. Brave, even as she watched me slowly put the gloves on and grab ahold of the knife. Even as I approached her, she stared at me, daring me to do it.

"No, don't," she begs, and I ignore her, even as she begins to scream and thrash wildly in her chains. My main concern is Winter's safety and finally getting rid of this danger, once and for all.

"You have to die," I growl and walk to the back of her, placing the dagger at her throat, her eyes wide in disbelief. Feeling no remorse, I pulled the dagger across her neck, blood spraying the walls before her. Her screams suddenly stopped. Now there's nothing but silence, and it's beautiful. *Sorry, Langdon,* I think with a wince. Hopefully, he did what I suggested and accepted the rejection before I tortured and killed her.

I drop the knife to the ground, making a large clattering noise, and turn to the guards, who look nervous now. "Take care of that," I hiss, indicating the corpse hanging from the ceiling. "Clean up this mess. Do you hear me?" I growl, my eyes pitch black. They nod quickly as I tear the gloves off and go bounding upstairs. No doubt, Winter heard Candice's screams stop and knew what I'd done, but I did it to keep her and everyone else safe. She has to realize that.

Langdon meets me at the bedroom door. "She's pretty distraught," he comments. "Won't stop crying. She thinks she's a monster for what she did to Candice."

60

I'm incredulous. Winter had gone easy on Candice, at least as far as I'm concerned she had. I would have tortured the bitch for far longer and worse than she'd done. But Winter had never tortured anyone before. Up till now, she was the one who'd been beaten and tortured. Was it any wonder she was conflicted? I don't think so. But she's not a monster. She would never be a monster to me.

"I had to do it," I tell Langdon, feeling sorry for the man, but he just nods and looks away, his claw clenched.

"Don't apologize," he mutters. "You did what was right. Winter will understand that too."

I nod and then enter the bedroom, closing the door cautiously as I hear Winter's quiet sobs from the bed where she's lying, curled up in a fetal position. They tear me apart. She sounded so devastated. I perch on the end of the bed, trying to think of what to say and how best to comfort or at least distract her, but I'm coming up empty. I'm not good at this sort of thing, and it shows.

Come on, man. There's got to be something you can say to make our mate feel better, Kai.

What do you suggest, Storm?

I don't know, how about I'm sorry you're hurting right now?

I could, but nothing would make her feel better right now.

No, but at least distract her from her misery. Her crying is making me want to cry.

Really?

No, but I feel very uncomfortable from the crying. Fix our mate.

You can't just fix someone.

Do it anyway.

Stupid wolf, I grumble, focusing on Winter, weeping into the pillow. I reach out and touch her hair, stroking it softly. "Winter... Winter, will you look at me?"

She continues to sob, but her eyes glance up at me, tears trickling down her cheeks. She looks stricken. "I'm a monster!" she wails. "A horrible human being."

I'm confused. Why would she think that?

"Winter," I say delicately. "You're not a horrible human being. Why are you saying that about yourself?"

She cries harder as I wait patiently, sitting closer and rolling her to face me.

"Because," she stammers. "Because I enjoyed hurting Candice," she cries. "That's what makes me a monster."

Oh, the poor sweetheart. She thought that because she'd enjoyed it, that made her horrible. After all the times she'd almost died at Candice's hand, she had every right to enjoy inflicting pain on the woman responsible. That didn't make her a monster. If anything, that made her human.

"Winter, she's almost killed you several times since you came to this pack. She's hurt you in so many ways and not just physically. Are you enjoying hurting her back? That was revenge, and it doesn't make you any less of a person. That makes you human," I tell her honestly, trying to project compassion into my voice. *Please, God,* I think to myself. *Let this work.*

Should we get a tub of ice cream and some wine? That always helps when chicks are sad in the movies.

Storm, this isn't a movie.

I still think it's a good idea, Kai. Let her binge her problems away and her sadness.

How do you know she won't bang us over the head for your stupid suggestion?

Chocolates, then, what woman doesn't like chocolates? Or flowers.

You're uncomfortable with her crying, aren't you?

It makes me feel odd, Kai. I wouldn't say I like it. Make it stop, throw some jewelry at her, or something.

Do you want to take over and comfort her?

Would you let me?

Hell no, you'll get us both banished from the room.

You have so little faith in me, Kai.

No, I'm just a realist.

"You don't think I'm a monster," Winter says in a wavering voice as she wipes the tears from her eyes and sits up, now meeting my eyes.

"Of course not," I tell her. "If anything, I was slightly impressed with how you held it together. Winter, you don't enjoy hurting people, and that's all right. Your kindness and your inner strength are one of the things I love about you," I say and watch as her tears begin to fade away, and the stricken expression falls from her face. Now there's a tentative smile there instead. I open my arms, and she falls into them, sniffling against my shirt, her eyes closed. I kiss her head, grateful that she's calmed down somewhat.

"Kai," she says. "I love you."

It's like an arrow pierced my heart. I'm in awe at how she says it, how easily. Like it's second nature to her. My heart is thudding wildly in my chest.

"I love you," I say, stammering back, but I mean every word. I have fallen in love with Winter. It's taken me this long to admit it to myself. She's everything to me. I don't think I can imagine my life without her.

She wrinkles her nose and sniffs, looking up at me repulsed. "I think we should freshen up," she says grimly. "You have blood on you, and so do I," she sighs. I give her a wicked grin. "You could join me in the shower," I say with a wink, and she bats her hand at me with laughter.

"No, thank you. I'm thinking more that I soak in the tub while you shower," she says pointedly.

"But what if I want a bubble bath?" I ask, whining.

Dude, I'm not getting in a bubble bath. It's not manly.

Chill, Storm. It's not like it affects you.

It affects my image and my reputation.

Really, Storm? I think you're getting a bit obsessive over how you're perceived.

Need to be more obsessive. You get in that bubble bath, and I swear I'll refuse to speak to you for a week.

Well, now it sounds tempting. Besides, bubble baths are relaxing.

I don't like the feel of bubbles! All right! No bubbles!

Sheesh, my wolf has serious issues.

"Do you want the tub after me, then?" Winter asks, breaking up my thoughts.

I laugh and shake my head. "No, I'll take a shower. That way, I get to feast my eyes on you naked," I tease as she blushes. God, she's adorable. Even after that fantastic night together, she still gets embarrassed about showing her perfect body to me.

I start the water in the tub first, Winter turning her back to me as she struggles out of her clothes. I look at the bandages and quietly help her peel them off. God, her wounds are healing, but it's clear that she has new scars over the old ones. I trace them with my finger, swallowing past the lump in my throat.

She climbs into the tub and fills it, soaking in it luxuriously as I shrug out of my clothes and fling them to the floor. I'd also have to organize fresh sheets on the bed, but that could wait until we were dressed.

I've barely stepped into the shower, moaning as the water hits my muscles, when that dratted Langdon decides to mind-link me.

Alpha Kai, we have a situation.

Whatever the situation, Langdon, I'm certain you're more capable of dealing with it, right?

Well, yes, but you should consider this. Does it affect Winter after all?

Speak plainly, man what the hell is wrong then, Langdon?

God, I was going to murder Langdon with my bare hands. My hands clench into fists in my anger, and Winter looks at me startled, seeing my eyes glazed as I speak to Langdon, my back slightly to her. Surely, Winter was not going to be affected by anything else? Shit. Then I remember the reason for Alpha Laurence coming through. Could this be to do with that?

Patrol caught two shifters near the boundary line. Both are male, and both are teenagers.

Well, throw them in the dungeon, as we do with all trespassers. Candice should have been removed now, and the guards were told to clean up. I need help understanding the problem here.

The thing is, Alpha Kai, they say their names are Johnathon and Damien. Damien claims he's looking for Winter, and he's her brother.

Fuck. This is the last thing Winter needs right now. I guess we have no choice. Have them escorted to the study then and guard them. They better be who they say they are, or I will strangle them both.

What about Winter?

I'll inform Winter, but we'll both come to the study in a few minutes. Do not tell them anything. Is that clear?

Perfectly, Alpha Kai. I'll see you in a few minutes.

I break the mind-link, cursing silently, turning around to face a very puzzled and concerned-looking Winter.

"Kai," she says tentatively. "What's wrong?"

I take a deep breath. I'm just going to have to break it to her. Even though she's just had a traumatic experience, she may be happy to hear about her brother Damien. I'm pissed that Johnathon, the son of a bitch who dared to reject her, is also there. My hands itch to teach him a lesson. Then again, if he hadn't rejected Winter, I wouldn't have her by my side as my mate.

"Winter," I say slowly. "That was Langdon. He caught two shifters near our boundary line."

"Oh," she says, relieved. "So it was just a patrol thing."

"Not quite," I admit, my eyes gazing into hers. "Their names are Johnathon and Damien. One of them is claiming to be your brother."

I watch the myriad of expressions across her face. First, there's shock, then surprise, fear, concern, worry, hope, and a small spurt of happiness. Damn it! She's glad to find out he's come all the way here.

"Damien's here," she breathes out excitedly, her eyes dancing. "My brother came to find me," she says, hastily standing up and sending water sloshing over the tub. "He must have been so worried," she whispers, almost leaping over the side of the tub in her haste.

I quickly turn the water off and reach for the towel. "Steady," I warn her. "We don't know why he's come, and I get you're excited, but I don't want you to get hurt. We'll go see them together."

She clasps her hands together with glee. "My brother wouldn't have come here to hurt me," she says confidently.

Maybe not, I think to myself bitterly, *but he had no issues hurting you in the past, or have you forgotten about that already, Winter?*

Chapter 83

Damien's POV

The rogue was nice enough to abandon us near a pack, the boundary line nearby. "Good luck," he muttered, and the next thing we knew, he was gone as though he'd disappeared along with the wind. Damn, he was fast when he wanted to be. He was a damn decent bloke too.

"Lovely," muttered Johnathon, scowling darkly in the direction the rogue had gone.

"He was nice enough to show us the way," I protest. "He didn't have to."

"Who's to say he wasn't lying? This could be any random pack. In which case, he just wasted our time."

"We won't know until we approach the pack," I mutter, walking forward, my hands in my pockets, feeling quite casual. At the same time, Johnathon continues to swear silently how everyone puts up with him as the Alpha of his pack is against him. I'm ready to strangle him with my bare hands. He's been that much of a nuisance and a whinger.

What if it took another two weeks to get here? That was nothing, not if we came across Winter. Johnathon needed to lighten up. At least the rogue hadn't killed us; trust me. He'd had plenty of opportunities to attempt it. All he'd asked for in return was food and water, even helping to hunt down some food we all shared. I enjoyed the company. He'd made a nice change from just Johnathon and his constant whining. Not to mention had all sorts of interesting stories to tell. I felt sorry for the rogue at the end of it. Maybe he'll find a pack to take him in.

A low growl stopped us both in our tracks. Several large wolves came out of the woodwork, so to speak, their heads lowered, their eyes focused solely on the both of us. We must have been closer to the boundary line than I'd assumed. I held my hands up in surrender, noticing that Johnathon, thankfully, was showing common sense for once and doing the same. One of the wolves shifted, his eyes staring hard at the both of us. I sniff, wondering why I was smelling the most delicious scent of apple and cinnamon coming from him. I'm almost drooling at the man. He looks so fucking god-like standing there, naked and completely at ease. What the fuck is going on with me? I'm not into guys. I like chicks. But I'm drawn to this one, like a moth to the flame. My mouth goes dry. The man's eyes are intense, but another expression is on his face. It's hard to tell if it's pure anger or something much deeper than that. I can't stop staring at him.

"State your business," the man growls, and my wolf purrs in my head.

Oh, fuck no, I know what this is. My wolf begins to prance around in my head, almost dancing triumphantly. If I can feel it, shouldn't he be able to feel it as well? If he is, he's doing a damn good job hiding it from me. Without thinking about it, my mouth opens and speaks of its own accord. "Mate," I growl, but the man looks away, his jaw clenched tight. My heart sinks.

"You must be mistaken," he mutters lowly, but it's enough to anger my wolf.

"Mate," I growl louder, Johnathon looking wildly between the man and my concern on his face. At least he has the decency to avoid interrupting.

"State your business," the man booms back. I can't believe he's ignoring the mate bond. Bastard.

I scowl at him and then remember the reason that we were here in the first place. "We're here looking for my sister Winter," I say quietly. "She's been missing for a few months now, and I'm worried about her."

The man is silent for a moment.

"What are your names?" he asks with a raised eyebrow.

"I'm Damien," I say shyly, my wolf pouting in the background.

"I'm Alpha Johnathon," Johnathon says, sounding very arrogant. God, could he act normal for once? Who cares if he's Alpha? He's on someone else's territory.

The man's eyes are glazing over, and I can tell he's probably mind-linking their Alpha, whomever he is. We're so far from my old pack that I don't even know what this pack is called, let alone how far away it is from mine. I couldn't tell you who the Alpha was.

"Come with me," the man orders, the other wolves dispersing. He ducks behind a tree and begins to get dressed, to my and my wolf's annoyance. We'd enjoyed staring at him naked.

"Wait," I say with annoyance, and he stops to glance at me. He's slightly older than me, but that doesn't explain why he's not acknowledging the mate bond. "Why won't you accept that we are mates?"

He groans out loud. "Now's not the time for that," he snaps. "I have to get you to study for Alpha Kai. We can discuss the mate bond thing later," he hisses, and I smirk. Well, at least he's willing to discuss it later. I'm not sure what to think. I'd never really dreamed that my mate would be a guy. My mind was in turmoil, and I was conflicted over the whole damn thing.

"Is Winter here then?" I ask eagerly, and he shoots me a wry look.

"I can't confirm or deny it," he says arrogantly. "The Alpha wishes to speak with you, so that's what he'll do."

The pack house is glorious, beautiful, with lush gardens and a huge monstrosity. A lot larger than the one in my pack, that's for sure. I guess my pack is small potatoes compared to this one. Even Johnathon seems to be in awe. For once, the other boy is speechless.

"My name is Langdon," the man says quietly as he opens the door to the pack house and motions us inside. We enter slowly, our eyes taking in all the details and elegance, yet it still seemed homely. Like a pack house should feel.

"Langdon," I repeat, the name rolling off my tongue. It seemed to suit the man, and I liked it a lot. So did my wolf.

"Down this way," Langdon ordered, leading down a corridor from the main entranceway. It seemed rather long, but the room he directed us to was none other than the study.

"Sit," he orders, gesturing at the two armchairs in front of the rather large, impressive desk.

We hastily sit, and he stands behind us, his arms folded in front of his chest, scowling. I fidget nervously in my chair.

"They must have Winter. Otherwise, why go to all this trouble? Besides, don't you think they would have shoved us in the dungeon?" Johnathon whispers, leaning back in the chair and looking like he doesn't have a care in the world.

"Maybe, or maybe the Alpha wants to tear us a new one for being near his land before taking us prisoner," I say back to him, frustrated beyond belief.

I could tell my mate was listening but not saying anything, which pissed me off even further.

"He wouldn't dare put another Alpha in the dungeon," Johnathon said with certainty.

I wasn't so sure. After meeting Johnathon, the Alpha might be too willing to throw him in the dungeon after discovering the boy's annoyance. I hope he keeps his mouth shut during the meeting.

"How much longer?" I ask, turning around and facing Langdon.

He stares at me. "As long as it takes for Alpha Kai to come down and see you," he spits out. "Show some respect and wait patiently. He's a very busy man," he adds. Of course, he is. Still, he was the one who wanted us to wait in the study, so you'd think he would hurry the hell up.

Sigh. Johnathon's busy taking office in, looking out the window at the greenery. "Man, your pack is awesome," he tells a very unimpressed-looking Langdon. "You've got a sweet operation here."

Chapter 83

Thanks, Johnathon. I'm sure that impressed Langdon, but not. I hope this Alpha arrives soon because my hands are itching to wrap around his neck and squeeze until Johnathon's massive head falls off.

I can't help it anymore. The words burst out of my mouth before I could take them back. "Are you going to reject me?" My voice is wavering, and I'm near tears. The thought of being rejected was slowly killing me inside. No wonder Winter had run away after Johnathon did what he did. I felt so embarrassed at divulging my feelings like this.

"Reject you," Langdon mutters, sounding surprised. Then his eyes narrowed. "We will discuss this later," he sighs, but he doesn't sound as annoyed or angry as before. Instead, he sounds remorseful. "I have no intentions of rejecting you if that helps," he says lightly. That does help. My wolf is a lot happier hearing that.

I see Johnathon stiffen in his chair and know he's thinking about Winter and how he'd done that. I rejected my poor sister without getting to know her first. I wonder how she's being treated in this pack, whether she's made a home here, and if she's being treated kindly. I hope so. I hope she's found what she's been looking for and wanting all these years. Now I feel uncertain. What if Winter didn't message me because she didn't want me to be in her life anymore? I could have made this trip for nothing.

No, not for nothing. I quickly correct myself. Johnathon and I had made this trip to warn her about Thomas, whom we, thankfully, didn't come across. One could only hope he'd gone in the complete opposite and wrong direction. If Winter didn't want me to be in her life, I would respect her wishes, although that might prove hard, considering my mate was from this pack. If it means keeping my sister happy, I may have to reject Langdon or let him reject me. God, that stings. Just the thought of it is making tears form in the corner of my eyes.

"Screw this," I hear Johnathon mutter and turn to see him stand up from his chair. "I'm not going to sit around and wait for this

71

bloody Alpha to show up," he snarls. "I don't wait for nobody, do you understand."

Fucking great. Of course, Johnathon had to get impatient. Are all Alpha's hotheads like this? It's a miracle they survive if they are. I go to put a warning arm on Johnathon's shoulder, but he shrugs it off, glaring at Langdon, who merely raises an eyebrow and looks nonchalant.

"You will wait as long as it takes," Langdon repeats, rolling his eyes.

"Johnathon, we've come all this way, for God's sake. Don't ruin it now when we're so close to getting answers," I plead with him. "I have to know if Winter's here. Can't you sit for a few more minutes?"

He looks like he wants to protest, but I shoot him a beseeching look, and he sighs, plonking back down on the chair and folding his arms across his chest, a pouty look on his face.

"Fine," he sulks.

I swear Langdon is fighting back a grin. Johnathon looks like a sulking schoolboy instead of a big bad Alpha. It's not something one wants to see. Langdon's eyes glaze over. I guess he's mind-linking someone because he ushers us to our feet. "Alpha Kai will be in, in a moment. Stand and be respectful," he advises, and I nod.

Johnathon shrugs, and I almost lose my cool at him. I hope Alpha Kai throws him through a window at this rate. Wouldn't that be a sight to see? I can hear footsteps now and frown. It sounds more like two people coming instead of just one, but Langdon stays silent. They get louder. My heart is thumping in anticipation. Johnathon looks completely unfazed. But I know him better than that. He's just trying to pretend he's cool.

The door bursts open, Langdon shifting out of the way. A pair of feet scurry across, and someone throws themselves into my arms. They are light as a feather, and I stare down at the face of the girl I've been hoping to find all this time as she beams up at me and hugs me tight.

Chapter 83

"Winter," I breathe, embracing her tight. "Thank God, I finally found you," I mutter fervently. Finally, the search was over.

Chapter 84

Winter's POV

Kai and I continue to argue with each other as we walk downstairs.

"I don't understand how you can easily forgive him for everything. Besides, what if this isn't your brother?" he asks, angry.

I eye him pointedly. "I forgave you everything," I pointed out, and he looked taken aback. I have a point, though, and he knows it.

"I never beat you," he protests. He falls silent at the look on my face. He sighs.

"Look," I sigh, turning to him at the base of the stairs. "I know it doesn't make sense to you, but Damien was afraid of our father. He did everything he was told; otherwise, our old man would have turned on him. It might not make it right, but try and put yourself in his shoes. If you were afraid of your father, wouldn't you do anything to keep him from being angry at you?"

Kai looks thoughtful but no less angry. I shrug. He would eventually see reason. Maybe after he's met Damien, he'll loosen up somehow. Besides, Damien is my brother and the only family I have.

We approach the study, my footsteps getting louder as I rush in excitement. I know Langdon is guarding my brother, and I assume Johnathon is with him. I almost slam the door open and bounce in. Straight away, I see him, my older brother, standing there with his eyes twinkling at me. I throw myself into his arms, enjoying how his arms feel around me, his scent, and how I've missed him. I don't want to let go of him. But in the end, an "ahem" and a loudly cleared throat force me to step backward and look at my mate, who is glaring

74

profusely at poor Johnathon, who looks distinctly uncomfortable. I understand my brother coming after me, but why on earth is Johnathon with him?

"Damien," I say quietly. "This is my mate, Alpha Kai. Kai, this is my brother Damien and his friend Johnathon."

"Nice to meet you," Kai says between gritted teeth, and I shake my head at him, my eyes warning him to be kind.

Kai shakes their hands, and I notice both Damien and Johnathon wince. Is he squeezing their hands hard, eliciting his warning toward them?

Kai lets go and strides to his seat behind the desk while I perch on the corner, absolutely beaming at the both of them.

"I can't believe you're both here," I gush, and Damien sits tentatively while Johnathon's more relaxed, plonking himself down.

"I can't believe you can talk," Damien says in awe, staring at me wide-eyed. "It's like listening to music," he adds, and I grin. He was always a charmer when he wanted to be. Even though I swear, my voice is nothing like music.

I wonder about Langdon, however. He looks like he's swallowed a bunch of sour grapes. His arms are folded across his chest, and he hasn't made a single move, let alone cracked a smile. Hmmm, there's a story to that. Especially since Damien's eyes keep shooting to look at him over his shoulder, that's very interesting. I have an inkling of what might be the problem, but that's something to bring up later.

"Let's cut to the chase, shall we," Kai growls as I stiffen. "You better have a good reason for coming here because if I think you're trying to bullshit me, I'll throw your sorry asses in the dungeon."

I scowl at him.

However, that made the two boys blink and sit upright.

"I came because I was looking for my sister," Damien says huffily. "Do you have any idea how worried I've been? You've been gone for months, and I haven't heard from you," he exhales. Man, he sounds pissed. His concern is touching. I hadn't realized I'd worried him so much. Or maybe I hadn't realized how much he cared.

"I was worried about her too," Johnathon says sourly. I almost laugh in amusement. He sounds like a petulant child.

"I'm sorry, Damien," I apologize softly. "I was going to write you when I was fully settled in. I just have been busy," I add hastily.

Yes, busy. Busy not being killed and dealing with a stubborn jackass of a mate who refused to reject me. I don't think bringing that up to Damien is appropriate. The last thing I need is a fight between my mate and brother.

Damien's eyes darken. Is he that angry at me? Why the hell was Johnathon here anyway. The last I'd heard, we were officially no longer mates. Maybe he and Damien had become good friends in my absence. It's the only explanation I can think of, at any rate.

"We can get to that later," Damien says slowly. "Johnathon and I came here for another reason as well. You're in danger, Winter," he says, and I look at him, confused.

In danger from what? I'm safe, aren't I? Candice is finally dead. I can finally breathe and relax. I begin to hyperventilate. No, whatever this was, it couldn't be too serious. Kai would keep me safe. Damien as well. All I need to do is clarify what he means by danger, but Kai gets to it first.

"Explain yourself," Kai hisses, and Johnathon glowers at the man. Geez, what is his problem?

Langdon has dropped his arms and sidled closer, his hands going to the back of Damien's chair. Damien fidgets slightly, and I swear there's a flush on his face. I hold back a smile.

"Winter, I don't want you to freak out," Damien says nervously.

It's a little too late for that. I want to scream out. *Tell me already. Tell me, damn you.*

"Well, Thomas isn't dead, Winter."

Thomas isn't dead. Thomas isn't dead. Thomas isn't dead. The words keep repeating themselves, and I'm at a complete loss. Of course, Thomas is dead. I killed him myself. I hadn't meant to, it was self-defense, but he was dead. Damien had to be mistaken.

I give a short laugh as Kai surveys me. "Good one, Damien," I say, forcing my voice to sound light. "But not a funny joke, don't you think."

He looks apologetically at me. "Winter, Thomas is alive. I saw him with my own eyes."

I can feel myself shaking now. "Not possible, Damien, he's dead. There was no coming back from what I did. It's impossible. Now stop. The joke isn't funny."

Kai pulls me onto his lap, stroking my hair as I turn into him, gripping his arms tightly. I can't even bring myself to look at my brother anymore.

Johnathon speaks up. "It's true. He's no longer just a shifter, either. He's a hybrid."

No, no, no, that was impossible. How on earth did he become a hybrid? Only one race would have saved Thomas, and that would have been a vampire. It's a miracle he survived the transformation.

Kai continues to soothe me. "It's all right, Winter, we'll be all right. I'll protect you."

But I can't help it, beginning to sob on his shoulder. I can't deal. I just can't. Candice is finally gone, and now someone else is after me. Why can't I just be left alone?

"What's he a hybrid of?" asks Kai calmly.

"Vampire and shifter," Damien says bitterly. "Money does buy everything."

"That's a potent combination, especially when you're not born one. Amazingly, he lived through the transition," Kai murmurs.

"We didn't mean to distress you like this," Johnathon says as I slowly turn and look at him. "But we wanted to warn you before it was too late."

"I don't get it," I shout, growing angry. "What does he want? What does he have to have so badly that he can't leave well enough alone? Is it revenge he wants for killing him?" I trail off and see my brother and Johnathon go pale. I'm trembling all over now, and still, they stare at me. *Somebody speak,* I beg in my mind. *Speak.*

"He wants you, Winter, but not for revenge," Damien says.

"He's still obsessed with you," Johnathon says above a whisper, and I stare at them both, tears trailing down my cheeks.

I knew Thomas' obsession with me, but now it seemed much worse. I'm terrified, and it shows.

"Winter, look at me," Kai says sternly, and I turn my head around, my eyes meeting his, which is pitch black. "You are safe here. He will not get his hands on you, not ever. I will protect you. Stop panicking, sweetheart," he said, kissing me on the cheek. It works. I begin to relax. I'm in a strong pack with strong warriors. Thomas won't stand a chance if he attempts to get at me. Not to mention this time, I have my wolf.

Exactly right, girl. We kick ass. You're bigger now, stronger. Did I tell you that Johnathon looks hot right now?

Sabriel, Thomas is on his way to find us, and you're still checking out other men?

I'm not blind, Winter. I appreciate beauty when it's right in front of me. Like smelling the roses, sort of.

Um, it's nothing like that. Johnathon rejected me, remember?

Oh, yeah, my bad. How about after this, we pee on him?

Um, no thanks, Sabriel.

Bite him in the ass?

Tempting, but still no.

Kick him in the man bits?

Also no.

Change his shampoo to hair dye so it goes a purple color.

No idea how you came up with that one, but still a no. Let's leave him alone.

Fine, you never let me have any fun.

You'll survive, Sabriel.

We should increase the patrol. Kai instructed Langdon, who was standing there nodding, mind-linking as they spoke. *No one gets near the boundary line without being thrown in the dungeon,* he growls. *And,* he adds, looking at Damien, *anyone that matches this Thomas' description will be killed on sight. Is that clear?*

Yes, Alpha Kai, Langdon says obediently.

"As for the both of you," he says darkly, shooting Damien and Johnathon a black look. "If it were up to me, you'd both have your hides in the dungeon right now. It's only because Winter has requested that I don't that's saved you from it."

They both went quiet and silent.

"Kai," I say sweetly. "I would like my brother and I to catch up. Do you think you could give Johnathon a tour of the grounds? Show him the pack house."

Johnathon looks annoyed, but I could care less. Kai looks just as pissed.

"I can do that," Kai says between gritted teeth. "But if he so much as does anything that upsets you," he growls, pointing at Damien.

"He won't," I promise.

Kai gets up, pecks me on the forehead, and looks at Johnathon with a scowl. "You're coming with me," he snaps and irritably stomps out of the room.

Johnathon hesitates, but something on my face must have told him to leave because he gives a long-suffering sigh and follows Kai out the door. Good, one less thing I need to worry about.

Langdon is still there and looks hesitant. I don't even worry about it, blurting out what I know must be the truth. "You two are mates, aren't you?" I ask.

Langdon blushes. "Yes," he mutters, looking away.

I couldn't be more thrilled, but I also know that Langdon is going through stuff right now, especially as that bitch Candice was his first mate. Damien looks concerned.

"I couldn't be happier," I declare. "But I also think you must work out what you both want. Damien," I tell him with a wicked grin. "You and I can catch up with each other again. But right now, I think you and Langdon must discuss this properly. Langdon," I say, turning to the man who looks startled. "Don't let your past mate ruin what could be a good thing. Let her stay in the past where she belongs." He gives a small nod.

"Damien," I say lightly. "You so much upset Langdon, and I will throw your ass in the dungeon. Langdon deserves to be treated respectfully, and I suggest you remember that," I say, a deadly look on my face as my brother stares at me and gulps.

"I'll remember," Damien whispers, and I give a smile of satisfaction.

"Fantastic," I beam. "Then I'll see you both at dinner. We're all going to eat as a family."

Langdon is about to protest, then thinks better of it. I head to the doorway and give them a casual wave. "See you later," I sing out and leave the both of them staring at each other, completely speechless.

Chapter 85

Kai's POV

I'm not even remotely sorry about what I'm going to do. My whole body is trembling in indignation as I take Johnathon for a tour of the pack house and pack grounds. He, the little pup, arrogant, cocky bastard, has said nothing as I take him outside, scowling and just looking like a petulant teenager. My hands itch to strangle the bastard around his neck. I'm pissed that Winter asked me to take him on a tour.

"She was mine first, you know," he says suddenly, and I halt in my tracks, anger making my head whip around quickly, my eyes flashing between black and normal as I glare at him. He did not just say that to me, did he?

"If I recall what Winter told me, you rejected her on sight, didn't you," I snap, and he shrugs, looking nonchalant. I'm tempted to throw the bastard across the grounds with my bare hands.

"Doesn't mean I can't change my mind," he says softly.

My hands clench into fists. "I've already marked her, and she's mine now," I hiss. "You had your chance with her, and you blew it."

"I shouldn't have rejected her," he muses as I stare at him. Does this kid have a death wish or what? "But I was too much of a coward to think about having a mate. I should have gotten to know her first," he adds sadly.

"You've left it too late," I snap. "She wants nothing to do with you." My God, I'm going to kill him.

He raises an eyebrow at me. "Are you so sure about that, Alpha Kai?" he challenges.

God, I'm dangerously close to ripping this moron's head off. I'm damn sure Winter wants nothing to do with this miserable excuse of an Alpha, but there's always the slightest chance I'm wrong.

"Winter's made her choice," I say evenly. "Whatever she decides is up to her."

He looks annoyed now, like he's trying to push my buttons. "That's it," he explodes as I glower at him. "You're not going to yell at me or even fight me? I've been waiting for you to hit me, and you haven't even tried!"

Great, he wants me to hit him. Storm is more than ready to oblige. I can't get a handle on what this kid wants. "If you want a fight, I'll give you one in the training ring."

His eyes light up. He must have wanted this from me because he gave me an arrogant grin. "Bring it on, Alpha Kai."

Sigh. The kid has a death wish. The worst thing is I can't even kill him without getting into trouble with Winter. Not to mention, I guess I owe him for bringing us the news of Thomas. Still, I was happy to fight and vent some of my frustration to him. The kid has no idea what he's in for.

We approach the training ring. "Clear the grounds," I thunder, and the small crowd quickly disperses, leaving Johnathon and myself alone, sizing one another up.

"A friendly fight, nothing more," I say between gritted teeth. No matter if I would prefer to the death. Winter would never forgive me if I killed him.

He gives me a nod of agreement, and the two of us shift. I stare in disdain at his wolf. Like mine, his is black, but I'm pleased to see his is several inches smaller than Storm's. Already I have the upper hand. *Size does matter,* I think smugly to myself.

I don't waste time circling and tackling him to the ground with a large snarl. He kicks me off, and we begin to circle each other, waiting for an opening. He jumps, and I meet him halfway, sending him flying to the ground, my body landing on his as I bite and claw at him, backing away hastily as he kicks out and gets to his feet. He growls lowly in his throat, and I can tell he's taking this seriously.

Another tackle, but I sidestep and swipe, clawing across his midsection, careful not to gouge him too deep. The last thing I need is for this arrogant, cocky pup to end up in the hospital. Winter would never forgive me. He races towards me, and I leap overhead, twisting and turning, my claws scraping against his back as he lets out a howl, a chilling sound that fills the otherwise silence. He's injured now, not severely, but enough that I'm hoping he'll have the common sense to stop because he crashes towards me and sends me rolling across the grass, hitting a tree trunk. I swear silently in my mind before returning to my feet. Now he's becoming a nuisance more than anything. A real annoyance.

He snarls, and I snarl back, opening and closing my jaws, my eyes focused on my target. I need to end this. He's starting to piss me off, seriously. Why is he so intent on fighting? We circle each other, both of us with moderate injuries, and I wait for him to attack. He lowers his head and pushes off, but I jump, landing on his back and immediately clamping my jaws down on his neck, not letting go as he frantically bucks and kicks out, trying to get me to release him. It's not happening. This fight is ending with me as the victor.

I clamp down harder as he whimpers. *Concede,* I think to myself furiously, *concede already, you obstinate brat.* My jaw is getting tired, but finally, Johnathon lays down on his stomach and bares his neck, submitting and conceding defeat. Finally, I let go, crinkling my nose at the smell of his blood, and backed away from the prone body, giving him time to get up on his own. He does and stares at me for a minute before getting to his feet and shifting back to his body.

I shift back to human form as well and stare him down. I fold my arms across my chest. I also feel angry and a little sorry for the young man. It must be hell to realize you've made a mistake, found the mate you rejected, and now want to be with someone else. I feel sympathetic towards him.

"What the hell was that." I almost explode, staring at him. "Why insist on fighting? You must have known you were going to lose! I have several years on you. It wasn't exactly the fairest fight."

He looked slightly sheepish. "I was angry, and fighting was the only way to cool my temper. Besides, I wanted to see what kind of man you are."

He wanted to see what kind of man I was. How did he tell that just by fighting me?

"You wanted to see what kind of man I was," I repeat, narrowing my eyes at him. "Well, what kind of man am I then, Alpha Johnathon?" I sneer.

"Strong," he says promptly. "Brave, but also kind and protective of your mate. You would fight to save Winter in a heartbeat. Even I can see that." He sounds sad.

"I could have been pretending," I point out.

He shakes his head. "No, you were fighting fair without trying to fight dirty. You could have. Heaven knows you're pissed off I'm here, but you still fought fairly."

He was right. I could have easily fought dirty and caused a major accident where he couldn't walk for several days. But that wasn't my style.

"Why didn't you?" I say quietly. "Why didn't you give her a chance?"

He's silent for a moment, a gutted look on his face. "My father abandoned me and my mother for someone else. I told myself that true love doesn't exist and makes people vulnerable. I told myself that having a mate would be a hindrance and make me weak to have one. So instead of getting to know Winter, I rejected her immediately."

"Stupid thing to do," I commented. "Having a mate is meant to make you stronger, not weaker. Not that I was any different towards her. If anything, I've been more of an asshole than you were to her," I'm ashamed to admit.

"I know it was stupid. I had to reject her twice to get the mate bond to sever, but she doesn't know that, and I'd prefer you not tell her."

I give a low whistle. "For the mate bond to not sever the first time, you had to have not been certain about the rejection. What made the second rejection work?"

"I realized I wanted her to be happy, and it wouldn't be with me. So I had to let her go," he explained.

We bend down and retrieve our clothes, getting dressed as the cool breeze makes us shiver. He hesitates and gives me a sidelong glance. "Tell me," he says softly. "Is she happy here? I know she was bullied at school and in her old pack, but she looks like she's thriving here. She's gained weight, and her face has more color."

I hesitate. "I think she's happy. God, I hope she's happy," I exhale. "She's certainly had her issues in this pack, and I've not made things easier, but I'm trying to show her how much I love her."

"You love her then?"

I give a small nod. I feel partly embarrassed about this, but he needs to know he's got no chance of getting Winter back. Not if I can help it. "I do love her," I admit. "She's everything I could have ever asked for in a mate. It's just taken me a long time to see it."

"Then I guess I can't ask for anything more," he shrugs. "I'm happy for her."

Just like that? Now I feel like a right bastard. He was testing the waters. He wanted to make sure I was going to take care of Winter. I guess he's not that bad after all. I shake his hand and notice he winces as he shakes. I hadn't hurt him that badly, had I?

"Do you need medical assistance?" I ask, and he shakes his head.

"They'll heal," he mutters.

We hear a shout and turn to look at Winter, who is racing across the grounds. "What on earth do you both think you are doing?" she is shouting, incensed.

"Having a friendly fight," I say guiltily.

Johnathon looks just as guiltily at her. "Don't get upset at Kai. It was my idea," he says hastily.

Winter glares at both of us, her hands on her hips. It's quite adorable. "Don't you think we have enough to deal with?" she roars as we flinch at her voice's anger. "Without the two of you acting like stupid teenagers."

"Sorry, Winter," Johnathon murmurs, and she turns to stare at me. I gulp.

"Sorry, sweetheart," I say, trying to get her to smile. She looks at me frostily.

"We have Thomas possibly coming, and you both decide a fight between the two of you is in order? Are you both complete morons?" she huffs.

We both look at the floor. She throws her hands up, exasperated, and inhales several nonsensical things.

"I thought you were going to catch up with Damien," I say hastily, stopping her mid-rant.

She raises an eyebrow at me. "That can wait until dinner," she says crossly. "We're all eating together, that is," she glares. "If you two think you can be civil enough to eat together!"

"We'll be civil," I assure her gruffly. She doesn't look like she believes me.

Johnathon clears his throat awkwardly. "Where is Damien? I might go and talk with him if that's all right."

Winter's hand shoots out and prevents him from walking any further. She shakes her head adamantly. "No, can do," she says with a catch in her voice. "He's spending time with his mate, and I don't want him interrupted."

Well, that was news to me. I wonder who on earth Damien's mate could be in my pack. My eyes narrow. If his mate is here, it might mean he stays here permanently. Damn it! Then another thought springs to mind. "Winter," I say with my jaw clenched. "Who happens to be Damien's mate?"

She takes a deep breath. "Langdon."

Chapter 86

Damien's POV

When the door closes to the study, I eye Langdon with uncertainty. He looked so powerful, handsome, and slightly older than me. I have no idea what to think or feel. I always thought my mate would be a girl, a woman. I never, in a hundred years, would ever have thought my mate would be a male. But what stung the most was that my mate didn't even seem to want me or like me very much at all. I hadn't anticipated this when I searched for Winter, and now that I've found her, I have another issue to deal with. Why is life so difficult sometimes? I don't even know if I want to be mates with a male. But my wolf is going berserk in my mind. He refuses to reject our new mate. Part of me, a small part, doesn't want to either. I'm so confused.

Langdon peels away from his stance by the door and reluctantly sits beside me. He looks a bit annoyed, and I bite my lip. Is he angry at me? Like it's my fault this has happened? He eyes me with a sidelong glance.

"Listen, kid," he mutters, and my temper flares.

"I'm not a kid," I snap. "I'm an adult, and I'd thank you for remembering that." The audacity of him!

He shrugs. "I don't know what to do about the whole mate thing either," he says slowly. "I mean, I wasn't expecting it to be a man or a teenage boy. I'm still getting over my first mate," he explains. I wince.

That hurts. The knowledge that I'm not even his first mate. That he's already had one. But if that's the case, what happened to them? It hadn't been a male.

"What happened to her?" I ask, his eyes hooded as though debating what to tell me.

"She rejected me," he exhales, and my eyes widen in shock. What kind of insane person would let this beautiful hunk of male slip through their fingers?

"Why?" I ask timidly. God, this is hell. I'm normally so confident. He looks away for a moment.

"She didn't want to be the Beta's mate when she could have a chance to be Luna of the pack. She pursued Alpha Kai instead," he admitted lowly. I feel a pang of sympathy for him.

My god. *What a bitch,* I think to myself sourly. That must have been so painful for Langdon as well. To see his mate every day with his Alpha, right in his face like that. It's a wonder he didn't go insane with jealousy, even if the mate bond had been severed. No one should have to go through something like that.

"You should know," he says, staring directly into my eyes. "That she tried to kill Winter numerous times. She almost succeeded. My mate was that desperate to be Luna."

I stay silent. I'm angry that someone's tried to kill Winter, but I also can't blame Langdon for his mate's choices. It's not like he had encouraged his mate to do any of it. I feel so bad for him. The pain he must be feeling inside right now and then having to deal with another mate he's unsure about. One that's male as well.

"Is that why you don't want to be mates?" I ask shyly, and he looks away, avoiding my stare.

He runs a hand through his hair in frustration. "It's not that I don't want to be mates," he bursts out as my heart swells with happiness. "It's just... I don't know. You're a man," he points out. Well, isn't that obvious, I think, annoyed?

Yes, I'm a man. I'm still coming to grips with the fact that my mate is also, but a small part of me wants to see where this leads. Maybe he feels the same.

"I know I'm a man, but does that even matter? Doesn't this happen all the time in packs? Male shifters finding their mates amongst other males?" I ask.

"It does," he says lowly. "There's a few in this pack."

"Then why are you so scared?" I push. "Are you ashamed of being with me? Ashamed of being with another man? Are you some homophobe?"

Okay, even I know that was hitting below the belt. But I need to get some reaction from him. I'm getting angry now.

It works. Now he looks angry. "I'm not a homophobe," he spits out. "I'm trying to adjust to the idea, that's all. I would never be what you just accused me of being."

I shrug. It incensed him further. "You have no idea what kind of man I am," he growls, and I watch in fascination as his eyes flicker between dark and normal. His wolf must be dangerously close to the surface. It means I'm getting somewhere.

"Maybe I want to find out," I point out, staring at him challengingly.

He cocks his head at me. "What if I scare you?" he hisses. "What if I'm too much for you to handle?"

I almost laugh but keep it to myself. Now he's trying to frighten me away, and it won't work.

"I'm not afraid of you," I answer honestly, and he looks disappointed. I wonder what else he will try to get me to reject him or leave.

"Maybe you should be," he says with a catch in his throat. Now he looks miserable.

I shake my head and move closer, my eyes staring into his as he gulps, seeing his Adam's apple move up and down in his nervousness.

"Maybe I just want to get to know you a little better," I breathe and watch his body wriggle uncomfortably in the chair. "Maybe this could lead somewhere," I continue persuasively. "But we'll never know if we don't give this a try. What do we have to lose?"

He looks thoughtful and slightly impressed with me. Because I haven't run away from him? Or because I'm pushing back despite his objections? He seems to be wrestling with himself now. Some internal conflict. He was debating with himself. Suddenly his eyes narrow on me, and I feel him move closer to me, his eyes never moving from my face. My breath hitches.

God, I can smell his intoxicating scent wash all over me. It's like an aphrodisiac. My heart is thudding wildly in my chest. He looks so serious now. His muscles ripple underneath his shirt as he stands, overtowering me and making me sit back, feeling slightly apprehensive. He smirks now. Looks dangerously in control of himself and his emotions. He pulls me upright, kicking the chair behind me and slamming it into the wall.

I feel like I can't breathe. He's so intense, and his eyes are pinning me down. His arms caress and grip mine, sparks and tingles flying throughout my body. His eyes are incredibly dark now, a fierce expression on his handsome face. I shudder, feeling his breath on my skin as he bends his head, mine raising to meet his.

His lips are incredibly soft. That's the first thing I notice as they descend onto mine before they become more hungry like he's trying to devour me. His arms move to my waist and grip me tight. I feel like I'm swimming underwater. His tongue slowly caresses my mouth, demanding access, and I give it to him, moaning as my lips open and his tongue delves inside. He begins to caress my own, forcing my mouth even wider as he plunders me, my hands reaching up of their own accord and twining around his hair, my body pressing hard against his. It wants more. It's craving more.

Oh, God. I can feel his arousal pressing into my leg. He's hard as a rock, but to be fair, my cock is twitching and becoming hard. The more we kiss, the more I feel myself losing control. My hand lets go of his hair, which begins to trail down his chest, and slowly comes up his shirt. I can feel his bare skin against my hand and his taut muscles. My body is trembling, and I'm so horny I'm almost ready to throw him on the floor and ravish him. I'm not sure how much of this I can stand. He doesn't look like he's faring any better.

"Langdon," I moan, and he gives a low growl deep in his throat.

"Say it again," he hisses. "Say my name again."

"Langdon," I repeat, and then I feel his hands grip my waist, lifting me effortlessly, sitting me on the desk without breaking the kiss. I shudder and quiver, my whole body aflame.

His hand moves under my shirt and feels me along my abdomen as I lean into him.

"So delicious," he's muttering, and I stiffen, feeling his hand slowly move underneath the waistband of my pants.

I pant, my cock erecting as he slowly slides his hand toward my boxers. I wriggle in pleasure on the desk. At this rate, we will end up doing it on the desk, and while my wolf more than wants it, I think my first time should be a little more private.

"Langdon," I gasp, peeling away from him reluctantly. "I'm not ready for..." I trail off helplessly, and he seems to understand, his hand slowly coming back up from underneath my waistband while letting go of my hair with the other one. He seems to be a little dazed and disoriented. But there's a wide smile on his face, and his eyes are twinkling. On the other hand, I feel like I'm gasping for air, like I can't get enough oxygen.

"Fuck," he mutters shakily, eyeing me with concern. "Did I go too far?" he asks, sounding worried.

I shake my head. I let him go that far, and if I hadn't stopped him, I would have let him go even further. "No," I answer honestly.

He gives a broad grin. "I think we can safely say that we have chemistry. "

Oh, boy, do we have chemistry?

"So what do we do now?" I ask, feeling completely out of my depth.

He eyeballs me. "What do you want to do?"

What do I want? Christ, after that makeout session, I only want to be with him. I can't stop staring at his lips and tussled hair. I take a deep breath. "I want to see where this goes if you're willing to try."

He laughs out loud. I feel slightly hurt. Does this mean he has no intentions of trying? But then he explains, "I want nothing more than to see where this goes. But I have conditions," he says firmly.

"Name them."

"I want you to stay with me in my house," he says, and my heart skips a beat. "I also want you in my bedroom," he adds.

My head is swimming. He wants me to stay with him? I'd been planning on staying in the pack house with Winter, but to be fair, she did have her mate to contend with, and I'm not naive enough to think that they're staying in separate bedrooms. It might be a good idea to have some space between us.

"Deal," I say decisively. "I think it's a good idea," I add. He looks pleased.

"I think it's a good idea," a voice sings out as they come crashing through the study door. Winter looks at the both of us, taking in our disheveled hair and clothes, the puffy lips, and the way we're staring at each other, and gives a small laugh.

"You're both so cute," she beams. "I'm so happy for you both," she adds. Then gives us a wicked grin, Kai and Johnathon peering in with curiosity. "Let's go and get some dinner now and catch up properly," she exclaims, fairly bouncing back out the door.

I stifle a grin. Winter's excitement is contagious, and to my shock, Langdon takes hold of my hand and leads me toward the dining room. I say nothing, just enjoying the feeling of him holding my hand. Maybe this will work out after all, then.

Chapter 87

Johnathon's POV

We all sat down for dinner like a family. Seeing Langdon's fellow fawns all over Damien like that was laughable. It wasn't comforting. Not because they are both males, don't get me wrong, I could care less about that, but because they couldn't stop touching each other long enough to eat. I also feel like a fifth wheel, sitting all by my lonesome while Winter sat with Kai and Damien sat beside his new mate.

I can't stop glancing over at Winter. She's filled out some. Not in a bad way either, just in a good healthy way. Her skin is golden brown, and it is clear she's been getting outside some. The biggest shock for me was that she could now talk so much for her vocal cords being damaged beyond repair. The doctor had completely gotten it wrong. I scowled at that. Poor Winter had been told not to have any hope, and now look at her. I'm glad to see how much she's changed and how much she seems to glow.

She looks so happy. It's almost painful to watch. All I can think about is whether we would have been this happy if I had just accepted Winter as my mate. Would we have been this close? Are they friendly with each other? I feel like I ruined my best chance of being happy, and it's not a nice feeling at all. Would my life have turned out differently with Winter as my mate?

"So Winter," Damien says as there's a lull in the conversation, Winter turning towards her brother with an eager look. It's clear to see how much she's missed her brother. Had she missed me at all? "What made you run away so suddenly? I found the note on your desk, so I know you were planning it, but you didn't even bother to come home to grab clothes or anything. You just vanished," he said quietly. "And I had no clue where you were."

She stiffens and looks down at her bowl of soup as though she's debating what to tell us. I wait, wanting to know the reason as well. She'd just up and left and hadn't given us a chance to change her mind. Not that she would have been talked out of it. I'm fairly certain that she'd bothered to write a note that meant she'd made up her mind.

Winter looks at us guiltily, and Kai looks interested, very interested. Has Winter not told him the reason, either? Well, this should be good. At least we're not the only ones in the dark, then. Damien looks concerned. Is it my imagination, or has she gone extremely pale?

"Well, the thing is," she starts to stammer, and Kai reaches over to grasp her hand, squeezing it as I glare at him. It's stupid, but I can't seem to help myself. "I didn't have much choice," she explained.

Damien and I look at each other confused. What on earth does she mean she didn't have a choice?

"I know I was late that day," Damien began. "I didn't mean to be. The headmaster kept me back with Johnathon." He sounds apologetic.

She shook her head. "It wasn't because you were late, Damien," she said, breathing heavily. Whatever happened, it's not a pleasant memory judging by her reaction. I tense. Something had made her run away. She just needed to spit it out.

"Jessica and her groupies attacked me," she finally said quietly as my blood began to boil. *That bitch,* I thought to myself furiously. I had told her and everyone else that they weren't to touch Winter anymore, and they'd gone and done it anyway. When I got my hands on them, they would pay big time for their actions.

"I'm sorry, Winter, we should have..." I trailed off. She shrugged.

"Look, it would have happened eventually," she interrupted me as Kai looked on silently. "They blamed me for Thomas' death, and if I hadn't managed to get away, I would have been killed." She laughs bitterly as the room goes silent. "Isn't it ironic," she commented. "Blaming me for Thomas' death, and it turns out he's still alive," she said sourly. "And still wants me."

"He's not going to lay his hands on you. I swear to God," Kai growled, and Damien echoed.

"Winter, we'll keep you safe," I promised thickly. It was the reason I had come, after all.

"You guys can't stay here forever," Winter said with determination. "And I can't keep relying on everyone else to save me. I'm grateful you traveled all this way to tell me, but this isn't your fight. It's mine," she finished, and I stared at her in awe.

She's like a completely different woman. Stronger, fiercer, and more stubborn. I'm unsure if I like the change, but Kai adores it. He leans over and kisses her. I look away.

Damien looks at her pointedly. "I may not be leaving at all," he says quietly, Langdon reaching over and grasping his hand. "It depends on how Langdon and I work out," he adds quietly.

Winter looks stricken. "Oh, my God, Damien, I wasn't thinking…" she trailed off sheepishly. "Of course, you want to stay here with your mate. Forgive me," she added, twirling her fork and staring at it.

"No apologies necessary," broke in Langdon. *So he does have a voice,* I think, a tad bit sourly. I hadn't heard him speak since we'd sat at the table.

"We need to make a plan," Kai said decisively. "Because Thomas is a hybrid, he may be faster than a shifter."

"If he was that fast, wouldn't he have made it here first?" asked Damien, puzzled. "We stopped at every single pack so that we didn't make a wrong move and go in the opposite direction. You left a pretty decent trail," he told a glum-looking Winter. Guess she wasn't trying to do that.

"That is strange," Kai agreed, stroking the stubble on his chin. "He should have beaten the two of you here without problems," he added. "Unless he went in the wrong direction and traveled too far," he said thoughtfully.

"What do you propose we do?" cut in Langdon, looking at his Alpha seriously, seeing the worried expression on Kai's face. I say nothing. I'm not going to propose anything unless I'm asked to. This isn't my pack, this is Kai's, and as such, anything he says goes. I'm not about to interfere in his business. As it is, I'm not sure if I will stay or leave them to it. God, now I feel like I'm acting like a spoilt brat or a complete asshole.

"We've already increased patrol," Langdon assured his Alpha, who gave a grim nod. "And they are checking the woods far more often for intruders. I've even got two warriors capable of being snipers around the perimeter as a backup. I'm not sure what else we can do."

Kai looked thoughtful, and I admit they've covered all the bases. I'm impressed despite myself. I wouldn't have thought they were capable of such plans. The sniper bit is awesome. I'm organizing that when I get back to my pack.

Winter looks grim, fidgeting relentlessly with her hands, dropping her fork to the table and staring into the distance. Kai looks concerned. "Winter, what are you thinking?" he asks her. "Because I can tell something is on your mind," he adds softly.

Well, duh, I think to myself sarcastically. Any idiot could tell that there was something on Winter's mind. All you had to do was look at her, for heaven's sake.

It is barely above a whisper when she speaks, and I have to strain to hear her. Kai even moves closer, his eyes darkening as he hears what she utters. "We could use me as bait."

The words echo in my mind, and I inhale a sharp breath. There was no way I would let Winter use herself as bait in hell. No matter how much sense it seemed to make. No, she could end up killed or worst.

"No," bursts out Damien furiously. "He'll kill you or take off with you before we can follow. Have you forgotten what he tried to do to you last time?" he almost growled. "I can't bear you to be hurt, Winter."

"We'll find another way," Kai told her gently. "I'm not letting you put yourself in danger, Winter. Your brother is right. It's too dangerous."

"What do you propose we do?" Winter bursts out, sounding extremely frustrated. I raise an eyebrow, surprised at her vehemence. She's really determined. *Way to go, Winter.*

She turns to Kai. "I can't spend who knows how long looking over my shoulder, wondering when he's going to attack, what he's going to do? It will drive me insane. Can't you see that," she pleads. "It's my life, and I won't spend it like this. I'm not asking, Kai. I'm telling you this is what we must do."

"Winter, you were broken after his attack," I say harshly, ignoring the tears welling in the corner of her beautiful eyes. "You couldn't speak and moved around like a ghost at school. It was horrible to watch, and now you want to give him the opportunity again? Are you insane?" I spit out?

She looks shocked. Good. She needs to think this through.

"I'm not broken anymore," she hisses at me, her hands clenching into fists. "I'm stronger now, and I have Kai beside me. I might have been a coward at school, but I'm not afraid anymore. I want to do this. I want to show Thomas he has no hold over me anymore."

Kai looks torn. *Say no, you moron,* I want to shout at him. *Tell her no. You can't have her put herself in danger. Tell her there are other ways to deal with this!* I almost growl at the other Alpha in frustration. He taps his hands on the table.

"You'll carry weapons on you," Kai says firmly, his eyes staring into hers as I listen in disbelief. "And you'll do everything I tell you to do. Is that clear? Otherwise, it doesn't happen," he says, folding his arms across his chest and staring directly at her. Damien makes a strangled noise in the background, but I'm staring at Winter and

Kai, wanting to intervene and knowing I can't. Shit. He's going to let her become bait in a trap.

My own hands clench into fists under the table. I can't believe she wants to do this. I want to beg her not to. I didn't come all this way, travel through so many packs so that she could put herself in harm's way, the idiot!

"I'll do everything you ask of me," Winter answers, and I sigh. Well, that was that. I guess I'm staying after all and helping. Winter reaches down and takes hold of Kai's hand. "I'm tired," she says gently. "Let's go to bed."

She looks at all of us, but I look away, feeling very disgruntled and angry. Damien will sleep in Langdon's house, and Winter will be with Kai. I've already been shown the guest room. They take their leave, and then Langdon turns to Damien. "Shall we?" he says, offering his arm to Damien, who reluctantly takes it. I stare obstinately at the table, wanting to smash my fist right through it. I feel sick to my stomach. If Winter were to put herself as bait, I would constantly be patrolling, whether Alpha Kai liked it. I'm not letting Winter be hurt, not under my watch, not again. I wasn't going to fail her this time. I promised myself I would save her this time, even if it were from herself.

Chapter 88

Winter's POV

I say goodnight to my brother and Johnathon, still not quite believing they are here or that they traveled so much to warn me about Thomas. I know I've made them angry and annoyed at my suggestion of being bait, but this is my life, and I refuse to live it afraid of one man who is after me. I've managed to survive Candice and everything she's done to me, so I refuse to let this one person, Thomas, best me now. Not when I feel stronger and more assured of myself than ever. Kai seems to sense my determination because, to my shock, he agrees with my suggestion. Maybe he, too, knows I'm desperate for this all to end. I want to live my life without constantly checking over my shoulder.

We walk upstairs to the bedroom, and I feel well-inspired, feisty, and brave simultaneously. I'm on edge, and I don't know why. Sabriel is purring in my mind.

I think it's because you want him again after all the day after our first night together was ruined.

I want to take the initiative this time. Is that surprising, Sabriel?

Not really. You're becoming more confident and self-assured. Unsurprisingly, it's also starting to flow into other aspects of your life. You're growing as a person but, more importantly, as a woman. If you want him, then show him.

How do I do that, Sabriel? I don't want to make a fool of myself.

Something tells me you'll work it out, and trust me, babe. You won't make a fool of yourself. That man wants you, and he wants you badly. He's probably just waiting for you to make the next move, especially with what you went through.

Guess I'm doing it, then.

That's what I'm talking about, girl. Get some! Sabriel cheers.

Kai is staring at me, probably wondering what I was talking to my wolf about. I'm not about to enlighten him. I like my conversations with Sabriel too much to divulge anything we do or discuss together. Instead, I stare at him directly and stride, gently placing my lips against his as he starts in shock.

God, his lips are rough, but he tastes so sweet, and I lightly trace them with my tongue until he opens his mouth up, delving inside and lightly dancing with his tongue. His hands grip me tightly around the waist, pushing his lips harder against me as I moan. I feel his hands moving under my shirt and reluctantly stop him as he stares in confusion. I smirk.

"I'm in charge," I rasp, and his eyes widen in disbelief, but he stands there, waiting as I lick my lips and look at him hungrily. My hands go to his chest, and I slowly, carefully, teasingly undo his shirt's buttons, letting it drop to the floor. My hands move over his chest, my head lowering to kiss him along his navel as he trembles beneath me. I take my time. I want to feel him all over. I want to make him feel as adored as he makes me feel.

I drop to my knees, and his eyes glisten down at me as I slowly, reverently, pull his pants down. He's not wearing underwear (not a complete shocker, considering it's one less piece of clothing to deal with when dressing in a hurry), and his cock is already rock-hard and standing erect. I almost drool. I want to taste him. My mouth was watering already. He looks like he's about to pull me up, and I shake my head.

"I want to taste you," I say and watch his eyes darken, his body tensing as I slowly bend down and lick the shaft of his penis as he shudders. I grip his legs and open my mouth, slowly taking him inside, inch by inch, as he tenses and his breathing becomes heavy. He feels smooth, and his scent is so delicious. I've never done this before, but I know what to do instinctively. I move my head back and forth, hearing him moan out loud as I take as much of him in my mouth as I can. I like listening to him. His hands are gripping the back of my head and twining around my hair, and I increase the pressure and the timing of my thrusts as he begins to pant heavily from above me.

"Baby girl," he pants, his hands grabbing me and pulling me up, even as I want to protest. "You keep going, and I'm going to cum," he growls, and I pout. I wouldn't have minded. But he seems determined that I have my fun too, almost dragging me to the bed and dropping me on it. He uses his claws to shred my clothes off, apparently too impatient to take them off nicely, and I can see his wolf is dangerously close to the surface.

He pulls my legs up, exposing my pussy to his gaze, licking his lips. Before I can say anything, he begins to trace along my clit with his tongue, and my body tenses up. Goddamn, it feels fucking amazing, and the pleasure is intense, even though he takes his sweet-ass time. I'm panting, my hands clenching in the bedcovers as he makes a growl of satisfaction, enjoying my small cries and moans. "Kai," I moan, my whole body shivering and quivering. "God, I can't take much more," I gasp, and he chuckles, lowering his head and flicking his tongue quickly against my clit. I unravel completely and scream his name, cumming hard against him as he laps up my juices, prolonging the orgasm even more. I come back down to earth with a crash.

He looks like he's about to come back up, but I grab his arm and shake my head. "I want to be on top," I tell him, biting my lip. His eyes light up, and I stand, waiting for him to lie down. Now I'm incredibly nervous. It's not like I've done this position before, after all. But he smiles at me reassuringly.

"Take your time," he rasps out.

I kneel over him, slowly guiding his cock inside me as he groans loudly.

"Fuck you're tight," he moans, and I kneel, riding him as he looks at me in appreciation.

His hands skim along my waist, and his eyes are dark. He doesn't move; I realize it's because he will let me set the pace. Slowly, I move up and down, watching his hands touch me all over without halting my progress. He cups my breast in one hand, and I moan as he squeezes it. I feel full, incredibly stuffed in this position, and his cock slides against my clit with every movement back and forth. It's fucking intense, and I moan, whimper, and mewl as I move.

"Fuck," he moans, and I smile, leaning down to kiss him, whirling my tongue inside his mouth. I begin to move faster, loving that I'm in charge and setting the pace. His hands grip me around the waist, helping to guide me back and forth. But I can see he's getting impatient, and I know it's just a matter of time until he takes over, unable to take the teasing anymore.

Sure enough, he grips me on the waist with both hands and slowly lifts me as I protest. "No more teasing," he growls and places me on the bed, positioning me on my hands and knees. I look over my shoulder and see him approach. He positions himself at his entrance and pushes inside with one hard thrust that takes my breath away. If I thought he felt big in the other position, it was nothing compared to this.

I arch my back and whimper as he thrusts in and out of me. He's not gentle. Instead, he's taking me rough, wild, almost primal. I move back and forth to meet him. I can hear the sounds of us moving back and forth together, his hands in my hair, pulling my head back gently, my eyes looking up at him. He's dominant in this position, but I don't mind. I'm reveling in it, happy to be submissive now that I've already had fun with him.

His hand reaches down between my legs, and I tense up as he begins to finger my clit while he continues to pound inside of me. Fuck. It's like my body can't handle the pleasure between everything happening, and I mewl, almost sobbing with the intensity of the pleasure. My whole body is tense. I can feel an orgasm approaching, and apparently, so can Kai.

"Cum for me," he rasps, biting my shoulder. "Cum for me, darling," he croons.

I shrieked, and then the orgasm washed over me, Kai wasting no time pounding into me even harder and faster as I whimpered. It feels incredible. Then I feel him stiffen, his body tensing behind me, and then, with a shout, he spills his seed inside of me and collapses on the bed next to me.

I lie down, and he rolls me over to snuggle, my back pressed against his chest. He's breathing heavily, one hand over my stomach in a possessive move that I've gotten used to from him.

"That was amazing," Kai tells me, kissing me on the forehead. "I'm especially impressed at your wanting to be in charge. Sorry if I ruined it," he apologizes sheepishly. "Storm couldn't take not being in charge."

I laugh. Trust his wolf to want to be the one on top. Besides, I hadn't minded. I can still taste his cock in my mouth and lick my lips.

"You didn't ruin it," I assure Kai. He smiles. He was looking very relieved.

There's a slight stinging pain between my legs, and I feel a little uncomfortable. Kai, the gentleman that he is, senses it.

"Wait here," he says, kissing me on the nose. I watch him disappear into the bathroom and then hear running water. God, I hope it is for the bathtub. I need to soak in water and get rid of this stinging pain. He comes back with a washcloth.

He spreads my legs and then gingerly begins to wipe me down, cleaning me up as I wince from the stinging.

"Bath," he says firmly, and I nod, standing up and walking towards the bathroom, Kai whistling behind me. Well, he's in a good mood, but then who wouldn't be after sex?

Ahhh, the blessed relief of the water is divine as I sink into it. I lean back against the bathtub, Kai having a shower while I eye him like candy. I'm already feeling aroused and look away, embarrassed, even as my mate smirks at me.

"I'd take you again, but I think you might be in too much pain," he says with a grin.

I blush despite myself.

"So that you know," he teases. "You can take me anytime you want, princess."

I throw a shower puff at him as he laughs. Then I settle back against the bathtub. I'm too relaxed to be mad at his teasing.

I feel myself yawning. After that sex marathon, I feel completely drained. Kai sees me almost falling asleep and wraps a towel around himself. "Winter," he says softly as I stare up at him, my eyes blurry. He chuckles and drains the water, picking me up and wrapping me in a towel, heading back into the bedroom and making a beeline for the bed.

"I'm cold," I protest when he places me naked in bed.

"I'll warm you," he growls, climbing beside me. He pulls me against his chest and throws the bed covers over us. My eyes are closed as his body heat begins to warm me up. Before long, I'm sound asleep. The last thing I remember is Kai kissing me on the forehead.

Chapter 89

Langdon's POV

I take Damien out to what I like to refer to as my bachelor pad. Not that it will continue to be one, not if I now have a mate. He looks so timid. Does he honestly think I will jump his bones right here and now? Especially since we're both adjusting to our mate being another male? I never in a million years thought that would be the case. I'm not against gay people. I just envisioned a female as my mate. That doesn't mean I feel too disappointed, either. After all, mates are meant to be a blessing from the moon goddess herself. I doubt she makes mistakes. Or at least I like to think she doesn't. She is a goddess, after all.

I'm holding Damien's hand, and his cheeks are flushed as he gazes around the small house I own. He looks impressed, but I'm far more interested in him.

"Is Winter going to be okay?" he asks suddenly. "I mean, in that house with that man. He looks fierce," he says apprehensively, narrowing his eyes. I almost scoff at him. Kai is a big teddy bear once you get to know him. But he does have a reputation to uphold.

Indeed he's not serious? Sure, Kai was an asshole initially, but he wouldn't hurt Winter, at least not now. The man was utterly besotted with her, and she was with him. I've never seen such a perfect couple. They are completely infatuated with each other, and I know that Kai's told her he loves her. The furthest he's ever gone in a relationship.

"Kai loves Winter," I say, turning to Damien indignantly. "She loves him as well, you should know."

His eyes widen. "I didn't think it was that serious," he says lowly.

Is he completely oblivious? I'm starting to wonder about his intelligence. "Winter and Kai have gone through a lot together. Trust me when I tell you she's completely safe with him."

He doesn't look convinced, and I sigh, leading him into my bedroom, where he stops short, looking terrified. "I, um, thought you were joking about sleeping in the same room," he blurts out, letting go of my hand.

I stiffen. I wasn't joking. His face goes ashen. Is he really that terrified to share the same room as me? I consider him, taking in the way he's breathing unevenly, the flush on his cheeks. He's either scared or embarrassed—or both.

"I told you we were only going to share the bed, nothing else," I say, a little annoyed. "Surely you're not that much of a fraidy cat."

His eyes widen. "I'm not afraid," he tells me, and I just cock my head at him, a small smile on my face. Oh, he's scared, all right, he doesn't want to admit it. My wolf tells me he's cute, and I have to agree. I know he's slightly older than Winter, which means there's less of an age gap between us than between Kai and her.

"Then what's the problem," I huff out.

He blushes and looks away. "It's just that. How do I know you won't try anything," he mumbles.

"How about because I've given you my word," I growl, and he gasps as I walk up to him, my eyes staring into his, my face only inches away from his own. He looks like a deer caught in headlights. "All I want to do is sleep in the same bed as you," I say firmly. "That's all."

He bites his lip but nods. Thank God for that. He's making me grumpy, and not because I'm tired. Suddenly I can't look away from him, my eyes gazing deeply into his, those lips tempting me. I try my best to hold out, but suddenly it becomes too much to bear, being this close to him and smelling his delicious scent.

I close the gap between us, holding his head in my hands and leaning forward to press my lips against his. He flinches and then moans as I lick his lips, demanding access. He opens his mouth, and

I begin to plunder it. God, he tastes so fucking good and feels incredible as I deepen the kiss, my hands moving down to the back of his neck as I hold on tightly. My hands begin to caress his arms, and he makes no move to stop me, his eyes closing in what I hope is bliss. My whole body is thrumming with desire and the need to ravish him, but I'm careful to step slightly back, not wanting Damien to feel the erection poking through my pants. The last thing I need to do is scare the poor kid with that. He'll run away if he knows.

I feel my wolf coming dangerously close to the surface and will him to stay back, focusing on the kiss and feeling of my mate in my arms. His moans turn me on, and I'm barely holding it together. I pull back Slowly, reluctantly, watching Damien's eyes flutter open. He looks to be in complete shock, whereas I'm smirking at him. I can't help it. He was so damn responsive to the kiss that it makes me wonder how responsive he'd be underneath me as I take him.

"That was..." Damien murmurs, trailing off.

"Fantastic, mind-blowing, orgasmic," I suggest cheekily, folding my arms across my chest. He gives a shy nod.

"I didn't know it could feel like that," Damien mutters. "I've never felt like this with a girl."

Neither have I, although I suspect it might have felt something like this with Candice if she'd been willing to be mates instead of rejecting me in favor of Kai. I'll never know for sure.

I turn back to the bed, and he sidles closer to me, not looking anywhere as apprehensive as he'd initially been when we entered the room.

"Do you have a preference?" I ask him, and he blinks at me, looking confused. "I mean, as to what side to sleep on? Does it matter?" I clarify, and he slowly shakes his head. "Feel free to sleep naked," I say wryly, watching his face turn red like a tomato.

"I think I'll sleep in my pants," he says shyly, taking his T-shirt off as I watch. My God, I think my heart just skipped a beat. He's glorious to behold, his abdomen taut with a six-pack. There's no hair on his chest, either. My eyes involuntarily dip to the waistband of his sweatpants, my own body tightening with arousal.

Keep it together, Langdon, I mutter to myself in my mind. I shrug out of my shirt, and Damien looks flustered. Is it my imagination, or is he staring down at a particular part of me? Well, how interesting is that?

"How about you climb in first," I suggest. It's the part closest to the wall, meaning he'd have to climb over me to get out of bed. I don't even feel wrong about that.

"All right," Damien mutters, walking forward and gingerly climbing into the bed, scooting over quickly.

"Do you want some water or anything first?" I offer, trying to be a good host, at least.

He shakes his head. I shrug. Well, I can't say I didn't try.

I get in, pulling the bed covers over us both. I'm not surprised when Damien rolls over with his back to me. I swear he's trying to drill holes in the wall with his staring. I move over until I'm almost touching him and pull him back slightly as he wriggles in surprise.

"What are you doing?" he sputters indignantly.

"Cuddling with my mate," I say calmly, pulling him so his back is against my chest. My arm is over the side of him.

"But I don't want to cuddle," he exclaims, and I sigh. Shame. I let go of him, and he scoots back close to the wall. I'm not going to lie. That stung, but I'm not about forcing him to do something he doesn't want.

I try to content myself with the fact that he's at least in bed with me. That's progress. His body is so stiff and tense that I can't see him falling asleep comfortably. I spread myself out. Just because he's curled up into a small ball doesn't mean I must be uncomfortable with him. It looks like it's going to be a long night.

Much to my astonishment, though, it's only several minutes later when Damien begins to snore, his body relaxing in his sleep. *Man, he's loud,* I think to myself with a chuckle. But he's definitely out of it. He's even spread himself out somewhat, so his leg is touching mine. He's also come a lot closer to me, and as I watch, out of the corner of my eye, he backs up so that he's pressed against me. I have to smile. Even though he denies wanting to be near me, his body seems to have a mind. Or maybe it's the mate bond working. It's hard to say.

I pull him against me, feeling his back against my chest. My cock twitches in my pants in response to feeling our mate, my body tensing up against his. He feels so good, so warm. His breathing evens out, and his snoring goes quieter as I tentatively place my arm over the side of his body. His hair spreads out on my pillow, and I wrinkle my nose as his hair touches me. I settle down, but I can't stop staring at him. Everything about him is utter perfection. His jaw is strong, even clenched in his sleep, his hair is silky, even after spending so much time in the woods, and his skin is deep golden and tanned from being outdoors so much. There's a roughness to him, the stubble on his face making him look more masculine. Just the way I like it, I realize, touching his hair softly with my hand. He wriggles in response, and I stop before I accidentally wake him up.

My eyes close. I try hard not to think about my first mate, but Candice always comes to mind, whether I want her to. The pain of her rejecting me is still as fresh as the day it happened. Maybe with my mate, Damien, the pain will fade and go away. That is if he decides he wants to be mates. The whole male thing has thrown both of us for a loop, even though it's not uncommon with werewolves. I don't want to reject him. My wolf has already wholeheartedly accepted Damien, wanting him just as much as I do.

The tension in my body begins to fade, and I feel myself becoming drowsy. I wonder what Damien is dreaming about. Maybe he's dreaming about me? I feel my breathing evening out, and my eyes are becoming heavy. I'm tired, drained from the day's events. I'm exhausted. I know Kai will want to see me early tomorrow morning, especially with Winter's dangerous plan. I enjoy my mate's company by my side and tighten my grip on him possessively. Damien is mine, and no one will take him from me. I don't care what it takes to persuade him to remain mates, but I'm willing to do whatever it takes. I'm not about to let my second chance mate reject me either, not if I can help. I fall asleep, my snores mixing with Damien's, my body curled up against his, my lips pressed against his head. Neither of us moves away from each other during the night while we sleep, and when I wake up the very next morning, there is a massive smile on my face. You really cannot fight the mate bond. It was pointless even to try.

Chapter 90

Winter's POV

I wake up to Kai kissing my nose. I giggle at him. "Good morning, sweetheart," he chirps. I guess he's one of those annoying morning people that wake up happy. I curl up in my blanket and eye him sleepily. I would much rather stay in bed.

He knows I'm not a morning person because he releases a giant huff of resignation as he climbs out of bed. He makes a beeline for the bathroom, and I close my eyes, so sleepy that I want to go back to sleep.

Then I hear running water, and he comes back out, smiling. *Damn him for looking so cute,* I think grumpily. It made it hard to be mad at him for waking me up.

"Winter, we really should get ready for the day," Kai tells me, and I groan and roll over.

It's so nice and warm under the blankets, and I whine as he tries to take them off me. "It's too cold," I mumble, and he laughs out loud.

"I started the shower for you," he offers as I blink up at him, unamused.

He picks me up as I shriek, kicking and wriggling in his arms. His eyes are gleaming now, and he places me in the bathroom, folding his arms across his chest and staring me right in the face as I glare at him, my teeth chattering together from the cold.

"Shower," he orders, and I reluctantly get in and glare at him some more. Ahhh.

The water is warm, perfect, just the way I like it, and as I warm up, I begin to eye Kai, who's standing there naked, smiling. I can't believe it, but I open my mouth and almost purr. "You could come to join me."

Yes, girl, get adventurous. That's the spirit, Winter.

I cannot believe I just said that to him.

You better believe it all right. I'm so proud of you.

I don't think it's something to be proud of, Sabriel. I sound like a real horn bag.

So?

Kai opens the shower door, and I back up to give him room. His eyes are black now, his wolf close to the surface, and I swallow nervously. What have I done?

He smirks at me as he grabs the washcloth. "Calm down," he teases me. "This was your idea, wasn't it?"

Yeah, but I hoped he wouldn't take me up on it. Stupid really.

He begins to wash me everywhere as I gasp, down my breasts, across my stomach, and even between my legs as I moan. Fuck. I'm becoming aroused, but a quick look at him shows I'm not the only one. His cock stands to attention, and my eyes hone in on it. I'm almost drooling at the thought of that cock inside of me.

He turns me to face the tiles, my hands up to keep my balance, spreading my legs out wide. I'm panting heavily at this stage, my head looking over my shoulder. He comes up behind me, one of his hands coming down to my pussy and slowly fingering along my folds as I gasp.

"Oh, God, Kai," I choke out, and he moves closer so my back is right against his chest. He circles my clit with his finger as I stiffen against him. Fuck. It feels so damn good. My whole body is trembling, the shower water still cascading over us.

He inserts one finger inside me, slowly pumping it back and forth as my back arches. He kisses the back of my neck simultaneously, and I moan, my legs barely holding me up, the pleasure becoming extremely intense. Another finger is pushed inside of me, stretching me, filling me, pumping inside and out as I stand there, helpless to do anything but feel.

"You're so fucking tight," Kai whispers from behind me, a low growl. I cry out in response.

I feel him curl up his fingers and pound into me faster and harder. I scream, almost sobbing from the pleasure, his fingers hitting my G-spot with astounding accuracy. My orgasm washes over me, and I scream "Kai" as I cum hard against his hand.

Kai's panting heavily behind me. He slowly withdraws his fingers and then moves them up to my mouth. I open my mouth, and he places them inside as I taste my juices. Then he pulls them out and licks them himself, his eyes never leaving my face.

"Delicious," he growls as I shudder.

He bends me at an angle, my hands against the tiles again, legs spread apart. I can feel his hard cock at my entrance, and I prepare myself as he thrusts into me, hard, all the way inside, as I whimper.

"I didn't hurt you, did I?" he growls, and I shake my head, feeling full, my walls clenching around his rock-hard cock.

"No," I pant back. "You didn't hurt me."

He withdraws, and I want to cry at the loss of his cock, before he thrusts back inside, this time extremely slow, filling me inch by inch as I scrabble at the tiles.

"You like that," he grunts, holding firmly to my waist.

"God, yes," I sob, feeling completely out of control. He withdraws again and then pushes back in, just as slowly as I mewl the last time. God, I want him to move harder and faster, but he's setting the pace, and something tells me that he's well aware of the reaction he's getting from me.

Another thrust, and I mewl. He chuckles behind me. "Please, God, Kai, move," I beg him, and he shakes his head.

"I'm setting the pace," he growls.

At this rate, he's going to kill me. He withdraws and slowly slides back in, prolonging it, going even slower than before, my eyes widening as he stuffs me full.

"Beg me for it," he growls, gently pulling me by the hair. "Beg me for my cock."

He doesn't even need to ask me to do that. I'm already begging. "Kai, please, God," I pant out heavily. "Please fuck me harder."

He withdraws hard this time and slams back in. Fuck. That's more like it. My hips move back of their own accord to meet him as he slams into me, hard, fast, and raw. I'm screaming his name at the top of my lungs. He's thrusting as hard as he can. It's primal.

"I can't take much more," I moan, feeling the pleasure rising within me.

Kai grunts and continues, holding me tightly by the waist with his large hands. I can hear our bodies smacking together. He bites me on the shoulder, and I shriek, loving the feel of his teeth gently nipping me.

My orgasm rips through me. I scream as I cum, his cock still inside of me. Kai thrusts me repeatedly as I tremble, prolonging the orgasm even more. He goes even harder and faster, slamming into me at a furious pace, then I hear him growl and stiffen, spilling his seed inside me as his body relaxes.

"Fuck," he groans, his head on my shoulder as I relax against him, his cock slowly sliding out. "You're too damn irresistible," he complains.

"Same here," I mutter. "You're too good-looking for your good."

He snorts. "I think I'll leave you to finish getting washed up before this turns into round two," he says with a grin. I watch him walk away reluctantly.

We could have gone another round, Winter. Should we call him back?

Um, no? I'm sore right now, and we have things to do today.

Fine, but I must tell you, that was hot right there. I'm all hot and bothered.

Sabriel!

All right, all right. I'm going. But I still think you're getting pretty adventurous, and I like it.

I finish washing myself up, especially between my legs, and stumble out of the shower. Kai, I notice, slightly disappointed, is already dressed in his comfortable sweatpants and shirt. I would have liked to watch him getting dressed. Damn. He smiles at me.

"Can I steal your sweatpants and top," I mumble, wanting them as comfort and because they smell like him.

He raises an eyebrow but shrugs and fetches them for me, throwing them as I catch them easily.

I put them on.

"What's the plan?" I ask, in a far better mood now than when he first woke me up. I guess the endorphins will do that to you. Or maybe it's just getting laid in general.

He smirks. "Breakfast and talking to your brother and butthead," he mutters.

"I think you mean Johnathon," I say wryly with a roll of my eyes. He chuckles. "Please don't call him butthead," I mutter. "It's not polite, Kai."

"I can think of a hundred different names I'd like to call him," Kai argues back, and I sigh. I'm not about to get into an argument with the stubborn man.

"Let's go downstairs," he says, holding his arm to me and waiting for me to take it. "We'll get some breakfast and discuss this plan of yours properly. Besides, Langdon has mind-linked me, and I know he and Damien are waiting for us in the dining area."

I smile. "Can you believe that Langdon and my brother are mates?" I ask enthusiastically. "I wonder how last night went."

"I think you should not ask that," Kai laughed. "Some things between a brother and sister should remain private. Unless you want to tell him what we were up to last night and this morning?"

"Ew, no," I exclaim, seeing his point.

We begin to walk downstairs and into the kitchen. Kai gives me a peck on the cheek. "What do you want for breakfast?" he asks.

I eye him thoughtfully. I'm sure he can't cook because I haven't seen him in the kitchen, and Omegas normally fetch him food.

"Cereal," I answer, watching as his face looks relieved. Yep, pretty sure the man can't cook. Still, at least he was nice enough to offer.

I join the others at the table, seeing that Langdon and Damien have already finished eating and Johnathon is scowling down at a bowl of cereal. Did he not like it?

Kai comes back and shoves a bowl in front of me. I start to eat, Kai sitting beside me, and then push the bowl aside when I'm finished. No one speaks. But, I do notice, with a smile, that Langdon is holding Damien's hand under the table. How adorable is that?

"So," Kai says, all business now that he's finished eating. "We need to discuss the plan Winter came up with last night."

"About that," I pipe in. "If I'm going to be bait, then you need to reduce security measures, not increase them. You have to allow Thomas to come and get me."

Kai looks displeased by this, and Johnathon looks pissed.

"It's a stupid plan," Johnathon mutters, looking at me coldly. "You'll get yourself killed this way."

I'm hurt. "Johnathon, this is the best way. Otherwise, it's going to take too long. You want to be away from your pack for a long period?" I ask pointedly.

He looks away.

"Look, Winter has a point. I might not like it, but I can see where she's coming from," Damien sighs. "I think her plan is the best one to go with. We must be extra cautious and plan for every contingency we can think of."

I agree with that. So does Kai.

We bend our heads together, and the whole table begins to speak in hushed whispers as everyone offers their opinion on what to do. Everyone, except Johnathon that is.

Chapter 91

Winter's POV

I'm not sure exactly how this is going to work. I've been walking in the woods for several days now, and there hasn't been a single peep or attempt from Thomas. Maybe he decided it wasn't worth it to come after me? A girl can hope, right? Perhaps he even found his mate on his travels. Wouldn't that be something? Then he wouldn't need me, would he?

Girl, you are way too optimistic for your good, Winter.

Isn't it better to be an optimist than a pessimist, Sabriel? Besides, it could happen, right?

Maybe, but at this rate, you're just avoiding the truth. He hasn't found his mate, and he's still coming for you. You can't afford to let your guard down, girl.

But it's been days, Sabriel, not just a few. It's been almost a week, and nothing's happened.

That doesn't mean we let our guard down. That man is insane, or have you forgotten the last incident? I might not have been there for that, but I can access your memories; they're not good ones.

I know. But I was weaker back then with no wolf. Now I have you.

Your confidence in me is very humbling.

I love you, Sabriel.

Love you the most, girl.

I sigh. The sun seems to set soon, and my legs are tired. Damien, Johnathon, Langdon, and Kai, are all stationed around the grounds. There are two snipers, but I'm not holding my breath. Being in the forest means taking a shot is complicated with all the trees and overhanging branches. My stomach is growling with hunger.

I mind-link Kai, feeling annoyed and very hungry. Both are not a good combination for me. It makes me extremely grumpy.

Kai, I'm going to come in, in a few minutes. Nothing's happening out here. I don't think he's out there.

I don't sense anything in the woods, either. Damn it! This wait is driving me crazy.

How do you think I feel? I'm the one who's out here for bait!

I know, sweetheart, I hate waiting.

Well, so do I. It would be best if you told the others to head inside. This is just a complete waste of time. Plus, I'm hungry.

Do you want the snipers to stay?

Yes, at least until I've returned to the pack house. I feel safer that way.

No problem, I'll meet you back at the pack house.

See you there.

I shut the mind link off and sighed. *At least the sunset is beautiful,* I think to myself wryly. I always did like to watch it set. Would spending a few more minutes out here before heading inside hurt? Considering it is fairly safe. I wish Kai were out here to watch it with me. It would have been very romantic, except for the tension of waiting for Thomas to make his bloody move. If he didn't make it soon, I would go insane.

I can see the glint of the snipers as I wander slowly back to the grounds. The sunlight makes it stand out, and I make a mental note to let Kai know about that. The sound of rustling leaves makes me stiffen and slowly turn. But there's a breeze which explains the noise, but then I hear the crack of a twig. My heart begins to thump wildly in my chest. *Get a grip, Winter,* I chide myself. *Remember that the snipers are still out there, and you can mind-link for help if need be. Stop being such a wuss.*

A rabbit, a fucking rabbit, comes out of the woodwork and skids upon seeing me. I almost laugh at the absurdness of it all. I just let myself be frightened by a goddamned animal. I shake my head and chuckle. Wait until I told Kai this. He'd laugh his ass off. So would Damien. I smile at that.

Damien and Langdon have gotten closer in the last few days. Not so close that I think they've done the deed, but close enough to show some signs of public affection. They hold hands, and I've even caught them kissing once or twice. Damien went as red as a beetroot when I saw them. I think it's sweet. They look so handsome together, and Langdon is a good catch, at least as far as I'm concerned. After being rejected by Candice, he more than deserves to be happy. I hope Damien doesn't break his heart as Candice did. He still hasn't decided to continue to be mates with Langdon, but how they work around each other gives me hope that they'll agree. Besides, Damien seems to be into him, and I know Langdon feels the same way.

I still can't work Johnathon out. He constantly seems to be in a lousy mood and scowling at me. I don't understand why he felt the need to travel all this way and help me after all this time apart. Not to mention, he chose to reject me, not the other way around. Is he upset that I've finally found happiness with my second chance mate? Because he had his chance and he made his choice. If he's regretting it, that's on him, not me. I wish he'd smile more or try to be happy for me. Instead, he's coming across as a jealous ex-boyfriend, and that's alarming me right there. What if he turns out to be another Thomas? I don't care how nice he seems to be. When it comes to Johnathon, I'm not letting my guard down. I think he's here for some other ulterior motive, and even Sabriel agrees.

Kai seems to readily accept Damien and Langdon being mates, even though I know he still holds a grudge towards my brother for the past and how he treated me. They might not get along well, but I can see that he's slowly softening towards Damien. All I wanted for him to do, was try to get along. After all, there's every chance that Damien will want to stay with Langdon, which means he'll most probably, fingers crossed, end up living here in this pack. Then I'll have my brother close to me. That sounds awesome. Especially since Damien is making every effort to spend quality time with me whenever he can, well at least when he can force himself away from his mate Langdon, they make such a cute couple. Langdon looks happy. After Candice, he deserves a mate that cares for him, so if Damien stuffs this up, I will kill him.

I sigh and breathe in the cool evening air. It's getting slightly chilly, and the sun has fully set. I've been so lost in my thoughts that time has passed without awareness. No doubt Kai is probably wondering where I am and what's taking me so long to return. But it's only been a few minutes from what I can tell, so he shouldn't be too angry. After all, I am entitled to peace when I can get it, right? Especially since I've been on edge for hours now.

I walk to the edge of the grounds and lift my arm. That's strange. The sniper rifles can't be seen anymore, but then I realize that with the sunlight gone, I won't be able to see them. I shrug. Then I hear a strange whirring sound and spin around, only to feel something embed itself in my leg. It stings.

"Fuck!" I curse out loud, glancing down to see a tranquilizer dart in my leg. *No, no, no, this can't be happening,* I chant to myself. Why didn't I return to the pack house instead of wasting time here? I can smell the scent of wolfsbane and stiffen, pulling the dart out, blood trickling from the wound. Great, now I can't even mind-link for help.

My eyes frantically scan the ground. No sign of anyone exists. I begin to limp toward the pack house, but there's a sudden rush of wind, and the next thing I know, I'm being swept up off the floor by a pair of incredibly strong arms. My body feels too heavy, and my limbs don't want to cooperate or move when I try it. I'm turned away, and the person, whoever it is, takes me deeper into the woods instead.

My vision is blurry, and I blink several times to focus. I open my mouth to scream, but all that comes out is a gurgle. How much wolfsbane was in that dart? I stare up into the person's face, confused. This wasn't Thomas? Was it? His eyes were glowing red, his arms were heavily muscled, and his body thicker than I remember. He stares down at me, smirking, his arms gripping me so tightly it's painful.

I'm helpless, feeling like a rag doll as he runs. He's fast. Incredibly fast. The trees pass by in a blur. Even with my blurred vision, I can tell he's faster than a shifter. Is this the result of him being a hybrid? I can also smell the metallic scent of blood on him, seeing tiny droplets on his clothes. Who did he kill? I suck in a breath. Did he kill the snipers? Was that why I couldn't see them? Or had he killed patrol warriors? My God, I'm responsible for someone's death. At least Damien and the others were safe in the pack house, or I hoped they had been.

Has Kai noticed I'm missing yet? I can't mind-link to my frustration, and my stupid body won't move, not that I want Thomas to drop me. So far, the bastard hasn't said a single word. I can feel nausea and realize it's due to the wolfsbane he's given me, my stomach rolling and bile rising in my throat. It's taking all my concentration not to be sick of him.

"I finally have you," he chuckles darkly, and my spirits plummet.

I would know that voice anywhere. It haunts me in my dreams at nighttime. It's Thomas.

I try to speak again, but again just a garbled mutter.

He laughs. "Don't worry. The wolfsbane isn't a fatal amount. It will wear off, and then I'll give you another dosage," he tells me.

Not exactly reassuring. If he continues to give me wolfsbane, it means keeping me weak, and if I'm weak, then I can't fight back. I shudder at the thought of him having complete control over me. I don't even want to think about why he wants full control, not after the last incident. I already know.

I would rather die than go through that again. He's careful, leaping over branches, the wind blowing my hair around every which way. My eyelids are heavy. I struggle to keep them open. The last thing I want to do is fall asleep. Thomas' face has a crooked smile, and I notice the large fangs protruding from his mouth. It's true, then, that he's half vampire, half shifter now. *God, please don't let him drain my blood,* I think. Although I'd prefer that to him forcing me.

"Not long now," he murmurs, and I'm astonished at how much ground we've covered and disheartened. How was it that Damien and Johnathon beat him to my pack? When can he run like this for long distances? He must have made a mistake and gone in the wrong direction. It's the only thing that makes sense.

I'm terrified by what he'll do to me when we reach whatever destination he has in mind. Something tells me it's not in a pack. No, I think desperately, my eyes beginning to shut. *Not now. Please don't do this to me,* I plead in my mind, but my body isn't listening to my desperate pleas. My eyelids close shut and refuse to open. My body is beginning to feel like it's floating. The tranquilizer is starting to set in, and I curse in my mind. The last thing I remember before falling into a deep and heavy sleep is Thomas kissing me on the forehead and muttering. "Soon, you'll be mine forever, Winter, till death do us part."

Chapter 92

Kai's POV

I head inside after telling Damien, Johnathon, and Langdon that it's all over and dusted again for today. There's been no sign of this asshole Thomas, and it's frustrating as all fuck. Where was the bastard hiding? Was he even coming for Winter, or was this all made up by Damien to keep his sister afraid? I'm suspicious of the lot of them, and I wouldn't say I like that Winter is out there, putting herself on the line as bait. It's not fair. It's wrong to ask her to put herself in danger like that.

Our mate will be okay, Kai. She's strong and has an inner strength that will do her well.

Yeah, well, I don't trust Damien and Johnathon. What if they're lying to us?

Why would they lie?

Because of Storm, Johnathon wants Winter as his mate. Don't think I haven't seen the way he looks at her when he thinks I can't see him. He thinks he can get another chance with her.

He's not getting his hands on our mate, but I don't think he's lying. I believe that you're jealous.

Are you telling me you're not, Storm? He was her mate first, even if he rejected her.

I'm jealous, but if he steps out of line, I'll rip the bastard to shreds. You're just being too nice. It's unlike you.

That's because Winter will kill me if I do anything to harm them. I promised her I wouldn't.

True, give them a chance. After all, if Winter trusts them, then we should as well.

I'll think about it, I tell Storm grumpily, cutting him off.

The boys head into the study, which becomes dangerously crowded and confined with everyone there. It's very claustrophobic.

"We should have stayed out there longer," Damien protests. "Isn't he more likely to strike at nighttime?"

I glower at him. Johnathon fidgets in the chair, and Langdon looks completely neutral. Bastard. Where's the loyalty? Stupid mate bond, making him all googly-eyed at Damien. I scowl at both of them.

"I do not have Winter out there at nighttime," I say dangerously quietly. "It's bad enough that she's out there until now. Nighttime is just asking for trouble," I huff.

"It could be why he hasn't attacked, though," Langdon speaks up, and I scowl at him. Now he wants to talk! He sees the look on my face and falls silent. Smart man. My hands are itching to place themselves around someone, anyone's throat.

"She's not going to be out there at nighttime," I reiterate, and Johnathon just sighs and stares out the window. What the hell is his problem? Would he dare ask his mate to do the same thing? I don't think so.

"I think that's a mistake," Damien protests while Langdon clears his throat, pointing at me. "He's a hybrid now, remember? Don't vampires prefer the nighttime?"

I eye him coldly. "For a brother, you seem keen to put your sister in danger," I growl.

He goes pale. I'm not finished yet. I lean against my chair and intertwine my fingers, regarding the lot of them with contempt, except for Langdon. I stare at him, annoyed. "For all I know, you've been lying about Thomas coming for Winter," I thunder. "And if that's the case, it would be best for you to come clean right now."

Damien explodes. "We wouldn't have traveled all this way to lie about this. I understand you're my sister's mate, but I'm her brother and love her. I want her to be safe," he snapped.

"She wasn't exactly safe from you, however. Was she back then?" I ask, and he trembles beneath my glare. He knows precisely what I'm talking about because he avoids my gaze, rubbing the back of his neck and looking remorseful. Part of me enjoyed getting that slight dig in.

What in the hell is taking Winter so long to come back? I frown. I know how much she enjoys the sunset, but she could have at least mind-linked me if she was planning to watch it. I try to mind-link her and frown. Nothing. I can't get through to her at all. I start to feel slightly panicked and turn to Langdon.

"Can you mind-link Winter at all?" I ask slowly, and he blinks at me, surprised but trying while I watch. A frown comes onto his face, and I begin to panic. Fuck. This isn't good.

"No," he breathes. "I'm not getting through to her at all."

She hasn't blocked me then, not that I thought she had.

My eyes meet Damien's, who looks panicked. "The snipers," I say and try them, perplexed when I can't mind-link them either. I stand up. Either the snipers are out of commission and can't mind-link, or it's worse. I feel dread in my gut. Don't let it be what I think it is. I race out towards the nearest sniper and halt in my tracks. The smell of blood is potent, drifting in the air, and my stomach churns with disgust. I'm forced to step around the tree, and one of my pack members, a trusted sniper, is lying there. That wasn't the most horrific thing, however. It looked like he'd been drained of blood, he was incredibly pale, but Thomas had done far worse than that. The sniper's guts were ripped open and left all along the floor, vital organs missing. I feel nauseous and am fighting not to be sick. In all my years as an Alpha, I've never seen anything so horrendous. He showed no mercy or compassion to the poor shifters who were now dead.

"Mother of God," whispers Langdon, kneeling beside the body. The eyes are blankly staring up at the sky. "I bet the other sniper is in the same condition," I say grimly.

Johnathon and Damien are quiet. "We need to find Winter," Damien says shakily, his eyes never leaving the body in the open. Patrol is mind-linking me, and I close my eyes, listening.

Alpha Kai, there are signs of a struggle in the forest where Winter was last seen.

Stay there. I'm coming. Any sign of Winter?

None, we're all searching now for her. We didn't hear any screams or signs that she was in danger. I'm sorry that we've failed you, Alpha Kai.

Never mind, get the best trackers we have out here. I want every available one out there searching for her.

Already done it, Sir.

Right, give me a minute, and we'll meet you there. Don't move.

I will be right here waiting.

I cut the mind link off. "Come with me," I growl at everyone, and we head towards the forest where Winter was last seen, where she'd been pacing back and forth for Thomas to come to get her. I feel disgusted with myself. How many times am I going to fail my mate? How many times am I going to curse myself for my stupidity? She could be going through hell right now, and it was because I let my guard down.

Seth, the warrior who mind-linked me, met me at the forest's edge. She must have been coming back in when she was attacked. He brandishes something at me that he's clutching in his hand.

"What is it?" I growl, and he hands it to me.

It's a small tranquilizer dart. I give it a sniff and raise my eyebrows. "Wolfsbane," I mutter. "No wonder I can't mind-link her."

"We're wasting time," Johnathon shouts as I stare at him. "Winter is out there with a madman, and we're wasting time when we should be looking for her. Are you insane?" he almost screams at me.

I'm being patient. After all, the little pup is distraught, but I will fling his ass into the dungeon if he continues.

"Calm down, pup," I mutter and turn to Seth. "Was she wearing the bracelet that I gave her?"

He gives a smirk and a nod. "Yes, Alpha Kai, she was."

"Excellent, fetch Morgan," I demand, and he nods, disappearing slightly.

"Who the hell is Morgan?" asks Damien.

"Wait and see."

Sure enough, Morgan comes trailing towards me. He pushes his large spectacles up his nose and greets me grimly. "Sorry about Winter, Alpha Kai," he says remorsefully.

"Never mind that," I cut in impatiently. "Can you bring up Winter's location?"

"Sure," he says easily, opening up his laptop.

"Kai," Langdon says, apparently cottoning on. "Did you put a GPS tracker on Winter's bracelet?"

"It's embedded in it. Winter doesn't even know that it's tracking her movements."

"Genuis," whistles Langdon, and even Damien looks far less hysterical now.

Johnathon continues to scowl in the background. I shrug. I can't help everyone. But if he doesn't stop soon, I will wipe his anger off his face with a well-aimed fist.

It takes a minute for Morgan to locate the GPS signal, but when he does, he shows it to me on screen, his eyes wide in disbelief. "It's moving incredibly fast," he breathes. "Faster than a shifter can move. It makes tracking it difficult because it keeps jumping off the screen," he adds, annoyed. Shit.

"Can you keep tracking it?"

"I can," he says slowly. "But your best bet is to go in the same direction and hope he eventually stops. Otherwise, you'll never catch up to him," he murmurs, peering at his laptop screen. Damn. Fucking hybrid bastard.

"Right," I say decisively, turning to the small group. "I'm leaving to go after Winter. Morgan, do you have earpieces we can use to communicate with you?"

"Of course," he says, putting the laptop down and retrieving another case I hadn't even noticed until now. "But they're not going to work in your wolf forms. You'll have to go by car," he says.

"That's fine. It will be slower, but as you said, he has to stop at some stage," I murmur. "We'll just have to rely on that."

"I'm coming too," Damien growls.

"Me too," Johnathon snaps.

I roll my eyes and look over at Langdon, who fidgets nervously. "Let me guess," I say wryly. "You want to come as well."

"I would," Langdon says formally. "But if you require me to stay back at the pack, I'll follow your instructions, Alpha Kai."

"No, you can come. That way, you can stop her brother here," I point to a stunned Damien. "From doing anything stupid," I finish, even though I suspect that Johnathon is the one that I have to keep an eye on.

Morgan hands over the earpieces. "It's a pleasure to help you, Sir," he says shyly, and I have to remind myself that he's only sixteen years old as I place the piece in my ear. "You should be able to hear me now," he adds, and I nod, impressed. This gadget is fantastic.

"Right, Johnathon, you're coming in the car with me," I growl while mind-linking several warriors to follow us. "Damien and Langdon, you can go together in Langdon's car."

They nod. Good. I'm not wasting time with arguments. I thank Morgan and run towards the garage, getting into the driver's seat and waiting impatiently for Johnathon to enter the passenger seat. I don't say a word, turning the key in the ignition and pulling out with a squeal of my tires.

"Head southeast," Morgan's voice comes into my head. I already have a GPS tracker installed in my car, as does every other pack member, so he can quickly locate us. I follow his instructions, Langdon and Johnathon right behind me.

Hold on, Winter, I think grimly, trying not to think about what she's going through. *Just hold on a little longer, baby. We're coming to save you. Be brave, sweetheart, be brave. I will kill that fucker for daring to lay a hand on you.*

Chapter 93

Winter's POV

It's dark. That's the first thing I notice when I open my eyes. My eyelids feel gritty, and I wipe them with the back of my hand, cursing at the feeling of silver restraints preventing me from doing much else. Fuck. This brings back some horrible memories of the last time, but when I glance around, there's no one there. I don't know where I am, let alone how far we traveled, but something tells me it had to have been a fair distance. My bracelet was taken by Thomas, the one Kai gave me.

Hopefully, Kai has noticed I've gone missing, but I'm not sure how well they'll do at tracking me when Thomas can move so unbelievably fast. He's twice as fast, maybe triple what a shifter is. I scan the room, and frown, puzzled. Pews are sitting in the room, and when I try to whip my head around, I can see an altar of some kind, a large cross in the background. Candles are burning in the far corner, but other than that, there's no other lighting at all.

Where the fuck am I? I suck in a breath as realization dawns. I'm in a church. Thomas has taken me to a fucking church. I can't even tell if it's abandoned or if he's killed anyone that lives here. I desperately hope it's the former. Maybe he's just brought me here to sleep? But my heart is thumping wildly in my chest, and my mouth feels parched. I'm so thirsty, and my stomach is growling with hunger. How much time has passed since Thomas kidnapped me?

My legs are chained together, and I hiss, uncomfortable as the silver digs into my skin, burning it. Still, I struggle and persevere, getting to my feet without toppling over—a small success. I mind-link Sabriel. She answers immediately.

Winter, you don't have much time until Thomas comes back. I don't know if this is a good idea.

What do you want me to do, Sabriel? Lie down and wait for him to come back, to do God knows what to us? No way, I'd rather die.

I'm sure Kai is trying to track us down. He knows we're missing by now, and don't forget that Damien, Johnathon, and even Langdon will be out searching for us.

I still don't want to rely on them to save me, Sabriel. I'm getting sick of it, to be honest.

Don't talk like that. There's nothing wrong with needing help, Winter. It doesn't make you weak.

But it makes me feel weak, Sabriel, and I'm tired of feeling that way.

She says nothing more to me, but I sense her anxiety as I awkwardly hop toward the pews. I have no plan other than to get out before Thomas returns from wherever he's gone. I make it halfway, cursing, panting, sweat dripping off my forehead, when I sense I'm not alone. Fuck. I waited too long, took too much time. I raise my head as the doors bang open, two glowing red eyes glaring at me. I swallow nervously and lose my balance, toppling over face first. Sabriel was right. I should have just waited instead of trying to escape.

I shriek angrily as Thomas picks me up like a sack of potatoes and deposits me, hard, back in my original location as I scowl at him. He looks pissed off. He's also clutching a grocery bag in his hand. I hope his eyes weren't glowing while he was supposedly shopping or stealing. For all I know, we're residing in a human town.

"Seriously, Winter," he barks. "You try to escape the second I'm gone," he explodes.

I cringe at the anger in his voice. But what does he honestly expect from me? To lie still and be a good little prisoner?

"Here," he mutters, throwing the bag at my feet.

I look at him tentatively and reluctantly reach for it. There's a bottle of water and a bagel in it. I eye it, my mouth watering as Thomas folds his arms over his chest.

"It's not poisoned," he says when I shoot him suspiciously.

I debate my options. I can't trust Thomas, but my stomach hurts. It's in that much hunger. The water bottle looks relatively safe, and I unscrew the lid and take a long swallow, feeling the cold against my dry throat in welcome relief. The bagel looks all right to me, and I tentatively take a bite, almost moaning from the taste of it, my stomach churning in appreciation.

I swallow the food and take another bite, Thomas' eyes on me the entire time.

"Thomas," I rasp out, finishing the last few bites of bagel and feeling satisfied, even though I'm not full. "Why am I here? It's not to be friends, so spit it out," I almost snarl, my temper igniting again. Sabriel is still quiet in my mind, and it's a bit disheartening. Is she that afraid of Thomas?

"Of course, it's not to be friends," Thomas laughs lightly, sounding incredulous and giving me a disbelieving look. "I want so much more than that," he growls, coming closer. My heart sinks. I thought this might be the case, but to hear it come from his lips is causing me to become paralyzed with fear.

My heart beats painfully, reminding me that I am still alive. He comes close, and I shiver as he reaches over and grasps a large chunk of my hair, sniffing it and giving a low growl. "You smell so nice," he almost purrs, and I shudder. "But then you always did smell so sweet to me," he says cocking his head. "Like a meadow of flowers. Not like all those other girls," he scowls. "They just reek of cheap perfume and cigarettes. By the way, you can thank me," he adds, and I stare at him, confused.

"I know what the girls did to you," he says softly. "The way they tried to kill you for my supposed death? Jessica was the main culprit, wasn't she? I took care of her for you."

Chapter 93

I feel bile rising in my throat and close my eyes, forcing myself to breathe and not throw up the meager contents of my stomach.

"What do you mean, you took care of her?" I ask, and he gives a slight chuckle.

"I guess I have to spill it out for you," he says, amused. "I killed her and not quickly either. I did it before I left our small town," he says calmly. "Which is why it took a little longer to get here. I had to hide the body and the evidence. You should have seen the look on her face when she saw me. She was so happy," he chortled, shaking his head. "And then when she realized why I was there, well," he paused. "Then you should have heard her screams. Ah, they were delightful," he murmurs. "Worth being a little longer so I can show you how much I love you."

I stare at him, horrified. He killed Jessica. I can't believe it. As much as I had hated that bitch, she hadn't deserved to die at Thomas' hand on my behalf. I can't even imagine the torture he would have put her through, either. I can't help it. I lean over to the side and puke my guts up while Thomas hastily backs away and wrinkles his nose.

"Winter," he admonishes me, and I look at him helplessly as he wipes my mouth with the back of his shirt and gives me more water. Tears prick the corner of my eyes.

"I also thought I took care of your damn brother," swears Thomas. "But I should have been more careful. I saw him and that annoying son of a bitch Johnathon at the pack. I'm not stupid, not to mention the Alpha and you."

"The Alpha and me," I say quietly, watching his eyes go even redder.

"You're mates, aren't you?" he spits, his hands clenching into fists. "I saw how you looked at each other when you thought it was safe. I see the mark on you," he hisses. "I can't believe you would betray me like that," he whispers.

I haven't betrayed you, you psychotic son of a bitch, I want to yell out loud, but instead, I bite my lip and look away, Thomas breathing heavily in what I'm hoping is an attempt to calm the hell down.

"It doesn't matter," he murmurs. "I can undo the mark, and we can still be together. You will be my chosen mate," he vows, and I look at him, panicked.

What did he mean by removing or undoing my mark? That's impossible. I decided he had to be lying, trying to scare me, but a small part of me wasn't so sure. Especially with the way he's licking his lips.

His fangs slowly come out of hiding and gleam in the darkness with the candlelight flickering over them. It's almost like being trapped inside a horror movie. He cocks his head at me as my eyes widen.

"Thomas, we can work this out," I plead desperately, hoping to distract him.

"We are working this out," he mutters. "Don't think I'm unaware you're being tracked," he snaps. "By that precious Alpha mate of yours and that annoying brother. They're ruining my plans," he snarls.

I try to back away but can't as he kneels over me. He licks his lips again. "I'm hungry," he whispers. "And I want that mark gone, Winter. You'll only bear my mark for now and forever," he says vehemently.

I stare at him, tears trailing down my cheeks. "Thomas, don't do this to me," I beg. "Please, don't drain my blood."

He laughs loudly, his head thrown back. "I'm not going to drain your blood," he sneers. "I just want a taste, plus I need to bite you to mark you," he growls.

I feel his hand grip the back of my neck as I begin to sob, his grip strong enough that I can't move as he pushes my head to the side, exposing the nape of my neck to him. He trails a finger down it, tracing my mark as I sob.

"Don't worry," he whispers to be reassuring. "It will only hurt for a minute," he promises. I say nothing, trying to wriggle my body, but it doesn't do any good. His grip is just too strong. I feel ashamed. Kai is going to be upset if our mark is removed. It was his official claim on me, and I treasure it.

I feel his fangs slowly piercing me, right in the center of the mark, Thomas biting down as I shriek at him to stop. Pain floods my body as I feel him sucking at my blood, his hand never moving. It's excruciating. It feels like I'm slowly dying. How much blood is he going to take? I'm so hazy now. My entire body is tense, though, as he continues to make small moans as he feeds on me.

"So delicious," he mutters, and to my relief, I feel his fangs slowly withdrawing, the pain fading. I shudder at the feel of his rough tongue on my skin as he seals the wound closed. I frantically look at the nape of my neck, and my heart skips a beat. Kai's mark is gone. It's completely gone; instead, my neck has puncture marks. Thomas looks pleased. "Now all I have to do is bite you with my shifter teeth, and you're mine," he crows.

I'm in shock, my body feeling like it's floating. I make a strangled noise of anguish as I fall face down to the floor. Thomas rolls me over, and I see his eyes looking down at me. "I forgot to mention that it will make you pass out again," he says nonchalantly as I close my eyes in resignation. His voice is the last thing I hear before succumbing to the darkness surrounding me. "Get ready because I want you to perform the ceremony when she wakes up."

Chapter 94

Damien's POV

I'm fuming when we get in the car. Kai's so-called plan for keeping my sister safe was an absolute joke. Look where it's called us! Winter's been kidnapped by Thomas, despite us warning her. He sucks as a mate for my sister. I should have trusted him with her, no matter how much Winter tried to convince me to. As it is, my hands are clenched into fists when we begin to pull out. If I could have gotten my hands on Alpha Kai, I would have hit him for failing her and us. This was all his fault. Part of me, though, recognizes it's my fault as well and that I should share the blame for this.

Langdon reaches over to take my hand, and I reluctantly let him, feeling the usual sparks tingling in my body when we touch. Straight away, I calmed down, knowing it was because of him. He looks grim, focused on the driving, shooting me sidelong glances occasionally to make sure I'm all right. I'm not. All I can think is that I've failed to protect her again. I should have fought harder for a different plan instead of going along with it. I should have come up with something that would have been better than this failure. My God, I'm a useless excuse of a brother.

The car swerves, sending me flying into the window, Langdon efficiently doing way over the speed limit and looking unconcerned about it. "Hey," he says as I straighten myself back up again. "It's going to be all right. We're going to find your sister," he adds vehemently. I blink at him. He doesn't understand. How much does he know about Thomas and what he attempted to do to her the last time? How much has Winter divulged to him? Something tells me she held some stuff back.

"What if we're not in time?" I asked dully. "What if we're too late to save her."

He falls silent, and I stare out the window, glaring at the stupid scenery.

"You and Winter are close, aren't you?" he asks slowly.

I have to think about the answer. To be truthful, we're not as close as I'd like, but I like to think that we're at least good friends.

"We're sort of close," I answer Langdon, who nods and pulls into the next lane.

"I know about your father," he says softly, and I'm stunned.

Had Winter divulged her past to Langdon, or had Kai spilled her secrets?

"Your sister told me," he says casually.

My heart sinks. Does that mean she told him about me and what I'd done? My spirits deflate like a lead balloon. He notices my distress.

"She told me all about you, Damien," he says quietly, reaching over and gripping my hand tightly. "I know what you did, how you bullied her at school and home. But I also know that you had a drunken alcoholic son of a bitch father that encouraged you to do those things and whom I know you were afraid of. I'm not judging you here. You did what you had to do to survive. Anyone would have done the same in your shoes."

"That doesn't excuse any of it," I say harshly, yanking my hand back. Watching as the scenery passes by in a blur. "I could have stood up to him and told him no. I could have stopped bullying her at school and let her be at peace there. Instead, I made her life a living hell." My voice trembles.

He gives me a sympathetic look, but I'm not looking for sympathy. I deserve everything that happens to me and more.

"She also told me about how you changed not long before she ran away. How you became the big brother, she'd always wanted and needed. She talked about you all the time, Damien. You were always in her thoughts. I can only imagine her guilt when she didn't communicate with you once she reached the pack. She loves you, Damien," he tells me firmly. "I believe she always has, despite everything."

I'm silent. How Winter can love me, and forgive the past, continues to astonish me. That kind of nature caused her to be bullied so relentlessly. Because back then, she never stood up for herself. My eyes meet Langdon's. "I don't know what I'm going to do if we get there too late," I choke out. "I can't bear to think of her being hurt…" I trail off. "Or worse." I don't even want to think of the worse. I want to get my hands on Thomas, choke him, and ensure he never hurts poor Winter again.

Langdon sighs. "We can't predict the future, Damien, all we can do is focus on the present. But I will say, and point out, that Alpha Kai is beating himself up right now over Winter being kidnapped. Just like you are," he points out with a sigh.

I don't want to hear it. I blame Kai for all of this. "The plan was his idea," I point out angrily. "I said it was a stupid one."

Langdon sighs. "Winter agreed to it, Damien. She even added to the plan. Do you think Winter is stupid?" he points out, and I scowl at him blackly. How dare he imply that. I don't like how he turned my question around—stupid logical Langdon.

Suddenly he pulls over. "What are you doing?" I ask nervously.

He holds up a hand and gestures for me to be quiet. It must be the earpiece. I frown. I hadn't been given one, only Kai and Langdon. I would kill to know what was going on right now. It must be necessary for Langdon to have pulled over when we were only just behind Kai as it was. Langdon is listening intently. There's a bewildered look on his face, and he looks pissed. He's cocking his head and shaking it. I wonder what the person on the other end of the earpiece is saying.

What the hell is going on? I almost want to grab him by the shoulders and shake him back and forth, screaming in his face for answers, and it's taking all my self-control not to do that and to wait patiently for him to finish. When he finally turns to me, his eyes show a nervous look. Something tells me I'm about to lose it, especially since Langdon's making no move to touch or calm me down in any way, shape, or form.

"I need you to remain calm," Langdon says evenly.

Big mistake. He should have led with something else because my temper, which is close to the surface anyway, ignites.

"Spit it out," I snarl. "Tell me what's going on, Langdon. Why did we stop?"

He bites his lip and looks away for a minute. I think he's trying to gather his thoughts and is thinking about what to say. I fold my arms across my chest impatiently.

"Okay, well, the thing is," he starts after exhaling heavily. "That Winter's location has disappeared. It looks like Thomas has either gotten rid of Winter's bracelet or managed to break the tracking device."

I swear, long and loud, wanting to do nothing more than thump the steering wheel or break a window. Fuck. Now what are we going to do? We were relying on that tracking device, for heaven's sake. How are we going to find her now?

"But," Langdon says tentatively. "We do have her last location. It's our best shot," he answers, looking grim. "We'll have to find her once we reach there."

I glare at him. "What good is knowing her last location if they decide to start moving again," I explode. "What you mean is that we've lost her, and we've lost her for good."

"Not true," denies Langdon. "Morgan said they'd been in the same location for over an hour. They may have stopped to rest, and we can catch up with them," he says calmly. He's too damn calm for my liking.

He steps back inside the car. "What are we waiting for then?" I growl as he starts the car back up, glances in the rearview mirror, and then peels out.

"Morgan lost our location, which is why I had to stop the car," he answers. "Otherwise, he couldn't give us directions, and we'd be going nowhere."

Oh. Now I understand. I feel a little sheepish, but not so much that I'm about to apologize, even if I feel bad. Langdon doesn't deserve me taking all my anger out on him.

"How far out are we?" I ask nervously.

Langdon glances at me. "We're about two hours away, depending on traffic conditions and if we speed or not. I'm currently speeding, so who knows."

"Two hours," I say, dismayed. "They'll have moved by then for sure."

Langdon shakes his head. "We just have to hope they don't. Winter is a smart girl, smarter than you give her credit for. You need to realize she's also stronger than you believe her to be. Don't think it's all hopeless because it's not. There is always hope."

His eyes glaze over, and I realize he's mind-linking someone. Probably that asshole Alpha Kai. I wonder how Johnathon's doing, being in the same car as that fucker. He's probably pissed off, but someone had to go in the car with him, and it sure wasn't going to be me. Johnathon could deal with the big angry asshole Alpha.

"Kai is going ahead. He's several minutes ahead of us. He'll meet us there. He's not going to wait on us."

Of course, he wouldn't. He's a big bad Alpha. He won't wait for backup, even if it makes sense. He must show off his prowess and strength to his pack and us. He's going to be a show-off. I know it. He better not do anything reckless and get Winter hurt, or else I will kill him.

"Fine," I tell Langdon dismissively. "But I don't want to be too far behind him. I don't trust him not to make another mistake," I added bitterly.

His jaw clenches, and I know he's upset with how I talk about his Alpha, but I'm beyond caring as he puts his foot on the gas pedal and goes even faster. After this with Langdon, I will discuss our relationship and where we want to go. Once Winter is safe, that is. I don't even know what I want yet. All I know is that when Langdon touches me, I get goosebumps. I want to be by his side all the time. I like waking up next to him in the bed, even though all we do is cuddle each other. But is that enough for me to stay with my mate forever? I don't even know what Langdon's thinking. Where he sees this relationship going. Right now's not the time to question him either.

We're so close, I think to myself a little desperately. *Winter, we're so close, and we're coming. I don't care what it takes, what you have to do, you need to stay in that place until we can get there. You need to fight if you have to because all of us are coming for you, and when we get there, Thomas is a dead hybrid who will never hurt you again. Please be safe, sweet sister of mine. Please be alive,* I think frantically and glance down at my clock. One hour and forty-five minutes to go until we got there. I would be counting down the minutes until we reached her location. *Please stay there,* I think desperately. *We're coming.*

Chapter 95

Winter's POV

This time when I open my eyes, there's a piercing pain in my neck, which is still there and excruciating. Not only that, but I still feel dazed, out of it and highly disorientated. I don't know how much blood Thomas decided to help himself to, but it feels like it was a lot. Otherwise, why would I be so damn weak? Sadly, I trace the mark, which is now non-existent on my neck. I loved that mark. Now I would have to get Kai to mark me again, and there were no guarantees he would want to. *Damn you to hell, Thomas.*

A coughing noise draws my attention, and I glance up towards the altar, where it appears to be coming from. My eyes widen in disbelief. Tied to the altar is a man dressed in a priest's uniform, not just any man. I take a long sniff and crinkle my nose. I can't sense him being a shifter; I'm sure he's not a vampire. Why was he there? How could Thomas have tied up a human, for heaven's sake? I had thought this church was abandoned, but it wasn't. Where were the rest of the people? Thomas couldn't have killed them all, could he?

He's gagged, so he can't speak. I sigh and then move my hands, my eyes looking down in shock as I realize that while they are still restrained, they aren't shackled to my legs anymore, giving me some freedom to move around. The silver burns, but it's a slight annoyance in the grand scheme. That's not the worst part, however. I shudder. I can't believe how violated I feel. He touched me while I was sleeping and saw my naked form. I'm no longer wearing the clothes I had initially put on. Instead, I see with dread that I'm wearing a white gown that resembles a wedding dress. I feel the bile rise in my throat. Had he taken liberties with me while I was sleeping? Surely not. I feel sick to my stomach. Bad enough, he dressed me while I slept. I wish I had the bracelet that Kai gave me. Thomas took it, and I don't know what he did with it.

Where is he? Then I see the pair of glowing red eyes behind the priest and swallow. He looks mad, half crazy. His hair is disheveled. I wonder if it's due to the result of being a hybrid and one that hadn't been born but created. He steps forward, and I cringe, curling up into a ball. I'm afraid my teeth are chattering. He seems to be unhinged, and that's what frightens me the most. As for Sabriel, I cannot hear her, and I'm wondering if he gave me more wolfsbane while I was unconscious. I would have given anything to have listened to my wolf at that moment, even if it was just for some reassurance. She would have kept my spirits up in a heartbeat.

"How do you like your dress?" Thomas asks smoothly, stepping forward.

I glance at him in contempt. He has gotten dressed up and is now wearing a tux. It doesn't take a genius to put two and two together. He's trying to get us married. It explains the poor priest who's tied up at the altar. This is not how I envisioned getting married in my dreams.

"I can't say I like it," I spit out at him, and his eyes narrow. Before I can stop him, he steps forward and swings his hand forward, slapping me directly across the face. It's the first time he's hurt me since he's taken me, and I put a hand up to my stinging cheek, staring at him as he looks apologetic suddenly.

"I'm sorry, Winter," he croons at me, looking worried. "It's just that I went to so much trouble to get that dress for you, and then you insulted it."

"I'm sorry," I say automatically. Man, he was stronger than he realized. The pain was much more than just a simple slap.

He looks pleased with my apology.

"Good, good," he mutters, helping me to stand and supporting me as I sway back and forth on my feet, feeling dizzy and lightheaded.

"This is no good. You can barely stand," he says, slightly annoyed. Then he places me leaning against the altar and darts forward. He begins to untie the poor fellow tied to the altar, and I know it's not because he's about to let the man go free.

"Stay back from me, demon," the priest says shakily as he's untied. I see Thomas roll his eyes at the man, and his fangs slowly protrude from his mouth. The man flinches. I see two marks on his shoulder and realize Thomas has also taken his blood. The poor priest must feel as dizzy as I am.

"I'm not a demon," Thomas roars at him. "But, help me, I can turn into one if you don't do as I say. Don't make me kill the rest of them," he snaps, and I realize he must have stashed the other people somewhere so that the man would be forced to do his bidding.

"What do you want from me?" the priest asks shakily, swaying back and forth on his feet. He's pale, ashen, and sweat beading on his forehead. He looks unwell. I wonder if I'm faring better simply because I'm a shifter and not wholly human like this poor guy. My shifter blood probably replenishes the lost blood far more quickly than if I was human.

"Isn't it obvious?" Thomas growls grimly, gesturing towards me as I lean against the altar, feeling weak as a newborn kitten. "I want you to marry the both of us."

All the blood drains out of my face. I don't want to marry him, but I can't exactly force my body to move, to run. If I managed to, he'd snatch me up in a heartbeat, much quicker than I am at running. *Stupid hybrid powers,* I think, miserably. *I wish Sabriel were here.*

God, where was Kai when I needed him? If I was to marry anyone, I wanted it to be him. I even pray that he, Damien, Johnathon, and Langdon are all searching for me. If only I could have left some clues for them to follow! But I'd been unconscious for the majority of it all. *Maybe they had a backup plan,* I think to myself. I was violently hoping that if they were to find me, it would be soon.

"I cannot marry someone unwilling," the priest says quietly, trembling. "And the young lady does not look like she wants to get married."

I want to smile at the man, but Thomas is furious. "Marry us," I say before he can threaten the innocent people he's got tied up somewhere. "It's for the greater good, priest, if it means saving innocent people," I say pointedly.

Thomas gives the man a wicked grin and returns to my side, holding me firmly at the waist as tears come to the corner of my eyes. "After the ceremony, I'm going to mark you as mine forever," he promises, and I stifle a sob. This was my worst nightmare coming true. The priest looks uncertain, but I give him a pleading look. I don't want people killed because of me, not when I can prevent it.

"We need witnesses," the priest says uncertainly.

"The hell we do," snarls Thomas. "Just do it already. You can pretend there are witnesses. Now get a move on," he threatens.

I say nothing. If I do, I might be sick all over myself.

The priest takes a deep breath, a bible lying on the altar before him, a nervous expression on his face. He looks at me apologetically, but he's not to blame for any of this. Instead, I blame myself. I was so sure I'd killed Thomas back then, but I'd failed. This is all my fault. It's karma getting back at me. I close my eyes as the priest begins to speak.

"Ladies and gentlemen, we are gathered here today to witness the union between this man," he motions to Thomas, who speaks. "Thomas," and this woman. "Winter," Thomas fills in "today."

I can't bear to listen to the words as he speaks them. I tune out. I feel numb, dead inside. I know what Thomas will do after this ceremony, and I'm tense, preparing myself. I would rather die than let him mark me. I won't let him violate my body like that, let alone have a wedding night of nightmares. If I have to kill myself first, I will, but I'd rather fight until the end. I'm pretty sure the priest is going on and on, prolonging the ceremony for as long as possible. When I open them, I thank him with my eyes, but it's all for nought.

Unless Kai comes bursting in, but the more time goes by, the more deflated I feel.

"Not much longer," Thomas whispers, licking his lips as I stare at him in revulsion. "Just think about our wedding night, Winter. I'm going to make it so special for the both of us," he whispers. Tears trail down my cheeks, and the priest pauses, seeing it. I move my head, imploring him to continue as Thomas's eyes turn even more red in his anger. The priest looks at me helplessly as he continues the ceremony.

"If anyone should object to this holy matrimony," booms the priest. "Let them speak now or forever hold their peace."

There's silence. Then the doors to the church burst open, and a disheveled Kai comes racing in with Damien, Johnathon and Langdon. His jaw is clenched, and he looks furious, especially when he enters the scene. A growl fills the air. The priest looks like he's about to faint.

"I object," Kai growls as Thomas grips me tightly, hissing, holding me before him.

"She's mine," Thomas hisses. "You no longer have a claim on her Alpha Kai," he adds triumphantly, indicating my bare neck.

There is silence as Kai looks at my neck and sees his mark is gone. Then all hell breaks loose. "You son of a bitch!" Kai roars, and their low growling comes from the rest of them as they shift to their wolf forms. Thomas moves my head to the side, even as I try to fight it, his fangs pointing out. "Come any closer, and I'll drain her blood before you get to me," he threatens.

Kai is pissed and stuck. He makes one move, and Thomas takes the blood from my body. He's too frightened to put me in danger. The priest makes a bolt for it, and Thomas lets him go, more focused on keeping me from moving. He lightly places his fangs against my neck as I shudder. Kai's eyes widen.

"Don't do it," he cries, and Thomas grins.

"Back away," he orders, and Kai slowly backs up, the wolves doing the same, although they look angry, snapping their jaws up and down at him. Thomas ignores all of them.

"How dare you ruin my wedding day," he says, and Kai looks nonplussed.

He's crazy, I speak to Kai, and he nods.

"Winter is mine, mark or no mark," Kai says firmly. "She is my mate, and I love her. You are a crazy shit hybrid that needs to be put down," he spits out, angering Thomas. Great. Both of them are fighting with words. *Screw this,* I think to myself and tense my body up. I have one shot at this, and if I fuck up, then I'm a goner. But would that be such a bad thing if Thomas would kill me anyway? At least this way, I would have attempted something instead of standing there and letting it happen.

I look at Kai, trying to convey that I was about to do something. I hope he gets the message. His eyes darken at the look on my face. Without further ado, I smack my head back into Thomas and drop to the floor as he gives out a howl. Next, I see a large black wolf leaping over my body, aiming directly towards a stunned Thomas.

Chapter 96

Kai's POV

W e're almost there. We're so close I can taste it. I pull up in front of what seems to be an old abandoned church in the middle of a small town. *Winter better be here,* I think grimly. It's the last coordinates that we received before they went missing. I almost leap out of the car, Johnathon doing the same.

"We should just go in," Johnathon mutters, and although I'm tempted, I want to wait for Langdon and Damien. They're not far behind, and I'd rather have them as backup. The warriors are a little bit behind them.

I sidle closer to the doors and sniff. My eyes widen. Winter is in there. I can smell her. My heart begins to thud loudly in my chest. Another car pulls up. It's Damien and Langdon, thank God, because I'm having a hell of a time preventing myself from storming inside. I motion for them to follow me. I kick the doors open to the church. The son of a bitch is in there, I'm sure of it, and I'm going to kill him.

I pull up at the sight of Winter in a wedding dress, Thomas behind her, wearing a tuxedo. I know he's trying to marry her against her will. My fury ignites.

"I object," I growl, the sound filling the otherwise silent church.

There's a priest behind them, and he looks petrified. I sniff. He's human. Incredibly the last thing we need to deal with. Thomas grins at me. *Cocky little bastard.*

He presses his fangs to Winter's neck. They are gleaming in the darkness of the church, threatening to take her blood. Even as the others shift, I'm helpless, ready to take Thomas out immediately.

Chapter 96

There's no mark on Winter's neck anymore. Somehow the asshole has managed to remove it. I'm so angry, I can barely see straight, but I'm holding it together for Winter's sake. She's so pale, and I can see a bite mark already on her neck where the bastard has already dug his fangs into her. Winter is giving me a look, her eyes trying to convey something, and my eyes turn black. She's going to do something, I can tell, and my body tenses in preparation. Whatever she's about to do, I can't afford to take advantage of it.

I watch in disbelief as she throws her head back into Thomas' and throws herself down. I don't hesitate. She's given me the opening I so badly needed, and I shift, throwing myself over her body and sending Thomas flying against the altar. I expect him to give up. After all, he's outnumbered, but instead, he laughs, getting back up and sending smiles our way. Is he that crazy?

"That was nothing," he sneers and throws himself at me. He's still in his human form, but he's incredibly strong, grabbing hold of me and throwing me across the room, sending pews flying everywhere.

Damien's wolf snarls and leaps, Thomas grabbing him by the tail and sending him flying into Johnathon and Langdon's wolves, sending them crashing to the ground. This fight isn't going to be easier. I spare a glance at Winter. She's still on the basis, and I hope she stays down. It's safer at the moment. I notice the priest has dashed it. Thomas begins to shift, and I watch in astonishment. His wolf is large, larger than my own. Is this because he's a hybrid? More powerful than even an Alpha wolf? Fuck.

I tackle him, his jaws clamping on me as he shakes me back and forth like a rag doll and sends me crashing into the nearby wall. Damien growls, charging him, and I watch as Thomas easily dodges and then turns, swiping Damien across the midsection. He howls and backs away. Langdon takes the opportunity to charge and gets thrown into the wall, his back hitting it solidly and his body making a huge thumping noise as he crashes to the floor.

Johnathon leaps, landing on Thomas's back, biting furiously, his jaws clamping down on Thomas. Thomas reaches back and bucks him off, sending him to the floor. At this rate, we're never going to win the fight. I never anticipated that he was this strong. He's holding his own against two Alphas, for heaven's sake. That in itself is remarkable. Then I hear more snarls coming from the back of me, and I know that the warriors have come and shifted. *Game on,* I think to myself, watching Thomas. *You've nowhere to go, you bastard. You're dead meat.*

I see fear in Thomas' eyes for the first time since this fight began. He hadn't expected me to bring so many reinforcements. Or he had been banking on us not being able to track him. He was that arrogant. I snarl. Winter slowly gets to her feet and moves sideways. I wonder what on earth she's thinking, but thankfully Thomas doesn't appear to notice. All his focus is on me and everyone else. This means that for now, Winter is safe, so long as she doesn't bring any attention to herself.

I leap, and he swerves. He jumps and takes out two of my men, attempting to sneak up behind him. They skim into some of the other wolves, upending them off their feet. I jump simultaneously as Johnathon, both of us landing on him, our jaws clamping down. He howls, jumping and bucking, as I claw at his sides. He manages to twist enough to get both of us off. But there's something strange. I can see the blood trickling down from his various injuries, but they're healing incredibly fast, right in front of my eyes. No wolf can remedy that quickly. This is because of his mixed blood. Shit. We will have to work together and break his neck so he can't heal. Something difficult even at the best of times.

Damien and Langdon attack, Damien clamping his jaws onto Thomas' leg and bending it until it makes a sickening crack. He's managed to break it, and they both dance away. But within moments, the damage is undone. Everyone is panting heavily, but Thomas hasn't broken a sweat. He even looks like a rogue with his red glowing eyes, even though he doesn't smell like one.

Chapter 96

I can see Winter behind the altar, digging around like she's looking for something. I try not to look too hard. I don't want Thomas to swing his head around and stare at her. She could be coming up with some plan. Whatever it is, I hope she keeps herself safe at the same time.

Thomas leaps and meets me in mid-air. We both kick and claw simultaneously, falling to the ground and rolling repeatedly as everyone else tries to chime in and help. I feel his jaws clamp down on my leg and kick, bucking and writhing until he lets go and backs away. Damien and Langdon are up, but as my eyes swing to them, I can see that both are covered in various injuries and won't be able to continue much longer. My warriors have fared slightly better, and they go dashing for Thomas, but he sends them flying. I barely dodge in time as a wolf almost careens into me.

Winter is standing now. I eye her. She's brandishing something in her right hand, shimmering in the darkness. I have to hone in, and when I do, my eyes widen. She's found a knife, a silver one, at the altar. It could be our only shot, but it would have to be plunged into his heart, and even then, he still had his vampire side to contend with. *Throw it,* I think to myself. *Throw it, Winter.* She raises her arm and throws the dagger at me as I return to human form and catch it. Thomas looks at me but seems nonplussed, changing back into his human form.

"You really think that's going to change anything," he growls and moves fast, but not as fast as me. I hold the dagger up and stab him directly in his chest as his eyes open in disbelief.

He lets out a short cry, a gurgled sound, and I let him drop to the ground. I push the dagger even harder, making sure it enters his heart. I'm not taking any chances. The other shifters surround me. I drop him to the floor as his eyes blink up at me. Winter sidles closer.

"Fuck you," he breathes, and I push the dagger in even more as his eyes widen. Then just as suddenly, he stares up at the ceiling, his eyes blank. Winter comes to my side, and I place my arm over her shoulder, but she shrugs off. "We have to make sure he's dead," she says, sounding slightly hysterical. Before I can stop her, she bends over Thomas' body and grasps hold of the dagger. However, before she can pull it out, his eyes shoot open, and his arm raises. He hits her, sending her flying, her head and back hitting the church walls as her body slides to the floor.

"Son of a bitch," I growl and reach down, gripping hold of his neck and his body as he weakly tries to stop me. I twist his head until his neck breaks and continue until his head is severed. I drop it to the floor as everyone returns to their human form.

"Clean this up," I say tiredly. "And contact the chief of police. He happens to be a shifter. He's going to need to know what went down tonight."

Langdon nods, helping Damien to sit. Johnathon is already clutching his ribs and breathing heavily, sitting on some pews.

I race over to Winter. She's breathing, thank goodness, but blood is matted in her hair at the back of her head and some along the wall. She hit the wall hard. I'm worried about her being concussed and that the damage might worsen. I need to get her home. I glance over at my shoulder. Johnathon is definitely in no state to be in the passenger seat. He needs to be lying down with those cracked ribs. Good thing the warriors had several cars.

"Langdon," I say, bending down and picking Winter up. Geez, she's light as a feather.

He comes over to me, glancing over his shoulder at Damien. "Yes, Alpha Kai."

"I want you to organize transportation and any medical assistance anyone needs. I'm taking Winter back in my car," I explain gruffly. "But Johnathon needs to be lying down. He won't be comfortable sitting up in my passenger seat."

Langdon nods his understanding. "Leave it to me. I'll organize everything," he says confidently.

I have no doubts he'll clean this mess up. I gingerly take Winter to the car, her body flopping limply in my arms like a rag doll. I'm careful to place her in the back of the vehicle, uncaring about the blood that stains the seats. She's far more important. I buckle her in securely and find a blanket to place over her. She's been through something traumatic, and any small thing I can do for her, I'll do without hesitation.

I start the car, easing it out onto the road. I'm still naked, but I could care less when we arrived. I can steal some scrubs or something from the hospital. The drive is long and painfully slow as traffic forces me to a standstill several times. Even this late at night, the roads are busy. When we finally return to the pack house, I'm nearly prepared to cry in relief, pulling up right in front of the hospital and carefully getting Winter out of the car. I walk inside, clutching her tightly to me.

Please, God, let her be all right.

Chapter 97

Winter's POV

There's so much beeping. It's frustrating the hell out of me. Why is it so loud? It's piercing my eardrums. I want to shut it off. It's making me so mad, so angry. My eyelids flutter open. I look around me, perplexed. Why am I hooked up to all these machines? Something is in my arm, and I pull it out, ignoring the blood trickling from the wound. It stings a little, but I'm more fascinated by the room. Or disgusted. Disgusted would be more accurate.

It's so sterile, so white. I glance down and see that I'm in a gown. I touch it. It's rough. Not soft at all. The blanket is coarse and thick. *It's warm, at least,* I think to myself with a shrug. I'm barefoot, and the window blinds are up, showing a large house in the distance and lovely grounds. I wonder if I live there?

Where am I? I'm so confused. I can't remember how I got here, no matter how much I tried. Did someone bring me here? I know I'm in a hospital of some kind but not where. Everything seems to be jumbled in my mind. The room is empty. Should I ring for a nurse? My head is pounding, and it feels like it will split open. I grimace. Bathroom business first. I push the machines to the side and climb out of bed. A quick check of the room and I find the bathroom attached, going inside and doing my business.

I stare at my face in the mirror. A stranger stares back. I touch my hair, and so does the reflection. I purse my lips, and so does the mirror. But I don't recognize the face. I can't tell if that's me. It's like I've never seen this girl before in my life. Who is she? I slowly walk back out of the bathroom. I'm at a complete loss as to what to do. Should I go and find someone, maybe?

A doctor and a man come into the room. I stare at the man. He's handsome in a rugged masculine way. He has scars across his face that make him look a little ferocious, but I'm not frightened of him. Instead, a small part of me wants to touch them. I frown. Am I familiar with this man? Because he looks much older than the girl in the mirror. I sit on the bed and stare, wanting to know who they are.

The doctor smiles at me. He looks nice. The other man is beaming and folding his arms. I stare at him. Why is he so happy?

"How are you feeling?" the doctor asks me.

I think for a moment. "My head is pounding, and I have a bad headache," I told him reluctantly.

He scribbles in his chart. What is it about doctors and charts?

"That's to be expected," murmurs the doctor. "You hit your head pretty hard. From what I can tell, there was no concussion, but I want you to be on the lookout for other side effects."

"Like what?" I ask, frowning.

"Nausea, vomiting, blurred vision," he lists. I nod and grimace. Big mistake. The pain in my head flares up.

The other man speaks. "I'll keep a close eye on her doctor. Don't you worry."

Why would he be keeping a close eye on me? Then it hits me. He must be a family member. It explains the age gap. Maybe he's my brother.

"Winter, are you feeling all right? You're being very quiet," the doctor says, concerned.

I blink at him, confused. Is he talking to me?

"Who?" I ask. "Who's Winter?"

There's nothing but silence in the room. The man with the scars is chewing his lip and staring at the doctor, who looks incredibly nervous and slightly upset.

"Your name is Winter," the doctor says worriedly. "Do you not know your name?"

I shake my head. I'm trying not to feel too panicky, but that's easier said than done. The doctor glances at the other man, who's gone pale.

"What about this man?" asks the doctor, pointing to the other.

I shake my head again. "Is he a family member?" I ask, turning to the man with scars. "Are you, my brother?"

His mouth drops open in disbelief. "No, I'm not your brother," he growls, and I stiffen.

What's his problem? It was a genuine mistake. He doesn't have to get so angry over it.

"What's wrong with her?" The man glowers at the doctor, who gulps and looks at me with concern.

"I'm going to have to do some tests," the doctor mutters to him. "But I suspect she's suffering from amnesia due to the injury she sustained on her head."

"What?" explodes the man with scars as I nervously jump. "How on earth does that happen? How do we fix it?" he snarls.

"You can't just fix it. Her memories must come back on their own," the doctor explains.

The man does not look happy.

"Who are you?" I ask, and he looks at me, his eyes softening momentarily.

"I'm your mate," he says quietly, holding my hand.

I shiver as tingles run up my hand and arm. It feels nice. The word mate echoes in my mind as I should instinctively know what it is.

"Can she still feel the mate bond?" the man asks rather desperately.

"She can, but she won't know what it is," the doctor says reluctantly. "All she'll know is that she's drawn to you for some reason."

Hello, I'm sitting right here, I think to myself sarcastically. They don't seem to notice, but I'm not listening.

"I like you," I tell the man with scars as he squeezes my hand. "You seem nice," I say, yawning and incredibly tired.

The man looks taken aback. "I like you too," he mutters. He seems a bit out of his depth. We like each other, but it surprises me, considering the age gap. But then, does age matter when you're in love? I want to believe it doesn't.

"I'll come back in a little while," the doctor says. "And get those tests started."

The man looks displeased. "You said I could take her home today."

"You still can. I want to confirm everything first," the doctor says, scurrying out of the room as fast as his little legs can carry him. I guess he's afraid of the man with scars. I don't blame him. The man is intimidating but oh so handsome. I feel like I'm drooling as I stare at him.

"What's your name?" I ask shyly.

"It's Kai," he says gruffly.

Kai. The name sounds familiar. Like I've heard it before. I like it. I like the person attached to the name. I'm sure of it. He squeezes my hand.

"Winter, we live together," Kai says, his eyes staring directly into mine as I suck in a breath. "We share the same bedroom. We both love each other. Do you remember any of that?" he asks, rather forlorn.

I strain but can't remember. I feel miserable as I shake my head again. "I'm sorry," I whisper. "I don't remember," I add.

"It's not your fault," he tells me. "Don't blame yourself. We'll get through this," he adds firmly.

I admire his optimism. There's another sound and voice at the doorway.

"You're awake, little sis."

I look at the doorway. There's another man at the door, clutching a teddy bear and smiling. He looks slightly older than me. I frown. Did he call me his little sister? He pulls me into a hug, and I awkwardly pat him on the back before he hands me the teddy bear. He sits on the other chair next to Kai and smiles.

"So, how are you feeling?" he asks breezily.

Kai glares at him. "She has amnesia, so she doesn't know who any of us are," he barks.

The man's face falls. "Really?" he says in a whisper, pointing at himself. "You don't know who I am?"

I feel bad. "No, I don't know you. I'm sorry."

"I'm Damien, your older brother."

Damien. The word rolls off my tongue. It sparks something inside of me, but I can't say what. I hug the teddy bear to my chest and breathe. I'm starting to feel overwhelmed.

"It's all right. We can get to know each other again later," Damien says hastily.

I give him a tentative smile.

The doctor reappears, and I shrink back. Kai holds onto me, running his fingers down my arm. It's soothing and relaxes me. It helps me to calm down. "I just checked the X-ray, and there was some damage to her skull. It's minor and will heal itself, seeing as she's a shifter, but it means the amnesia is real. I can't say how long it will be until Winter returns her memories."

Kai looks disappointed. I'm disappointed too. Now what am I meant to do? Just take everyone's word for it when they tell me who they are and how they relate to me.

"When can I take her home?" asks Kai, and I stiffen.

"You can take her now if you want. But I need to check up on her in a few days," the doctor warns. Kai nods his head.

"Winter," Kai says softly as I look at him, fear in my eyes. "How about we get you some clothes, and then I can take you back home to rest."

I'm unsure, but the doctor trusts him, so I will also. I obediently let him help me out of the bed, and the doctor hands me some clothes. They look new. I don't bother to ask, going into the bathroom and slowly changing myself.

When I return, Damien is gone, and Kai is standing there.

"Where's Damien?"

"He went back already," Kai answers. "We didn't want to overwhelm you."

He hands me the teddy bear, and I clutch it.

Kai puts a hand on my back and leads me out of the hospital. We go through the main doors and walk outside. The sun is bright and warm. My eyes water at the brightness of it. The sky is a beautiful clear blue with fluffy clouds in the sky. The grass looks soft and lush, bright green against the pathways. It's a perfect day, and I appreciate the scent of pine and earth. He holds my hand, and I let him guide me toward the large house in the distance.

"Kai," I say quietly as we walk. "I don't want to stay in the same bed as you until I have my memories back." I flinch. Is he going to get mad and hurt me?

He looks hurt instead. "I can understand that," he admits, and I let out a giant whoosh of relief. "But I'm at least going to put you in an adjoining room instead. That's as far as I'm willing to compromise."

I think about that. It seems fair enough. He is compromising, considering we share a bed and bedroom.

"Thank you," I tell him shyly.

We enter the large house, and he leads me upstairs. We bypass a few bedrooms, and then he stops showing me one. "This is our room," he explains as I look around, seeing nothing to spark a memory. He opens another door and motions me inside. It's a pretty basic room, but it's nice and next to where he will be sleeping. I sit on the bed.

"Lie down," Kai tells me, and I lay on the bed. He places the covers on me. I snuggle into the bed. It feels so damn comfortable compared to the hospital one.

He pulls a loose strand of hair from my face and kisses my forehead. "Try and go to sleep," he murmurs. "You need to rest and recover."

"How did I end up in the hospital?" I ask curiously.

He hesitates. "We can discuss that later."

I sigh but nod. My eyes begin to flutter closed. They feel heavy now, and I feel exhausted. I hug my teddy bear to my chest and start to fall asleep. The last thing I hear before darkness surrounds me is Kai's voice.

"Damn that bastard for causing this."

Chapter 98

Johnathon's POV

"You mean she has no memories of us at all?" I ask in disbelief, the others hanging onto my every word as we crowd around in the study. Kai looks at me angrily, but I don't care. How the hell does Winter manage to lose her memories? I didn't think her injuries had been that serious. Now I feel like an idiot.

"None," Kai says heavily. "She doesn't remember me, her brother, or any of you guys," he adds, indicating myself and Langdon.

I scowl at him. "For how long?" I ask irritably.

"It could be days, months before she gets her memories back," Kai shoots back. "We can't force her to try and remember."

I don't have months, however. I sigh. Damien understands the reason for my angst and shoots me a sympathetic look, but I don't want his sympathy.

"So what are we supposed to do in the meantime?" I ask, and Kai looks frustrated.

"We just encourage her to remember. Remind her of things she likes and what we've done together."

Well, that's not helpful.

"I don't want to remind her of her past," Damien grumbles. "It's not exactly something that will make her happy," he adds, and I know his reasoning. After all, he, more than anyone, well maybe except his father, bullied Winter relentlessly at school and home. I don't blame him for not wanting to remind Winter of that.

"I don't think we should mention her father either," I shoot out irritably, and Damien gives a small nod, looking glum.

"So we tell her about all the good things," Langdon points out, arms folded across his chest. "All the little things. I know she likes purple flowers, for instance, roses in particular."

Kai looked thoughtful. "I can remind her of the first date we had together."

"Oh, and what about when you guys went for a run for the first time?" Langdon says to Kai eagerly. Kai nods furiously.

Well, I feel left out. There are no fond memories that Winter's going to have of me. Rejecting her at first sight, wouldn't make for a memorable moment. It would just leave a sour taste in her mouth. My heart feels sad. I wanted to show her how much I've changed for the better; instead, she's lost all my memory. The irony. I guess it's karma coming back to bite me in the ass. It's the least of what I deserve.

Besides, who am I kidding? Winter's never going to give me a second chance. Not when she has a mate like Kai. I didn't stand a chance of trying to persuade her to give me a shot. Besides, Kai seems to love her genuinely. For who she is, and every time he glances at her, I can see the love in his eyes for her. I want that. I've given up on thinking I never want a mate. Now I see just how special it is. Even Langdon and Damien make a cute couple and can't seem to keep their hands off each other. It's adorable.

"The only memory she has of me besides being here is me rejecting her," I say softly, meeting Kai's eyes. "I'd rather she not remember it."

"She's going to want to know who you are," says Kai gruffly.

I look him directly in the eyes. "I plan on avoiding her until I leave tomorrow."

He looks surprised. "Why avoid her? Even if you're just friends…" he trails off.

I take a deep breath and steel myself. "Because it hurts too much to be near her and not touch her," I say honestly as Kai looks taken aback.

Chapter 98

"Johnathon," Damien says softly. "You rejected Winter, remember?"

"I know," I answer. "And Kai, I wouldn't dream of trying to take her from you. But seeing her with you reminds me of what I don't have and what I let slip through my fingers. It's unbearable," I choke out.

"I understand," Kai assures me. "I would feel the same way in your shoes. But where are you going when you leave? Back to your pack, or will you continue to travel?"

I think about it. Mother is probably missing me like crazy by now, and to be fair, I miss my pack and the responsibilities that go with it. I've managed to do what I set out to do: save Winter. Now it's time I go back, and maybe, if I'm lucky, I'll even find a second chance mate like Winter has.

"I'm going back to my pack," I say quietly. "It's time for me to become Alpha again."

I look over at Damien. "Are you going back to your pack?"

You could have cut the tension with a knife as Damien tensed and Langdon looked up, scowling. They hadn't discussed the future yet. Ouch. I guess I put my foot in it.

"I don't know yet," Damien stammers, looking at Langdon with beseeching eyes. "I think I might stay for a while if it's all right with everyone else?"

"I have no problems with you staying in my pack," Kai answers quickly, looking at his Beta. "And I assume Langdon would like you to stay with him in the meantime?"

Langdon gives a big huff. "Of course, I want Damien to stay with me, but I don't want him to feel like he's being forced to."

"I'm not," growled Damien looking exasperated.

"Then that's fine," Langdon growls back.

Kai looks amused, and I'm also trying to stifle my laughter. They are so well matched to each other, especially with their personalities being similar. I feel envious of their relationship. They're just like Winter and Kai in some aspects, and it's sweet to see.

"At least I know that my mate isn't in any of the packs we traveled at," I say grimly. "So mine might even be back in my pack. I can hope."

"Do you want to say goodbye to Winter," offers Kai. "She's sleeping now, and I doubt you'll wake her up."

"You don't mind?"

"I wouldn't have suggested it if I did," Kai says wryly.

He stands up, and I follow suit, following him out to the corridor and quietly upstairs.

"As long as you don't make too much noise, she'll stay asleep," Kai whispers. "She's a deep sleeper."

Ouch. My heart skips a beat at hearing that. Of course, he would know that she was a deep sleeper. After all, they had been sharing a bedroom, well, until now, at any rate.

He gently opens the door and gestures to me inside.

I walk inside, and my eyes focus on Winter. She's snuggled under the covers, clutching a giant teddy bear. I frown. I'm pretty sure Damien was giving her a teddy bear when he visited. It must be this one. Her chest moves evenly up and down. Her eyes are closed, and her soft snores are filling the air. Her hair is spread out on the pillow, some even covering part of her eyelids. I want to touch it, push it back from her face, but I'm incredibly aware of Alpha Kai standing in the doorway watching me.

I do it anyway. Her hair is soft and silken, and I feel it with my fingers as I brush it aside, kneeling beside her.

"Hey, Winter," I whisper, a lump in my throat. "I wanted to come and see how you are doing. You look like you're okay."

I feel foolish and glance towards the doorway, relieved to see that Kai has gone, presumably to give us both some privacy. He must trust me not to do anything stupid.

"I wish I could tell you how much I hate myself for rejecting you and how much I wish I could take it back. You're a pretty special girl, Winter. You're strong, brave, compassionate, and loving towards everyone. Even with what I did, you didn't hate me for it.

You forgave me like it was nothing. Because that's the kind of girl you are."

I pause. "I know we can never be together, and I'm happy for you and Kai. He seems to love you, and I know that you love him. You deserve to be happy. You deserve to be loved. I hope from now on that your life becomes much easier and you continue to be happy every day. I wish I had the guts to tell you all this to your face and more. I can't stay any longer, Winter. I have to go back to my pack. You don't know who I am anymore, which hurts, but it's not your fault. I wish you all the best and tell you goodbye forever, Winter. I'm leaving tomorrow. I want you to know I love you, and you'll always have a special place in my heart."

I stop, feeling choked up. I gently kiss her forehead, watching her eyelids flutter and settle. I stand up and quietly walk towards the doorway, my shoulders slumped in defeat. I can't help looking over my shoulder for one last glimpse of her before gently closing the door behind me, leaving Winter to sleep.

Kai meets me at the head of the stairs. I wonder how much of that he overheard. But he says nothing. Instead, he gives me a small smile and walks me back toward the study. It's empty. Damien and Langdon have left to do something else. Kai closes the door behind him.

"Listen," he says firmly. "You did me and Winter a great service coming to her rescue and warning her about the danger. Is there anything we can do for you? Name it, and I'll arrange it," he breathes. I can hear the gratefulness in his voice. I cringe. There's nothing I want from him. Well, almost nothing. An idea sparks in my mind. "Maybe we can do each other a favor," I smile, leaning back in the chair. "How does a treaty between our two packs sound?" I coax.

He's silent momentarily, and I wonder if I've overstepped my bounds. But then he stares directly at me with a small smile. "I would be honored to sign a treaty with your pack. If anything should happen, I am more than happy to offer my aid, Alpha Johnathon," he breathes.

"Can we organize it before the morning?" I enquire. I don't want to delay my plans after officially saying goodbye to Winter. It would hurt too much to stay here and have to watch her with Kai. I need to get out of here.

"I can organize it within the hour," Kai grins, pulling out a bottle of bourbon from his desk. He offers me a sip, but I shake my head. I've never liked the taste of bourbon. He takes a swig before me, and then his eyes glaze over.

"Right, I've got a lawyer, a witness, and Langdon coming back to the study," he says, fixing his gaze on me. "Not to mention a notary. I told you I'd organize it quickly," he says proudly, and despite myself, I'm impressed. He's done it a lot quicker than I'd anticipated. This time when he offers the bourbon, I take a small sip, trying not to splutter as it burns my throat going down. I hastily give it back to him.

"To a treaty between our packs," Kai cheers, and I smile and nod.

"To the treaty between our packs," I say back, grabbing the bottle and drinking from it. This time it goes down a lot easier.

Within the hour, the treaty is signed, and I carefully place it in a bag Kai has produced for me, along with a small pile of clothes.

"I can send you in a car with a small group of warriors," Kai says. "It would ease my mind to know you're not traveling back alone."

I cock my head. It sounds better than traveling back on my own, and quite frankly, a car would be an absolute luxury as the weather is getting cold and quite wet.

"Can I leave now?" I ask quietly, and he hesitates and then nods.

"I'll arrange it. Is there any reason you want to leave so badly?"

"I hate goodbyes," I say calmly, and it's the truth. I'm in a car heading back toward my pack house within minutes.

Goodbye, Damien, Langdon, and Winter, I think to myself a little sadly. There was no telling if I would ever see any of them again.

Chapter 99

Damien's POV

I sigh. I'm not in a great mood. Johnathon up and left without saying goodbye to Langdon or me! I've been traveling with him for months, for Christ's sake. I guess he's not good at goodbyes. Besides, maybe it hurt him to be so close to Winter, knowing he had no chance with her anymore. Who knows. Damn, idiot.

Langdon can sense my mood. "Something the matter?" he asks, and I turn to look, taking in his folded arms across his chest.

I don't know why, but I explode. All the tension I'm feeling, the awkwardness, and the uncertainty comes to the surface.

"Is something wrong?" I vent. "What about all of it? Johnathon's gone. Winter's got amnesia," I say bitterly. "Which is ironic because now she has no idea who I am and this relationship," I mutter, gesturing towards each other. "I don't even know where to start with that."

Langdon frowns. He's so calm. It's unnerving. "What do you want in the relationship?" he asks coolly as a cucumber. "Because we haven't discussed what either of us wants."

Of course, we haven't. We've been a little preoccupied with the whole Thomas, dangerous thing, and now Winter has amnesia. The last thing on my mind is this entire mate bond thing with Langdon. But we have to talk, and I guess now is as good a time as any.

"I don't know," I tell him, almost shouting. "Because you haven't told me whether you want me or not. You don't give me any idea either way. It's infuriating," I add.

His eyes darken. "So what you're saying," he says quietly, his body tense. "Is that all hinges on me and has nothing to do with you? That you don't get a say at all?"

That's not what I mean. I want to scream. Instead, I flop down on the bed and glare at him. "I'm saying you've given me no indication of whether you want to accept me as your mate," I say bitterly.

He raises an eyebrow. "It works both ways," he points out. "I don't know what it is you're wanting either."

I blurt it out, blushing profusely. "I want to stay with you."

Awkward silence. I can't even look up at him anymore. My heart starts beating loudly in my chest. He doesn't move from the doorway. Tears well in the corner of my eyes. He doesn't want me. That's why he's so quiet and stiff. He can't accept the mate bond because we're both men. I'm an idiot for even thinking he would want me. I brace myself for the rejection I'm sure he's about to utter, but it never comes.

"You idiot," growls Langdon, and I look up, blinking furiously.

Did he just call me an idiot? What the hell?

"I've been waiting for you to tell me that because I didn't want to pressure you," he growls.

I can feel myself lighting up. "You mean?" I ask tentatively. God, I don't even recognize myself. Where is the cool, collected, and calm Damien gone? *Get a grip, you moron,* I think to myself furiously.

"I mean, I want you," he growls. "As my mate. I don't want anyone else, so help me god. It's you."

He saunters over, reaches out, and grasps my chin with his hand, his other one wiping the tears away as I look at him, ashamed. He bends his head down and presses his lips against mine, and it's heaven. They're coarse and rough, his hand gripping the back of my neck possessively as he plunders my mouth, forcing my lips open and caressing my tongue. I moan out loud, my lips mashing hard against his. I can feel my arousal, my cock twitching in my pants in response, but I don't care. He tastes so delectable that I don't want to stop kissing him, but eventually, we both have to pull back and draw in oxygen.

He's panting heavily, I see with satisfaction. I'm doing the same, however. His eyes are dark, and it's clear his wolf is close to the surface. He pushes me down onto the bed without warning, his fingers undoing the buttons on my shirt frantically. He shakes his head, and I lie still, eager to feel his flesh against mine.

His hands touch and caress my bare skin as I shudder, the feeling intense, pleasure coming over me in waves. He leans down and trails kisses from the nape of my neck to my navel as my body trembles beneath his. He looks like he's barely holding onto his control. I could stop him, but my body is feeling too much pleasure to want to, and I'm eager to touch him as well, even if he's preventing me from doing that right now.

"Fuck, Langdon," I moan, and he chuckles, pinning me with his gaze.

"You like that?" he asks huskily, and I give a shy nod, writhing beneath him.

I feel his fingers at my belt buckle, undoing it, and then his hand goes to my zipper, and I stiffen.

"You can tell me to stop at any time," he growls, his body stilling as I look up at him shyly.

"Don't stop. I never have…" I trail off helplessly. Then again, it's not like Langdon has either.

He pulls the zipper down, freeing my cock, which is fully erect, to my embarrassment. But Langdon looks pleased, licking his lips. I shudder. Indeed, he's not about to…?

But he is. His head leans down, and before I can prepare myself, I feel his rough tongue along my shaft, my hands clenching and clutching at the bedsheets in desperation.

"Oh, God," I pant, and he holds me down with his arms, slowly taking my shaft into his mouth, inch by inch, as I gasp and writhe.

Fuck, it feels incredible, and I can't keep still, moaning and mewling as he begins to move his head up and down my cock, putting all of it inside his mouth. The pleasure is incredible, and he begins to use a hand to move up and down with his mouth. At this rate, I'm going to explode in his mouth.

"Langdon," I whisper. "Langdon, I'm about to cum," I warn him, sensing it is coming.

I expect him to pull away, but instead, it's like his mouth clamps down, and he increases the pace until I'm shaking, my body stiffening as I shoot my load into his mouth with a big cry. He licks his lips and swallows the lot, looking up with a grin.

I feel exhausted. Completely drained, and yet my body is crying out for more. More of Langdon. Langdon stands up and slowly removes his clothes as I watch with wide eyes. He's so fucking beautiful, like a god from olden times. My mouth waters just looking at him. His cock is fully erect, and I stare at it in astonishment. It's huge. I doubt it's going to fit. He sees my trepidation.

"We can stop," he says quietly, but I shake my head. God, even now, I'm desperate for him.

He comes over and slowly rolls me onto my stomach. Now I feel slightly hesitant. Is this going to hurt? Langdon whispers in my ear. "Calm down. I want to get you ready first," he finishes with a low growl.

I feel something at my entrance and look over my shoulder. Langdon has a bottle of lube that he's fetched from God knows where and has spread some on his fingers. I relax. Slowly, he inserts a finger inside me. I jolt. It's not painful, merely uncomfortable, and I groan as he spreads me out, the lube cold but slowly warming as it's inside me. He sticks another finger inside of me, and I start to mewl. I feel stuffed. Full, the feeling is incredible. He slowly thrusts them back and forth, letting me get used to the feeling and take them in deeper.

"God, I can't wait anymore," he says from behind me, sounding desperate. "So if you want me to stop, tell me now before I lose control," he chokes.

"I want you inside me," I whispered, resting my head.

His fingers slowly withdraw. This time when I feel something at my entrance, I know that it's his cock. I take a deep breath and steel myself.

"Just breathe," he whispers and then slowly pushes his cock inside of me as I clutch the bedsheets.

It's a lot bigger than his fingers, and the feeling is more uncomfortable, but the further he goes, the more pleasure I feel, my hips slightly raised to allow him better access. He growls as he enters me, not stopping until he's in.

"Stop," I plead, feeling a slight burning pain. He stops immediately, hands gripping tightly to my waist.

I pant, trying to will my body to relax as it gets used to the feeling of Langdon inside me. Eventually, the stinging fades. "Okay," I whisper, and he slowly withdraws before plunging back in just as slowly. I moan. Damn, it feels fucking good. My head whips side to side as he continues in the same slow rhythm, the pleasure slowly rising inside me.

"More," I moan in a gruff voice. "Please, God, Langdon," I beg. I barely even recognize myself.

He increases the pace. My cock is rock hard again as he takes me. Soon he's built up to a fast and hard rhythm, our bodies slapping together in our eagerness. I'm unsure how much more I can take before I feel Langdon pull me up so that I'm on my hands and knees, rocking back to meet him. He reaches around me and grips my cock, making me cry out. He furiously pumps his hand back and forth as I whimper before I cum, shooting my seed all over the bed. He grunts and moves faster, holding me still, furiously slamming inside and out as I quiver, still coming down from my release. Then I feel him stiffen and become still, his seed spurting inside me as he yells out my name simultaneously.

We collapse, panting heavily. Langdon rolls me over so I'm cuddling into him, his head on my shoulder, a broad smile on his face. "That was," I breathe out, still in disbelief. "Amazing."

He chuckles and kisses me on the forehead. "Next time will be even better," he promises, his eyes dark as he stares at me with lust. I swallow. The sex we just had was pretty fucking fantastic. I can't see how it could be any better—my whole body tenses at the thought of sex again with him.

"Still want to be mates?" Langdon teases, and I give him a playful shove.

"Yes," I growl, taking hold of his face and giving him a quick peck on the lips.

We both glance at the bed and the rumpled sheets. "I think we might need to remake the bed," I say quietly as he grins. He motions towards the bathroom. "How about you get cleaned up, and I organize fresh bedding," he suggests. "If you take too long, I'll join you in the shower," he jokes. "I need to get cleaned too."

I don't know whether that's a promise or a threat, and I don't care either. I'm already drooling at the thought of Langdon showering with me and anything else that might happen. I thought I would be too sore to go again, but my body already craved another round. I wonder if shifter blood means that certain parts of you still heal regardless. It's an interesting theory.

I get up, and he gives me a smack on the ass. I turn to glare at him, and he raises his eyebrows at me. I laugh and shake my head, heading to the bathroom and turning the water in the shower on. As I step beneath the water, part of me, a small part of me, hopes that Langdon will come and join me, even if I have to stand in here for an hour before he decides to. My cock twitches in anticipation. Being Langdon's mate certainly seems to have its perks.

Chapter 100

Winter's POV

I wake up and stretch, staring out the window. It looks like a nice day outside. The sun is shining, big puffy clouds chase each other across the deep blue sky, and I can see trees swaying in the wind. But I'm hesitant to go downstairs on my own. The man, Kai, claims to be my mate, but I can't remember anything. I know I'm a shifter, but other than that, everything is blank. I feel the back of my head, where the stitches are, and frown. My hair is all matted with dried blood. The first thing I want to do is shower, but where are my clothes? I remember Kai placing me in an adjoining room to what was supposedly ours and tiptoed towards it. With any luck, he wouldn't be in there.

Luck was on my side. I spot a dresser and rifle through it, grabbing sweatpants and a shirt. I head into the bathroom and start the shower, my eyes closing in bliss as the water cascades down on me. It's relaxing, and I inhale the steam greedily. The water is hot, just as I like it, and I could easily spend forever in here if it means avoiding everyone downstairs.

Winter, honey, you know it's not so bad. Your memory will come back.

Who are you?

Your wolf Sabriel. I know you probably don't remember me, but maybe I can show you a memory or two of us. Would you like that?

I don't know...

It won't hurt, I promise, sweetling. I want to show you a memory of Kai and us.

All right then, I guess it can't hurt. I'm curious to see.

For a moment, there's silence, and I lean against the shower tiles, closing my eyes and waiting. Soon images are flooding my mind. I can see myself shifting, my bones cracking and adjusting. *We're beautiful,* I think to myself, taking in my wolf form. The man, Alpha Kai, is there with me, and I can't stop staring at him as he, too, begins to shift, his large beautiful black wolf called Storm.

We take off running into the forest, lightly nipping each other, Sabriel teasing Storm and playfully fighting with him as their wolf side takes over. There's no destination in mind, just the sheer pleasure of running, watching the trees and the scenery pass by in a blur, dodging over branches and debris, our paws thudding lightly on the ground. We're out there for hours, having fun, letting our wolves run free. It's so freeing.

We return to the grounds, and I shift back, placing my clothes on while Kai does the same. There's a broad smile on my face, even though I'm exhausted from the run. Kai is beaming at me, even as he shrugs into his clothes. We embrace, and he kisses my head as I lean into him.

If that was a memory, then it was a pleasant one. Even the feelings associated with it, the adrenaline, the carefree attitude, and everything else flashed through my mind. Sabriel had done well in showing me a memory. Alpha Kai seems far less intimidating to me now. I turn the shower off and wrap a towel around me, heading out to the bedroom and stopping in my tracks. I wasn't expecting to see Kai in the bedroom, and I can't help but tighten the towel around my body nervously, blushing profusely.

"I came to check up on you," he says quietly, not making a move to come any closer. I wonder if he can sense my nervousness. "How are you feeling?" he adds.

"Tired," I admit sheepishly. "Even though I've slept a lot, it doesn't seem to make much difference."

He frowns at that and looks a little concerned. I feel bad. I hadn't meant to worry him.

"Do you think you might want to visit a doctor at the hospital?" he asks kindly.

I shake my head. I've had enough of hospitals. The thought comes out of nowhere, and I'm puzzled. How often have I ended up in the hospital to feel that way?

"No thanks," I rasp. "I just need rest and food," I say wryly as my stomach lets out a loud growl.

He laughs. "How about I show you to the kitchen," he chirps, and I give a slight nod, my stomach churning. Man, I felt like I was starving. He holds out his arm, looking hesitant, and to my surprise, I willingly take it. He beams, looking so happy that I feel I've done the right thing. Kai leads me out to the hallway and down the stairs. He steers me into the kitchen, and I pull up short when I see two other men in the dining area. I don't know who they are. But they look at me with smiles, although one looks particularly upset. I do remember vaguely one of them. Were they at the hospital?

"Winter, you might not remember them," Kai says quietly. "But this man here," he indicates the upset-looking one. "Is your brother Damien and this other one is my Beta Langdon."

I stare at my brother. There's nothing there, no memory flashing in my mind. It's strange. I force my mouth to be open. "It's nice to meet you, I guess," I mumble, unsure what else to say. My brother's eyes flash with disappointment. Maybe he was hoping my memory would have come back by now. I wish it had. This would be a hell of a lot easier on me.

"Why don't you sit down," my brother says gently, pulling a chair out for me.

"Thank you," I tell him, sitting and looking at Kai helplessly.

"What do you want to eat?" he asks, and I hesitate.

I thought I was hungry, but my stomach felt a bit uneasy. "Dry toast," I request. "And juice."

Kai nods and sets the toaster up. "You don't remember me, do you?" Damien asks.

"I'm sorry," I say tentatively. "But I don't."

"It's not your fault," he assures me, Langdon reaching over to hold his hand.

"Are you both mates?" The way they touch each other makes it appear like they are, but I can't help asking anyway.

"Yes," Langdon answers with a smile. "Is that a problem?"

"No, of course not." I feel indignant that he even had to ask that. He flushes and looks apologetic.

Kai places the toast and juice in front of me. I grab the juice and swig it down, feeling incredibly thirsty. Kai grabs hold of the empty glass. "I'll get you another," he says, hurrying off. I take a bite of the toast and almost moan as it hits my tastebuds, my stomach beginning to feel slightly better.

He places the glass back in front of me, full of juice, and then sits in the chair beside me.

"I'm glad you're eating," he says, placing an arm over my shoulder.

I continue to eat, Langdon and Damien discussing their day in hushed voices.

"Winter, what would you like to do today?"

I have to think for a minute. Then it hit me, what I would like to do today. "I want to go for a run," I declare happily, and Kai's eyes light up, although he looks concerned.

"I don't know if that's a good idea. You're still recovering," he murmurs, but I interrupt

"Please." Sabriel had sparked my interest with the memory, and now I wanted to experience a run for myself.

"Only if I go with you," Kai says finally.

We go out to the grounds, and I strip my clothes off, Kai doing the same. I flush and look away from his body. It's instinctual.

I know exactly how to shift into my wolf form. Once I'm done, I howl at Kai, who hastily changes. I don't even wait for him. I head straight to the forest, my paws thudding across the ground. My wolf is large, and I frown. Something about the size of my wolf strikes a chord in me, but I can't remember why. But I'm not much smaller than Kai's wolf, and I easily keep up with him when he dashes ahead of me.

We play like wolves do. Nipping at each other, running as fast as we can, tracking down wild animals, and watching them run when they pick up our scent. We drink from a nearby lake and play fight with each other. It's bliss. For a while, I can forget that I've lost my memory, wholly absorbed in this run and spending hours with my supposed mate by my side. I have such a good time that time flies by, and before I know it, we're reluctantly heading back toward the grounds.

I shift, feeling sulky. I hadn't wanted to come back. Slowly, I begin to put my clothes back on. Then Kai shifts, and my mouth goes dry. God, he's sexy. He's the very image of masculinity, and I can't stop myself from staring at his abdomen and chest as he puts on his clothes.

"Winter," he says gruffly. "You keep looking at me like that, and I'm going to drag you to the bedroom and have my way with you," he promises, and I blush, biting my lip and looking away as he chuckles.

"All right, you can look now," he says, and I glance back over, seeing amusement on my mate's face.

He saunters over. "I've been wanting to do this for quite some time," he murmurs, his face now inches from mine as I stand there trembling. He bends down and captures my lips with his, gently pressing them against mine as I gasp in shock. His tongue slowly dives into my mouth and caresses mine. I moan, my hands holding onto his shoulders to keep myself upright as he intensifies the kiss. My whole body feels like it's on fire. Is this what it feels like to touch your mate?

His hand twines in my hair, keeping me firmly pressed against him. My eyes close as I let myself feel, let the sparks and tingles spread throughout my body. His other hand begins to trail down the side of me, sliding underneath my sweater so that I feel his bare hand against my flesh. It burns, but not in a bad way, but in a delightful sizzling way. My own hands clutch at him, holding tightly onto his sweatshirt. I'm panting heavily now, moaning as his hand slides up toward my breast and squeezes it gently. I've completely forgotten where we are, let alone who might be watching, wholly lost in the moment.

Finally, gasping for breath, I pull back, seeing Kai's eyes have turned black. His wolf is close to the surface, or I was kissing his wolf for all I know. His lips curl up in a wicked grin. "There's plenty more where that came from," he promises me, and I gulp. *Maybe I should let him drag me back to the bedroom,* I think to myself hazily. Then I notice his hands keep my legs from buckling and keeping me upright.

"I have a request for you," he says, looking down and staring directly into my eyes. "Something I think you'll enjoy and might help with your memory."

Now I'm intrigued. I cock my head to the side. "What is it you want me to do?"

He smiles. "I want to take you out on a date," he says.

"A date," I murmur. "What kind of date?"

"I want to take you to the same place that I took you for our first date," he says with a smile. "All you have to do is get yourself dressed tonight, and I'll take care of the rest."

Chapter 101

Kai's POV

I'm nervous. I can't believe it. All this time I've spent with Winter, and I can't entirely stop fidgeting with my hands. I get dressed in a separate room so that she doesn't feel afraid of me, spending time smoothing my hair back and making myself look as presentable as possible. I knock on the door gently and wait for her to call me in.

Whatever you do, please don't mess it up. She's vulnerable, remember?

Don't you think I know that, Storm? I know she's vulnerable. She's got amnesia, for heaven's sake.

Well then, treat her gently, like fragile china.

I'm not going to treat her like she's going to break. She's stronger than you think she is.

Please don't say I didn't warn you.

Enough, Storm!

"Come in," she calls in her raspy, beautiful voice.

I open the door and walk in, my mouth falling open. God, she's beautiful. She has no idea how much of an effect she's having on me. Her smile, those pearly white teeth of hers. Her slim legs were clad in leggings. She's wearing a dressy blouse and the leather jacket I got for her. Her hair cascades down her shoulders in waves. She's stunning, and for a moment, I'm speechless.

"Do I look okay?" she asks me nervously.

I gulp. She more than looks okay. "You look beautiful," I breathe, bending down and giving her a quick peck on the cheek. I'm not about to push it right now and try and get a long kiss, although I have to say it's taking a hell of much restraint.

"Where are we going?" she asks, curious, and I smile and shake my head.

"It's a surprise," I remind her, and she pouts at me. It's adorable, shaking her head so that her hair flies over her shoulder. I go to take hold of her hand, and she flinches.

"Sorry," I apologize. I guess she's still not too sure about me. It stings a little bit, but I can't exactly blame her. Who knows how I would act if I didn't have all my memories?

"No, I'm sorry," she says softly, holding my hand, sparks flying between us. "I didn't mean to."

"No harm done," I say with a friendly smile and begin to tug her out of the room. She giggles as we descend the stairs, laughing at my excitement.

"You'll love it," I promise her, helping her into the passenger seat. She nods, buckling up her seat belt and patiently waiting for me to enter the driver's side.

I start the engine, and she reaches over to change the music to country. I know she likes that type of music, and I'm willing to leave her to listen. She stares out the window, watching the scenery go by. She fidgets with both hands, and I know she's nervous. I don't know if she's nervous about me or going out in the first place. Soon, we've started our way into town, and her eyes light up with excitement as I maneuver through the streets, parking in front of a club that I hope will be very familiar to Winter. The neon sign reads "Club 666," the one I brought her to on our first date and the one I am the proud owner of.

I help her out of her seat as she stands and grips my hand tightly, tucking herself under my shoulder. "A club," she says anxiously. "Are you sure this is a good idea?"

"I promise you'll like it. If you don't, we can go home," I suggest, and that seems to cheer her up slightly.

I walk her down towards the line that's up the street. Seeing how many people are desperate to get into the club is great. I confidently head towards the front of the line, where my regular bouncer, Leo, is.

"Leo," I greet him, and Winter looks at him, biting her lip.

"Do I know you?" she asks him tentatively. "You look a little familiar."

Success. She remembered something. I want to fist pump the air. Leo looks bemused. "We met the last time you were here, princess," he says charmingly.

I glower at him. No one calls Winter princess but me. He grins, recognizing that he's pushed my buttons. Good thing he's an excellent employee.

"Oh," is all Winter says with a puzzled expression.

"Hey, what's going on? This guy's pushing his way in. You're not going just to let him through, are you? We've been waiting for ages," a young teenager shouts from behind us, sounding extremely pissed.

Leo shrugs. "I'm not telling the owner he can't get into his club. You do it if you're game enough," he says calmly, and the boy falls silent.

Winter looks at me. "You're the owner?" she asks eagerly.

I give her a wink. "I'm just going to take her through," I tell Leo smugly, gently pulling Winter behind me as we go inside.

Winter is bouncing in her excitement now, listening to the loud music and watching couples gyrate and make out on the dance floor. There's a broad smile on her face. "What do you want to do first?" I ask her.

She thinks for a moment. "Can we get a drink?" she asks. "I'm a little thirsty," she adds.

We go to a booth and sit down. A waitress comes up, and this time Winter orders a Dr. Pepper while I order a plain Coca-Cola.

"I think I need sugar," Winter says quietly. "I keep having this craving."

Come to think of it, now that I eye her. She does look a bit pale. We should have left tonight for a different day.

"We can leave if you want," I offer, but she shakes her head and smiles, leaning back against the seat.

"No, I like it here," she says.

A cute goth girl comes up. She has makeup plastered all over her face. She's wearing a tiny shirt that shows her midriff off, a short skirt with a little chained belt, knee-high boots, and fishnet stockings. She had lovely brown hair in pig-tails and would be roughly about Winter's age. She's also very drunk as she stumbles slightly into our table.

"Sorry," slurs the girl, and I frown. She's very inebriated. Surely the bartender should have cut her off by now? I make a mental note to check into that. In the meantime, the girl is staring down at Winter, who is looking at the girl, completely fascinated.

"Can I just say," the girl continues, tipsy and swaying on her feet? "That you are the most beautiful girl in the room."

Well, that wasn't something I saw coming. Winter looks at me helplessly, wondering what to say or do. I'm trying to stifle my laughter.

"Would you dance with me?" the girl asks hopefully.

Poor Winter looks like she's about to faint—enough of this.

I approach Winter's side, laying a possessive arm on her shoulders. "I'm afraid that I don't share," I drawl. "But my partner thanks you for the compliments."

Winter nods profusely. "Yes, thank you," she says, blushing.

The girl looks disappointed. "Well, if you change your mind," she grins. "Then come find me on the dance floor."

"Okay," Winter says quietly, both of us watching as the girl staggers away.

The second the girl is gone, we both burst into laughter. Winter laughs until she cries. "Oh, that was funny," she chortled. "Especially considering I was sitting with my partner. She's ballsy," she continues with admiration.

"Well, if you don't mind," I joke. "How about dancing with me?"

She's up instantly, and we're both on the dance floor. I'm not much of a dancer, but Winter doesn't mind. On the other hand, can move to the music, her hips swaying in time to it, her body pulsating on the dance floor. It's a complete turn-on, and I must work hard at a specific part of my anatomy not popping up in my tight trousers. It takes a lot of effort and self-control.

Several dances later, several women glared at by Winter for daring to approach me, and we're both pooped and ready to relax in a booth. Winter fans her face which has turned slightly red. I give her some cold water, and she drinks it, throwing it back in several gulps. "Thirsty," she wheezes.

I laugh. "You're not kidding."

She grins. "Dancing is hard work."

Man, she looks hot right now. Her body on that dance floor, I've got the enormous hard-on.

Storm, have you ever heard of giving too much information?

But we're bros, so we can say whatever we want to each other.

Still, I don't need to know you have a hard-on!

Why not? I know for a fact you were getting one while you were dancing with her.

Okay, that's enough. Goodbye, Storm.

I cut Storm off and put up a block before he could tell me anything else. Damn, that mutt. Bros indeed.

"Can you order me a Dr. Pepper again, please?" Winter asks, standing up and looking slightly unsteady on her feet. "I just need to go to the bathroom."

"Do you want me to walk you over there?" I ask, glancing at the bathrooms in a hallway off the dance floor. She shakes her head. "I'll be fine. I need to freshen up a little," she says weakly.

I'm not sure, but she starts to walk off anyway, and I keep a close eye on her to ensure she enters the bathroom. Only then do I flag down a server and order Winter and myself a cool drink. I'd give anything for a refreshing beer right now, but seeing as Winter can't drink, I'm not going to either. I'm not that much of an asshole. Give me some credit, at least.

The drinks come—still no sign of Winter. I'm concerned she might be sick in the bathroom. My fingers drum along the table top as I sip at my Coke. I don't want to embarrass her by trying to get in or getting security to check on her. I take a glance at my watch. It's only been five minutes. I'm getting carried away. I settle back in my seat and sip my drink, watching the dancers on the dance floor.

A drunken man shouts obscenities at the bartender, and I hover, wondering if I should investigate and possibly step in. He hasn't threatened violence, but as I listen, it's clear that the bartender has cut the man off from drinking, rightfully so. It's standard policy, and I appreciate that he's following it. The security team step in, so I don't have to, and I watch as the man is dragged away, kicking and yelling all sorts of things, before his voice fades away as he's dragged outside. The bartender looks relieved. I don't blame him. No one wants to deal with that crap, and bartenders have to daily. How hard is it to stop drinking when it's clear you've had enough? Too hard for some people.

Where the hell is Winter? I glance at my watch and begin to get concerned. It's been a little while now. What do I do? I can't precisely push into the ladies' room myself. Hell no, not even as the owner. There had to be a female member of security who could check on her for me. I turn my head to look and sigh. They're all outside still. I turn back and almost have a heart attack. Winter is standing there, pale, her eyes red and puffy. I hadn't even heard her approach, let alone smelt her scent, but there were so many people in the club that it would have been easy to miss.

"Are you all right?" I ask, leaning over to grasp her hand. God, they're so cold and clammy. I try to warm them with my own.

There's a tremulous smile on Winter's face. She swallows and then speaks. "I'm not feeling the best. Is it okay if we go home?"

If she's not feeling well, then, of course, we're going home. That's not even a question. I get up hurriedly. "Let's go," I say crisply, dragging her out of the club behind me. She feels so cold. It's odd.

"I didn't mean to ruin anything," she whispers.

"You haven't," I say firmly. "I had a great time tonight, and there'll be other nights too."

She gives me a small smile and nods.

I help her into the car and place the heater on for warmth. She curls up in the seat and rests her head against the window, watching everything pass. By the time we return to the pack house, she's fallen firmly asleep.

I frown. She must be sick or something. I gently gather and cradle her to my chest, walking toward the bedroom. I debate whether to put her in a separate room again, but she's cold, and I figure my body heat might help. I place her in the bed and take my shirt off, climbing beside her, pulling her up against me as she sleeps, and resting my head on her shoulder. This is where she belongs, where she's meant to be. I close my eyes. I would have to be content with her company and pray that her memories return soon.

Chapter 102

Winter's POV

I can see the crestfallen look on Kai's face when I ask to go home. But what was I supposed to tell him? When I went into the bathroom, my eyes, for a moment, looked like they were glowing red. That was enough to upset me. It also meant I remembered Thomas and everything that went on. My memories are slowly flooding back, but I can still feel Thomas' hands on me, see his fangs out of his mouth, and even feel the pain as his fangs pierce my skin. Everything was so vivid. It was like I was right back there again.

I'm trying to tell myself that the glowing red eyes were just a trick of the light, that it was a residue of the memories that came flooding back, but part of me isn't so sure. We get into the car, and I feel exhausted and drained. No matter how much sleep I get lately, it never seems enough. I'm always tired. I wonder if it's because my blood got drained. Maybe I don't have enough iron in my blood and need to get supplements?

I watch the scenery go by and feel myself drifting off. I'm barely aware of Kai picking me up and carrying me to the bedroom, but I can feel him as he cuddles close to me. I can hear his heartbeat beating slowly as he pulls me tightly against him. It feels nice. I stop shivering, his body heat helping to keep me warm underneath the blankets. Soon instead of being drowsy, I'm asleep and dreaming...

I'm running. It's dark, and the moon is shining overhead. I'm fast. Faster than I've ever been in my whole life, running as though my life depends on it. But it's not fast enough. Even as I flee from danger, it finds me. His voice drifts towards me through the air as I shudder.

Chapter 102

"Winter," he calls, and although it's barely above a whisper, I hear it, my whole body stilling in fear.

"Winter," he hisses, and I turn, desperately trying to find the source of the noise, my heart thumping wildly in my chest.

Where was Kai? Or Damien or Langdon. Why am I all alone? Has he killed them all? But I thought he was dead, how is he here? It wasn't possible. It can't be.

"You can't escape me," comes the whisper again as I force my body to move, crashing through overhanging branches and leaping over debris. For some reason, I'm in human form, and I don't know why. Why haven't I shifted to my wolf form? When I try, though, I find I can't. But I can run fast. Faster than an average human.

"Leave me alone!" I scream hysterically. My feet are bare and covered in scratches, blood flowing from several cuts. It has a metallic smell that makes my nose crinkle. It smells strong.

"Winter," he calls, and I stop, seeing him up ahead.

It's like living a nightmare. He's standing in front of me, a wicked grin on his face, his arms held out in surrender. "You can't escape me," he says again, his voice chilling. He's so pale, so stiff. His body is covered in various injuries; weirdly, they haven't healed. I'm trying to remind myself this is a nightmare, but it seems real. So, so real.

"You're dead," I say, my voice shaky. "We killed you."

He laughs, throwing back his head. "But did you really?" he asks, a smile on his face, an expression of amusement. My throat goes dry. I'm starting to second-guess everything. But we had killed Thomas, hadn't we? Nobody could go back from what we'd done to him.

"Why are you here?" I ask shakily.

His grin grows wider. "I'm here to see my handiwork," he says, and I frown.

What on earth did he mean by that?

"Did you think you would escape me, Winter?" he asks, bewildered. "That I would just let you go without a fight."

"Why are you so obsessed with me!" I shout across at him, the wind howling in the distance. "What did I do to make you want me so badly?"

"You didn't do anything special. I've just always loved you," he says. My heart sinks. He's like a paranoid stalker. Was he going to stalk me in my dreams as well now? Give me nightmares that won't go away?

"Please, just let me go, Thomas," I beg him, tears trailing down my cheeks. "You have to let me go."

"I can't," he rasps, his eyes glowing red in the darkness, his body moving closer.

My own body is stiff, paralyzed with fear. No matter how hard I try, I cannot get my limbs to move. He reaches out and touches a strand of my hair as I gurgle. Now my voice has betrayed me.

"You're so beautiful," he murmurs, his fingers trailing down my face, stopping at my neck.

"Please," I manage to whimper, but it doesn't stop him.

"You'll thank me one day," he whispers. "You were supposed to be mine forever."

I belong to Kai, I want to shout at him, but my mouth won't move now. Instead, I'm forced to feel his clammy hands on my skin as he grabs my hand and presses it against his lips. Yuck. His lips are cold. His eyes are glinting with triumph.

My whole body is trembling. He can sense my fear, making him smile, his eyes staring directly into mine. They're so bright, so vivid. He stares at me. His head cocked to the side.

"One more, for old time's sake," he mutters, and before I can even comprehend what it is he's getting at, he bends his head down and presses his lips against mine, forcing a kiss on me. My stomach is roiling, and there's bile rising in my throat. I'm going to puke, but he stops, places a hand against my chest, and smiles.

"I gave you a gift," he murmurs, and then, in a puff of smoke, he's gone, just like that.

My mouth opens to scream, and suddenly, I burst awake...

I press a hand to my lips, trembling. The dream, or rather a nightmare, had been so real. So vivid. Like I had been there and Thomas was alive. I sit up, careful not to jostle Kai, who's sleeping peacefully in the bed. I don't want to wake him, but I can't sleep either. I crawl out and make my way downstairs and into the kitchen. Whenever I was little, my mother would make me some warm milk when I had trouble sleeping. I wanted comfort right now, and luckily, the kitchen was empty.

Girl, that was some nightmare. Gave me the heebie-jeebies.

Me too, Sabriel. What do you think it means?

It means nothing. He's dead. We killed him. You were having a nightmare.

It felt real.

I know, but it was just a nightmare. Trust me, Winter. He's gone. He can't hurt you anymore. Maybe you should talk to Kai about the nightmare?

I don't want to disturb him with something like this. It's just a nightmare. I'll get over it.

Well, it might help, but it's your decision.

I'll see, Sabriel.

I place the milk in the saucepan and put it over the burner on the stove. I stir it constantly, humming under my breath. With luck, this will make me sleepy again. I pull it off the stove and place it in a mug, sitting at the table and sipping away. The stuff warms my throat and makes my belly warm. This is what I needed.

My hands cup the mug tightly. My stomach growls lightly like it's hungry. But it is the early hours of the morning, and to be honest, I'm still tired. I focus on drinking, trying to reassure myself enough to go back upstairs and back to bed. But the nightmare stays fresh in my mind. I can still feel Thomas' clammy hands and freezing-cold lips on mine. I shudder.

I finish the milk and reluctantly place the mug in the sink. If I cuddle up to Kai again, my body will relax and go to sleep. It's worth a shot. I walk upstairs, my heart thumping in my chest. I can't believe I let a nightmare scare me this much. God, I'm such a coward. I go into the bedroom, and Kai sits on the bed, looking disheveled as my throat goes dry. He glares at me. Uh oh, I guess I'm in trouble, but for what?

"Do you have any idea how panicked I felt when you weren't in bed next to me," he hisses. I gulp. That thought hadn't even crossed my mind. Maybe I should have woken him up to tell him where I was going. "Anything could have happened to you," he continues to vent. "You could have been out for a run and attacked by rogues. You could have hurt yourself and fallen down the stairs. You could have been kidnapped again," he almost shouts, and I flinch, cringing at his words. He was pissed. Not that I blamed him. After Thomas took me, Kai had trouble keeping me out of sight.

"I'm sorry," I apologize softly, and he huffs, running a hand through his messy hair. He's not wearing a shirt, and my eyes stare at his chest appreciatively.

"Where did you go?" he asks finally, trying to keep his voice calm. His eyes stare directly at me, and I swallow nervously.

"I went down to the kitchen for some warm milk," I answer quietly, fidgeting with my hands.

He exhales. "Why didn't you wake me up? I would have come with you," he says, annoyed.

I flush. "I didn't want to disturb you. Besides, I was only going to the kitchen downstairs," I explained. He nods.

"Couldn't sleep?" he asks, and my heart skips. He didn't know the heart of it.

"A little," I admit. "I'm tired now, though."

He sighs. He pats the bed. "Come here, let's get you tucked in," he says, and I come over, letting him place me into the bed and tucking me under the bed covers.

"I'm going to go do some training," he mutters. "If you need to get up, then mind-link me, please," he says grimly.

I give him a nod.

Chapter 102

He bends down and gives me a peck on the forehead. "Get some rest," he says, walking towards the doorway and eyeing me sternly. "I order you to," he adds and then leaves. I close my eyes in relief. Now I could try and get some sleep, but there was something that wouldn't leave my mind. Something very concerning to me. In the dream, Thomas had mentioned he'd given me some gift. I knew it was just a nightmare, but that wouldn't stop going through my mind. I can't help wondering what Thomas had meant by gift. From my memories, he hadn't given me anything, not that I remembered.

It was just a nightmare. I remind myself. It didn't mean anything. Stop letting it mess with your head. Thomas is dead. There is no gift. The nightmare was just that. A nightmare. It wasn't real. There was nothing real about it. It's just something that you need to move forward from. At least, that's what I was trying to tell myself. But another small part of me wonders if there was something to the nightmare, some small part of it in my subconscious that was trying to tell me something or warn me. Either way, the nightmare would stick in my mind for now and the foreseeable future, and I would have a hell of a time trying to forget about it.

Chapter 103

Langdon's POV

Life's been different with my new mate. Sometimes it's hard to know his thoughts, but we get along well, and the sexual chemistry is there. I blush, thinking about how responsive my mate is to being touched and the sex itself. God, his little cries turn me on, and my cock twitches just thinking about doing it again.

Damien comes out of the bathroom and looks pensive. I know he's worried about Winter and this damn amnesia. Especially since he's been traveling for so long to find her, and now he's lost his chance to reminisce with her. I know he's still beating himself up for everything he's done to her. He'd done many horrible things to poor Winter while she was growing up. But I know it was also due to his father and Damien's fear of him.

"What's wrong?" I ask softly as he sits on the bed, frowning. I move behind him and knead his shoulders and the back of his neck muscles in a soothing, circular massaging motion.

For a moment, there's nothing but silence and his heavy breathing.

"I just want to spend quality time with Winter," he says, disappointed.

"That's a bit difficult while her memories are mainly gone," I point out and hear his exhale.

"I know. Do you think she'll forgive me again?" he asks, putting his hands up and stopping me from continuing the massage, his eyes staring beseechingly at me. "Do you think she'll be upset remembering what I've done?"

Chapter 103

I have to pause and think. It was challenging to say one way or the other. But Winter's a kind, compassionate, caring girl. I couldn't fathom that she would hold a grudge against her brother, not when she'd already forgiven him once. But I could also understand why my mate was so concerned.

"I think you'll find she forgives you," I say slowly. "After all, she forgave you before, so what's to stop her doing it again?"

That makes him smile slightly. "But the things I did... Langdon," he says thickly, and I hold a hand up, stopping him with a shake of my head.

"What you did is in the past. What you do now and how you treat her matters now."

He falls silent, brooding. I can't help but stroke his hair, and he lets me. It feels so soft and silky, running through my fingers.

I've noticed his breathing has hitched again and smile knowingly. I remove my hands and sit across from him, staring at him challengingly. "It's time," I tell him firmly as he looks at me, confused.

"I need to know that you want this relationship and this mate bond. I know we've had sex, but that doesn't mean anything if you're thinking about walking away now."

He looks puzzled. "Why would I walk away?"

"You tell me," I shoot back. "Since we've had sex, you've been quiet, depressed, and detached. It's like you can't hear me half the time," I say, trying not to sound like I'm sulking. I feel like a pouting teenage boy, however.

"Oh," breathes Damien, his eyes seeking mine. "I'm sorry. I didn't realize I had made you so concerned," he said thoughtfully. "Honestly, I've been lost in my thoughts for the last few days."

"Really," I say, skeptical. Surely he wouldn't lie to me, though, would he? But what kind of thoughts are so pressing that you fail to communicate with those around you? It didn't make sense.

"Really," he repeats. "I've just been trying to come to terms with everything."

I wonder what he means by everything. It's not just about Winter, then. I fold my arms and patiently wait. Damien blushes, how adorable, his cheeks bright red, as he bites his lip and looks away.

"Explain," I say softly, and he begins to fidget with his hands, looking down at the bedspread. His ears are red as well. That's interesting.

"The thing is, I'm trying to come to terms with this mate bond thing," he says softly as I flinch. Was he saying he didn't like that we were mates?

"Is it that you don't want to be mates?" I ask, and he shakes his head. Thank God for that.

"I just needed to accept that my mate was a male, and I can't stop thinking about the sex we had. How different it was and how well," he pauses and looks at me shyly. "How great it felt."

I can understand that. I'd found the sex to be mind-blowing as well. I'd known instinctively what to do, and my wolf had grumbled because I wouldn't let him take control.

"Then what's the problem?" I ask delicately, reaching over and taking hold of Damien's hand so that he stops his damn fidgeting.

"The problem is I don't know how you feel about me," he breathes.

Oh, Damien. The poor kid was at a loss and looking around him, anything to avoid looking directly at me.

"Do you want to know?" I ask quietly. He gives me a nod.

"I adore you," I tell him firmly. "I love waking up to you each morning and snuggling against you at night. I hate when you're not with me, and want to protect you. You're always in my thoughts. When you smile, I smile. When you're sad, I'm sad," I say with an exhale. "I honestly can't even remember my life before I met you. All I know is that I no longer feel lonely or miserable."

He looks stunned. Crap. Maybe I had told him too much information. I feel vulnerable, naked, and exposed, and I hope I haven't scared him away.

"I feel the same way," he whispers as I look at him in shock. "I want to be with you, Langdon. I don't want to be with anyone else," he says with a hitch.

I watch, mystified, as he stands up and sits on my legs, facing me, his hands wrapping around my hair, his face inches from mine. It's the first time Damien's initiated contact, and my heart almost swells with joy at that fact, my wolf prancing around happily in my head.

"You're the only one I want," he breathes, then leans forward, pressing his soft lips to mine as I gasp. He's gentle, a little unsure, his lips moving, his tongue diving into my mouth and caressing it. I moan. The boy turns me on, my cock twitching in my pants and becoming hard.

I can't get enough of him. The softness of his lips, the delicateness. He tastes so mind-numbingly good that time seems to stop still, and there's just the two of us making out on the bed. I'm panting, and I can see his erection as well. When we pull back, our eyes are dark, and our wolves are momentarily coming to the surface.

I close my eyes, trying to regain control, which is made extremely difficult by Damien's bottom sitting on my lap and wriggling around. He was going to kill me with this torture. My hands were itching to touch him. But I hold back because there's an idea brewing in my mind that I want to ask my mate, and I need him to hear what I have to say, even if we both are itching to ravish each other on the bed.

"I want to prove how much I want you," I tell Damien, grabbing his face between my hands and staring intensely into his beautiful eyes. He looked confused. I almost want to smile, but this is serious.

"How?" he mutters once he's got his breath back.

"Let me mark you," I growl, and his mouth falls open in shock. "Let me claim you as mine so everybody can see it."

Have I gone too far? Was this too much, too soon for Damien? I'm starting to doubt myself as his eyes slide away from my own and his body tenses on my legs.

I open my mouth to say we don't have to when he speaks first. "Yes."

Have I heard him correctly? Did he say yes to me? "Yes?" I clarify.

"Yes," he growls back. "And I get to mark you as well."

"Fine by me," I hiss. "But I get to do you first."

I stand up, hold him firmly, and lay him on the bed. He looks apprehensive now, but I give him a reassuring smile. I climb over him and lean down, pressing my lips to his mouth, rougher than he had been, demanding access and plundering his mouth with my tongue. He moans, and it makes my entire body jolt. Fuck, that sounds hot. I can feel the sparks between us as I push harder against his lips. My hands caress his chest underneath his shirt, and he begins to pant as I touch him. Slowly I pull back, trailing kisses down his neck until I stop at the nape, his neck exposed, bare, and smooth. Reluctantly, I let my canines pop out, and as he lays there, my hands still touching him, I bite into his neck, hearing him cry out as I do. I pull my head back and then lick the wound, sealing it closed, looking at a wolf's mark in satisfaction. He's mine now. The mark is there for everybody to see. No one will dare try and touch him now. Not unless they want their heads ripped off their body.

Damien surprises me by gripping me by the waist and laying me beside him. He climbs over and kisses me fervently, his hard-on rubbing against my leg. I moan, his hands touching me hesitantly underneath my shirt as he begins to mimic what I did to him. I grip him around the waist. My eyes closed as he slowly broke off the kiss and began to kiss the nape of my neck. My breathing becomes heavy as he tilts my head to the side, giving him better access to the nape of my neck. I feel a sharp piercing pain as he bites into my flesh and then the roughness of his tongue as he seals the wound closed. Now I had my mark from him. I, too, have been claimed by my mate.

"Sorry," he says timidly, sitting up. "I didn't mean to hurt you."

"You didn't," I growl. "So don't apologize."

Chapter 103

God, he's sitting atop me and looking so fucking cute. We've just marked each other, making tonight even more special. I wonder how Winter will react and then remember the amnesia. It's a shame. She was so excited to discover that her brother and I were mates. She would have loved to find out we had marked each other. Maybe when she gets her memories back, she'll be excited.

Damien's moving to get off me, and my hand shoots out, preventing him from moving. He's rubbing slightly against me, and my eyes narrow as I smell his arousal. My hand moves to cup him at the front of his pants in the crotch. He sucks in a breath. I smile, gently rubbing him as his breathing deepens. He's so responsive. Within seconds I have him flat on his back, blinking in shock. I begin to pull the zipper down on his pants. He clutches the bedsheets between his fists. Fuck. I haven't touched him yet; he looks like he's about to blow. *This was going to be much fun,* I thought with a smirk.

"I think tonight calls for a celebration, don't you," I say gruffly.

His eyes widen. "Celebration," he squeaks. "What kind of celebration?"

I undo the zipper on his pants and reach in, grabbing his cock and gently stroking it. "This kind of celebration."

Chapter 104

Johnathon's POV

Aaaah. It's good to be back home. It only took one hell of a car drive, a plane ride, and a car rental to get back as soon as possible, and I stared at my pack house with satisfaction. I've been gone for so long, but now I can focus on my pack and duties. I feel older somehow, more responsible. I feel a pang in my chest, remembering my goodbye to Winter. She doesn't even know who I am, let alone is going to be worried about my leaving. I guess I can take comfort in the fact that she's all right and that, in the end, we were able to save her from that son of a bitch, Thomas.

I pull up in front of my pack house and take a moment to look at it with new eyes. It might not be as big as Alpha Kai's, but it's a beautiful wooden-style cabin with two stories and modern amenities. It was nothing to be ashamed of. Neither was the pack, even if it wasn't the largest in the country. I was going to change all that. I would make my pack one of the strongest in the world. I had big plans.

I exit the car and shut the door, my feet pounding into the gravel of the driveway as I walk to the front door and let myself inside. I barely make it into the foyer before there's a whooshing sound. My mother comes running in and throws herself into my arms. I feel tears trickling down her face onto my shirt, and I feel immensely guilty. Even though she knew where I was heading, I hadn't fathomed it would be as long as it had. *I was a terrible son,* I thought to myself, to make her so worried about me.

"You were gone for so long," she sobbed as my arms awkwardly surrounded her. "I didn't know if you were coming back."

I patted her lightly on her back. "Mother, I was always going to come back," I remind her gently, frowning at the wild look in her eyes. "I am sorry it took so long for me to return, though," I finish.

She continues to cry as I hold her. I don't dare move, even though her tears slowly drenched my shirt.

"Mother," I say quietly. "I'm sorry."

She pulls back, sniffling, wiping the tears from her eyes with the back of her hand. "It's just that I didn't hear from you, and Mason has been stepping in for you as the Beta, but even he was getting concerned and..." she trailed off helplessly.

"Mason is perfectly capable of taking care of pack business," I assure her. "That's why I left him in charge. You shouldn't have to concern yourself with any pack business while I was gone."

I motion for her to follow me, heading to the trusted study where all the paperwork and boring stuff gets handled. Somehow I'm not surprised to find Mason sitting behind the desk, furiously scribbling away. He'd always been pedantic about ensuring all the work was done. Mason leaps up as soon as he sees me.

"Alpha Johnathon," he says formally, bending his head respectfully. "It is a pleasure to see you again."

I wave my hand at him. I don't care much for the title anymore. It leaves a sour taste in my mouth, although I can't say why that is. "Just call me Johnathon from now on," I say firmly. He nods, looking speechless.

He moves out from behind the desk, and I sit in the large chair, motioning for my mother to sit down, Mason sitting in the other chair, one of his legs folded over the other.

"Did the warriors keep up with training while I was gone?" I ask, turning to Mason.

"They kept to the rigorous schedule. We will have to find a new head warrior soon."

I'm puzzled. "What happened to Nick?"

"He found his mate and is moving to her pack to live with her," answers Mason smoothly.

Damn. Imagine that. "Who's been taking care of the training in his absence?" I ask suspiciously. Man, I've only been home a few minutes, and already I've gone into Alpha mode.

"I have, between all the other duties," Mason answers.

I stare at him in shock. The poor man must be exhausted going from one thing to the other. He hasn't delegated any of the work. He was that pedantic. He would rather do it himself and burn himself out doing it.

"Mason," I say very calmly and quietly. "That is going to end. It would be best if you had some idea of who's the best warrior by now. Ask them if they'll become head warriors. I want it done by the end of tomorrow. If they won't do it, then go to the next best, and so on. However, considering its many benefits and perks, I have no doubts that the first one will agree."

Mason looks upset and a bit sulky. Maybe he doesn't like that I've returned, and he's back to being the Beta again. Too bad. He can deal with it.

"I'll arrange it by the end of tomorrow," he assures me, and I nod.

"You've changed," my mother breathes, staring at me, her tears long gone. "It's like you've become more mature somehow. You seem more responsible," she adds, putting her hands to her face and looking at me in astonishment. It's unnerving.

"Mother, are there any maintenance issues in the house or gardens that you would like taken care of?" I ask in the hopes of distracting her. It works.

She cocks her head and thinks about it. "Well, there's a loose step in the staircase," she murmurs. "Which could be dangerous. Other than that, I really can't think of anything else."

"Consider it fixed," I tell her, watching Mason scribble it down. I doubt it will be fixed by tomorrow's end if Mason has anything to say.

"What about rogue attacks while I was gone?" I ask, leaning back in the chair.

Mason looks concerned. "We had one rogue attack while you were gone, but it was easily handled."

"Were they killed?" I ask. "Or thrown in the dungeon?"

Now he looks nervous. "We killed them. Should we have taken one prisoner?" he asks, puzzled.

I shake my head. "No, but if you had taken a prisoner, then I would have wanted to know," I explain. "You did well in handling the rogue attack. Were there very many?"

"About five," Mason answers. "Luckily, patrol spotted them straight away. The other good thing is that we had men injured, but there were no fatalities. None of our people received life-threatening injuries."

God, I'm tired. Although not long, the plane ride has taken it out of me. Or maybe it's the last few weeks spent stressing over finding Winter and saving her from that hybrid Thomas. That's probably it. However, it was a far better way to travel than by wolf or foot. If I have my way, I'll only ever be traveling by car from now on.

"Did you find the girl?" my mother asks unexpectedly. She leans forward and looks at me eagerly.

"Yes, we found Winter. Just in time, too," I explain. "Her brother is staying there. He found his mate in the same pack."

My mother claps her hands together. "How sweet," she gushes. "But no girl caught your eye there?"

I shake my head. No, the only girl who had caught my eye was Winter, and due to my stupidity, I had lost her. I had no one to blame but myself. If I could turn back time, I would do things differently, but she was with Kai now, and she was happy, and that at least was something to hold onto. Who knows if she would have found that happiness with me?

"The only girl I am happy to see is you, Mother," I tease as she laughs and shakes her head at me.

"We have to have a celebratory dinner," Mother grins.

I almost laugh. I had anticipated that's what she'd do. She always loved to cook when she had the chance, giving her the perfect opportunity.

"What do you want? I'll make anything you'd like," she offers.

"Anything you feel like making," I say honestly. "A homemade meal is great. It's been a while since I've eaten one."

She looks stricken. "My poor little man," she croons, and I cringe. My God, how embarrassing. "I'll have to fatten you up with some decent food. I'm going to go and start cooking right now," she cries and sails out of the room, almost skipping in her happiness.

I dissolve into laughter, Mason's shoulders shaking in his chair.

"I don't know why you're laughing," I tease him. "You know you're expected to attend dinner as well."

"It's just…" he chokes out. "She called you little man." He bursts into laughter. I scowl at him.

"Don't forget I'm your Alpha," I growl warningly, but he continues to laugh, tears forming in his eyes.

"All right, all right," he finally says, leaning against his chair and surrendering his hands. "I'll stop."

"How is the pack running? Tell me the truth now. Mother's not here," I order.

He looks perturbed. "The pack is running fine, smoothly. Everything else has been smooth sailing except for the head warrior position needing to be filled and that rogue attack."

I relax. The pack had been in good hands while I was gone. Mason had done an excellent job of keeping things running. I take note of the fact that he has dark circles under his eyes. When was the last time that he had a decent sleep? I also need to organize a Gamma to help lighten the load.

"Mason," I say gently. "I think we need to look at filling the title of Gamma as well. It's too much work between us, and you've had to shoulder the burden the entire time I've been gone."

I swear his face brightens up. He thinks this is an excellent idea. "That would be fantastic. It would be far easier if we had a Gamma to help delegate some of the work to."

"Any ideas on who the Gamma should be? I feel like it should be a decision made between us rather than just myself deciding."

That shocked him. "What about Jordan? He's also the best warrior and could fill both positions. Training could be a part of the Gamma's duties?" he suggests.

It's brilliant. It's like killing two jobs with one stone. "I think that your idea is brilliant," I say honestly. "Let's talk with him in the morning. It's best to get it done quickly."

He nods, and I smile. Everything is going well. I'm about to stand up and go to the kitchen, where Mother is no doubt cooking furiously. When something comes to mind, I sit back down hastily.

"How is the prisoner doing?" I ask him.

Mason looks blank for a moment. The prisoner, I want to yell at him. You know, the only one that's been there in the dungeon for the last couple of months. That prisoner. The one I swore to Damien would never cause trouble again.

Come on, Mason, I think impatiently.

Then he looks at me and bites his lip. Now I'm feeling suspicious. What isn't he telling me? Why is he so quiet?

"About that prisoner," Mason says in a hushed voice. "Um, the thing is," he stammers.

"Spit it out, Mason," I growl, watching him wriggle in the chair, clearly nervous.

"There was an incident, and he managed to escape," he bursts out. He looks away nervously.

For a minute, there's just silence as I digest his words, not fully comprehending them. Then realization dawns. I stand up, towering over him, as he cringes back in the chair. My eyes are narrowed, and staring directly at him.

"How does one," I say, dangerously quiet. "One measly little prisoner manages to escape the dungeon?"

"See, the thing is, there was an Omega, and they got too close and..." he trails helplessly.

I can't believe it. They let the prisoner escape. One that I intended to keep locked up for the rest of his miserable fucking life. My hands clench into fists. "How does he get away from a whole pack, Mason? Did no one track him down?"

"He escaped just before the rogue attack," Mason explains miserably. "By the time we ended the fight, he was well and truly gone. I didn't see the point in wasting the tracker's time."

I give a loud huff and punch the wall, venting the anger coursing through my body. "Get out," I say between gritted teeth. "Before I lose control completely."

He's out the door in a flash. I breathe, counting to ten, trying to keep my wolf from taking over, willing my body to relax. My whole body is tense, my muscles stiff, I'm breathing heavily, and I'm so angry. All I feel is pure rage right now. Finally, I sit back in the chair and cover my face. How will I tell Damien and Kai that Winter's father has escaped his prison cell and it was all my fault?

Chapter 105

Kai's POV

I don't know what's going on with Winter lately. I know she's lost her memories, but it's something more than that. I just can't quite put my finger on it. Last night on that date, she told me she felt sick but disappeared for warm milk this morning because she couldn't sleep. Who can't sleep when they are sick? It doesn't make sense. Or maybe I'm just being paranoid. Who knows.

I meet Langdon. "Training grounds," I mutter to him. "I need to work out some of my frustration."

He looks taken aback but does as I ask. There's no sign of Damien; I figure he must be sleeping. I wonder if they were up late last night. Then I stop and halt in my tracks, reaching out a hand to look at Langdon properly. There's a massive smile on my friend's face, and there, on his neck, is a mark. They marked each other!

"Congratulations, man," I say, patting him on the back. It was awesome news. More than anyone, Langdon deserves to be happy with his second chance mate. Especially after what that bitch Candice put him through.

"Thanks," Langdon says quietly. "We did it last night."

I look directly at him. "Are you happy then?"

His eyes sparkle. "Very."

We start to walk across the grounds, both of us lost in thought. Winter doesn't have my mark anymore, and while I would love to claim her again, I'm uncomfortable doing it while she still has amnesia. Storm, on the other hand, has no such qualms about it.

She's our mate. She should bear our mark!

Storm, we've been over this. We can't just do it without her consent.

Why not? We did it the first time.

Exactly why we can't just do that to her this time. We should never have done it without her consent; this time, we must be more respectful of Winter.

I wouldn't say I like that she doesn't have our mark anymore, Kai.

I don't either, Storm, but we must be patient. She'll let us mark her again eventually.

She'd better. She's ours, no one else's.

Trust me. She knows that, Storm.

Man, my wolf is more possessive of Winter than I am. He's very protective of her as well. I guess Damien is lucky that Storm hasn't torn him to shreds for what he did to Winter in the past because, my God, he wanted to. He wanted to. If he hadn't been Langdon's second chance mate... he would have been in serious trouble.

We reach the training grounds. Jeff, the head warrior, gives us a wave and jogs over to us. I can see two warriors in the ring sparring, both not giving an inch, covered in sweat from head to toe. How long have they been out here?

"Alpha Kai, Beta Langdon," Jeff says with a smile. "It's nice to see you out here. Is there something you need?"

Oh yeah, there's something I need all right. I need to vent some of my anger and frustration by fighting. My whole body is tense, and even Langdon looks like he could use a fight.

"I came out here to train," I say, and Jeff looks at me, completely taken aback.

I'm a little indignant. It's not like I don't come out here. It's just that Langdon and I normally train by ourselves together to save time. But I come out here occasionally to see how everyone else is going and train some men and women.

"We'll, that's fantastic," beams Jeff. Man, he's so chirpy in the morning. It gives me a headache. "Who are you wanting to train against?"

I turn and eye Langdon who looks resigned. "I'm guessing it's me," he tells Jeff wryly. Jeff nods. He gestures for the warriors to leave the training ring.

"Wolves or human form?" asks Langdon as we get into the training ring and separate, staring at each other.

"Wolves," I growl, and he nods.

Without hesitation, both of us begin to strip off our clothes. Then I spot Damien in the crowd. He's come out here to watch. I consider pointing him out to Langdon, but I don't want to distract him from our fight.

I shift, bones cracking loudly in the otherwise quiet air. There's a small crowd gathered around us, something that I'm used to. They rarely get to see their Alpha fight another in the ring. Langdon shifts into his wolf as well. I've always liked his wolf. It's a dark grey color all over except for a small patch of white on the nose. He's large, only a few inches smaller than my black wolf. We glare at each other and begin to circle one another.

I'm looking for an opening, any opening at all that will help. Langdon is the first to race towards me, and I meet him halfway, both of us clawing and swiping at each other. I get on top of him, and he bucks me off, sending me flying. I shake my head and run towards him, stopping just in time as he dodges to the side. Damn, he's fast, but I'm faster.

We begin to circle each other, snarling, our jaws opening and shutting. This time he leaps towards me, and I jump, meeting him in mid-air, my jaws clamping onto him as I land, shaking him and throwing his body into the nearest tree. He hits the tree with a large thud and crashes to the floor. It doesn't stop him, however. He's up on his feet within moments. This will be a hard fight, how I like it.

But then I spot someone's face in the crowd. Someone I hadn't expected to see, considering that I had left her tucked in bed in the room. What on earth was Winter thinking coming out here? Was she insane? She should have stayed inside the pack house if she'd gotten up instead of coming outside and into the cold air. We were going to have a serious discussion once this was over. Damn it. Now I'm distracted.

I dodge to the side as Langdon attempts to tackle me. I turn and swipe him across his midsection and hear him growl in response. I jump and land on top of him, only to get sent flying through the air as he twists and kicks me off. I'd forgotten just how good Langdon was at fighting. Then again, there was a reason I had made him my Beta, and it hadn't been just because we were best friends. This time I stalk over to him and tackle him to the ground. My wolf is bigger and more dominant. I clamp my jaws onto him, and he wriggles and kicks. Then I go flying again. *This is becoming a nuisance,* I think to myself. We're so evenly matched that the fight could go on forever.

I look over at Winter, and her face is completely ashen. She's standing next to Damien, a hand in her mouth. She looks worried. Langdon also looks over and realizes Damien is in the crowd. Damien is just as pale and looks concerned for his mate. I don't think I can continue, not with Winter looking so frightened. Langdon appears to be thinking along the same lines.

I shift. Langdon does the same with a smile on his face.

"Good fight," I tell him as we bend and retrieve our clothes. "I just couldn't continue…" I say, looking over at Winter pointedly.

"I know," Langdon says softly. "I understand."

We both get dressed.

Then we make our way over to Damien and Winter. Damien's eyes are shining. "You were awesome," he tells Langdon. "I can't believe how well you fight."

"Thank you," Langdon says with a chuckle. He takes hold of Damien's hand. "Do you want to do some training while I watch," he offers. Damien looks thoughtful. "I wouldn't mind doing some training. I haven't had the opportunity to in the last few months," he admits. "Even at my old pack, I tended to skip it."

"Well then, there's no reason not to train here," Langdon answers, looking at his mate sternly.

I glance over at Winter, who is looking and listening intently to both of them. There's a smile on her face. She does love that brother of hers, even with amnesia.

Damien glances at her. "Winter, would you like to stay?" he offers. "I would love to spend time with you."

She frowns. I guess she still doesn't have much in the way of memories regarding Damien. "I don't enjoy watching the fighting," she says slowly. "It makes me feel sick to my stomach."

There's a disappointed look on Damien's face. Winter sees it. "But maybe later, after the fighting, we could talk. Maybe you could tell me about our childhood," she says.

Damien goes even paler. He swallows. "Sure, we can do that," he says faintly. She gives him a beaming smile. Now Damien looks miserable. I guess he's going to have trouble explaining her rough childhood. I don't feel even an ounce of sympathy for him.

Winter looks at me. "I know you probably wanted me to stay in bed," she says quietly as Damien and Langdon move away from the both of us.

"I would have preferred you did," I growl, and she looks at me, upset.

"I can't spend the rest of my life in bed," she points out. "Not when I need to get to know you as well, considering that we're mates," she adds with a frown.

She has a point. That doesn't mean I'm any less upset with her. I mind-link Langdon.

I'm taking Winter back to the pack house. Let me know if you need me.

I will do that, Alpha Kai.

Thanks.

I gently take hold of Winter's hand and kiss it, noting how cold it is and frowning. I shrug out of my jacket and drape it over her. "Cold?" I ask, and she gives a small nod. No wonder she's so pale. It's a surprise her teeth aren't chattering together.

"Let's go home and have breakfast," I suggest, and she walks along with me obediently. I sigh. I don't want Winter to feel like I'm being possessive of her, but I'm afraid to let her out of my sight after what happened with Thomas. Even though that bastard is dead, I feel like I failed her. I'm not going to fail her ever again.

Is it my imagination, or is she walking funny? Her body is stiff, and her movements are slightly jerky.

"Are you feeling all right?" I ask softly.

She bites her lip. "I don't know. I feel strange," she admits. "I don't know how to explain it, but I know I'm thirsty," she says. "Even though I drank plenty of water before coming out here."

"Maybe you're just hungry," I suggest, steering her towards the pack house. I'm concerned but trying not to show it. Something seems off about Winter. But I'm not sure what it is. Her movements are strange. Like she's having trouble walking. She's not all right. Then I see her stumble, and although I move fast, she drops to the ground in a dead faint as I stare down at her. I scoop her off the ground quickly. Her lips are blue now. Her hands are clammy.

I change directions and head toward the hospital, Winter securely cradled against my chest. I scold myself for not getting to her sooner and hope she hasn't injured her head. That's the last thing she needs. *Hold on, Winter,* I think to myself as I run. *We're almost there.* Hopefully, the doctors know what caused her to faint because this doesn't seem like she's sick to me.

Chapter 106

Winter's POV

When I wake back up, the doctor examines me, shining one of those damn bright lights in my eyes. I frown. I knew I hadn't felt well when I walked out to the grounds, but I hadn't realized I would faint. How embarrassing. The doctor looks concerned. "Your iron is severely depleted. I can tell just by looking at you," Dr. Jameson says. That's what his name badge says, anyway.

"What do we need to do?" asks Kai anxiously.

"Well," the doctor pauses. "I would suggest eating iron-rich foods, such as plenty of red meat and spinach, but I also might suggest supplements. You might have been drained when that hybrid took your blood, and it's struggling to replenish itself."

Kai nods, looking grim. I feel woozy.

"Everything else appears to be fine and healthy. Winter, I don't want to see you in here again," jokes the doctor as I struggle to sit upright. "You can go home," Dr. Jameson says to me. "But I suggest you take it easy and rest when you can. Especially since your amnesia still hasn't gone away."

"Thank you," I say meekly.

Kai sighs. "I'm carrying you back to the pack house," he says shortly. I frown at him. I'm perfectly capable of walking back, but something in his facial expression warns me not to push it.

"Good luck, Winter. Come back for a checkup in two weeks," suggests Dr. Jameson. "We'll check your iron levels and give you a transfusion if needed."

I nod and climb out of bed, my legs almost buckling beneath me. Kai's hand whips out and supports me, preventing me from sliding to the floor.

"Careful," mutters Kai admonishing me. Like I did it on purpose. I give a huff, feeling annoyed at him. I'm not some delicate piece of china that's going to break. I was getting tired of being treated like it. He scoops me up, and I shriek, kicking and wiggling.

"Stop," he growls, and I pause, my body tense as he cradles me against his chest.

I sniff involuntarily, and my mouth waters. Man, he smells delicious, his scent strong and pungent. I can't get enough of it. His arms tighten around me.

"I'm taking you back to the pack house," he murmurs, and I don't bother to argue. Instead, I force my body to relax against him rather than fight against him. He looks relieved. Slowly, he walks out of the hospital room and heads towards the main entrance.

"Where's Damien?" I ask out of nowhere, and he looks at me, jaw clenched tight. Damien is a sore spot for him for some reason. But I remember speaking to Damien just before I fainted. Plus, he is my brother.

"He's waiting in the dining room for you, along with Langdon," he grunts as we make our way out of the hospital and onto the grounds.

It doesn't look like much time has passed since I've fainted. At least judging by the sun's position in the sky. I curse that I don't have a watch or a way to tell time. I snuggle against Kai. His body is nice and warm. He easily walks with me in his arms like I don't weigh more than a feather. It's a nice feeling. He's quiet, but looks concerned, all of his focus on the pack house ahead.

My stomach growls loudly, and he chuckles. "I guess you're hungry," he laughs. I blush. But it's true. I'm starving. Suddenly ravenous. It feels like it came out of nowhere.

We enter the pack house, and he walks to the dining room.

"Winter," cries Damien as Kai reluctantly puts me down, one arm snaking around my waist as I lean against him. "How are you feeling."

"I feel a little weak and shaky. I didn't mean to worry anyone," I answer softly. Damien leans forward and then hesitates. He looks uncertainly at Kai and me. I don't know what makes me do it, but I close the gap and fling my arms around him. His arms instantly go around me, and he hugs me tightly. I breathe in his scent, recognizing it's familiar. A memory comes to me...

I'm so small. Just a little girl running around the grass while her mother and father watch her. Her older brother is sitting on the ground, looking bored. I don't want to play by myself. It's boring.

"Come get me, Damien," I cry. "Come play chasey."

At first, he ignores me. But my mother gently nudges him, and he slowly gets to his feet. I shriek and run, Damien's footsteps behind me. I giggle and shriek, running as fast as my little legs carry me.

"I'm going to get you," he shouts as I speed up. I dodge around trees and jump over branches, ignoring that I'm getting dirt all over my dress, wanting nothing more than to play with him.

Then he tackles me to the ground, and I giggle, wriggling underneath him. He grins at me. "I got you," he says, and my eyes shine adoration at my older brother...

The memory's gone just as quickly. But it's enough for me to feel some love and tenderness towards Damien as I give a small sob and hug him. Slowly he pulls away. "Why are you crying?" he asks me, slightly panicked, Kai scowling darkly at him.

I wipe the tears from my eyes. "Just a memory," I tell him softly. "A nice one."

Why does he look so relieved to hear that? Kai relaxes slightly as well. My stomach lets out a loud growl, reminding Kai why we came to the dining room in the first place.

He pulls a chair out from the table and motions for me to sit. Langdon and Damien join me. "Have you guys eaten?" asks Kai gruffly as he gets behind the kitchen counter.

"We have, but we could always eat again," Langdon grins.

"That would be nice, all of us eating together," I beam. Kai falls silent at my happiness, shooting dirty looks at Langdon and Damien when he thinks I'm not looking.

"Winter, what do you feel like?" he asks, perusing the refrigerator and its contents.

Hmmm. I have to think. But I'm craving meat like nobody's business, and the first thing that comes to mind is what I call out. "Steaks," I say hopefully, and they all look surprised.

"Steaks," Kai repeats, looking taken aback. "Anything else?"

I only want the steaks. Honestly, the thought of anything else is making my stomach churn. "Maybe some juice," I answer slowly.

"I'll just make some steaks and eggs with toast," declares Kai, shooting the others a look. "If anyone wants something different, they can make it themselves."

"That sounds good," declares Langdon, and Damien nods fervently. Good, no one seems to be too bothered by the steaks. I have to admit it's a strange craving to have. Maybe it's the lack of iron?

I sniff appreciatively as the steaks get removed from the fridge, my mouth watering in anticipation. Even though they haven't been cooked yet, they smell delicious. I can't wait to get my teeth into one. Langdon gets up and grabs the juice, pouring a glass for everyone.

"Here," he says kindly, pushing a glass toward me.

"Thanks," I mutter, staring at the orange juice with revulsion. It seemed like a good idea then, but now that it was right in front of my nose, it made my stomach heave. I tentatively take a sip and almost spit it out. It tastes strange, like it's gone off, but when I glance at Langdon and Damien, they don't seem to have a problem with the juice. Strange. I gently push my glass to the side and glance over at Kai.

He's got the frying pan ready, and the eggs are cooking, toast in the toaster ready to be buttered. Now he just had to deal with the steaks. "Winter, how do you like your steaks?" he asks.

I have to think for a moment. Normally I would go for well done, but my body wants something different. Before considering what to do, I call out "rare" and lean back in my chair.

If Kai thinks my decision is weird, he doesn't say anything, and Langdon and Damien opt to have their steaks medium rare. Within minutes Kai's finished everyone's breakfast.

He brings mine over first, and I can smell the tantalizing odor of the meat on the plate as he places it in front of me. My stomach growls loudly, and my mouth begins to water. Kai gives me a peck on the cheek. "Breakfast," he growls, giving the others their food before plopping onto a chair opposite me. I stare down at the steak in fascination. There's blood oozing underneath it. The eggs look like runny liquid, and I scrape it to the side, not wanting to taste it. I nibble lightly at the toast, but my stomach doesn't like the taste.

"Thank you for breakfast," I tell Kai, and he gives me a small smile, diving into his breakfast. He's given me the biggest portion of steak, and I reach for the knife and fork. As soon as I press on the steak, blood oozes out. It's rare, I see with satisfaction. I cut a tiny piece off and place it in my mouth, chewing slowly and almost moaning as it hits my taste buds. It's so sweet, so tender. I'm desperate for more. This time I take a slightly larger piece and plop it in my mouth, closing my eyes in ecstasy. It's so juicy. So soft. It's the best thing I've eaten in a very long time.

I begin to dive into the steak while the others eat around me.

"So if you want to start training, how about together, the two of us go out there tomorrow morning?" Langdon.

"Are you sure?" Damien.

"Of course. You can only learn by training. Heck, I'll even train you as well." Langdon.

"That's brilliant. I can't wait." Damien.

I ignore them. All I want is this beautiful steak. I almost want to cry when I've eaten the entire piece. Kai shoves a small piece at me. "I wasn't sure if you would want more," he explains, eyes on the broken steak. At least I'm eating. I want to tell him indignantly.

Soon though, that piece is gone, and I'm still craving more. But I don't know what. I stare down at the small pool of blood on the plate. I inhale, and the metallic scent is strong in the air, but instead of filling me with revulsion, I feel hunger instead. Without thinking, I place the toast and eggs on the tabletop and lift the plate in both hands, staring at the blood with fascination. I tip the plate towards my mouth, and the blood slowly trickles into my open mouth, trailing down my throat as I swallow it all greedily. It's so good. I lick my lips. I even lick all the blood off the plate and smack my lips together.

Utter silence. That's the first thing I notice. Everyone is staring at me awkwardly. Kai, of course, looks like he's about to faint. I stare back, wondering what's wrong. They look like they've seen a ghost. What the hell is wrong with them? I wasn't acting that strangely was I? Now that I'm thinking about it, I feel energized rather than weak, like earlier.

Kai is the first to speak. "Winter, are you feeling all right?"

"I feel great," I tell him honestly. "Fantastic."

Langdon and Damien are shooting Kai sidelong glances. "Um, all right, do you want to try and rest?" asks Damien.

I shake my head. "Maybe I could join in on training? Or go for a run or something?'

"I think a run would do some good," Kai agrees. "But you just fainted not long ago, so how about taking it easy until I can run with you?"

I pout. "Fine, I might go read a book," I say grumpily. I get up and storm upstairs. Why were they all acting so freaked out all of a sudden?

Chapter 107

Unknown's POV

God, I can't believe I escaped that horrible dungeon. Those bastards thought they could keep me there forever, but I showed them. I showed them all. That Omega, I don't even feel sorry for messing around with her feelings as if I was in love with her. She's about the same age as my daughter Winter. Still, she served her purpose, So I can't complain about that, can I? She was just so easily fooled. That's what they get for using Omegas to bring my food to me. It was a matter of time until I managed to sweet-talk one. Stupid pack.

My feet crunch on the grass. How fortunate it was that there was a rogue attack as I was escaping. Even I can't believe my good fortune. It was like the moon goddess herself was urging me to escape. I take my time walking. There's nothing but clear blue sky for miles and no sign of rain or anything gloomy like that. The sun is warm, which is good because the only thing I have on is pants. They left me shirtless in that damn dungeon. I could shift, but I'm still weak from my injuries and find it easier to travel in human form and allow my wolf to recover.

I frown at the ground. I've managed to cover a large area of space. That bloody Alpha Johnathon was missing from the pack, and rumor had it he'd gone searching for my daughter Winter, with my son no less. They thought I couldn't hear them, but I paid attention. Even when blood pooled from my wounds, I listened and remembered everything they spoke about. They should have been more careful. Sometimes I'd faked being unconscious to get them to talk even more.

I know all sorts of things. Winter being mute, my son's apparent guilt over the whole thing. I spit at the ground in anger. That bastard son of mine stood up against me and all for her. What had made him change his mind about hurting Winter? How dare he stand up and tell me no. This was all his fault, well, his and Winter's. I would forever hate my daughter, no matter how much her big eyes pleaded for me to stop or the tears she cried in front of me. Once upon a time, I would have stopped instantly and hugged her, but now I can't even bear to think of touching the little bitch.

I could leave and go in another direction. But I want revenge. Revenge for what happened to me in that dungeon. It's all Winter and Damien's fault that I ended up there. It's their fault that I was tortured. It's their fault for my miserable existence. As I walk, my hands clench into fists, my head lowered to avoid stepping on anything sharp or pointy with my bare feet.

Slam. The door swings shut on the cell in the dungeon as I race to it, my fingers curling around the bars, ignoring the burning sensation of the silver against my flesh.

"Let me out!" I roar, and the boy, Johnathon, stares at me with anger on his face.

"You sold your daughter for money," he hissed, and I stared at him and shrugged.

Of course, I had. I needed it to pay back some debts. How did this concern him? It's not like it affected him at all. He should butt the hell out of my business.

He motions to the guards. "Shoot him," he orders, and I notice for the first time that the guards are holding tranquilizer darts. I have no doubt they contain wolfsbane. I can smell it from here.

I back away, but it's too late. The darts hit me, one in the chest and another in my thigh. I roared and pulled them out, but it was too late. My body flops to the ground.

"Get him chained," Johnathon says coldly from above me.

The guards haul me up, even as I kick and fight, chaining me against the wall, my back exposed to them.

Chapter 107

"You bastard," I snarl, trying to look over my shoulder.

His eyes are dark. There's an unreadable expression on his face. He's holding something, but I can't determine it from my position. I refuse to let some young lad intimidate me like this.

The first crack of the whip surprises me more than it hurts. But I can tell it's silver because my back burns until he pulls it away. I let out a howl, my whole body shuddering.

"I'll kill you when I get free," I promise him, my voice shaking.

The boy is silent. "The only reason I'm not killing you is Winter," he says. "God help her, but she still thinks of you as her father, despite everything you've done to her."

Crack.

Shit. The pain is excruciating. I cry out at the second strike.

"This is for Winter," he grunts, and the whip slashes my back. This time it's so powerful that I scream involuntarily. He certainly put most of his strength into it.

"This is for Damien," he mutters as the whip slashes me again. My whole body is shaking now. I'm unsure how much more I can take, but I don't want to give the bastard the satisfaction of seeing me fall unconscious. My hands clench into fists.

"When I get out of here," I mutter slowly. "I will kill you and my children with my bare hands."

Crack. This time I'm prepared for the whip. Then there's silence. It's nerve-wracking. I can't tell what he's doing. There are the sounds of things being moved and touched. That's when I realized he was going for something else. He has to be.

"Take him off the wall and let him dangle from the ceiling," he orders, and I feel the guards moving me around as I stare down at them with hatred. Soon my feet are dangling off the floor, and my hands are stretched over my head.

Johnathon walks in front of me, brandishing a silver dagger. I suck in a breath. He can do some serious damage with that. He caresses it, touching the tip, his hands covered in gloves to prevent himself from being burned by the knife. He cocks his head. "You know, I suspect Winter has scars all over her body from you. It would explain her loose baggy clothing," he hisses, and I flinch. He would be correct. His eyes light up at my reaction, and I swear as I realize I've given myself away.

He plunges the dagger into the side of my midsection, and I scream, my skin bubbling and burning bright red. He pulls it back out and examines it.

"Get the doctor," he snaps over his shoulder and moves close to me.

"You were going to let your daughter be raped," he breathes, his face inches from mine. "I think it's only fair that we ensure you can't physically do anything like that to anyone. You sick, twisted, son of a bitch."

I have no idea what he's talking about. A man comes down to the dungeon, looking uneasy. Johnathon looks over his shoulder and gives a quick nod. Then I feel him. He's cupping my manhood and clutching the dagger. Oh, God, no. I start to writhe in my chains, kicking and screaming. His hands tighten, and I howl. He's going to crush them at this rate.

I don't see it, but I feel it as he severs my ball sack from my body, my mouth open in an endless scream as I sob hysterically. The doctor injects me with something that makes me fall unconscious. When I wake up, there are stitches, and my scrotum is gone forever. I'm no longer a man, and it's because of them.

I shudder at the memory of it all. My gaze unconsciously goes to my nether regions, and my lip curls with hatred. They have ruined me forever. He ruined me forever. I spent months recovering from that ordeal, planning my revenge and plotting. Then I began to hear the rumors of Winter, and I listened. I know which way to go and which direction to follow, and it's because Johnathon's Beta lets lose the information.

I sit beneath a tree, needing to rest. I had half expected them to send out a search party for me, but maybe they thought rogues killed me. Fuck. I need a drink like no one's business. But I don't dare walk into town. That would make it far too easy to find me. Although they even have half a brain, they would know exactly where I was going. I plan on dragging Winter back with me. She can still earn me money, but Damien would have to die. He had become too much of an overprotective older brother, and I could no longer trust him to do what was right.

There's the crack of thunder in the distance. So much for there being clear skies. Now I can see fucking storm clouds gathering. Is everything going to be going fucking wrong today? I don't have the energy to make a goddamn shelter. I pause, debating my options. There's a pack not far from here. I could pretend to have run into some rogues and need assistance. But it's risky. Especially if that fucker Alpha Johnathon has put the word out to keep an eye on me. I scowl. I need to make a goddamn shelter. How fucking annoying.

I slam branches down in the right mood. My wolf is telling me to calm down, but I ignore him. Since we lost our balls, he's been particularly sulky. It's exasperating me. I slam the shelter together. Taking all my anger and frustration out on it. The stupid thing is barely waterproof, but I don't care. The rain is starting to sprinkle down on me, and I poke my tongue out, letting the raindrops fall on it and swallowing gratefully. I'm thirsty. It's been a long journey. We haven't come across any lakes or streams yet.

I slowly climb into the shelter, keeping my head poking out. The rain begins to get heavier, and soon it's hailing down. There won't be any moving until it's passed. It could take a while. I remind myself that I have time. So much time isn't funny. This isn't a race, not for me. I would rather be slow and cautious than be caught before taking revenge. The wind begins to get heavier. I hope my shelter doesn't go flying. Maybe I should have put a bit more effort in. My wolf is smug. I scowl and put a block up, refusing to talk to him.

At least there won't be any rogues. They hate water and when it rains. That means I'm safe for now, which is good. I'm not particularly in the mood for a fight right now. Even though it might help my anger out, lie on my back, and close my eyes, I ignore the thudding sounds of the heavy rain and the whoosh of the air as it causes branches to move back and forth. I drown out all the sounds and instead begin to picture my son and daughter in my mind's eye. I remember what they look like. I remember everything about them. Winter is no match for me. She never was, and I doubt she's gotten stronger even with her wolf. Damien might prove to be more difficult, but I can handle him if I need to. But it's Winter I want, Winter whom I will take back with me. I don't care how long I must wait to move. My daughter is returning to the house, whether she likes it or not.

Chapter 108

Damien's POV

I've spent some time with Winter, trying to make her remember me and the small, rare, good parts of her childhood, but it's been difficult. She still can't fully remember, and it makes it awkward. We feel like strangers rather than family that we are. Poor Kai is devastated. It can't be easy seeing the mark on her neck suddenly gone. Plus, he's too nice to mark her without her consent. I know if that happened with Langdon, I'd be pretty upset.

Langdon's been pretty quiet lately. I've just gotten into the shower, wondering where he's gone to, when the door opens, and he comes waltzing in. I raise my eyebrows. He leans back against the vanity and folds his arms, his expression unreadable. "Do you want to join me?" I offer, but he shakes his head.

Damn. I was hoping he would.

"Thanks, but I'm enjoying the view," he purrs, and I can't help but blush. Even now, I still react to the man. My body does it automatically.

"If you got undressed, I could enjoy the view too," I grumble as he chuckles.

"Are we training today?" I ask him eagerly. He's been super wicked at showing me the ropes and training me. It's been fun. But he looks pensive.

"To be honest," he says calmly. "I thought we could do something else today instead."

Now I'm intrigued. "What kind of thing were you thinking of?" I ask slyly.

He grins. "It's a surprise."

I groan out loud. I'm not fond of surprises, but if my mate wants it to be, I'll accompany him. Besides, now that I'm looking at him closely, he looks more excited than usual. It has to be something pretty important, then.

"Does Kai know about this surprise?" I ask suspiciously. After all, as the Beta, Langdon can't just walk away from the pack for anything without permission.

"Of course," Langdon says lightly as I turn the water off in the shower and wrap a towel around my bottom half.

He follows me back out to the bedroom. Man, he must have been up early today to be dressed and showered before me. I thought I was an early riser, but he's even worse.

"How should I dress then?" I say, exasperated. "Formal, not formal?"

"Wear something comfortable and loose," he says, and I eye his clothes with raised eyebrows. He's wearing trousers and a shirt, so I should do the same. Except for that, I go for black jeans and a white shirt. He looks impressed, licking his lips. I give him a wink.

"Follow me," he orders.

We walk down to the garage, and I expect to see his car. But instead, he retrieves two helmets and hands one to me. Well, that's a surprise in itself. I hadn't known he had a bike. Now my own heart is thudding wildly in my chest. I've always wanted a motorbike but could never afford one. Besides, getting one hadn't made sense when I had a perfectly working car. He leads me to a Harley, and I drool at it. It's a fine piece of work with leather seats, a huge motor, and one large piece of beauty. Langdon laughs at the expression on my face. He gets on and flips the helmet over his head.

"Get on," he shouts, his voice muffled by the helmet.

I gingerly get on behind him, wrapping my arms tightly around his waist for balance. He starts the bike with a roar, then slowly peels out as I tremble in excitement.

We head out of the pack house and onto the main roads, swerving between the traffic. Langdon seems to be a pro at handling the bike, and it's so fast that it easily surpasses the cars on the road. The wind is rushing through my hair, and I feel free, free than I've ever felt. To my disappointment, we begin to slow down once we reach the city, and he pulls into a parking lot full of cars. I narrow my eyes. Has he brought me to a carnival? Sweet, uptight Langdon? Surely not.

I climb off the bike and pull off the helmet, Langdon climbing off slowly, a wide smile on his face. "I hope you like carnivals."

He teases. My heart skips a beat. Man, I love carnivals. I wonder who told him or like me. He loved them as well.

"Brilliant," I breathe out, handing the helmet to him and watching him place it on the handlebar.

"I thought it was time we went for our first date," he announces, grabbing my hand and leading me to the entrance. He pays for our entry, and then we head inside.

My head swings everywhere. Where did we go first? There were so many choices. Then I spot the rollercoaster, and my eyes light up as I drag him over. Langdon clutches the front of the seats, looking green as we go up and over, spinning around fast. When it's finished, I have to help him, his legs swaying slightly as he walks. I have to stifle my laughter.

"How about that one?" I ask eagerly, pointing to a ride that went up high and dropped quickly.

Langdon goes pale. "Sure," he stammers.

"We don't have to," I protest, but he shakes his head.

"No, let's do it."

The poor sweet man screamed the entire time we dropped. He also went so pale that I thought he was going to faint. I helped him out, feeling slightly guilty. I should have insisted on doing something else.

"Langdon, do you even enjoy carnivals?" I ask suspiciously.

He looks sheepish. "I kind of heard you say how much you like them, so I thought it would make a perfect date," he mumbles. "I'm not too fond of them, honestly."

I'm so touched. He was doing something special for me, even though he didn't enjoy it.

"How about the Ferris wheel," I say softly. Surely that ride would be all right for him.

His eyes light up. *Score one for Damien,* I think to myself.

"Let's do that last," he suggests. "Get some ice cream and fairy floss first?"

Man, I'm down for that. Not to mention the endless games that are waiting for me. Langdon seems content to stand and watch me, eating the fairy floss and stealing mine. Not that I mind. I'm having a blast. We even do a ring toss game together. He's relaxed out here, and it's a good side of Langdon that I'm seeing. He's not so uptight out here, away from all his responsibilities of the pack. He's even content holding my hand, despite the strange looks we are receiving and the occasional insult under someone's breath. It doesn't seem to bother him at all. It doesn't bother me. I thought it would, but honestly, all my focus is on him and the enjoyment of the date. Everything else around us seems to fade away.

"Man, I'm stuffed," I growl, patting my stomach. So much fairy floss and ice cream, not to mention the hot chips and hot dogs I've eaten. I feel like I'm about to explode. Langdon hasn't faired much better but mainly stuffed himself on fairy floss. It's a weakness of his.

"I feel like I'm going to need to be rolled back to the motorbike," grouses Langdon. "I shouldn't have eaten so much."

"You ate less than I did," I point out with amusement. "You really should have tried one of those hot dogs."

He wrinkles his nose. "Do you even know what's in a hot dog?" he demands.

"No," I groan. "And I don't want to know. Not unless you want me to be sick, at any rate."

"Are there any other games or rides you want to go on?" Langdon queries.

Chapter 108

I shake my head, then remember. "We were going to go on the Ferris wheel," I mutter. It's not as crowded at the carnival now, not when it was starting to get late. We'd spent out here.

"Oh, yeah," Langdon said quietly.

We turn towards the ride, grateful to see hardly anyone waiting. Langdon pays for our tickets, and I swear he's talking to the ride operator because it takes him ages to come back.

"Everything all right?" I ask him.

He looks taken aback. "Yeah, everything is fine," he babbles.

My eyes narrow. He's up to something, I'm sure of it.

We get to the head of the line and sit down, putting the safety bar over us. The ride begins, and the view is amazing. You can see over the city, the bright lights, the sunset, all of it. It's beautiful. I'm in awe. I'm glad we decided to do this ride last because the view is spectacular. Then the ride stops suddenly. I glance downwards nervously, but Langdon has a wide grin. Did he know the ride would stop when we were at the very top?

"Langdon," I say. "Did you do this?"

He smirks. Then moves closer. His hands grab hold of the sides of my face, his eyes staring into mine as I swallow nervously. God, he's beautiful. He moves forward, his face inches from mine, and then slowly, tenderly, he places his lips against mine, one of his hands going to the back of my head and holding it in place. I moan out loud, his tongue diving inside, touching mine and caressing it as I push my lips back against his, giving as good as I've got. It feels like time has stopped everything around us, the noise, the lights, fading away into the background. My hands go around his neck, pushing deeper into the kiss, my tongue eagerly dancing with his. My hands itch to explore and feel him all over, and I'm only dimly aware that we're out in public.

Then the ride starts again, causing us to pull back reluctantly. "That was so romantic," I tell Langdon, who looks pleased.

"I bribed the operator. That's why I took so long," he beams. I grin back.

I'm sad to see the evening is over when we get off the ride. It was such a nice day, and spending it with my mate made it more special. I sadly take hold of Langdon's hand.

"What's wrong?" he asks.

"Nothing, I'm just sad the date has ended," I try not to sniffle. After all, there will be plenty of dates. Won't there? Langdon looks confused.

"But there'll be loads of other dates," he points out, stifling a smile. "I promise you that. Plus, we still have to ride the motorbike back," he says, and I cheer up. There is that.

The drive back is quiet. With all the bike and wind noise, it's hard to talk anyway. We return to the pack house, and Langdon puts my helmet away. I'm about to turn and head to the pack house with him when he pulls back on my hand and stops me.

"Just a second," he says quietly. "Damien, I want you to know that I genuinely care about you. I'm not taking this mate bond for granted. There will be other dates."

He exhales as I listen, a smile on my face. "I'm not good at expressing my feelings. But I can do better. In the meantime," he says with a chuckle, holding out his hand with the motorbike key.

I stare, not comprehending. What was going on? What was this?

"It's yours," he clarifies. "The bike. I got it for you. I know you've always wanted one."

"It's mine," I whisper, and he nods.

I fling myself into his arms. "Thank you so much," I utter repeatedly as I hug him. He pulls me back, and then I astonish him with a massive kiss. One that gets my heart racing, my body beginning to get turned on by touching him. Pull back and grab Langdon by the hand, the key firmly held in my other one.

"What do you say we take this to the bedroom," I breathe, about to show him how much I appreciate him. The perfect end to what had turned out to be the perfect day.

Chapter 109

Kai's POV

Winter's been acting strange lately. Even Damien has noticed it, and her memories aren't returning. At least not completely. Is it possible that's the reason for it all? I still can't get the image of her eating steak for breakfast and then licking the blood. Sure, shifters crave meat, but I don't think even my cravings have gone that far. Maybe she's pregnant? Like having weird cravings? But wouldn't she know if she was? Besides, I don't think bringing up the possibility is a good idea. She'll most likely start yelling at me, for now. It's safer to put that idea by the wayside.

I'm sitting in the study, perusing my paperwork. There's so much of it. But that's the life of an Alpha. Everything has to run smoothly in the pack. The phone rings, and I frown. Only certain people, mainly other alpha's, have the phone number in the study, and it's a small amount at that. I pick up the receiver.

"Alpha Kai here," I growl.

"Oh, Kai, thank God I got hold of you," the voice says. I stare down at the receiver. The voice is somewhat familiar to me. I'm almost certain of it. This has to be Johnathon. What the hell does he want?

"Johnathon, this better be an emergency," I say tightly.

There's silence on the other end.

"Well, I wouldn't quite say it's an emergency," his voice says quietly.

"Johnathon cut the bullshit. What on earth is going on?"

A large exhale. My hands clench into fists. He isn't even here, and he's driving me insane. Fuck sake. What does the moron want now?

"Look, it was an accident," Johnathon begins. Not the best way to start a sentence. "Winter's father was being held at my pack as a prisoner." I roll my eyes. Tell me something I don't know.

"I already know that," I growl. "So what about it?"

"Well, while I was gone, at your pack," Johnathon says delicately as I listen intently. "Her father managed to escape. I am assuming he will make his way to your pack. He knows where Winter and Damien are."

"Shit," I swear, slamming my hand onto the desk and placing a large dent. I close my eyes. For once, can't we get a break? Especially Winter. She's had enough to deal with.

"How could you let this happen?" I snapped irritably. "What good is your pack if it lets someone go free?"

"I'm just as upset as you are," Johnathon growls. "But what's done is done. I just wanted to give you a heads-up. Because he's a piece of work, let me tell you."

"Thanks," I mutter. "I'll get my men to keep an eye out. But damn it, Johnathon, I'm pissed off at you."

"I can live with that," Johnathon says easily. "Good luck with everything." Damn it, he's completely ruined my day, and I bet he doesn't give a shit about it, either.

I slam the phone down and put my head in my hands. Great. Another thing to deal with. Winter's father was abusive to her her whole childhood. No doubt she felt safer with him, a prisoner. How on earth do I take that sense of safety away? Do I even tell her? Maybe there's a way to keep her out of the loop and deal with this problem simultaneously.

Let's mind-link Langdon and Damien. *Can you both come to the study? It's important to come straight away, don't dawdle,* I warn them. I hope Winter is sleeping upstairs. She seems to sleep a lot lately.

Chapter 109

A knock on the door. "Get in here now," I snap, and they walk in, sitting in the chairs opposite the desk, while I hastily close the door behind them.

"We have a bit of a situation," I say grimly. "Johnathon just rang to inform me that they've had a prisoner escape."

"That shouldn't be a problem," Langdon says, confused. "Why doesn't he just track the prisoner down." He folds his arms over his chest.

Huh. I should have asked the little bastard when I had him on the phone.

"I'm guessing because the prisoner's now too far away to track," I say wryly. "Normally, it wouldn't be our problem either, but the prisoner happens to be…" I trail off, not wanting to finish the sentence.

Damien pipes up. His face was completely ashen. "Mine and Winter's father. Isn't that right?" he adds quietly. I give a small nod.

Langdon exhales. "How long do we have?"

"Until he gets here? Could be weeks, could be days, especially if he makes his way here without stopping anywhere else," I say grimly.

"Fuck," whispers Damien. For once, the boy doesn't look cocky. He looks like he's going to be sick. Langdon grabs hold of his hand and squeezes it.

"It's all right, Damien. We'll keep a close lookout for him. He's just one shifter and not even a strong one at that," Langdon said, trying to soothe his mate, who looked distraught.

Christ, if this is Damien's reaction, then there was no way I would entertain the thought of telling Winter.

"He can't be that bad," I say to Damien. "Can he?" I ask, sounding uncertain.

He looks grim. "He tortured Winter for her entire childhood. I'm also to blame, but he enjoyed it," he whispered incredulously. "He derived pleasure from hurting his daughter."

231

God, I want to beat the man into a bloody pulp. With luck, I'll get my chance to.

"Is he a strong fighter?" I muse, and Damien shakes his head, then looks at Langdon, biting his lips.

"He's a lot stronger than me," Damien tells his mate. "I never could stand up against him."

"We still have plenty of time until he gets here," I tell them both. "Patrol will also be on the lookout, but I don't think he poses much risk or danger. Someone from patrol will likely round him up and put him in the dungeon. He doesn't sound that strong to me."

"I agree," Langdon says firmly, looking directly at Damien, who is unconcerned. "You have nothing to fear, not when Alpha Kai and I will protect you and Winter."

Damien looks slightly calmer. "What are you going to tell Winter?" he asks. "She thinks she's safe and that he's a prisoner in Johnathon's pack. Well, she did," he mutters. "With her amnesia, I'm unsure if she even remembers that."

I shrug, trying to look carefree. "I'm not going to tell her anything," I say lightly. "I don't want anything to stress her out anymore than she already is."

"You can't just keep the truth from her," Damien protests. "She needs to know to keep herself safe. You'll only make her angry by not telling her."

"I'm trying to protect her," I thunder. "She doesn't need to know. What good would it do? She constantly looked over her shoulder and jumped at every little noise."

"She's stronger than that," Damien counters. Langdon stays silent in the background. I scowl at him. His mate is challenging my decisions, and it's pissing me off.

"I won't let this harm or put her back from her recovery!" I shout, getting to my feet and sending several things flying off the desk. The door swings open. Winter stands there, her arms folded, with an angry expression. Damien gulps. Langdon looks nervous, and I give her a small smile. How long has she been standing there and listening?

She strides forward and puts her hands on the desk, her body leaning forward, her eyes staring directly into mine. Fuck. This isn't good.

"What is it that you don't want to tell me?" she says quietly but ominous enough to make even Langdon cringe. It's blatantly clear that she's furious.

"Listen, Winter," I say hastily. "It's not that big a deal…" I trail off, her eyes narrowing as she glares at me. She's not buying it at all.

"She has a right to know," Damien hisses. "After all, it concerns her."

"Fine," I bark at him. "The both of you get out of here," I thunder.

Damien peels himself off the chair and tugs Langdon to the doorway. Langdon gives me an apologetic glance over his shoulder before he leaves the room with his mate.

Winter folds her arms across her chest and stamps her foot impatiently. "Well," she says snarkily. "What is it you're hiding from me, Kai? Don't lie to me," she warns.

I sigh. "Fine, your father has escaped from Johnathon's prison. He's on the way here."

Silence. Awkward silence.

She falls back into a chair, a hand to her mouth in shock. Tears form at the corner of her eyes. She clearly remembers her father then. Shame. I would have preferred she never remembered him ever again.

"You're sure?" she asks me, almost desperately. "You're sure he's coming here and not somewhere else?"

"I'm not sure, but Johnathon says he knows where you and Damien are, and I need to act accordingly."

"You were going to keep this secret from me," she says, scandalized. "How could you, Kai? I have a right to know that he's coming for me. Even if it means I must stay inside to be safe, you should have told me immediately."

"I only just found out," I explain heavily. "Damien and Langdon were my priority. I didn't want to stress you out," I say, flinching at the look on her face.

"You have no right to make decisions for me without my consent," she says, throwing her hands up. "You wouldn't like it if I did that to you."

No, I wouldn't, I have to admit. "I was trying to do the right thing," I argue.

"Well, stop making decisions for me," she cries. "I'm an adult, Kai. I can make my own. Promise me you won't try to hide anything from me again."

Her voice is soft, pleading with me. Her eyes are beseeching me. I can't resist the tears that are forming in the corner of her eyes. She's more upset than I imagined she would be.

"I promise I won't hide anything else from you," I say sternly. "But you have to listen to me and keep yourself safe. Is that fair?"

She gives a nod, a small smile on her face.

"Kai," she says gently. "I will try and keep myself safe, but I won't lock myself in a room while everyone else goes about their lives. I might not be prepared to fight my father, but I won't let him take over my life and living."

"Good," I smile, "Because I don't want that for you either. Winter, how would you feel about visiting the training ring over the next few days? Get some training in? I'm sure Sabriel is missing it."

For some reason, she looks inexplicably sad. Have I said something wrong?

"I, um," she hedges. "Haven't been feeling well lately, so it might not be a good idea to visit the training ring until I'm fully well again."

Now I'm concerned. She hasn't been feeling well for a while now. "Do you think you need to see a doctor?" I ask. "Maybe just for a checkup?"

She shakes her head. "No, I think I'm just under the weather," she admits. "I'm sure I'll start feeling much better soon with plenty of rest and fluids."

I'm not so sure about that. But she reaches over and takes my hand, squeezing it gently. "I remembered a little bit more today," she tells me eagerly. Her memories have returned in dribs and drabs, which is a good sign. Even if it's slightly frustrating, it's completely sporadic and random because there seems to be no order for when they come.

"What did you remember?" I ask, and she gives me a grin. Then I notice that she's blushing, her cheeks red. Whatever she's remembered, it is something good. I bet I know what it is too.

"I remembered our first night together," she breathes, kissing my hand. "And how special you made me feel."

I tenderly bend down and kiss her, Winter melting in my arms. "I love you," I tell her, and my heart skips a beat when she repeats it to me.

"I love you too, Kai."

Chapter 110

Winter's POV

*S*mack. *I can feel the sting as he slaps me directly across the face. I put a hand on my cheek. His face is inches from mine, and I can smell the sour taste of his breath. "You stupid bitch," he hisses. "Where's the beer."*

I had forgotten we were out. My job was to keep the fridge fully stocked, but it had slipped my mind between school and studying. I should be thankful that he left money for his beer but hardly anything else for food.

"I forgot," I mumble, dropping my head to my chest and hoping he might show mercy. But he shows none. Instead, he grabs my arm and twists it as I cry out from the pain, shoving me in front of him and down to the basement, the one place I fear most.

"Please," I beg, but he ignores my pleas for mercy, shoving me so hard down the stairs that I almost trip and fall. I catch myself on the railing just in time.

"Move," he snarls, and reluctantly, I place one foot in front of the other until I'm standing at the base of the stairs, his large frame thundering after me.

I can see it, and my whole body trembles. I don't want to go in there. All that's waiting in there is more pain. More abuse. But he shoves me towards it, and my body smacks to the ground. He curses under his breath.

"Move, you little bitch," he growls, and I get back up, feeling woozy and lightheaded. His eyes are gleaming in the darkness, and there's a twisted smile on his face. The bastard is enjoying this.

Chapter 110

I stand in front of it, willing my body to move. But I'm paralyzed with fear. He laughs loudly and pushes me hard, my body flailing as I fall inside the silver cell he's created just for me. I turn around, and he brandishes the whip that digs into my flesh and gouges at me.

"Father, don't do this," I beg, and he shakes his head.

"You are no daughter of mine," he spits. "You are a murderer."

I fall silent. I am a murderer. If it weren't for me, my mother would still be alive. I'm the reason she's dead. I'm the reason my father and brother hate me.

"Lie down," he orders me, and for a moment I waver. What would happen if I defied him? Refused to do as he said? But another part of me knows I'll only make it worse if I try. I lie down on the hard, cold concrete ground, my back exposed. I know what's coming. I bite my lip, trying to hold back the cries.

Thwack. The first hit of the whip lands between my shoulder blades. Even with my clothes on, it's digging into my skin, and when he pulls it back, I can feel large chunks of flesh being pulled along with it. The pain is excruciating.

Thwack. He doesn't hold back, using all his strength to whip me. I begin to scream, the sounds echoing throughout the otherwise empty basement.

Thwack. I stop counting after the first five. My whole body is now numb with shock. I can't hold back my screams. And if anything, that makes him smile even wider. My father enjoys hearing me scream from the pain.

Thwack. Blood is pooling around my body on the floor. The whip has silver on it. I can feel my flesh burning and bubbling as it touches the strips where my clothing has ripped and torn.

Thwack. I don't know if I will make it out this time alive. It's the longest he's beaten me for, and he shows no signs of letting up. Am I going to die right here in the basement?

Thwack. I barely feel the smack of the whip anymore. I feel like I might be dying. He grunts.

"You stay in here, you miserable, worthless piece of shit," he declares, and I hear the door to the cell closing. Part of me is relieved he's finally finished, hearing his footsteps as he storms up the stairs and slams through the basement door. Another part of me is worried I won't live through the night.

I lay in my blood, my head resting on my arms. I can't move. Every single tiny movement I make brings pain. I'll heal from these wounds. It will take time without a wolf. Not only that, but I'll be left with many scars on my body to join the old ones. What if I were to kill myself, comes a voice in my head. Finally, give Father what he wants and my brother as well. I try to tune out the voice, but it's persistent, constant, and not letting go. That was the first night I seriously started to contemplate killing myself. While I didn't go through with it, it stayed on my mind for the rest of my days...

I blinked, looking up at the ceiling. Since Kai informed me that Father had escaped Johnathon's dungeon, it seems like my memories are returning in small pieces of everything my father and Damien have ever done to me. I can feel the pain, the hurt in the memories. My hands trace the scars on my back and stomach, realizing where they have come from. I never realized why I feared my father so much, but if the memories indicated, he was a monster, an evil bastard who needed to be stopped. The old Winter would have been afraid, would have stayed out of the way, and tried to keep herself safe, but the new Winter, the new Winter, wanted to be stronger, more courageous. She didn't want to spend the rest of her life in fear.

I get up and wander to the mirror, looking at the back of myself, craning my head over my shoulder. There are all sorts of ugly scars, crisscrossing over each other, long white lines that snake around and cover me. They were put there by my father and my brother. I feel sickened. How could someone derive such joy from hurting someone?

I think back to the rogue attack that took my mother from me. But I don't remember much. Everything's a blur. I remember being a little kid, out for a picnic with my mother, sitting underneath a shady tree. This had been her idea. She had wanted to be outside, and Damien and her father had refused, wanting to stay indoors. Then she'd smelt something, stiffened, and told me to run. But I didn't want to leave her behind. I knew something was dangerously wrong…

"It's rogues, Winter. You have to run," she shouted.

"But, Mummy," I had cried out.

"No, you need to go," she growled and shifted.

I don't remember much more than that, other than running across the grounds screaming my head off, bursting inside the house while Father and Damien looked at me.

"Mummy, Mummy," I sniveled, pointing.

Father had gone as white as a sheet. "Stay here," he demanded, telling the both of us to stay put.

He went racing out.

When Father finally returned, his shoulders were slumped, and his head was down. He looked miserable, sad. I hadn't known what to do and had gone to hug him, but he pushed me back.

"You," he hissed, and I stared at him, my lip quivering. "This is all your fault."

"What's wrong, Daddy?" I'd asked.

"She's dead," he'd growled. "Because of you."

Being a little girl, I hadn't understood what he meant, but from that night onwards, everything had changed, and not for the better…

"Winter," Kai said softly, distracting me from my thoughts. "Winter, are you all right?" he asks me, concerned.

I try to smile at him but fail miserably. "I'm remembering things I would rather not," I say lightly. I'm trying to play it off like it's no big deal, but Kai sees right through me.

"Oh, Winter," he murmurs, grabbing hold of me and embracing me tightly. "You don't always have to act so brave, you know. I know what your father did to you. I know what Damien did. I don't expect you to get over that," he explained.

239

I stifle my sobs, but suddenly the gates come crashing open, and I'm crying loudly on his shoulders as he holds me. Why can't I be the strong girl I know I can be? Why does the past affect me so much? Kai holds me, saying nothing, and I soak his shirt in tears.

Winter, you went through something traumatic. It's all right to cry and to show weakness.

I hate doing it, though, Sabriel.

Well, the past is shit, no kidding, but the future, the future, is what we make of it. This handsome man is most definitely a part of our future.

I like the idea of looking forward instead of backward. But I don't think I can avoid my memories coming back, Sabriel.

I'm not asking you to. You need to accept the past to move on to a better future.

Thanks, Sabriel. Your advice is something I'm going to consider.

I heave a shuddering sigh and burrow into Kai's shoulder. God, he smells delicious. That scent of his is mesmerizing. My mouth is watering, just smelling him so near. I can hear his heartbeat, and it's so loud, thudding in his chest. Why is his heartbeat so loud? He pulls back from me.

"I think you need to spend some time with Damien if those memories are returning to haunt you," he says, and I shake my head.

"He hurt me, Kai," I say indignantly. "He didn't stop my father, and he even joined in. What kind of older brother does that to his little sister," I add, hurt.

Kai sighs. "It's in the past, Winter, and he did come good. Heck, he even traveled all this way to find you. I don't know if you remember how excited you were to see him, but you flung yourself into his arms."

"But what if he hurts me again?" I ask in a small voice. I sound like a small child instead of a grown woman. So much for being brave and confident.

Kai looks thoughtful. "I don't think he will, not intentionally. He seems to love you, Winter, and your amnesia hasn't been easy on him either."

Ouch. That hurt. Big time. Who cares about Damien? Not when I was the victim.

"Maybe if you're there, I'll spend time with him. Or if Langdon is there," I say slowly. "But I don't want to be left alone with him, at any rate. When he shows me I can trust him, I'll see him alone."

"That's fair enough," Kai agrees, giving me a long lingering kiss with my knees knocked together. "But how about you at least come downstairs? We can all sit together in my study or have lunch in the dining room?" he suggests.

That sounds too much like being a family, which we are not. I think about the study idea, but I'm not ready to face Damien yet. I need time to process everything. I need time to be alone and not be pressured to do something I don't want to do. Quite frankly, I just don't want to see my brother just yet.

"Maybe next time," I answer quietly. "I think I'm just going to spend time here and read a book."

He looks like he wants to protest but sees the look on my face and nods. He quietly leaves.

After he's gone, a thought comes to me, and I sigh. I might have to see Damien after all. Because not once did my father ever tell me or show me where he buried our mother.

Chapter 111

Kai's POV

"No, there haven't been any sightings of the son of a bitch just yet," I snarl, holding the receiver tight to my ear and imagining it to be Johnathon's neck as I squeeze it tightly.

"I've sent my best trackers out, but too much time has passed to pick up his trail," Johnathon says on the other end, not sounding remotely apologetic. Does he not realize the full magnitude of what he's done? How on edge have Winter and Damien been since they heard the news? Does he think this is a game? My anger rises with every word that he speaks.

"I've sent mine out. There's nothing there. Are you sure he's coming for them? Maybe he got smart and decided it wasn't worth dying over," I hiss. Maybe the man possessed some common sense. It was entirely possible.

There's silence on the other end of the phone.

"I don't think he'll give up on them quite as easily as you seem to think he will," Johnathon says quietly.

I glower at the telephone. This was all his fault, to begin with. This man would still be in prison if it weren't for him and his bloody useless pack. Well, a dungeon, at any rate. Instead of heading here and traumatizing my poor Winter all over again.

"How's Winter and Damien going?" he dares to ask me.

I grit my teeth. "Damien is on edge, expecting to see his father at any moment. As for Winter, she's holed up in the bedroom, and it's bringing back some bad memories. She's about to have a nervous breakdown," I growl.

"I'm sorry for that. By the way, we forgot to tell you about the rogue. You won't understand, but Winter will. The rogue she saved showed us the way to your pack. That's all she needs to know. It might be enough to cheer her up some."

I frown. What the hell did he mean by the rogue she saved? No one saved a rogue. They would kill you as soon as you look at them. Johnathon had to be playing a cruel trick. Was he messing with me?

"Yeah, sure," I say dryly. He senses my unease about it.

"It's not a lie. Talk to Damien about it. He'll tell you it's the truth," he defends hotly.

I roll my eyes. Sure, I'll get right on that. He's silent momentarily while I fume on the other end, fighting back the urge to hurl the receiver at the closest wall and break it.

"Do you require some assistance?" he asks. "Because I can come back and help until he's been captured again."

The hell he would. I don't want him anywhere near my pack, let alone near Winter, making those googly eyes at her again. Besides, for heaven's sake, my pack was fine to deal with one lone shifter. It was laughable that he thought we might need his assistance. I'm one of the strongest packs in the country and one of the strongest Alphas. Now I was viewing it as an insult.

"Thank you for your concern, but that won't be necessary," I tell him with a sneer.

"Kai," Johnathon says lowly, and I have to strain to hear him. "Take care of Winter because if she so much as gets a tiny bit injured," he pauses. "Then I'm coming for you. Take care of her or else," he snaps, slamming the phone and hanging up on me.

Did that little bastard hang up on me? I stare at the phone incredulously, but the beeping sounds mean that Johnathon has hung up. That little asshole. No one hangs up on me. I slam the receiver down several times, banging it hard, taking out all my anger and frustration. I keep banging it until there's a knock on the door.

"What?" I growl, and Langdon walks in without Damien, which is a surprise.

"Not in a good mood, I see," Langdon says with a smile of amusement as I scowl at him.

"What do you want, Langdon?" I say a bit sulkily, almost pouting like a child. Damn that, Johnathon. He's put me in a foul temper. I feel like punching something; if Langdon isn't careful, it will be him. I scowl at him.

Langdon flops down in the chair. He looks tense, a crease across his forehead, and his usual jovial smile feels forced. This isn't like him at all. Maybe I should be listening to what he needs as well. He was as affected by the possible threat of the father as I was. After all, Damien was his son. No matter how strong and brave Damien comes across, even I know he must have been terrified to have a father like that as a child.

Langdon puts his head in his hands, looking older than his twenty-three years. His brown hair is shaggy, tied back in a small ponytail. He doesn't look like the cool, confident, put-together man I knew.

"Man, I hope this asshole turns up soon," mutters Langdon. "I don't know how much longer I can keep Damien calm. He's terrified, Kai. A young man, an adult male, is terrified of his father. What kind of monster would this father have to be to cause that much reaction in his son?"

I sigh. So Damien wasn't faring too well either. Langdon looks exhausted. "He's not eating properly. He's not sleeping. When he is sleeping, he has nightmares. It's all I can do to get him to hold it together. Then to top it off, Winter has stopped speaking to him, which has put him in a depressive mood. I don't know what else to do. I left him sleeping to come to see you. If he knew I was gone…" Langdon trailed off. I got the hint. Damien needed Langdon to be by his side.

"Winter's not faring much better," I admit, clogged in the throat. "She's sleeping but not well, and I know she's having nightmares. All of this has started to bring her memories back. Her childhood trauma is all returning to her, not to mention Damien's part. That's why she's not speaking to him. I can't force her to either. That has to be a decision she makes for herself."

Langdon sighs.

"How is patrol going?" I ask, leaning back against the chair. My temper has soothed somewhat, and I no longer felt like punching the walls or poor Langdon.

"I've increased it, but there have been no sightings. Patrol is on the lookout, and I even got several pack members hiding in the trees, keeping a lookout over the forest. If this man comes, we will see him before he goes onto the grounds."

I harrumph. At least we were well prepared. But Langdon and I felt helpless when it came to helping our mates.

"All you can do is be there for him, Langdon," I tell him. "I don't think Winter or Damien will rest easy until their father has been caught. Until then, we do our best to comfort them."

Langdon grimaces but gives a small nod. "Maybe Damien will join me at the training ring," he says quietly. "It will allow him to vent his anger and frustration and make him exhausted enough to get a proper sleep."

"I think that's a great idea," I tell him with a small smile. I watch the poor man leave, his shoulders slumped, looking like he was carrying the world's weight on his shoulders.

I groan. Winter hasn't come downstairs again today, which only means one thing. She's holed up in our room again. This doesn't bode well. She was so afraid she couldn't bear to leave the room. Doesn't she understand that I will protect her? That nothing is going to get past me and sink its claws into her?

I walk upstairs and pause outside our bedroom. I can hear the sound of sobbing and crying, which wrenches my heart. She sounds so broken, so upset. Should I disturb her? But my hand knocks on the door anyway. If she tells me to leave, then I'll honor her wishes. But instead, to my shock, the bedroom door is wrenched open, and she flings herself into my arms. My hands go around her automatically, even as she wraps her legs around me, and it feels like I'm carrying a koala. Her head rests on my shoulder, and I can feel her tears beginning to soak my shirt. Her whole body is trembling as well.

"Winter," I say cautiously, rubbing her back as I sit on the bed. She refuses to look at me. "Winter, honey, what's wrong?" I ask, hearing her sniffle. Her small cries are painful to hear.

"I remembered," she whispers. "I remember everything."

Hallelujah. She finally got her memories back as the doctor had originally said she would. My arms tighten around her. I'm well aware of what painful memories she might have regarding me and the complete asshole I was to her originally.

"My father is a monster," she whispers. "And so is my brother."

Ouch. It didn't look like Winter was about to forgive Damien any time too soon. Still, I remember what Langdon said about Damien being completely miserable and deciding to try at least to make Winter see reason.

"Winter, your brother was just as afraid of your father as you were," I say, hearing her sobbing stop. "He went along with your father because he was afraid your father would hurt him if he didn't. That doesn't make it right or any less wrong, but he did go good for you, didn't he? Start to care for yourself properly. He even traveled all the way here to save you from Thomas."

She was quiet. Like she was digesting his words, maybe he'd gotten through to her. She took long shuddering breaths. Encouraged, Kai continued to speak to her.

"Langdon says Damien isn't sleeping well. Is barely eating, and he's completely miserable because you've stopped talking to him."

She finally pulled back, and I could see her face. I hold in my grimace. She has dark circles under her eyes, red puffy eyes, matted and disheveled hair, and she's ashen, completely pale. Paler than I've ever seen her. Whatever she's been doing up here hasn't been to sleep.

"Is Damien upset?" she asks, climbing off me and sitting on the bed, her arms folded across her chest.

I give a small nod. "To be honest, I think Langdon misses you as well," I say pointedly as she looks away from me for a moment, looking thoughtful.

"Kai," she says. "It's just that the memories won't stop coming, and I'm afraid. I'm afraid to close my eyes in case it's another nightmare. I've had so many nightmares, and they all seem so real," she whispers, her body shuddering.

My God, I hadn't realized how badly she was affected by all this. No wonder Langdon looks so miserable and exhausted. He kept as close to his mate as possible, whereas I have been doing all my work and leaving Winter to hole up in the room by herself.

"What if I stay with you while you sleep?" I suggest quietly.

She stares at me for a moment, fidgeting with her hands. Then a look of relief covers her face. "You would stay with me?" she asks uncertainly.

"Yes," I say, getting up off the bed, pulling everything off it, and pulling the bed covers back. She gets in slowly, lying on the pillows, her face staring at me as I sit beside the bed. I pull the covers back over her and kiss her forehead. I frown. She feels warm but doesn't seem to be too phased by it. Her eyelids slowly flutter closed as I watch over her intently. Slowly her breathing evens, and I push her hair away from her face. There's a small smile on her face, and she looks a lot more serene. I settle against the bed. I will stay here as long as she needs me until she wakes up alone. I hadn't realized how afraid she was. I need to be a better mate.

Chapter 112

Winter's POV

I'm screaming at the top of my lungs while thunder crashes in the distance and the rain pours outside. It helps to muffle the sounds coming from the basement. My father is grinning, enjoying the sounds of my screams while Damien stands in the background. My eyes meet his, pleading for help, but he looks away.

Slap. My father's hand slaps me directly across the face as I dangle in the cell, my hands chained over my head, my legs dangling uselessly. It hurts, but no more than what he's already put me through. I feel the knife's sharp, stinging pain as he trails it lightly across my back.

"Should I write something," my father sneers as I try to stifle my sobs and remain quiet. Besides, it's not me that he's asking, but Damien, who hovers in the background like the coward he is.

"I think she's had enough," Damien says lightly. "If she can't attend school, they'll know something is wrong. Winter's never missed a day in her life."

For a brief second, a brief moment, I had thought he was trying to save me. I should have known better.

"Nah, she can take more," my father mutters.

The blade's tip pushes in harder as he drags it across my skin. My flesh burns and bubbles from the silver, a sharp cry emitting from my throat. Blood trickles down to the floor.

"Your turn," my father says quietly, and my head whips up to see Damien. He looks like a deer caught in the headlights. But my father shows no mercy. He hands the knife to Damien, who, I bitterly realize, has already gloved up like he was expecting this to happen.

Damien eyes the knife, twisting it repeatedly in his hand, a dark look on his face.

"Do it already," my father barks out, and Damien slowly wanders over to me, the knife held firmly in his grasp, his eyes looking up at mine.

My body tenses in preparation. He plunges the knife into my side, stabbing me, and leaves the knife in as my father crows with delight in the background. I scream hysterically, trying to dislodge the knife with no luck, my legs kicking and my body bucking wildly. Tears are trailing down my cheeks. It's with relief that I feel Damien pull the knife out, but just as quickly, he plunges it into my abdomen, blood pooling around the wound. When he yanks the knife out, I feel woozy and dizzy this time. My body's been pushed past my limits. I no longer care if I live or die. I want the pain to stop. The torture. The torment.

I'm lowered to the floor, and the chains are torn off. My father hums under his breath. "Make sure she gets food and water," he tells Damien. "Can't have her dying on us now, can we?"

I stare at my brother hazily, and for a moment, I swear I see regret on his face. But it's gone just as quickly as it had never been there in the first place...

Another flashback. Another piece of the so-called puzzle slotting neatly into place. I try not to rock back and forth on the bed, even as tears come. How anyone could do that to their daughter and sister defies all belief. Was I not good enough? Besides apparently killing my mother, was I such a terrible person that I deserved punishment? Why else would Damien have taken such joy in it?

You're not a terrible person, Winter.

Sometimes it's hard to tell, Sabriel.

Why don't you ask him? See Damien face to face? He owes you an explanation.

You're right. He does. He can damn well start explaining himself.

You go, girl, sock him one if you have to. Get those answers you've been asking for.

Right. I'm going. My hands clench into fists. Damien does owe me an explanation for everything. Kai is currently in his study, but I know that Damien and Langdon have been walking around the house lately and staying close by. I yank the door to the bedroom open and stomp down the stairs, now in a full-blown foul temper. No matter how much I eat and drink lately, nothing seems to satisfy the hunger and thirst I seem to have. This makes me angrier.

I check the house first. No sign of Damien. I even check the grounds outside quickly but don't venture too far. For some reason, I can't bring myself to go too far from the bedroom. The bedroom is safe and secure. It feels like a haven to me. I sigh. Something tells me the person I want must be in the study or Langdon's house. I'm betting on the study. Damien is clinging to Langdon lately and doesn't like being too far from him, just like I don't like to be too far from Kai.

I walk down the corridor and reach the study door. I sniff and wrinkle my nose. I can smell them all in there, but they smell weird. Slightly unpleasant, which is odd because Kai's scent should smell delicious to me, at least. I must be getting sick or something. I shrug. I'll deal with it later. I tense and then smack the door to the study open. As I suspected, Kai, Langdon, and Damien are all discussing God knows what.

Kai goes to get out of his seat. "Winter now's not the time," he begins, but I ignore him.

I focus all my glaring on Damien, who's cringing in his chair. He can see just how much of a temper I'm in.

"This is between me and Damien," I say calmly. "Both of you can get out."

Kai opens his mouth to protest, but Langdon shoots him a look, and they both excuse themselves. I fold my arms across my chest. Damien stays silent.

Finally, I can't take it any longer. "How could you?" I burst out. "You tortured me with Father, and you didn't do anything to save me," I almost screamed in my rage.

Chapter 112

"You don't understand," Damien mumbles, and I turn to him, my eyes flashing and my lip curled up in a sneer.

"You're right. I don't understand. I don't understand how a brother can take part in torturing his sister. How you just kept quiet. How you didn't try to stop him, not even once, and how you even occasionally participated with him."

Now he looks pale. "I didn't have a choice," he pleads. "You think he wouldn't have done the same to me if I'd refused?"

I think Damien's full of shit. "Father never laid a finger on you," I scoff. "You were his precious son. It was his daughter he hated. You weren't responsible for Mother's death. I was."

Damien stands up, sending the chair he's sitting on to the ground with a large crash. "You have no clue how hard it was to stare into your eyes and still torture you while you cried."

"No, because I was the one being tortured. Maybe you should have seen how much that hurt from my side," I say sarcastically. He swallows nervously.

"Look, I was terrified of Father," he admits. "Enough that I would have done everything he said if it meant he didn't hurt me instead."

"You were a coward," I spat out.

"Yes, I was a coward!" he yells, spreading his arms wide. "And I regret what I did to you every damn day. I have nightmares about what I've done. I know that no matter how hard I try, I'll never be able to make it up to you."

He's damn right about that. My rage feels like it's spiraling out of control. My breathing is heavy, and my hands won't stop clenching and unclenching as I stand there and grit my teeth. I want to punch the lights out of him, but I can't hurt him even now. Damn it. My eyes fall on the desk instead, and before I can stop myself, I pick it up, which astounds me. I didn't know I was that strong, and I threw it against the wall, shattering the desk into splinters while Damien stood there in shock. I feel mildly impressed with myself. Fuck, I'm strong.

"How did you do that?" breathes Damien in disbelief, staring at the ruins of the desk on the floor.

"I used my anger," I snap at him, trying to breathe and still feeling the urge to kill him.

"Look, Winter, I don't know what you want from me," Damien says quietly, wringing his hands and standing on the spot, putting his weight on one leg, then the other. "I am truly sorry for everything I did to you in the past. I can never make it up to you because you're right. I was your brother, and I should have protected you instead of doing what I did. There are no excuses. I stuffed up, made a horrible mistake, and you suffered because of me."

It's like he's taken the wind out of my sails. I'm starting to feel deflated. Instead of rage, I'm starting to feel overwhelming sadness. "I have scars all over my body that won't go away," I choke out.

"I know," he whispers.

"The memories, they'll never fade," I continue.

"I know," he whispers.

"I have nightmares, Damien," I say, bursting into tears. "And I'm afraid all the time. Why couldn't Johnathon have just killed him," I howl. "Because waiting for him to come is killing me."

"I know," he whispers. "Because the same thing is happening to me. I can't eat, sleep, have nightmares, and feel constantly looking over my shoulder. I feel the same way you do, Winter. I would have lost my mind if it weren't for Langdon."

I sniffle. If it wasn't for Kai, I'm sure I would have had a nervous breakdown by now. He's been my rock this entire time.

Damien's eyes are shiny with unshed tears. "I can't make up for the past, Winter," he says with determination etched on his handsome face. "But I can try and have a future with you. That is if you're willing to let me. I don't blame you if you never want to forgive me, but you forgave me once before. I do love you as a sister, and I want to show you that I can be the brother you deserve."

I'm openly crying now. My emotions are a mess. He closes the gap between us and hugs me, pulling me tight against him as I rest my eyes and place my head against his chest. His hands grip me tightly around the waist, and I breathe in his scent, which still smells strange.

We stand there for several minutes, clutching each other and saying nothing. I finally let go of all the anger I've been holding onto with Damien. There's no point holding onto an old grudge. He can't change the future. He did travel this way for me. Despite everything, I know he loves me; a small part of me loves him back.

There's a tentative knock on the door, and then Kai and Langdon step in, looking at the destruction of the room with raised eyebrows.

"Sorry," I apologize sheepishly. "I let my anger get the best of me."

Kai looks at his desk. "Who broke the desk?" he asked, curious.

"I did," I say very quietly.

He looks amazed. "That desk is so heavy and solid that I struggle to lift it on my own, and you managed to throw it across the room," he exclaimed. "Strange," he mutters to himself.

"Is all forgiven?" asks Langdon, and I give him a nod, stepping away from Damien.

"All is forgiven," I say and mean it, sailing out of the room. Kai and Langdon look at the desk as I leave and shoot each other a glance full of meaning.

Chapter 113

Damien's POV

I'm too little to understand, but I wouldn't say I like watching him hurt my little sister, Winter. I pull on his arm. "Stop, Daddy," I tell him, Winter cowering on the ground to stop his fists from hurting her face. She's crying, and it makes me feel sad for her.

He glares at me. "Your sister is a murderer," he spits out. "She's the reason that your mother is dead. She killed her, and now she gets to pay. Don't get in my way, or you'll be next," he threatens. He waves his arm and sends me flying, my back hitting the wall as I crumple to the ground before he starts hitting poor Winter again, who is crying and begging him to stop.

It's raining, and there's thunder in the background. Winter is in the cell that Father purposely built just for her, crying and screaming as he whips her. I can smell the blood in the air. I'm older now but no less afraid of him. I can barely stand the screams, the crying as he hurts her. She's lying there on the ground, completely helpless. She's much weaker than us, and having no wolf makes her even more helpless. It also means she's slow to heal, something that the older man takes sadistic pleasure in.

"Please stop!" she screams as I watch, feeling numb.

Whenever she gets hurt or because I'm carrying it out, or numb when Father does it. Her voice is pitiful and weak. She's begging for mercy, but it's pointless. She should know by now. It's been years that Father is incapable of mercy or forgiveness. He's incapable of anything but drinking his precious alcohol and inflicting pain.

I can hear the thwacks of the whip as it meets her flesh. The sound of her cries in the small basement. The sizzling sound of the silver *meeting and touching her bare flesh. The smell of burning flesh is sickening. I gag.*

My father is smiling. He's not holding back, using his strength to whip her, and I can't even remember why. It takes very little to make him angry these days. But I wouldn't say I like the cell. It's monstrous. But what I fear the most, which makes me ashamed, is that he'll use it on me one day when I make him angry. That's how much of a coward I am.

"Please," Winter sobs, her hands scrabbling at the cold concrete floor, her body covered in gouges and scratches, and her voice hoarse from screaming. "Please... stop..."

Father hits her again, and she falls silent. Her head turns to the side, and she looks at me. I suck in a breath. Her eyes are dead, staring blankly. The light's gone completely from them. It's like she's given up completely, no longer making a sound as the whip strikes her back. I feel sick. I'm a coward. But if I step in, who's to say Father won't turn on me with the whip? The bastard is a lot stronger than me. To my shame, I say nothing, turning away and walking upstairs as my father continues to torture the little sister I've long since stopped trying to protect. Now, I protect myself, no matter what it takes...

The flashbacks are coming more regularly now. More intense, more in my face than ever before. I don't know what's caused it. It could be my argument with Winter or that I know Father is coming. I place my head in my hands. Why can't I stop remembering? It's so painful. It sticks in my mind and won't let go. Every sound, pain, and feeling is there as I relive what I don't want to remember. My breath comes out in short heavy puffs. My heart is thudding wildly in my chest. I glance over at Langdon, sleeping peacefully, his brown hair all tousled and across the pillow. Thank God I haven't disturbed him. He needs sleep. I know he's gotten very little since I started with the flashbacks, and he hasn't left my side. He senses my fear, even though I've tried not to show it. How pathetic am I? Even fully grown with a wolf, I'm afraid of my father. I don't see what

Langdon sees in me sometimes. He could do so much better, you know?

I climb over him slowly, trying not to jostle him. If he wakes up, he'll insist on staying awake with me, and I can't have that. This insomnia is slowly killing me. I can't sleep. My whole body trembles as I get out of bed, putting on a heavy sweatshirt of Langdon's for comfort and slowly creeping into the kitchen. Warm milk is meant to help you sleep. At this point, I'll try anything. I open the refrigerator and grab the milk, pouring it into a saucepan. I grab a mug and place the saucepan on the stove, stirring constantly until the milk is warm. Then I sit at the dining table.

I yawn. I'm so tired. If I were this tired, you would think sleep would come naturally to me. But no. No matter how exhausted I feel, my body refuses to sleep. It's infuriating. I sip my warm milk. At least that's making me calm down somewhat. The milk soothes my sore throat, and I relax in the chair. I don't even mind that I'm sitting in semi-darkness. The only light there is coming from the few windows in the kitchen.

There's nothing to fear here, I chant to myself. It's just Langdon and myself in this house. I'm perfectly safe. But my body, even though it's slowly relaxing, refuses to stop trembling. Then I hear the sound of footsteps, and my heart sinks. I was sure I'd left the room without disturbing the poor bastard. Sure enough, Langdon walks in, his hair all disheveled, looking sleepy and adorable. He yawns widely, putting a hand to his mouth. I feel guilty that he's awake.

"Do you know what time it is?" he comments quietly.

I shake my head. His eyes soften as they gaze at me. "I'm guessing you couldn't sleep again," he said pointedly. I flush and look at the table.

He doesn't look angry. He looks calm, grabbing himself a hot drink of coffee and sitting opposite me. "I thought I told you to wake me up when you can't sleep," he chides.

Chapter 113

"I don't want you to sit with me when I have insomnia," I burst out. "It's unfair to you, and you need your sleep. Kai relies on you as his Beta."

He's silent for a moment. "Kai might rely on me, but I care about you, Damien. We're mates. I am happy to stay up with my mate and comfort them when they can't sleep."

I lower my head in my hands. "They won't stop Langdon. I can't make them stop."

"The memories," he guesses. "The flashbacks? They only started when Winter stopped talking to you, and you learned about your father escaping his cell. I think that your fear is producing them."

He's probably right. "You must think I'm pitiful," I say weakly. "To be afraid of my father like this. Not to mention disgusting. I treated Winter to save my skin," I tell him, tears forming in the corner of my eyes. "I could have stopped hurting or bullying her at school. Instead, I chose to keep going. It's a wonder that Winter's forgiven me when I can't forgive myself."

Langdon runs a hand through his hair, sticking it up in different directions. "Has it occurred to you that maybe you need to forgive yourself," he argues. "You were a kid, Damien, making the best of a bad situation. You already confessed that you were afraid he would torture you as well. You were trying to survive," he argues. "Even if it meant hurting another person. We're not perfect. None of us are. All you can do is look forward and try to make amends with Winter now. She wants a relationship with you. You want one with her. The flashbacks are preventing you from looking forward."

"How can you even stand to be with someone like me?" I ask him thickly. "You're so damn handsome, you're perfect, you're confident, and you make me feel like I'm the only person in the world for you. Not once have you even judged me for what I did?"

He gives me a small smile. "I don't judge you because you're judging yourself enough for the both of us," he says calmly. "And I am with you not just because we're mates but because you're funny,

257

kind, sweet, and pretty damn good-looking yourself," he adds as I blush. I'm pretty certain my cheeks are beet red-right now.

I glance down at my empty mug and push it away. I hadn't even been aware I was still drinking from the mug.

"Damien," Langdon says quietly. "Your father will not lay a hand on you or Winter. You are both safe from him. Kai and I have a patrol on the lookout for him. He's never going to harm either of you again. I wish you believed that," he said with a shake of his head and an exhale.

"I wish I could, too," I say, ashamed and angry. "But until the bastard's caught, I'm always going to look over my shoulder expecting the worst, and so is Winter. I want this all to end."

"It will," Langdon says firmly. "You just have to hold on for a little longer."

It was easy for him to say but not so easy for me to do. Still, he's trying to help, and it's sweet. My mate genuinely cares for me. I love that he cares so much, even when I feel guilty. After all, he's probably got other things besides me that need attention. Still, it gives me a warm feeling inside.

Langdon finishes off his drink and stands up. "Do you feel able to go to sleep?" he asks.

I feel wide awake but give a small nod. In the worst case, I'll lie next to him until it's time to get back up.

His eyes narrow on me, and he looks suspicious. Uh oh. Maybe I wasn't convincing enough? He comes round to me and grabs my hand. His hands are nice and warm, although rough with calluses from all the training he does. He rubs my hand gently. His eyes search mine, and then he bends his head down and gives me a kiss, soft, gentle, his lips soft against mine.

"Let's go to bed," he breathes, pulling back, and I willingly follow him as he tugs on my hand and leads me back to the bedroom. Langdon plumps mine up as I quickly go to the bathroom, and I slowly climb onto the bed and snuggle down. Langdon climbs in beside me and pulls the bedcovers over the both of us. His arm pulls me against him, so my back rests against his chest. His other hand reaches over, and to my shock, he begins to stroke my hair.

It's soothing. His touch is gentle. The last time I was touched like this had been my mother soothing me back to bed. Despite myself, my eyelids begin to flutter closed. It's so relaxing. Langdon smiles down at me.

"Sleep," he soothes. "Sleep, Damien."

I yawn, and my eyelids close. He never stops stroking my hair. My body relaxes underneath the covers, and I feel myself beginning to get sleepy. I can't even fight it, and I don't want to. My body begins to drift off, and the last thing I hear, or think I hear before I'm fully asleep, is Langdon's voice saying, "I love you."

Chapter 114

Winter's POV

The pain in my head is excruciating. It's unlike any headache or migraine I've ever had before. It's so bad that I'm lying in bed with all the blinds closed and curtains pulled, the darkness surrounding me so that my eyes don't hurt from the sunlight. My head is pounding, and I'm so incredibly thirsty. No matter how much water I drink, it doesn't negate thirst. I'm also incredibly hot. Like I'm burning up. Maybe I've caught a virus or something. Who knows. I thought shifters very rarely got sick. This is the first time I've gotten sick like this ever. I don't want Kai to catch it, but he says he has a great immune system. In other words, he doubts he'll get it.

I'm so lonely. Since I've gotten sick, I've been avoided like the plague. But it's much more than that. There's a voice inside of me, and it's not Sabriel's. This is the secret I've been harboring for days, not telling anyone. Because I'm afraid. I'm afraid of what the voice constantly tells me to do. Sabriel's voice has gone completely silent. She's stopped speaking to me, and I know it has something to do with the evilness inside of me.

Kill them, kill them all, Winter. They are all betrayers, can't you see that? Your brother hurt you would be best if you hurt him back. Show him what it feels like.

Please leave me alone. I don't know who or what you are, but please go away.

Don't you understand yet? My voice is yours, child. The thoughts in your mind that you don't dare speak of, all the bad things you think about daily.

Chapter 114

I would never kill someone. That's a lie.

Is it? Right now, you're thinking about killing someone, aren't you? The one person who has hurt you the most? You want to hunt and kill him for everything he did to you and your brother. You crave his death. You want him dead. Why do you feel like that is so wrong?

The voice falls silent as I give a small sob. They are not wrong. I do want my father dead. He ruined my life and Damien's. Why should he be allowed to continue to live and hurt us? But the rest of it, the rest of it frightens me. I would never wish my mate or brother dead, no matter what they did to me in the past. I wish I could talk to Sabriel. I give it one more try.

Sabriel, do you hear me? I'm scared. I don't know what's happening to me. I don't know what's going on. Please speak to me. Let me hear your voice. I'm begging you. I don't know what I will do if I lose you forever. I miss you so much.

I'm begging to hear her voice. Part of me is fearful that I've lost my wolf forever. That Sabriel has vanished because I can no longer sense her now. Which means I can't shift into my wolf form either. The only defense I have is with my father coming. Without being able to shift, I'm vulnerable, weak, and reliant on others to keep me safe. It stings, and it sucks big time. Not to mention, I'm too afraid to tell Kai I've lost my wolf. Because I know he would panic and want me to go to the hospital for all sorts of tests. He has enough stress at the moment without me adding to it.

You have more strength at your fingertips than you think, Winter. You are not vulnerable. You are a hunter and huntress capable of much more than a pathetic shifter can do.

I don't want to know. Please stop talking in my head. I can't deal with this right now. I want Sabriel back.

When the voice speaks again, it's harsh and brutal. *Sabriel is gone. Get that through your thick head. There's just me now, and you'll have to learn to get along with me, or it will be a futile struggle between us. It would be best to embrace the strength, uniqueness, and fire within you. Even the parts you consider evil are a part of you, even if you try to ignore them. I am your only friend now. Deal with it, Winter.*

I lie there, quietly sobbing. The voice is getting stronger, more insistent. It sounds like it's constantly hissing and doesn't like Kai or the others. It often comments that I should push or poison them down the stairs. The worst thing is that the voice is so hard to ignore. Unlike with Sabriel, I can't cut it off or put a mind block up because it just breaks through. It taunts me, mocks me, and calls me names. But it sounds like me, and that's the part that's so frightening. Because what if the voice is me?

A knock on the door breaks my thoughts. "Winter, are you awake?" Kai calls, and I give a small grunt, watching the door swings open and blinking furiously as light enters the room. He comes and perches on the bed.

"How are you feeling?" he asks concerned. He reaches out and touches my forehead. His hand jerks back in shock.

"You're burning up," he exclaims, crossing to the bathroom. I say nothing. I feel hot, but not too much. I've been hot the last few days.

I hear the sound of running water. Kai comes back out. "A nice cool bath should do the trick," he says quietly. "It should help bring your temperature down at any rate."

I burrow under the covers. I don't want a cold shower right now. I don't want to leave the bed. But Kai isn't taking no for an answer. He pulls the covers off as I let out a squeal, scooping me up in his hands and carrying me to the bathroom. He stands me up and strips off my clothing while I let out a small murmur of protest. Then he picks me up and places me gently in the water.

I let out a small hiss. The water is cold, and it takes time for my body to adjust. When I do, I lean back in the bathtub, letting my body sink as the water washes over me. I start to feel cooler than I have in days. Kai sits on the floor next to the tub, not caring if he gets wet. His eyes are intently watching me. I feel self-conscious.

"How are you feeling otherwise?" he asks.

Chapter 114

Like I want to rip your head from your body, you pathetic, dumb shifter.

I must ignore the voice, my heart thudding wildly in my chest. I need to make Kai believe that everything with me is all right.

"I'm okay," I murmur. "Just have a bit of a headache and a bit hot. Otherwise, I'm all right, just tired," I assure him.

He doesn't believe me for a second. "Winter, you're not just a little bit hot. You're scalding to the touch," he says firmly. "As for the headache, how many days now?" he prods.

It's none of your business, you stupid mutt.

"A few days," I answer weakly, trying to concentrate on Kai and not the ugly voice in my mind.

"I'm worried about you. So are Damien and Langdon. I think that you should visit the hospital and see a doctor."

Don't let him force you. He doesn't know what he's talking about. We could hold his head under the water right now if we wanted to.

"I'll be fine. I need to rest and recover," I tell Kai dully. I clench my hands into fists under the water.

Kai doesn't look convinced, but I shoot him a pleading look, and he sighs.

"Fine, but if this continues, I will insist you see a doctor. Is that clear?" he asks sternly.

Crystal clear, I think miserably. "Yes," I answer quickly.

He clears his throat. "Look, I came up here to share with you that there still have been no sightings yet of your father."

What a shame. It means we must wait some more before killing the old bastard. Never mind, we can think of different ways to kill the man to pass the time.

"Patrol is still keeping a close eye. I hope that helps comfort you a little bit," Kai continues as I blink and refocus on him. "I know it's not much of a comfort, but at least we know he's another few days away."

"That's good," I say automatically. The voice snickers in my mind.

"Would you feel safer with Damien and Langdon?" asks Kai. "His house is further away from the pack house and is easier to defend?"

The question should be will Damien and Langdon feel safe with you in Langdon's house? Should we tell him that?

"Um, I would rather stay in my bedroom," I say quickly. "I feel safer with you, Kai," I add, lying through my teeth. Kai looks pleased with my answer. The poor bastard believes what I'm saying, and a fresh wave of guilt floods me.

"Of course, you're safe with me," he answers. "I just want to make sure you feel secure here."

"Well, I do," I answer quietly.

The water is more than freezing now, and I stand up, shivering slightly as Kai hands me a towel to wrap myself in. I do, my teeth chattering, and make a beeline back to the bedroom. I would get dressed, but prior experience has taught me that I'm about to go hot again, and quite frankly, I can't be bothered putting clothes on. Not this time, at least.

Kai lets out the water from the bath and saunters in, looking worried. "You look like you've lost weight," he comments, and I glance down at my body self-consciously. I hadn't realized, but now that he mentioned it, food had been the last thing on the agenda.

"How about I send something up?" he offers, and I realize he will get more concerned if I refuse.

"I would like that," I say calmly.

He comes over and gives me a peck on the cheek. "I have to go back and do some work, but I'll check on you later."

"All right," I say automatically.

"I'll send that food up," he promises. I nod.

He vanishes out the door, and I sigh with relief. The idea of food makes me nauseous, but it wouldn't hurt to at least try to eat something. Kai is as good as his word, and within minutes, there's a plate with a burger and fries, plus a Coca-Cola by my side as I eye it. The smell is amazing, and my mouth waters. It looks delicious.

Slowly, almost reverently, I pull the burger out of the bun and hold it between two fingers. I sniff. I'm almost drooling. I take a bite and almost moan with the sheer flavor of it hitting my taste buds. I devour the burger within moments, licking my lips when I'm done. The fries smell almost as good, but the second I put one in my mouth, I spit it back in disgust. It tastes like charcoal. Yuck. I wipe my mouth and send the fries scattering to the floor. I sip the Coke, and my stomach churns. It doesn't like it.

I frown. It's Coca-Cola, for heaven's sake. Since when did I stop liking soft drinks? It's perplexing. Reluctantly I place the drink back down on the bedside table. I guess I'm not drinking that, either. But my body is craving something, something more rich and flavorsome. I wish I knew what it was. The one small hamburger wasn't enough to satisfy it. Then I glance over at the mirror above my dresser and freeze. Two glowing red eyes stare back at me.

Chapter 115

Kai's POV

When I check on Winter later, she's fast asleep in the bed, snoring away lightly. I walk closer and frown. There are dried tears on her cheeks and puffiness around her eyes. She's been crying. But why? Is she that fearful of her father? Or is it from not feeling well? I hesitantly touch the side of her face. Her fever seems to have vanished, or at least for now, it's gone. It seems to have a habit of coming and going at the moment. Poor Winter. I sit on the bed and stare at my mate. She's had a lot going on and is under much stress. Her memories are coming back now in dribs and drabs. Thankfully, I'm still unsure how much she remembered our time together. I can't bring myself to push.

She stirs and mumbles in her sleep. It's adorable. Cute. The blanket slides down under her breasts as it moves, and I suck in a breath, staring at those creamy globes and feeling a twitch coming from my cock. God, she's beautiful. Storm wants her badly. He's disappointed when I tell him we must wait until Winter is better. He pouts in my mind, and I'm forced to put a block up so I don't have to listen to his constant whining.

As it is, I feel like I need to leave, my hands craving to touch her all over. It would be rude to disturb her sleep for something so crass. But before I can stand upright, her hand grabs my arm tightly. I'm surprised at her strength. She has a firm grip, and it's almost painful. That's laughable. I'm a big bad Alpha. She shouldn't be anywhere near as strong as me.

"Stay," she mumbles sleepily.

Chapter 115

I watch her eyelids flutter open, her eyes focusing on me. She gives me a tentative smile. "Please don't leave," she begs.

"I won't," I tell her, wondering why she's so upset. Something's happened, but I don't know what.

She struggles to sit, letting the blanket fall to her hips.

Don't look, don't look, don't look, I chant to myself, feeling hysterical. Typically, my eyes shoot to her breasts. Damn, my body and my eyes. Thank God she doesn't seem to notice that I'm acting like a horny teenager.

"Winter, what's wrong?" I ask, and she bites her lip and looks away.

Silence. I can hear the clock ticking in the room. It's that quiet. "Nothing," she says finally. "Nothing's wrong."

Right, and pigs can fly. She's lying. But I won't pressure her for the truth, not yet anyway.

"Are you hungry?" I ask instead. "I can get you some food."

She wrinkles her nose. She hasn't had much of an appetite lately. "No, thank you," she answers.

I'm feeling helpless to do anything. Then she takes a deep breath and gets to her hands and knees, eyeing me suggestively. Her eyes stray towards my cock, which is covered, thankfully, by my sweatpants. She licks her lips.

"I think I'm hungry for something else," she purrs. I gulp.

She stands up and moves so fast that she's almost a blur. I blink in astonishment. Man, can that girl move fast or what?

She slowly slides my pants down as I stand there trembling, too afraid to move and spoil the moment. I like this side of Winter, the confidence, and the teasing she exhibits.

My cock springs free, hard as a rock and erect as fuck. She licks her lips again and then sinks to her knees. She slowly licks the tip as I close my eyes and groan.

"You taste good," she breathes.

Fuck is she trying to get me to blow my load? She puts one hand on the end of the shaft and slowly, inch by inch, takes my cock inside her sweet, pretty little mouth. God, the feeling is so intense. It's all I can do to hold onto my self-restraint and self-control. Part of me is itching to get her onto that bed.

She begins to bob her head up and down, and I moan. Her throat is fucking tight, and the suction is unbelievable. Her hand moves back and forth, and I'm a goner. I'm panting like crazy, barely keeping myself upright while Winter continues, smiling. She knows exactly what she's doing to me, the little minx.

When I feel the tingles of an approaching orgasm, I force her to her feet. She looks up at me with those big innocent eyes of hers, her eyes sparkling with joy.

"My turn," I growl, undressing her slowly, reverently, before placing her on the bed, lying spread-eagled, waiting for me.

I crawl onto the bed and grab her ankles, keeping them apart. I bend my head and sniff her mound. My mouth waters. I want to taste her. Slowly, I lick along the folds of her pussy and hear her let out a small cry. I grin. I love hearing her cry in pleasure; she's about to do much of it now. I slowly lick along her clit, hearing her gasp as I continue. I slowly build up the pressure as she pants and writhes beneath me, unable to move her legs and forced to endure everything I do to her. Soon her body tenses, and I can tell she's almost ready to cum. I insert one finger into her slowly and pump it back and forth, continuing to lick her pussy as she moans.

"Oh, God, Kai…" she moans over and over.

I give a wicked grin. The girl has no idea what's going to happen next.

I insert a second finger and curl them both up, thrusting back and forth while my tongue stays on her. I'm hitting the G-spot, and her mouth is open in a silent scream. Seconds later, she screams out "Kai" for real as orgasm washes over her. I keep it going, forcing her to have a second orgasm as she wails and writhes, her body tensing, and arching. She screams again loudly, and I give her a grin, slowly letting go of her ankles and sitting on the bed looking nonplussed.

Chapter 115

She comes back down to earth and stares at me hungrily. "Please, Kai…" she pleads, and I cock my head at her.

"Please, Kai, what?" I ask, prodding her. "Tell me what you want, Winter," I growl. "Say it, say the words."

She's almost sobbing now. "Please, Kai, I want your cock inside me…" she whispers.

Well, she doesn't have to tell me twice. I arrange her on the bed, on her hands and knees, that delectable little ass right in front of me as she looks over her shoulder, unsure about this position. If she doesn't like it, I'll change it, I'm not a complete asshole, but I want her to try it at least.

"Trust me," I tell her, and she nods. I slowly run my cock along her slits, teasing her a little. She whimpers. Damn, she wants my cock badly. I'm desperate to be inside her sweet little pussy.

I line up at her entrance. "Ready?" I ask her, and she nods, looking shy.

I slowly, inch by inch, push my way inside of her. She arches her back, making it easier to gain access, although she probably didn't mean to. It was mere instinct. Fuck. She's so damn tight. I can feel her walls clenching around my cock.

"Oh, God, oh, God," she pants as I push in. "You feel so big," she whimpers. "I feel full."

I don't answer. Instead, I slowly pull out and thrust in again as she tries to keep her balance. I keep doing that, pulling all the way out and going back in as she trembles beneath my body. I want to take my time and make her feel every inch of me as I take her. Her little bottom is rocking back and forth, meeting my thrusts. I grip it and hold it still as Winter whines at me.

I begin to move a little faster, thrusting in harder. She grips at the sheets, her head lowered now, breathing in and out deeply.

"Fuck," I moan, feeling her ass against me as I take her. I reach around and squeeze her breasts, making her gasp. Fuck they are so soft. Everything about her is perfect. Just right.

I want her to cum again. Cum hard while my cock is inside of her. I reach around with my hand and finger Winter's clit furiously as she moans.

"Cum for me," I growl. "Cum for me, Winter."

She mewls, scrabbling at the sheets, her body beginning to tense as I give a wicked grin. Her body is responding right how I want it. I increase the pressure. She almost bucks beneath me.

"Cum for me," I hiss, and she bucks before her body stills, her walls clenching tightly around me as an orgasm washes over her body. I grin triumphantly.

"Kai..." she sobs. "God, Kai, I can't take much more."

I withdraw and flip her over so that she's lying on her back. Then I push back in while she's still recovering from the orgasm. I can thrust harder and faster in this position while bending and taking Winter's breast into my mouth. Her mouth falls open. She gasps. I begin to thrust as hard as possible, Winter meeting me halfway eagerly. Fuck. My cock is tingling now, and I can't help myself. Her walls are still throbbing and clenching around my cock. I give a loud growl and then tense, shooting my seed inside her.

Before she can move, my hand snakes back down to her clit, teasing it, touching it while I remain buried inside her. She wriggles and moans. "Please, God..." she begs, and I begin to furiously circle her clit making her whimper.

"Kai!" she screams, going over the edge, her body shuddering. *That's how I like to hear my name,* I think to myself smugly. Once her orgasm has finished, I pull out and get off the bed, grabbing a washcloth and bringing it back to Winter, who's still looking stunned.

I gently wash around her pussy, clean her up and then throw the damn thing in the hamper. I pull her into my arms and stroke her hair.

"Kai, that was," she begins with a hitch in her voice. "Amazing," she finished.

Chapter 115

"You make it amazing," I tell her, and I mean it. Werewolves are sexual creatures by nature, but it's always better to have sex with your mate and intended partner. She blushes.

"Would you stay with me a while?" she asks quietly. "Even if it's until I go back to sleep again? I don't want to be alone right now," she finishes.

"Of course, I can. I'm pretty tired after all that anyway, so why don't I catch a nap with you," I suggest.

Her eyes shine at me. *Yep, huge brownie points right there. Way to go, Kai.*

"Yes," she whispers, turning her back to me, snuggling under the covers, and looking over her shoulder. "Will you hold me, Kai?" she asks.

I would hold her until the end of time. I climb in beside her and pull her against me. I can hear her heart beating. It's thudding loudly and rather quickly. It must have been what we just did.

"Winter, is there anything you want to tell me?" I whisper.

"No," she murmurs. "I just need you to hold me right now."

Well, at least it was something. But in the back of my mind is a suspicion that Winter is hiding something, and it's something big. Why won't she talk to me? I'm her mate. I can be trusted. Whatever it is, I hope she spills her secret soon.

Chapter 116

Winter's POV

The voice in my head is getting stronger, more insistent constantly. It's bloodthirsty, wants me to hurt the people I love, and takes all my willpower to remember who I am anymore, let alone avoid doing anything the voice tells me to do. Kai is suspicious of me; I know he is. He might not have said anything, but his eyes are so intent when he watches me, like he's waiting for me to do something in front of him. Does he suspect that I'm changing? Part of me hopes not, but the more logical part is screaming out that he knows and has come to his conclusions.

The fever is still ongoing. But the rest of it, the fatigue, the sore joints, all of that has disappeared, and I've never felt better in my whole life. But I still can't speak to Sabriel. I miss her like crazy. I want to confide in Kai, but I'm afraid of what will happen if I do. What if he decides to put me in the dungeon because he thinks I might be dangerous? I can't risk that. Not when he's put me in the dungeon before.

Can't you hear their little heartbeats racing along the voice hisses, and don't they smell delicious and juicy? Just take a small taste of Kai and see how delicious he is. You know you want to. Give in to your desires, and embrace what you are becoming. Why try to hide it? You are strong. You are powerful. You are more than just a shifter now. Stop being such a coward and let the instinct take over...

It's getting harder to ignore the voice. Because even though I'm up in the bedroom, I can still hear Kai's heart thudding in his chest. It's beating steadily, and I can even hear the blood pumping through his veins. I lick my lips, wondering how his blood would taste if I were to take a sip. I frown and shake my head, pacing back and forth in the room. Something is up. Kai's heart rate is increasing. Which means he's feeling stressed. I open the door and creep down the stairs. I can already tell that Langdon and Damien are in the room, but to my surprise, they leave the study just as I make it to the door.

"Hey, Winter," Damien says gently, and I give him a small smile and a hug.

"Hey, where are you guys going?" I ask lightly.

They shoot each other a look. "Back to the house," Langdon says lightly. "Maybe watch some television or a movie. Relax," he finishes, grabbing Damien's hand and leading him away as Kai motions for me to sit down.

I barely hear Damien and Langdon leave the pack house. All my focus is on Kai and the worried expression he has on his face.

"So, Winter, how are you feeling?" he asks gruffly.

I raise my eyebrows. He's hiding something, but I'll play along for now.

"Better, except for the fever. Everything else is fine," I tell him. "I feel so much better."

He gives a small smile. "I'm glad. I was getting worried about you," he said lowly. "And was considering the hospital."

Thank God he hadn't forced me to go. "Well, as you can see, I'm fine," I say with a forced laugh. "Awesome."

He regards me steadily. I gulp and look around the room nervously. I'm trying to avoid looking at him. It doesn't help that his heartbeat is so much louder in here. It's almost pulsating in my head. I want to scream out. It's that loud. But I pretend everything is normal. That nothing is wrong, and I'm the same old Winter I've always been. I have to keep the facade going for as long as possible.

"Nothing, seems off at all?" asks Kai.

I blink at him innocently. "No, why do you ask?"

He huffs and sits back in his chair. "No reason," he says quietly. Liar.

"So what's happening at the moment?" I ask between gritted teeth. "Because I could tell that Langdon was lying to me."

Kai grimaces. "He's always been a terrible liar," he admits.

I wouldn't have to ask if they had been discussing whatever it was like normal people in the study because I would have easily overheard them. They'd been smart enough to mind-link with each other instead, so I hadn't.

Kai gives a loud groan. "I don't want you to panic," he begins, leaning forward, his eyes watching me without blinking. "But there's a possible sighting of your father approaching the territory. We can't say it's your father for certain. It could just be a lone traveler."

I say nothing. I feel this inexplicable desire to know if it is my father heading toward the pack. My hands clench into fists. I feel anger flare inside my breast. This was it. This was the moment we'd all been waiting for. The moment has finally arrived.

"How far away?" I ask casually.

Kai looks at me warily. "He's almost an entire pack away. We wouldn't even know about him if they hadn't called to inform me of a stranger coming this way. It will take at least a day on foot or several hours as a wolf for him to arrive, Winter, so there's no need to be hasty," he finishes.

No need to be hasty! There was every goddamn need to be hasty. If it was my father, we should use surprise attack him and kill him. Why would we wait? It didn't make sense. I don't even care that it's just one shifter that we should easily be able to deal with. All I can think about is how much my father enjoyed torturing me and the fucked up childhood I had because of that bastard. I'm ready to deal with him myself.

"All we can do is wait," Kai says quietly. "You're protected here, Winter. Remember that."

My head isn't listening to him at all. Instead, the voice persists in my mind, telling me we must kill my father to take care of him alone. I let the voice wash over me. It's becoming soothing, saying everything I'm already thinking and feeling. It's right. We needed to do this on our own, not wait for Father to come here, but rather take the fight to him.

"Let's go get some rest," Kai says, and I stare at him incredulously.

Does he think I can sit around and relax right now? Is he kidding?

He gets up and walks around the desk, holding my hand and gently tugging me behind him. I was so stunned that I let him walk woodenly up the stairs and into the bedroom again.

He's trying to trick you, Winter. There's a reason he wants you in this room. Don't let him control you. Don't let him lock you up like an animal. Don't let him take away the chance to kill that evil father of yours finally...

I stare at Kai suspiciously. He's rifling in his pocket and comes out with a key. Son of a bitch. The voice was right. Kai was trying to lock me up in the bedroom. How could he do this to me?

"This is for your safety, Winter," Kai says quietly, going to the door as I stare at him with wide eyes. "You've been stressed out about your father for weeks; this way, you know he won't get to you."

"Kai..." I say slowly. "Don't do this. I'm begging you not to lock that door."

He looks at me sadly. "I need to know you won't try something stupid."

That's enough for me. I race over and grab his arm, squeezing tightly, using my new strength to get him to drop the key to the floor. His jaw drops open, and he wrestles with me.

"I won't let you lock me up," I snarl at him. "I'm not some animal you need to cage."

"That's not what I was doing," he grunts.

"Liar," I hiss. "I should have known I couldn't trust you."

We wrestle some more, Kai attempting to get the key. I move fast, faster than I thought possible, and circle him. Without hesitation and with a fair bit of anger, I raise my hand and punch Kai hard enough to send him toppling to the floor. He's laid out flat, and his eyes are closed. Shit. How hard did I hit him? Hard enough to knock him completely out. I hesitate and then take hold of the key on the floor. I feel slightly guilty and stare down at Kai for a moment. Then I gently shut the bedroom door, locked it with the key, and threw it down the stairs. He should never have tried to do this. This was his fault. Stupid man.

Well done, Winter. See how easily you overpowered Kai? That's how strong you are now. You don't need his protection. You don't need anyone to protect you. You are a force to be reckoned with. They should all be fearing you…

I start heading down the stairs. Relieved that Damien and Langdon aren't in the pack house. The last thing I want is to fight both of them as well. I do no doubt that they'll try to stop me. I head out onto the grass. Very few pack members are around, and those merely ignore my existence or wave quickly. This is perfect. I run towards the forest. I'm so fast that trees and scenery pass by in a blur. I'm faster than I ever was as a shifter. I easily get past the pathetic patrol we currently have on. Then I pause. I have no clue what direction to head in. But maybe the voice inside my head might know.

Smell him out. He's your father, so you will easily recognize the bastard's scent. It won't change. Let your instincts and sense of smell guide you to his location. You can smell things from miles away when you concentrate on it. You can also hear things from far away, such as footsteps. Listen for the sound of cracking twigs and crunching leaves. Even shifters make noises as they run, do they not?

I wrinkle my nose and then take a giant whiff. I'm almost sick as the pungent scent of alcohol and cigarettes hits my nostrils. The scent is reminiscent of my father, that's for sure. I can also smell strong body odor and old food. Yuck. He's on foot rather than in shifter form, which is surprising. But if he's drinking, it won't be too much of a surprise. He was always fond of his damn alcohol. It means he's moving slowly. As I'm listening, I can tell that he's not even traveling in a straight line. He's weaving back and forth. He's drunk. Good God, how stupid could he be? This was going to be way too easy. My lips curve into a smile. I have nothing to fear. He's incapable of fighting in such poor conditions.

This was my chance. Before Kai wakes up and before he's found. I take a deep breath and center myself. My eyesight becomes even more focused as I look in the direction I need to go. I clench my hands into fists and narrow my eyes. My heart thuds loudly in my chest. I begin to run, trees and scenery passing by. I smirk. My father is about to get a big surprise and a not-so-warm welcome from his only daughter. I relish the chance to finally kill the man who's made my life a living hell for most of my life. I feel sorry for Damien, who won't be able to do the same.

Chapter 117

He's close. The smell of his disgusting body odor and the blatant scent of cigarettes and alcohol is getting stronger, more pungent. My heart is racing in my chest. My hands are clenched into fists. I'm ready for this. Ready to face the monster who made my life a living hell and ruined my childhood forever.

We will slaughter him and leave his entrails for the animals to consume. Drain him of his blood and tear his body from limb to limb. He will never mess with us again, and he will never hurt another human being again. He deserves to die. You know that, Winter. He can not be allowed to live…

I'm also dangerously aware that Kai might have woken up by now or been found by Langdon and Damien. *He's going to be incredibly pissed when he wakes up,* I think to himself a little guiltily. But then, what had given him the right to think it was okay to lock himself up in the bedroom for my safety? Did he think I was that fragile and that frightened? Was I coming across as pathetic? If that's the case, I must show him how capable and strong I am.

He's an arrogant fool. You didn't need him to protect you like that. He tried to lock you up in a cage like an animal. The irony is that you are so much stronger than him, Winter. He's a fool if he hasn't realized that yet…

I try hard to ignore the voice, but it's persistent. It puts thoughts and ideas in my head as I run, and eventually, blocking them out is impossible. Or maybe I'm just tired of blocking it out. I run, my breath coming in short puffs, but I never get tired or out of breath. That, considering the distance, is a small miracle in itself. My eyes are sharp, taking in every minute detail as I go past. I jump, and it's a massive leap, taking me closer faster than running. But I don't mind taking it a little easy. After all, I'm unsure what to do when I encounter my father.

But I can't prolong the meeting any longer because I sense him and his presence up ahead. I slow down to just a walk, my eyes scanning ahead as he walks into view. He looks just like I remember him, with the same greasy dark hair tied in a ponytail, the small pot belly, the stained and dirty clothes, bare feet, and repugnant smells surrounding him. He hasn't changed one iota, not even after spending time in Johnathon's dungeon. It made no difference to the bastard at all.

He stops when he sees me, and I cringe at the wide smile on his face. I can tell he's drunk because he's weaving slightly as he walks instead of walking in a straight line. God knows where he got the alcohol from. Probably stole it on his way here.

"Winter," he says cheerfully as I glare at him. "It's been a long time."

Not long enough, I think to myself grimly, feeling rage inside me. "What is it you want, Father?" I ask angrily. "Why bother coming here?"

He pretends to look hurt, but the bastard does not fool me. "Why you're my family, Winter, you and Damien. I came to take you both back home, where you belong," he adds. "I am your proper guardian, after all."

"No, you want something else. What is it?" I ask patiently, as if he wants us to be a family. What a pathetic liar he's attempting to be.

His eyes narrow, and then a calculating look appears on his face. I knew I was right and that he had an ulterior motive.

"Fine, I figure that you and your so-called mate, he's an Alpha, isn't he? Would pay money to get me out of your lives. After all, I'm currently unemployed because of you and Damien. The least

279

you could do is set me up. I'm sure your mate has plenty of money at hand."

"You want us to pay for you to go away," I say lightly, incredulous at his demands. Is he this moronic and delusional?

He shrugs. "Why not. We both know you wouldn't want me anywhere near you after what I did to you," he says slyly.

My voice rises. "You tortured me. Don't pretend like that was nothing. You tortured and abused me for years, and now you want me to pay you money to go away."

He laughs. "I tortured you, you little bitch, because you reminded me of your mother. God," he exclaims. "Even now, you look just like the bitch. I can't stand it. I could never look past it. It's like she's there, constantly getting a dig in at me, reveling in my misery."

I blink, confused. From his speaking, it almost sounds like he believes Mother is alive. But he'd told us she'd died in the rogue attack. I begin to feel suspicious. "Mother didn't die in the rogue attack, did she, Father? You just told us that story to save face."

His face contorts, and he looks at me meanly. "What would that information be worth to you," he taunts. "Would it make you feel better, Winter? To know that she abandoned all of us to be with her precious lover? That she never came back for you or Damien? I cared for you both housed you, and fed you. In contrast, she stayed away, enjoying herself and forgetting everything she had left behind. Your mother was nothing but a whore in the end. She ran away from me and our life together, telling me she wasn't happy. Ha. You don't do that to your mate. You don't just leave them. The bitch had the nerve to reject me. I wish I had killed her. She deserved it."

I feel numb. The way Father spat out the words, his disgust evident in his voice, and the lingering hurt all felt like he was telling the truth. Had my mother abandoned me and Damien without a care in the world? Perhaps she hadn't thought Father could lay a hand on us. Maybe she meant to come back and couldn't for some reason. It all whirled in my mind. The only thing that remained crystal clear was that my mother was alive. She was alive and safe after all these years of being punished for her death. Tears come to my eyes.

"You're not getting a goddamn dime out of me," I tell my father, my voice dripping with hatred. "Leave now before it's too late." Although I suspect it's already too late as my bloodlust becomes overwhelming.

The voice in my head is getting louder, and it's becoming harder to ignore, particularly with the rage I'm feeling inside me. I want to tear my father apart.

"I'm not leaving," he spits out. "Why don't you make this easier on yourself and come to me, Winter? You've always been such a placid little thing."

I cock my head. I'm not placid anymore, but he doesn't appear to know it. As I eye him, I realize he doesn't see me as a threat.

"Where is she?" I ask bluntly. "Something tells me you know where she is, Father. Where did our mother go after she left your sorry ass?"

He glares. "I don't know where the bitch is. If I did, she would no longer be alive," he spat out. I believe him. He's so petty that he would have tracked her down. Hurt her like the coward that he was.

Kill him. He lied to you and Damien. He told you that your mother died in a rogue attack when he knew she was alive after all these years. You could have looked for your mother years ago if it wasn't for him. Don't let him control you anymore. Get rid of the asshole forever...

My steps are slow but steady. A triumphant grin comes over his face as I walk towards him. I pretend to look meek and weak like the old Winter he used to. I feel what feels like fangs come out of my mouth. His mouth drops open. He points at me. "Your eyes are red," he splutters, and before he can shift or do anything, I feel my body move so fast it's a blur. I lightly grip him around the throat, preventing him from shifting, my eyes glaring into his. I'm enjoying his weakness, his struggle. The idiot is so drunk that he couldn't have shifted successfully anyway. How stupid could one man be?

His hands clutch at mine, frantically trying to move them. I throw his body across the ground and watch it hit a tree. He gets to his feet, trying to shift, but after a few bones cracking, he returns to human form. You would have thought he would make sure he was sober when coming to the pack, but nope, he'd had one too many drinks.

I grab him and raise him high, delighting in how strong I am and how feeble he is compared to me. I lick my lips, feeling hungry, hearing his heart race in his chest and his blood pump through his veins.

"You bitch!" he wheezes. "Monster."

Maybe I am a monster. But he's not one to throw stones. Because he's the worst abusive monster I know. I slowly lower him so he's facing me and stare at the nape of his neck. The fangs or canines? Whatever they are, they protrude out of my mouth. Instinctively I place them against my father's neck and then push down.

Blood, so much blood to drink. It eases my thirst and soothes my sore throat. It feels deliciously warm, rich, and potent. I hum in ecstasy as I continue to drain him, his body struggling, then going limp as I continue. Soon enough, the blood runs out, and I give a small whine of disappointment. My father's body is limp, and I drop him to the ground, staring down at his ashen face. I still have so much anger inside of me. So much rage. My nails turn sharp like claws.

My hands thrust inside the body, and I pull out his heart, smiling with glee as the blood stains my hands. I throw it across the forest and return to the body, pulling out his intestines and entrails. I sniff, sensing that someone is coming up behind me. My body tenses. Would this be yet another enemy to destroy? Or a friend? The scent is familiar, but I'm in a haze. All I see is red everywhere. I desire nothing more than to keep killing, to find more blood to drink. I can already tell wild animals are nearby, and I lick my lips, hungry again.

"Winter, sweetheart, look at me," I hear from behind me.

Chapter 117

I frown, puzzled. I recognize the voice. I'm sure of it. Slowly the red begins to fade from my eyes. The anger begins to fade as well.

"Winter, look at me," continues Kai.

I'm reluctant. Now that I've returned to myself, I shudder at the dead body lying at my feet. I feel sick to my stomach. I stumble backward. What have I done? My God, what kind of monster am I? But then I remember everything, and it takes all I have not to kick the dead body at my feet, feeling nothing but disgust at the man who dared to call himself my father. I'm not sorry he's dead.

"Winter," Kai's voice persists, and I slowly, quietly turn around, cringing at the horrified look on everyone's faces.

Kai is the first to get over his initial shock. He blinks a few times, then slowly moves toward me. His eyes dart to my father's body, but he says nothing. I look down and see blood trickling down my shirt.

"Kai," I say, my voice shaking. "I don't know what to do."

He gathers me into a hug. "It's all right, sweetheart. We'll figure this out together."

I shake my head. "No, you don't get it. I know that Thomas turned me into a hybrid," I whisper, and Kai holds me tighter.

"I've suspected that he might have done for a while, but it's only now that I am certain about it," Kai tells me.

I shiver. "I'm a monster," my voice cracks. "I'm disgusting."

"No, you're not," Kai says gruffly, turning me away and walking back towards Langdon and Damien. "I don't care if you're a hybrid, Winter, we'll work it out. I still love you no matter what," he says firmly, his eyes staring directly into mine. "You are still the woman I fell in love with. I don't blame you for what happened here," he says wryly. "It might have been nice if you hadn't knocked me unconscious."

"Sorry," I whisper guiltily.

"I still love you, Winter, as well," chimes in Damien, patting me awkwardly on the shoulder.

"I as well," says Langdon gruffly.

I say nothing as Kai steers me away toward the pack house grounds. But in my head, all I can remember is that my mother is out there, somewhere, still very much alive. How was I going to tell Damien? Or worst, should I tell my brother that our mother abandoned us, even to save her life?

Chapter 118

Damien's POV

What Winter did to our father will remain in my memories forever. But if I have to admit to anything, she was determined to take him down alone. So what if she's half-vampire? She's a badass, as far as I'm concerned. The only thing bothering me now is her words once we got her back to the pack house. "Our mother is still alive, Damien."

I wanted to scream at her that she had it all wrong, that mother must have died in that rogue attack. Because if she didn't, then where was she? How could she have abandoned her children as though they meant nothing to her? What mother would willingly leave her children behind? But there never had been a grave to visit, a place to grieve our mother. Our father was a lying bastard. That was the truth, and now I had to deal with the overwhelming guilt that Winter had been tortured for a reason that never existed in the first place. That is, if he spoke the truth. He could be trying to mess with our heads again. It wouldn't surprise me. I bet he never thought Winter would be capable of killing him.

I think back to one of my favorite memories of her. It's nighttime. I was always one of those kids who could never fall asleep at night. Most parents would be furious, but my mother would smile at me and motion me to follow her. My little legs would follow her outside, and we would lie down in the grass, staring at the sky with all the twinkling stars above us.

"Damien, look," she would say, pointing to a direct constellation and telling me what it was. "That one's the archer," she told me, her hair rippling in the wind.

I would cuddle beside her, my head on her shoulder, snuggling in as she held me. She always smelt so sweet, like flowers, and her hair was soft and silky. She would kiss me on my forehead and hold me close. I was always so excited to spend this time with her. It was our little secret. Even my father didn't know we went outside to spend time together.

We would lie there until I started to get sleepy. As soon as I started to yawn, she would give a small peal of laughter and get to her feet, gently pulling me up as well. Sometimes I was so tired she would have to carry me, but she never complained. She would tuck me into bed, pulling the covers over me.

"Go to sleep, my little cub," she would tease, kissing me softly on the forehead and disappearing out of the room. I always felt bad that I woke her up, but she seemed to like our time together, or at least I thought she did...

As a little boy, I adored my mother and loved her beyond all reason. She was the one who hugged you and dried your tears. She made cookies when I felt sick and told me stories at bedtime. She always had a smile on her face and laughter on her lips. I remember how she hugged me for no reason other than feeling like I needed one. Winter and I had both loved her to bits. Our father had also adored her, or at least that's what I remember. Is it possible my memories are wrong?

I storm into Langdon's house, my anger rising as I think about my mother. Winter had misheard her father when he told her she was still alive. Either that or he was messing with her. That would be like the bastard, to mess with our minds and break our hearts again. My hands clench into fists. I wish I had gotten there sooner to hear the asshole tell it too. I would have known immediately that he was lying. Winter was just too gullible for her good, that was all. But I was lying, now, to myself. Trying to make myself feel better, and it wasn't working.

"Hey," I hear a soft voice and turn to see a concerned-looking Langdon. "I heard what Winter said. Are you all right?" he asks.

Chapter 118

I don't know what to say. Am I all right? No, I'm no way near all right. I take a deep shuddering breath.

"I don't know."

He reaches over to embrace me. "I'm here for you if you want to talk. Just want me to hold you. Just tell me what you need."

I explode, jerking out of his grasp and punching the wall, leaving a huge dent behind. My hand stings, but I ignore the pain, enjoying the numbness coming over me.

"She can't be alive," I went to Langdon, who was watching wide-eyed, his jaw clenched. "Father is doing what he does best and fucking with our minds!" I shouted, punching the wall again. "There's no way my mother would have abandoned Winter and me!" I almost scream, spittle flying everywhere. "No mother leaves her children behind, do they?" I ask him, turning to face him directly. "I'm right, aren't I? No mother willingly leaves her children behind?" I stifle a sob.

"Oh, Damien…" Langdon breathes, coming closer and gripping my face between his two hands. "Listen to me. You can't let this break you. Your father could be lying. We'll work it out. But don't break down now on me. You're stronger than this," he whispers.

I lean into him, my whole body trembling, my head on his shoulder now as he hugs me tight. The silence is comforting. I hurt so much inside that it's like a pile of daggers being stabbed directly into my heart.

Langdon grasps my hand, gently tugging me towards the stairs and the bedroom. I follow without resisting, lost in my thoughts and bitterness. We make it to the bedroom, and he pulls the covers down when I stop him, grabbing hold of his arm with desperation.

I kiss him hard, rough, needing to feel his lips on mine. He responds, his hand gripping my hair, making me delightfully moan. I need him with a fierceness that frightens me. But Langdon seems to know it too. His tongue darts inside my mouth and caresses my own as I moan. He tastes so good. My hands gripped his shoulders, my body swaying gently as we kissed.

His hands slowly slide underneath my shirt, and I shudder at how warm they are against my skin. He gently squeezes me and then, breaking off the kiss, slides my shirt up and over my head, throwing it across the room and letting it fall to the ground. He undoes the belt on my jeans and slowly pulls it away as I suck in a breath. He pulls my pants down slowly, looking up at me, his eyes gleaming in the room's darkness.

My cock stands erect as I blush at him. But he doesn't seem to mind, licking his lips with appreciation. "Someone's excited already," he teases before gripping my thighs and kneeling.

"Wait, Langdon," I say roughly, but it's too late. He's already lowered his head and licked the end of my shaft as I close my eyes and groan.

"Fuck," I whimper as he slowly places his mouth over my cock and takes me inside his mouth. He slowly moves back and forth as my body tenses, the feeling of pleasure overwhelming me.

"Hold still," he growls, and I obey instantly, whimpering as he moves even faster, taking all of me inside. My body is tense, and I can feel my impending orgasm.

"Langdon…" I whisper, trying to warn him. "If you keep doing that, I'm going to…" I trail off helplessly as he gives me a grin and continues. I shudder and then shout, spilling my seed inside his mouth. Langdon drinks it all up and stands up while I stand there, trying not to fall.

"Get on the bed," Langdon purrs.

I climb onto the bed and feel his arms adjust me so I'm lying on my side with my back to him. I glance over my shoulder and anxiously watch Langdon take off his clothes. Goddamn, that man is delicious. He chuckles, seeing my wide eyes and blatant staring.

"Like what you see," he growls.

"Oh, yeah," I mutter with a smile.

He comes up behind me, cuddling close. I feel his erect cock poking me in my bottom as I wiggle against him.

Chapter 118

"Just a moment," he says, sounding strangled. I smirk. I'm guessing he's dangerously close to his peak at this rate.

I moan as his finger enters me, slowly stretching me out as I pant and writhe. Langdon begins to kiss the nape of my neck, hard, rough, making me submit to him. I would submit to this gorgeous man forever if I had the chance.

Another finger, and I feel stuffed. He thrusts them back and forth slowly as I mewl, clutching the sheets. Langdon's breath is short and uneven as he bites me gently on the neck. "Can't take much more," he groans. "Are you ready for me?" he chokes out.

"Oh, God, yes," I moan, disappointed when I feel his fingers slowly withdraw. Then I feel him at my entrance, and my head falls back as he slowly enters me, inch by delectable inch, until he's inside of me, his hands gripping tightly to my waist.

He withdraws and then slowly thrusts inside again. God, he's fucking huge, and it feels goddamn amazing, considering how tight I am. He's gentle with me, careful, my body rocking back and forth to meet his thrusts in a frenzy.

"Fuck you're tight," pants Langdon.

"God, I can feel all of you inside me," I pant. "You're massive," I say gruffly.

He lets out a small snort of laughter, then withdraws completely.

"Langdon..." I complain, pleading.

He rolls me over onto my back and lines himself back up again, his eyes staring directly into mine.

"I want to see your face as I fucking cum," he says loudly.

He slams into me. Thank fuck. Right now, I'm desperate for some rough fucking. He lifts my legs over his shoulders and pounds into me repeatedly. I can't stop crying out. My whole body is quivering. He's hitting some spot, and my cock has gone fully erect again. My hands clutch at the bedsheets, and I'm repeatedly whimpering as pleasure washes over me.

"Cum for me," he growls. "Cum for me, Damien."

My mouth falls open. My head falls back. "I can't," I pant. "Hold on much longer."

"Don't," he roars, and that's all it takes. My body tenses and my cock spurs my seed all over the bed. Langdon gives me a wicked grin.

"Good boy," he says with a wink.

He's rougher now, with an intent look, his eyes pitch black, meaning his wolf is close to the surface. He's biting his lip. He's in a frenzy now. "Goddamn," he whispers, and then I feel his body stiffen, his seed spilling inside me. I cry out, Langdon slowly withdrawing his cock from inside me, collapsing beside me.

"I needed that," I admit to him as he gives me a quick peck on the lips.

"I know," he answers. We both look at each other with a grin. "But I also think we both might need a bit of a clean-up," he says wrily.

I chuckle. We both strip the bed and then wander into the bathroom. Neither of us is shy with each other. He starts the shower and motions me inside. I groan out loud and let the water wash over me. Langdon hands me the washcloth.

"Thanks," I mutter.

I wash myself, fully aware that he's watching my every move.

"Damien," he says lowly. "I know you're hurting right now, and that's okay. But would it maybe help if you told me a little bit about your mother and what she was like?"

I close my eyes under the water. "My mother was the most beautiful woman I'd ever seen," I begin, getting lost in my memories.

Chapter 119

Winter's POV

The dungeon is cold and dismal. But I don't dare complain. I had insisted they put me down here in the first place, for everyone's safety, even when they had tried to protest against it. But my actions seem futile, stupid. I should never have bothered. Because if I wanted to, I could easily get myself out of there. There's the smell of old blood in the air. And it's disgusting, my nose wrinkling in disgust. I huddle underneath the blanket Kai gave me, shivering profusely and wondering at my actions. Will this keep all of them safe? I doubt it. I can't get the image of my father out of my mind. What did I do to him? The perverse pleasure I took in pulling out his entrails from his lifeless body, the screams that echoed through the forest. It was like another person had taken over, a different Winter, one who was evil and enjoyed every bit of harm she did to him. Who, even now, wished he'd put up more of a fight so that she could have hurt him even more than she had.

I feel numb. It's hard to explain. I should have felt happy, satisfied, and joyful that my father was dead. After all, I certainly enjoyed killing him. But the happiness and satisfaction have worn off. Now I'm glad he won't ever touch or hurt me again, let alone Damien. He was a horrible person. The pack would be much better off without that drunken alcoholic loser member. I won't ever have to look over my shoulder again and wonder when the next hit is coming. Or feel his flesh as it smacks into mine, or feel his breath as he whispers things into my ear. That bastard is gone, and part of me is guilty that I feel nothing over it, no sadness or guilt.

We need to get out of here. Why do you keep us locked up, Winter? Why do you not embrace the power that you possess? You hunted down your father, and he'll never hurt you again. Did you not enjoy it, Winter? Hearing his screams and pleas for mercy. Forcing him to die as a pathetic human instead of a shifter? That man will never lay a hand on us ever again. Why won't you convince Kai to let us out of this pathetic prison? It won't be long until we drink again and sate our thirst...

The voice is persistent, ever present in my mind, even as I try desperately to tune it out. It's loud, however. More of a constant hiss than anything. A lot different to Sabriel. God, I miss her. I would give anything to hear a bad or lame joke from my wolf. She would make me laugh without even trying. Goddamn, she was a sassy wolf. Not to mention pretty. I'm sure she would have a solution to this problem. One that didn't involve a dungeon cell.

Heavy footsteps on the stairs. Kai walks down slowly, holding a food tray. He opens the cell door and places the food on the floor without spilling a single drop. Reluctantly he closes the door again. I eye the food with interest. There's juice, a muffin, a bagel, and some fruit. I reach for the juice first, but the second the liquid hits my throat, I gag and convulse, throwing up the contents. I wipe my mouth, feeling miserable, and slowly reach for the muffin. It tastes like dust in my mouth, I cough it up, and the food flies across the room. I look at Kai, who is staring at me grimly.

"I think we need to face the facts, Winter. You don't need food or drink. You need blood," he breathes.

I shake my head. I refuse to believe that. I don't want to face the facts. I want to shy away from them for as long as possible.

Idiot, we drained your father's blood, remember? It will only keep you going for a small amount of time until you need more. You will need more, I'm warning you. So I would start accepting that we are a vampire and get over it already. Unless you want to slowly starve yourself to death, which is a painful way to die, be free, Winter. Save yourself...

Chapter 119

"I can't drink blood," I tell Kai miserably. "I won't do it. There must be something else we can do," I say desperately, but he looks completely stymied.

"What if you just drank a little" he suggests quietly, a determined look on his face as he holds out his wrist. Surely he must be joking?

Something comes over me, and I stare at the veins, licking my lips. I can hear the steady sound of his heartbeat and blood rushing through his veins. I begin to feel thirsty as I stare at it. Kai moves it closer to me.

"Kai, no, don't," I say weakly, but he doesn't listen and shoves his wrist and hand through the cell bars as I look at him, completely horrified. Does he have any idea what he's doing to me right now?

Doesn't his heartbeat and blood pulsating through his body sound so nice? We don't have to take all of his blood. We can take just a little. Enough to keep us going and get rid of this hunger and thirst. It's better than killing someone for their blood...

Damn, this voice won't shut up. But it's beginning to make sense. God, I feel disgusted with myself. Kai is holding steady, his eyes staring directly at me.

"Winter, drink," he says with a low growl. "I want to see if you can restrain yourself from taking too much. I want you to do this for me."

I sidle closer. I feel my canines (I hate calling them fangs, so canines it is for now) slowly protrude out of my mouth. Kai's eyes widen, but he doesn't move. I grab his wrist tightly, making Kai wince in pain from the strength of my grip, and bring his wrist to my mouth.

Slowly, gently, I pierce the skin of his wrist, and blood rushes into my mouth. It's sweet and flavorful, and I moan as I suck, letting it trail down my throat. It's refreshing, and I drink until I see Kai's hand tremble. Feeling repulsed, I immediately drop his hand and move back away, wiping my mouth with the back of my hand.

I no longer feel thirsty or hungry. Instead, I feel amazing, refreshed, like I could run ten marathons and never tire. All my cuts and scrapes are miraculously healed, and I almost jog in place. Kai licks his wound, and I feel overwhelming guilt. "I'm so sorry," I begin apologizing, but he holds up his hand, stopping me.

"I told you to do it," he interrupts. "And I would do it all over again. You can't see yourself right now, but you're practically glowing and look much healthier." He sounds amazed, like a massive transformation before his eyes.

See how good we feel with fresh blood in our system? Don't you want to feel like this all the time? Be this strong all the time?

"I guess the vampire side of me is stronger than the shifter side," I mutter without thinking, still disgusted with myself.

"Maybe, but you held back from taking too much. Now will you stop being so foolish and come out of there?" he asks, exasperated. "I trust you, Winter, not to kill me if that helps," he says, trying to lighten the mood.

I can't help but laugh at that. But I'm still a little hesitant. Kai gives me puppy dog eyes. "Look, vampire chick or not, I still love you as my mate. This doesn't change that. I will stay by your side no matter what," he promises.

I sigh and step back. "Fine, will you let me out, please," I say lightly, and he grins, opening the doors to the cell at once. I walk out slowly. My eyesight has become sharper, even sharper than a shifter, as I take everything in. He grips my hand and gently squeezes it. We walk upstairs together. I spot Damien on the grounds with Langdon, training. As I slow down to watch, he looks ferocious, and I'm impressed at how well he's doing against his opponent. Kai follows my gaze. "I'm impressed that you can see the training," he comments. "Because while I can see it, I can't make out who is doing the fighting."

"Langdon and Damien," I tell him with a smile. "And Damien is kicking ass."

"He's gotten really good," Kai comments with a grin. "Langdon has been training him hard."

Chapter 119

"Are you sure I should be back in the house?" I ask nervously. "I still think the dungeon is safer for all of you."

"Let me decide what's safe for me. None of us wanted you to lock yourself up in the first place," Kai said sternly. "That was all you. I bet you're exhausted after spending a night there."

I shake my head. "Not really. I could go and run for hours."

"Well, I'm' hungry," Kai comments with a sidelong glance at me. "How about we sit in the dining room?" he suggests.

Sitting at the table while he grabs some sandwiches, I'm more than up for that. I swear the man can eat his body weight in food and still want more.

He munches on the food while I relax against the chair. I don't know how to feel. I should feel repulsed at being part vampire, but part of me what happened to me, although if Thomas weren't already dead, I'd be killing him with my bare hands.

"Kai, what if we can't find a way to turn me back?" I ask hesitantly.

He swallows hard. "I have an idea about that. The werewolf king's wife is a witch. We could maybe ask her for help. She might know a spell or ritual that would take away the vampire part of you so you would no longer be a hybrid."

I don't know how to feel about that, but I feel excited at the thought that something could be done.

"When can we do it?" I ask hurriedly.

Kai shakes his head. "The werewolf King is visiting packs on the other side. We can contact him once he's back on our side of the world."

"Oh," I say quietly, feeling a little deflated. I guess I shouldn't have gotten my hopes up so quickly. *Silly Winter,* I chide myself. At least Kai has come up with some plan. It was better than nothing. It was a possibility, and that was something to cling onto.

I twirl my hair with my finger, looking off into the distance.

You will not be able to get rid of me. I will never let you go. Foolish girl. Do you think a witch helps you? You are stuck being a hybrid whether you like it or not. It is time you accepted it…

"Your brother is a little upset at the moment, but once he's calmed down, I'm sure he'll want to see you," Kai suggests.

"He's upset about what I told him about our mother, right?" I ask lowly.

Kai gives a small nod. "How does he think I feel?" I snarl, scratching the tabletop. "Finding out after all this time that Mother was alive and Father was lying while torturing me. Does he think I found it easy to listen to it? Or does he think I'm lying?" I hiss.

"Calm down, Winter. I think he's finding it hard to accept the possibility that your mother is alive," Kai says delicately.

I grunt at him, feeling disgruntled. Stupid Damien.

My hand goes up to my neck subconsciously, tracing where the mark from Kai used to be until Thomas manages to remove it. I feel sad at the loss of it. Wait a minute. My eyes widen in disbelief. Is that why I can't hear Sabriel anymore because I lost my mark? My mind begins to race, a mile a minute. If that's the case, would having Kai mark me bring her back? My mind begins to go into overdrive. I feel a spark of joy at my idea.

I grab Kai by the hand, insistently tugging at him, almost dragging him up the stairs as he tries to keep up with my pace.

"Slow down," he exclaims, panting.

We make it to the bedroom, and I sit on the bed and regard him eagerly. He raises his eyebrows at the look on my face, clearly wondering what it is I'm thinking. I can't help but give him a goofy smile. *God, let this work,* I pray to myself. *Please let it work.*

I clear my throat. "Kai, will you mark me again? This time I'm asking you to and consenting to it," I point out and watch his expression turn grim.

Chapter 120

Kai's POV

I stare at Winter, unsure if I've heard her correctly. She's twisting her hands together, biting her lip, looking at me shyly, waiting for my reaction. I can't help but remember the first time that I marked her without her consent and flushed. This time she's asking me for it, but what if it does something to her? What if it causes her pain now that she's a hybrid? Is Winter willing to risk it to have her wolf back again? I have to make sure. I can't just go into this blindly. But I do feel excitement stirring in my breast at the idea of having my mark and claim back on her neck again, where it belongs.

"You want me to mark you?" I ask, repeating her words slowly and watching her reaction.

She gives a nod. "Please, it might bring Sabriel back," she whispers. "And maybe it will make the vampire side less, oh, I don't know," she says desperately. "Aggressive. Besides, I miss not being able to mind-link with you," she points out. Her voice is shaky now, her eyes pleading with mine.

I still feel hesitant, even as my feet move closer toward her of their own accord.

"We don't know what marking you will do, though," I say softly. "Are you willing to suffer whatever consequences there might be doing this?" God, help me. I'm considering doing this. All we can do is pray that nothing serious happens as a result. Besides, she's asking me, desperate to have Sabriel back, and I can't blame her. I wouldn't know how to cope without Storm, my wolf.

297

"I'll pay whatever price," she assures me, her eyes beseeching. "I just want to be marked again. Claimed as yours," she adds softly, longingly. My breath hitches in my throat.

Let us do it, man. It's been bothering me that she doesn't have our mark on her neck. How are other wolves going to know she's ours?

Storm, she's going through a lot right now, and you want to tell me her not having our mark is bothering you?

She said she was willing to suffer the consequences. Kai, we should do it. At least this time, the marking will be on her terms instead of ours.

I'm worried it will do something or cause some reaction. We could end up hurting her, Storm. Then what?

We won't know unless we do it. I think it's worth the risk. Besides, can you resist the fact that our mate is begging us to claim her again? She's our mate. Our mark belongs on her neck to show we are her mate.

Damn you, Storm. Why do you have to be so argumentative?

Damn, the wolf for being so persistent. I slowly tug Winter up by the arm as she obediently stands, inhaling her scent and crinkling my nose. Her scent has changed slightly since she changed, but it still intoxicates me. I bury my head in her hair. "I hope you're right about this," I murmur as she trembles beneath me. "Because once I've done this, there's no taking it back," I growl, my voice loaded with meaning.

She shudders. "I know," she stammers. "Please, Kai. I want this," she whispers, and I swallow hard. How can I resist her plea?

I move her head to the side, exposing her creamy skin and the nape of her neck. Where my mark used to be. I frown down at it. Storm's prancing around in my mind encourages me, and I'm forced to block him. Slowly my canines withdraw.

"Get ready," I whisper, and Winter stiffens. My head lowers, and slowly, I pierce her skin and bite down as she jolts. I revel in her taste as I withdraw and lick the wound closed, my eyes gleaming with satisfaction that it's worked and that the mark is again there for everyone to see.

Then Winter gives a long, horrific scream, her legs buckling beneath her. I sweep her up and place her on the bed. Her face is flushed, and she bucks and writhes on the bed, screaming her lungs out as I look at her helplessly. I have no idea what's going on. But I had dreaded something like this happening. I should have listened to my instincts.

"Hurts," she whimpers.

"What hurts," I say anxiously, kneeling beside the bed, desperate to do something to help her. "What hurts, sweetheart?"

"All over," she pants. "Feels like I'm burning from the inside."

I rush to the bathroom and fetch a washcloth, soaking it in cool water and rushing back, patting her down. But the second it touches her, she screams even louder. I drop the washcloth. It's not going to help. Not when she's in this kind of state.

Screw this. I mind-link a doctor to come straight from the hospital. I'd take her there, but I don't want to cause her any more pain than she's already in. Several minutes later, I'm hovering near the doorway while the doctor checks on an almost unconscious Winter.

"I can't tell you what's wrong," the doctor tells me, puzzled. "If I have to hazard a guess, though, it's either a result of her wolf trying to claw its way back to the surface or both sides fighting for dominance."

"Will the pain stop?" I ask quietly, Winter lying there, panting, sweat dripping down her face. Her whole face is contorted in pain.

The doctor shakes her head. "I can't say if the painkillers I've given her will help. She doesn't appear to be responding to them, but she's also not screaming as much. I wish I could tell you more about, Alpha Kai, but this is way out of my knowledge and experience. Hybrids are so rare that we haven't had a chance to study them. I apologize for not being able to help you as much as I would have preferred."

I don't blame the doctor. "Will this stop?" I ask, pointing to Winter. "Will it stop if one side becomes more dominant?"

She looks upset. "I hope so, but there's also every chance this will cause her to die if it drags on too much. Her heart could give out from the shock."

I swear and rub my eyes. I shouldn't have marked Winter. I should have known something like this would happen. Fuck. I feel like I'm slowly dying alongside her. If she dies, I won't be able to control myself. I feel helpless, a rush of guilt washing over me. Goddamn, it!

"If you should need anything else, don't hesitate to mind-link me again," the doctor says, and I usher her out, thanking her silently. Langdon and Damien come rushing up. "What's going on?" Damien blurts out, paling as he sees the condition of his sister.

"I marked her," I said, pointing to her. "And this happened. Now we could all sit here and lay the blame on me, or we can do what we can to make her comfortable."

Damien glowers at me and pulls a chair beside Winter, clutching her hand. Langdon sits silently in the background, occasionally glancing at her but giving myself and his mate privacy to be with the one we love.

"Mother," she cries out, and my heart beats. Damien looks at me, pained. "Why?" she sobs. "Why did you leave us?"

Damien clutches her hand even tighter. "Winter," he says quietly. "Winter, I'm here for you," he promises. Her eyes are closed completely now, and she's almost lifeless on the bed.

I suck in a breath. She's so pale all over. Her skin is almost translucent. While she's not exactly writhing with pain anymore, she's barely moving, and her whole body is heating up. My mark is visible on her skin, and I swallow, glaring at it. This could have been avoided if I had just told her no and waited to find out what would happen. This is all my fault.

"Damien," she moans, and he leans over her, looking anxious. "Damien, why do you hurt me?" she whispers, and he flinches.

Chapter 120

"I think it's the fever. It's making her delusional," I tell him gently.

He nods, focusing on her while I sit on the other side, smoothing her hair from her face. Christ, she's burning hot. I don't dare get the washcloth after what happened last time.

"Father, don't," she shrieks, and Damien jolts. He swallows hard, and he grabs her hand.

"Father's not here anymore," he tells her thickly. "Father, can't hurt you anymore."

She stiffens, and then her body relaxes again. Damien's voice must be getting through to her then. God, this is so painful to watch. I'm on edge, and so is Damien, both of us unable to relax even slightly while Winter's in such pain.

I glance out the window. It's nightfall. The moon is glowing brightly in the sky. It's a full moon tonight when shifters are stronger than usual.

"Maybe we should put her in the bath or something?" Damien says a little desperately.

I look at him. "When I tried to wipe her with a washcloth, she screamed bloody murder. Otherwise, I would have done that already."

He deflates. "She's just so hot," he comments.

Suddenly she sits upright. "I won't let you win!" she screams out loud. "I won't!"

She falls back down.

Damien looks worried. "This can't be good for her body to handle."

"It's not," I told him glumly. I feel helpless, and it's a shit feeling to have. My hands clench into fists. God, if there was something I could do rather than sit here and watch my mate go through whatever she's going through.

That fucking Thomas, I think to myself miserably. He's the reason she's a hybrid. If I'd known what he'd done to her, I would have killed and tortured him more slowly. He'd gotten off lightly, and it stung. Poor Winter suffered because of that bastard and his sick obsession with having her. Who knows what else he might have done to her if we hadn't gotten there? I wish now it was sooner. Maybe then we could have prevented this from ever happening.

There's a cracking sound, and Winter screams. Damien and I jump back as we see that her leg has changed to a wolf one. But it stays like that. Another crack, her arm changing to wolf form. She's still closed her eyes, and I wonder if she's even aware of what is happening. She's sobbing quietly now, and my heart is breaking. Transforming shouldn't be painful, but this is her first shift after becoming a hybrid, and it's not normal how she's shifting. It's way too slow.

"Aaarghh!" screams Winter as her other leg becomes a wolf, breaking and adjusting.

Her body begins to buck and writhe as slowly her remaining limbs and body begins to break and shift into her wolf form. I blink as finally, after several long minutes of pained screaming, a wolf remains on the bed, her eyes closed, curled up in a fetal position.

I tentatively touch Winter's wolf. It's hot to the touch as well. Her eyes don't even open. I glance over at Damien. "Got any ideas?" I ask wryly.

He shakes his head and sits back down, looking at the wolf appreciatively. I admire her as well. When Winter first got here, she was a runt, a tiny little thing. But her wolf has slowly grown; now, it's almost as big as mine. Such a lovely thing to look at. Now I have to wonder if Winter can shift back to humans.

She slumbers. Damien, Langdon, and I slowly fall asleep, my head resting on the bed from my sitting position. I can feel her soft fur beneath me.

I don't know how long I've been asleep, but my whole body springs back when I hear the sound of shifting. Damien lifts his bleary eyes and pushes his chair back as Winter's body returns to her normal human form. I touch her. Her body is now cool to the touch. Her fever has broken. Damien blushes as he realizes she's naked, looking away in discomfort. Langdon stretches from his position on the floor, where he's spent most of the night observing.

Winter's eyes open, and she sits up, stretching her arms with a small smile. She stands up, walking experimentally, holding her arms and watching them with wide eyes. "Kai..." she breathes. "I can hear her again. Sabriel's back inside my mind, and I can shift back to a wolf again. I can control my vampire side too," she almost squeals happily, rushing over to me and giving me a massive hug.

"I thought you were going to die," I said miserably, and she cuddled me harder.

"Sorry," she whispered. "But don't you see? Now I have both sides of me. The shifter side and the vampire side. I can be a wolf again and go for runs. I needed this, Kai. I'm sorry if I scared you, though." Her voice is apologetic. I almost laugh. She shouldn't be apologizing to me. If anything, I should be apologizing to her. Silly girl.

She'd done more than frighten me, but I can't blame her for wanting her wolf back. One thing floats in my mind, however. If she's strong as a vampire, will her wolf be stronger than an Alpha's now as well?

TO BE CONTINUED...

ABOUT THE AUTHOR

My pen name is Cat Smith, but my real name is Crystal Smith. I am 34 years old with a husband and three beautiful children. I have always loved to read and write from an early age and consider myself blessed to have been able to write for Dreame. I also have a mental illness and was diagnosed with Bipolar Type 2 Disorder a few years ago, making writing a bit more challenging. I use it as part of my therapy, finding solace in creating different stories and realities.

My favorite thing is to curl up with a blanket and a good book with a cup of hot chocolate.

I have several other books I have written that are available on the Dreame App, and they include:

The Ordinary Girl and the Cruel Vampire Prince
Taken in By an Alpha and His Family
The Gentle Witch and Her Fierce Alpha
The King of Werewolves and his Mistreated Omega Mate
Saved By the Bad Boy
Beauty and the Alpha Beast
The Beta's Broken Mate
The Hybrid's Second Chance Mate
The Dominant Alpha
Death is Only the Beginning.
I also have two books that I am currently working on called, The Alpha's Abused Mate and The Alpha's Rejected and Broken Mate.

You can also check her works on www.dreame.com.

ABOUT DREAME

Established in 2018 and headquartered in Singapore, Dreame is a global hub for creativity and fascinating stories of all kinds in many different genres and themes.

Our goal is to unite an open, vibrant, and diverse ecosystem for storytellers and readers around the world.

Available in over 20 languages and 100 countries, we are dedicated to bringing quality and rich content for tens of millions of readers to enjoy.

We are committed to discover the endless possibilities behind every story and provide an ultimate platform for readers to connect with the authors, inspire each other, and share their thoughts anytime, anywhere.

Join the journey with Dreame, and let creativity enrich our lives!

Printed in Great Britain
by Amazon

43853464R00175